WHITE ROCK

J. RENÉ GUERRERO

No one has written about this much murder, sex, and suspense in Dallas since J.R. Ewing left town! (Guerrero) brings each of the colorful and complex characters to life so much so that you put yourself in their shoes and experience their dreams, motives, and fears! Each chapter is more exciting and entertaining than the last!

Steve Kemble, America's Sassiest Lifestyle Guru

What a great book! I loved it, and I think everyone would. Very informative and entertaining... two great qualities!

Rosemary Rumbly, Texas Historian, Humorist, and Author

I gobbled up this book in a day and half. It's a great ghost story with interesting characters, lots of twists and turns, and plenty of chills and frights. I can't wait to get my hands on the second book in the series to see where the main character, Laura Milton's, curiosity, courage, and adventurous spirit take her next!

Mimi Schippers, Professor of Sociology and Gender & Sexual Studies, Tulane University, New Orleans, La.

If you're looking for a big, juicy paperback full of suspense and meticulous historical research, White Rock is the book for you. ...Guerrero's unpretentious writing style is perfect for a fast, creepy read about (the) dark secrets (of) the city of Dallas, both past and present. You won't want to put it down...

Bonnie Pemberton, Texas Author, "The Cat Master"

I read it from cover to cover on the beach-side pool patio at Loews Santa Monica (and) couldn't put it down. Riveting!!! Wowza!!!! Being set in my town with characters that I personally knew/know made it especially delicious and I can't wait for the second book!

Dena Miller, Former editor at 'Ask Miss A' online publication, Texas Socialite, and Local Personality

This novel
is dedicated to

the

LIVING

to Robyn F:
Thank you for giving me the courage
to believe in myself...

and the

DEAD

to Lupe G, Danny S, Patrick S, Alice V M, and Sacha T:
The rest of us who are stranded here
carry on bravely without you

Grateful acknowledgement is given to my editor and co-conspirator Robyn Flach. Without your mentoring and consistent support none of this would have ever come to fruition. Thank you thank you thank you thank you.

Even though it includes the names of private citizens and references true historical events, this book is a complete work of fiction. The main characters, incidents, and dialogue are drawn purely from the author's imagination or are used in a fictional manner and are not to be construed as real. Any resemblance to actual persons alive or dead is either entirely coincidental or their characterizations are outright fabrications by the author and have been placed in speculative events that in no way are meant to be taken literally.

Library of Congress Control Number: 1-2562320981
ISBN # 978-0-9990178-0-7 (Paperback Edition)

First printing May 2017.

J. Rene Guerrero, rene@reneguerrero.com

Robyn Flach, Editor.
Chas Blankenship, Proofreader.
Original artwork by Cabe Booth.
Cover design by Robyn Flach and J. René Guerrero.

www.ReneGuerrero.com
www.WhiteRockTheNovel.com

WHITE ROCK

J. RENÉ GUERRERO

Printed by CreateSpace, An Amazon.com Company

One

1958: White Rock Lake, Dallas, Texas: 1:45 AM

It is a crisp winter night with a canopy of stars blazing overhead. A soft breeze whispers silently across the expanse of open water. Beyond the jagged black of the southwestern tree line the buildings of a budding downtown Dallas glow in the distance.

A lone beat-up sedan backs away from the water treatment plant at the far west end of the lake. Max Lucas, a 42-year-old hydro-technician, still in his greasy overalls from the night shift, throws his battered Chevrolet Bel Air into drive and mumbles to himself as he eases out of the rutted parking lot onto the loose gravel of West Lawther Drive, just as he's done every night for the past seven years. The latest hip doo-wop single "Tears on My Pillow" by Little Anthony and the Imperials crackles through the AM radio.

> *'You don't remember me, but I remember you'*

The song is slow and sultry, evoking loneliness and despair draped in deep shades of blue. The voice is pained and full of youthful emotion as the words speak of a time not so long ago when the singer's heart was broken in two...

> *'Tears on my pillow, pain in my heart caused by you...'*

A bobble-headed Hawaiian girl does the hula on the dashboard as the car rattles and shakes down the crude road encircling the lake. The moon is a pregnant yellow orb suspended in the sky, its glowing shadow streaking across the icy water like glitter on black glass.

'If we could start anew, I wouldn't hesitate...'

To Lucas it is sadly amusing how a young boy could possibly take someone back who hurt him so, tempting the hands of fate... Ah, the whimsy of youth...

'Tears on my pillow, pain in my heart caused by you...'

Lucas wipes the windshield with his sleeve and squints into the dark. In his headlights he sees what looks like someone standing on the side of the road up ahead. As the car gets closer he realizes it's a young woman standing in her bare feet on the right shoulder of the road not 20 feet from the edge of the lake.

"*Dang–*"

He pulls up next to her and stops. She is facing away staring out at the black water. Lucas notices her long blonde hair and powder-blue dress are dripping wet. She must be freezing. He leans over and rolls the passenger window down.

"Miss? You a'right?"

The girl turns towards him with a confused look. Though it is dark, her body seems to shimmer with a light all its own. She is stunningly beautiful. For some reason the details of her face don't register, but Lucas is entranced by the way her hair drapes across her chin, her slender arms and shoulders, a tiny mouth that trembles as she shivers in the chill of the night. Her lips are blue and cracked. They look almost frozen. And when she finally speaks, it is in a soft child-like voice that reminds him of the tinkling of bells.

"I–I had an accident. Up the road. My car..."

"You poor thang! Can I do sumthin?"

She looks at him with the deepest blue eyes he's ever seen. Her little mouth moves but the voice seems to come from somewhere else.

"Will you take me home?"

"Git in, darlin'."

He slides towards her and reaches behind the seat, opening the back passenger door for her. She grasps the door handle with a petite wet hand and gets in the back seat, gently closing the door behind her. Moonlight fills the interior of the car with a silvery luminescence.

"It's just up on Gaston Avenue," she whispers. "Not far. 4750..."

Lucas drives off into the night, making small talk. Later, he wouldn't remember a single thing that came out of his mouth, only that he was trying to keep the girl awake in case she was in shock. What in God's name could have happened to strand a pretty girl like her out here all alone in the middle of the night?

In the rearview mirror, Lucas watches as the girl stares out the window at the water as if she's looking for something. He can't help but notice her dress, once a stunning gown, clinging to her shivering little body like a second skin. She looks like a movie star or an angel that fell out of the sky.

Turning off the main road, he pulls up to an old house on a tiny cul-de-sac facing the lake. It's an aged stone two-story mansion overgrown with moss and ivy. All the lights are out and it looks abandoned except for a single gas sconce burning blue next to the front door. The house number on the wall is 4750.

"This whare you said?"

Lucas looks up into the rearview mirror. The girl's blue eyes are huge and staring back at him. He senses her directly behind him, so close he can feel her cold breath on the back of his neck.

He turns around quickly.

The back seat of the car is empty except for some slivers of weeds and a dark puddle of water soaking into the seat where the young girl had just been sitting.

"Jee-zus in heaven!"

Lucas jumps out of the car and makes the Christian sign of the cross. He searches around frantically but the girl is nowhere to be seen. Looking at his watch, he realizes it's 2:32 AM. Where has the time gone? Behind him, the house looms like a sleeping giant.

Shaken, he stumbles up to the front door and knocks. Nothing. He knocks again, louder. Standing in the shadows he feels something press against his back. Slowly, Lucas peers over his right shoulder. He's completely alone in the dark. A wave of chills runs through his entire body strong enough to make him almost heave. He quickly knocks again.

Just as he's about to hurry off, the porch light comes on. An elderly man silently opens the door. A thick security chain keeps the opening to a sliver.

"Yes?"

"Beg pardon, sir. 'Don't mean to wake yew, but I's comin' back from th' pow'r haus an' picked up a pretty blonde girl by th' lake. 'Said she had an *acci*-dent. I brung her here an when I turned 'round she wuz gone. You know her?"

The door closes and reopens slowly, the chain undone. Onto the porch a frail silver-haired figure in a plaid robe shuffles into view. The old man stares at Lucas through tired, weepy eyes and breathes out a sigh. The winter wind rustles through the trees ever so softly.

"Thank you, stranger," he says. "Yes, that was my daughter. You see, she disappeared many years ago. And every year on this same night, her birthday, she tries to come home..."

Present Day, September, New York City 12:53 AM

Laura Milton looked up from her computer, her mind reeling from the story she just read. It was one of dozens of accounts she had devoured over the past few months from people who claimed to have met the disembodied spirit that supposedly haunts White Rock Lake in Dallas, Texas.

Since 1933, hundreds of people have described similar nocturnal encounters with a hitchhiking young girl, soaked to the skin, who disappears after they pick her up on a deserted stretch of road surrounding the lake. Each story had its own variations; what the woman looked like, what she was wearing, what was said, and where she was taken. But two things were common to them all: the woman's abrupt disappearance and the physical presence of water where she had been sitting. One of the stories even included an eyewitness account that stated the ghost was wearing a designer gown from the famed Neiman-Marcus department store. Regardless of the accuracy of the accounts, these people apparently saw something shocking enough to report to the authorities. And those reports have lived on for decades as the region's oldest and most documented urban legend, that of the White Rock Lady.

Though she began her college career at New York University studying journalism, Laura's concentration shifted over time to the origins of folklore and modern mythology and their influences on contemporary society. From her studies she was well aware of a standing archetype referred to as "The Vanishing Hitchhiker," a profile that dated as far back as the Napoleonic Era. Some of the variations of the story described these spectral strangers as 'vanishing prophets,' entities that appeared suddenly, made some form of prediction, and subsequently vanished never to be seen again.

Regardless of the similarities, Laura knew the legend of the White Rock Lady was not just some psychological meme that had taken over the minds of the good people of Dallas, Texas for the better part of a century. There was something very real about this particular urban legend. As a young girl Laura witnessed the power of this mysterious presence, whatever it was, first hand. And it had changed her life forever.

A chill shuddered through her. Laura stood up and went to the windowsill where Katarina, her black four-month-old kitten, was perched and gazing out at the night. Across the East River, the Brooklyn skyline stared back at them with absolute indifference. The thought of the disembodied spirit of a young woman roaming the earthly realm forever was horrifying. To be tied to Earth, damned to watch generations rise and fall for all eternity, never to rest... Hell, just the thought of getting through the school week was hard enough at times. How much pain and suffering could one lost soul endure? And how long before that soul, in its despair, decides to reach out to the living for sympathy and understanding?

She took a Bluetooth headset from a nearby shelf. Activating it, she spoke aloud, her voice breaking the silence. The MacBook Pro hummed to life and began recording her every word.

"I'm still not sure what I'm looking for in the story about the White Rock Lady. Is she just a simple urban legend that has been reincarnated generation after generation? Or is there really something behind the myths and ghost-stories that hasn't been discovered yet?"

Outside Laura's window, the Brooklyn Bridge loomed in the distance. Dallas seemed a world away, and yet this lonely spirit was somehow reaching out, trying to communicate with her, touching her soul and filling her with an intense sadness she couldn't understand. "Were you real? If so, who were you? Why can't you rest?" She pulled the Bluetooth off her head, turning it off.

"...and why can't I get you out of my dreams?"

Laura undressed, put on a pair of men's boxers, a muscle shirt, and went into the bathroom. From the mirror, a strange young woman stared back, long strands of dark brunette hair hanging from a loose ponytail, thin black-rimmed glasses sitting on an elfin face making her look younger than she really was. Irritated, she quickly took the glasses off and tried her best to shake off her melancholy.

It wasn't so long ago that Colin was there beside her, naked, laughing at themselves in the very same mirror after a long, hot shower. He always knew how to get her to relax and let go of her worries. And even though at times his logical brain wasn't able to accept some of her heavier emotional baggage, he always seemed genuinely happy to be with her.

Sighing, she pushed back her longing for him. Even if her ex-fiancée were standing there now, it wouldn't change the fact that in the last few years her life had yet again been turned upside down...

On the basin in front of her sat a small prescription bottle. Picking it up, she read the label as she'd done countless times before. It held 200-milligram capsules of Topamax, the latest in a long series of medications she's taken over the last few years. It was a strong anticonvulsant, a sledgehammer in capsule form. Or as she referred to it, humiliation in a bottle. Though she hadn't suffered a seizure in over year, she wasn't sure if it was her body's chemistry balancing out or just the meds keeping her stable. However, as much as she hated it, the drug was a necessary evil. Could shame, despair, and insecurity ever co-exist in a more perfectly engineered delivery medium? She thought not.

Opening the bottle, she popped the devil capsule in her mouth and chased it with a swig of water from a squeeze bottle sitting on the counter. She turned off the light and walked in the dark to her bedroom.

Climbing into bed, Laura silently chastised herself for, once again, missing her medication time by three hours. It was a detail that was still so easy to forget. The less she thought about her condition, the easier it was to pretend everything was fine and that she was nothing but a normal 24-year-old grad student. But nothing could be further from the truth... Katarina leapt up on the bed and snuggled in next to her.

As she nestled in, Laura heard her father's voice echoing from the past. *'Goodnight, sweetheart, well, it's time to go...'* When she was little he would always sing her to sleep with some golden oldie doo-wop song from the 50's. The memory of it made her smile sadly as she closed her eyes. God, she missed him.

Sleep took her almost instantly, the doping effect of the Topamax helping to calm her runaway thoughts and send her quickly into unconsciousness. Soon, she was breathing deeply and the night closed in.

* * *

Hours later, Laura began twitching in her bed restlessly. Out of the black of her unconsciousness, streams of images began flooding her brain.

A large body of water stretches out into the distance, a blonde-haired woman staring out at the turbulent waves. The sky is filled with thunderheads flashing overhead like bruised cotton meteors. A strange sense of panic takes over as the visions speed up. A car rumbling down a deserted road at night, small bare feet on gravel, a dripping tiny blue hand reaching for the door handle, a pair of enormous cobalt-blue eyes staring back in a rear-view mirror. Lightning flashing. A pair of cracked, quivering blue lips, fragments of color and movement darting everywhere, a flood of images and emotions that won't stop or slow down. And there, finally, the blonde woman facing away, staring out at an endless body of water churning in anger. Behind her, a mass of countless, faceless people hidden under the trees watching, bereft in sadness, a shuffling parade of mourning silhouettes all staring out at a demon lake...

Laura's eyes snapped open to find herself sitting up in bed, flailing her arms and sobbing uncontrollably. She stopped herself abruptly, her heartbeat pounding in her chest, her body bathed in sweat. The horror of being so far under the influence of the dream was unbearable. She always woke feeling so cold and alone. What the hell did all this mean?

She didn't know the answer, but deep inside Laura knew the source. As a child, she had seen this blonde woman before. The memory was hazy, but she distinctly remembered being with her parents in a car at White Rock Lake late one night. She had been gazing out of the rear window when something appeared behind the car. A blonde woman with glittering blue eyes seemed to float out of the mist itself, softly whispering Laura's name. Strange that Laura could hear her from inside the car... And ever since that first sighting, these nightmares had become part of her, starting first as fuzzy impressions and slowly over the years becoming more and more vivid and violent as she matured.

But in the past few months the dreams had become utterly terrifying, wrenching her awake, sometimes with her screaming out in the night. And for some reason, a single sentence always kept repeating in her head, "*Please take me home, I just want to go home...*" It meant nothing to her. After losing both of her parents tragically, Laura felt like she had no home. No real home...

In confusion, she wiped the streams of hot tears off her face and then started to cry in earnest; for the first time in years, Laura Milton was truly frightened...

Two

Nestled in the center of Greenwich Village in lower Manhattan, New York University is the largest private institution of higher education in the United States. Founded in 1831, NYU is steeped in the cultural and artistic innovation that has identified our country since its inception. The heart of the campus, Washington Square Park, has been a hub of cultural life in New York City since the early 1800's. Artists and intellectuals such as Edgar Allen Poe, Walt Whitman, and Mark Twain were active contributors to the artistic scene at NYU in its early years. Later, personalities that peopled the Village area included Jackson Pollock, Willem de Kooning, Allen Ginsberg, and Bob Dylan. This melting pot of creativity and bohemian diversity that drives the heart of the university is a major reason why New York City is regarded internationally as the seat of Western culture.

It was no wonder that Nathan Milton's deepest wish was to have his only daughter join the esteemed alumni of such a broad-minded liberal-arts college. His alma mater had been NYU's Gallatin School of Independent Study, where students personally created and plotted their own unique degree plans. He knew Laura would be provided with a general knowledge about culture to sharpen her already keen faculties of reason and judgment. The curriculum would feed her love of history and help cultivate a taste in art and literature in an atmosphere that promoted independent and critical thinking.

And, in retrospect, she agreed that there had never been a more perfect place for her.

There was a slight chill in the morning air as Laura passed through the regal Washington Square Arch on her way to the campus. Even though this was her usual route, the sight of the square was always comforting. The surrounding canopy of towering trees had begun changing colors ever so slightly hinting at the coming of fall. The massive circular fountain was shooting streams of water into the air in a dramatic display while the park was slowly starting to buzz with activity. Students were lounging in small groups on the grass studying or playing guitars; a few early-bird tourists were shuffling around taking photographs. The entire square felt vital, alive, and in perpetual motion.

Monday mornings were always difficult. For some reason it took a little longer to wake up and get into the rhythm of the day. However, once in class, everything seemed to make more sense; Laura always felt centered in a controlled environment. It was no wonder she was more than a little frightened by the thought of graduating in two more semesters. Life without school? It seemed like a foreign concept to her, a life without structure, without discipline. She feared she would drive herself crazy with too much time on her hands. But perhaps that was what real jobs were for. Note to self: *get an f'ing job.*

Of course, there were pills her doctors were always recommending to help with her pre-occupation with the futility of modern life, but anti-depressants were no longer an option. Laura had made the mistake of getting on them right after her father passed away. Instead of helping her cope with her depression, the drugs made her lethargic and callous. When she finally snapped out of her trance months later, she realized she had alienated Colin and his parents at a time when she needed them the most. She threw her prescription down the toilet and never looked back.

Besides, the Topamax made her more than loopy enough. Laura always felt more or less inebriated for at least an hour after ingesting the medication, and not in a good way. The drug made her disoriented, slow, and, for the most part, incapable of functioning. And that was the *only* reason she started getting up at 5 AM every day.

Her mornings were something like a scorecard: Yoga, check. Shower, check. Breakfast, check. Mind-numbing psychotropics, check. She got into the habit of planning in advance to take an hour-long nap to sleep through the worst of the side effects of the drug. Usually, they always wore off in an hour or so and she would wake feeling more or less normal. She learned the hard way to set an alarm to make sure she didn't pass out completely and miss a class. The whole procedure was a pain, but she was thankful; she was one of the fortunate ones. Some seizure disorder patients lived in a perpetual state of mind-numbing haze just to keep the attacks at bay. That could easily have been her. Life could be so much worse...

Shaking off her lethargy, she entered the building on Broadway and took the elevator to the 4th floor. She went through a set of double doors and silently slid inside the packed lecture hall. Working her way along the wall, she found an empty seat at the very back of the auditorium. Glancing at her phone, she realized she was running much later than she thought, but thankfully she was only auditing the lecture today.

Professor Robert Reilly, the department head of Mass and Alternative Media and Cultural Studies, was speaking, his orator's voice deep and deliberate. At 6 foot 3 he was an impressive figure, thin and angular, but with the brooding persona of a modern-day Hemmingway, sans the alcoholism and the self-destructive tendencies. A full beard and a few visible tattoos made him look more like the guitarist for a new hipster band instead of a college professor who had the distinguished honor of recently receiving the Advisor of Distinction Award, given to faculty advisers in recognition of excellence in advisement and mentoring. Laura knew many of the under-graduate girls openly lusted after him. They would register for his workshops and sit for hours gazing at him in absolute worship. Watching him speak, Laura could understand their attraction. The man sure knew how to work a room.

"Here in this arid geography," Reilly purred, "the body was found very much like investigators expected. More times than not, the location of a violent crime will reveal intimate details of the perpetrator's psyche. In this case, the desert mirrored the murderer's birthplace. Beryl Stalls grew up in the outskirts of El Paso, Texas, a bleak, arid region that represented something maternal to him. In all his homicidal forays he kept going back again and again to what was familiar, even halfway across the country. And in the intimacy of this geography, he felt safe enough to commit his atrocities. What we come away with is a crucial insight into the motivations and *poetic stylings*, if you will, of a sociopathic serial killer..."

Reilly picked up his cell phone and checked the time.

"If we can implement this detailed analysis of data earlier on in an investigation, perhaps we can get to the point where we're actually preventing murders and not just attempting to solve them. Food for thought. We'll take this back up on Wednesday, ladies and gentlemen."

The students gathered their books and started filing out of the auditorium. Laura waited for some of the human flood to subside before attempting to make her way towards him. Reilly's class had become very popular in the last few semesters, especially with the female under-grads. Good for him, Laura thought. He deserved the recognition. Reilly was a good man, one she trusted implicitly. As if on cue, he looked up and smiled at her across the room. She waved back.

Reilly's office was in the south wing of the building, a place in which she had spent a lot of time as a freshman. He was her advisor as well as department head and had helped her formulate the last several years of her scholastic career into a self-developed course of study that would become her own personalized degree. Even though Reilly was obviously taken aback by some of her preoccupations, she was eternally grateful to him for all his support. But for now, she was simply in need of some good old-fashioned encouragement.

Laura leaned on the edge of his desk while he put his things away.

"Thanks for making time for me."

"Of course," Reilly said. "So, I understand you'll be addressing the thesis committee tomorrow. What did you decide?"

She stared silently at him for a long moment.

"You're going to do the White Rock story, aren't you?" His tone betrayed his disapproval.

"I know it's unorthodox, but I've worked really hard on my proposal and I know there's something there worth investigating..."

Reilly looked at her gravely but knew better than to try to talk her out of her decision. That would only solidify her resolve. So he took the high road.

"What do you have so far?"

Her inner geek almost exploded out of her, she was so excited just to be talking about it.

"There are dozens of reported sightings of the ghost starting as early as 1933. All the witnesses have been from different socioeconomic backgrounds, different ethnic groups, age groups, and all under different circumstances. The only thing they have in common is that the sightings all happened at night and in close proximity to the lake."

“Is there an actual history of traumatic violence or death in the area?”

“Definitely. First of all, the history of the site itself is disturbing. White Rock is a man-made lake that was constructed in a valley that was once a major route into Texas from Mexico in the 1800’s. Thousands of people made that trek into the country; men, women, children, the elderly... Of course, not all of them survived the journey. Also, three separate communities thrived around the valley area where the lake was created until construction began in 1910. Each had its own cemetery.”

Reilly kept silent and let her continue.

“In 1927, the first person, a nineteen year old girl by the name of Hallie Enid Gaston, drowned in the lake. It’s speculated that her death is what started the rumors of the White Rock Lady. But I haven’t found any evidence of living relatives or any concrete death records, just obituary notices. Then, in 1934 a small plane is said to have crashed into the lake killing all of the passengers. It seems early on, death was drawn to this lake for some reason...”

Reilly tried to hide his irritation at her sensationalism, but it was apparent on his face. This spurred her on.

“Since then, there have been dozens of drownings over the years, many in which the bodies were never recovered. There have been six in just the last 3 years...

“Finally, there’re two confirmed cases of young women committing suicide in the lake, one in 1935 and another in '42. I’ve contacted an elderly woman in Dallas through social media who claims one of those women was her sister. I guess I'll start there.”

Riley sighed. “So you want to go to Dallas to interview her?”

“Her grand-daughter. Robert, everything searchable on-line is a joke. If there really is something behind the urban legend I'll have to go and find it. That's what I want to present for the board's consideration. The only inconsistency I've found is in the descriptions of the ghost. They are all different. It doesn't make any sense."

He smiled. "Urban legends don't make sense, Laura. They are just fires to consume the imagination."

"You're probably right. Worse case scenario: my wild ghost hunt goes nowhere and I have to submit a new thesis proposal... and put off graduation for another year."

"What does Colin think?"

She paused for a heartbeat. "I haven't told him. I just–I don't want our personal problems getting in the way of this. He's looking for a reason to be helpful, but–"

"You want to do it on your own." Robert smiled. "Laura, you're not just a student of mine, you're a good friend. You know I respect the hell out of you as an academic. And I know it's your personal business, but just remember; not every graduate student has an ex-fiancée who's being groomed for the executive directorship of the Smithsonian..."

Three

After her meeting with Reilly, Laura was listless and decided to walk a few blocks before catching the subway home. As she strolled through the Village, her thoughts ricocheted. The microcosm of her life had become increasingly fragile and complex over the past few years. She still found it hard to believe that she was now in New York City. Of course, her life would have been very different had it not been for the lifelong friendship her father Nathan had with Grace and Garret Jonah, Colin's parents.

Laura knew the story well. The three had met in college at Texas Tech in Lubbock, Texas and had stayed lifelong friends. It was Grace who introduced Nathan to a young liberal arts student named Terri Birch when they were sophomores. Grace and Garret married that same year and, after standing up as the couples' best man and maid of honor, Nathan and Terri started to fall in love.

A year after graduation, the Jonahs moved to Philadelphia and Terri and Nathan married and settled in Dallas where Nathan was offered a teaching position at the prestigious Southern Methodist University. Terri became pregnant almost immediately, and nine months later on January 9, she gave birth to their daughter, Laura Grace Milton, at St. Paul's Hospital.

After Terri's tragic death seven years later, Nathan decided he and little Laura should leave Texas and continue their lives somewhere uncontaminated by calamity. Garret suggested they come out to live in New Jersey. He and Grace had just purchased a sprawling home in the countryside and had a fully-furnished guesthouse on the property that was just begging for some company. Nathan knew relocating close to his best friends would be very healing for both him and Laura. Besides, the couple had an 8-year-old son named Colin who was also an only child. It would be good for Laura to be around someone her own age for once. Perhaps she would find a friend in him.

Nathan humbly accepted. Within four weeks he sold their modest two-bedroom house in the Lakewood area of Dallas and moved with his daughter to start the next chapter of their lives in Far Hills, New Jersey.

Their new home was a gorgeous wooden A-frame surrounded by colossal walnut and maple trees. It was situated down the hill from the main house on 15 acres of land in the center of Far Hills. It took a few months for Laura to get used to living in the country, but little by little she started adapting to the slower lifestyle. In Dallas, people were always in a hurry to do everything, but in Far Hills time stood still and the summer days seemed to go on forever.

When the children first met, they were both incredibly shy. They spent the afternoon on opposite sides of the lawn staring at one another. But eventually young Colin got up the nerve and asked Laura to follow him into the main house to see his greatest treasure. When she walked in, there in the center of the living room sat a 500-gallon saltwater aquarium filled with exotic fish from all over the world. Colin told her all about the different fish and where they came from. Laura had been completely spellbound.

As the years progressed, Laura and Colin became inseparable. He was her best friend and protector all through school until he went off to college at NYU in her junior year, leaving her to fend for herself through the end of high school.

And she almost made it. But before her graduation, Laura's father had a sudden heart attack and died. Having lost Colin to college and now her father, Laura humbly accepted Garrett's offer to continue to stay in the guesthouse as a permanent part of their family. She was incredibly grateful for their love and the chance to stay with those who had been her surrogate family for so many years.

Aside from Nathan, Laura's only other known family members were his elderly parents who were rumored to have relocated to Western Europe to protest his marriage to her mother in the mid 80's. For some reason they had never given the couple their blessings, making a silent enemy of their son, and were never spoken of, even when Laura was a child. As far as she knew, they were deceased and there had never been a reason to think otherwise.

In the weeks following Nathan's death, a lawyer contacted Laura informing her of a tremendous trust fund that had been left in her name. Ever since she could remember, her family had always lived a simple, comfortable life, but Laura had never dreamt Nathan had accumulated so much wealth. Perhaps the money had been an inheritance from her missing grandparents, whom she knew almost nothing about. But whatever the source, there was a small fortune that she would become the executor of by the time she turned 21.

The timing of Nathan's death had kept her from turning in her application requirements. She had just submitted her transcripts to NYU mid-term and knew she wouldn't hear back in time for the fall semester. Not wanting to sit out a year, she enrolled in a small private college in Far Hills. It was a Catholic-based school, but that wasn't the reason she made the choice–it was simply the best education she could get in the region. The Miltons had never been tied to any religious beliefs; Laura's mother had been remotely Baptist from growing up with her foster parents in Texas, but Laura's father was a scientist, just like Colin and his father–a total atheist. He had to see ironclad proof before believing in *anything.*

After all she had been through, the *last* thing Laura believed in was a loving, omnipotent God who was watching over everything and everyone. That was not her reality. But instead of applying her logic to the lengthy list of inconsistencies and obscenities she saw in the present incarnation of the Catholic Church, she chose to be indifferent and aloof about the subject of religion all together. Opinion and passion polarized people against things, but aloofness was the great diffuser. It created a gray area where she could just exist and opt out without having to draw a line of demarcation in the sand and declare all-out intellectual war on Christianity. In her heart, Laura believed there was something greater in the world, but at this point, she knew she would never be able to trust it.

During this time, Colin and Laura began to acknowledge their feelings for one another. She had just entered NYU in the Gallatin School of Independent Study and had left the guesthouse in New Jersey to move into a new apartment at the Stove Factory Lofts Building down by the East River. She and Colin spoke daily and he quickly became her confidant and sounding board. She even got to the point where she felt comfortable calling him up and collapsing on his shoulder in the middle of the night when she couldn't hold back her grief any longer over losing her parents. He would come over and stay with her for days at a time, insistent on sleeping on the couch, to help her though her waves of sorrow that never seemed to lessen. There, in her misery, she realized Colin was now the only constant in her life. It seemed like one day he was her best friend and the next she belonged to him, body and soul. He was unbelievably tender to her when she needed it the most. It was wonderful having someone she loved and trusted implicitly.

But having a confidant was both comforting and frustrating for her. Colin was a lot like his father; full of wonderful qualities, but his intellect made him cynical and in many instances he couldn't help but let his objective mind taint his particular view of the world.

The first time Laura ever told him about her ability to see spirits, he literally laughed in her face. Even though he was being playful, it crushed her and she couldn't face him for days. After waiting years to say anything to anyone about her abilities, not even to her father, fearful that she was simply losing her mind, Colin's mocking tone was just a kick in the teeth. She had spent so much time painstakingly researching the subject objectively, ultimately convincing herself that the phenomena she was witnessing were real, and the only man she trusted humiliated her. How could Colin be so callous when he knew nothing about the depth of her experience? It made her question if she could ever commit herself to someone who could so easily reject the most secretive and personal details of her life...

Colin was a scientist, a statistical logician hopelessly tied to, as it related to the paranormal world, an antiquated system of observation that clouded his vision with inaccurate data. When Laura told him about her reoccurring dreams, he thought she was simply overworked. Never in a billion years would he entertain the thought that there might be metaphysical forces at play. He even called her childish. *Childish.*

Damnit. If he had been any other man, she would have thrown him out of her life in an instant. But she just couldn't bring herself to do it. Colin was more than just a lover; he had been her best friend for most of her life. And even with his psycho-centric views, she couldn't imagine ever living without him.

Colin's father Garret was the acting executive director of the Smithsonian Institute in Washington, DC. The man was a wealth of information and resources, all of which helped Laura and Colin exceed all through high school and into college. Now, Colin was being groomed to succeed him after his father's impending retirement in a few years, an amazing honor as well as a royal pain in the ass for someone as free-spirited as she knew Colin to be. She still couldn't believe he had accepted the offer without talking to her, especially after proposing to her first. That was a huge part of why she got a major case of cold feet that April morning and, instead of betrothing herself to the man of her dreams, decided to drive to Chicago with her best friend Emily for a week, leaving Colin and his entire family, who had shown her nothing but unconditional love since she was seven, waiting at the church for a bride who would never arrive. The memory filled her with deep shame even still, and probably would for the rest of her life.

With his resources, Colin could help unravel much of the mystery concerning the White Rock story. But that was exactly what she didn't want from him. She simply needed to know he believed in her. That's all she had ever wanted from her father, and now that he was gone Colin had become the main male figure in her world, whether she wanted to admit it or not. And, in the context of their relationship, all she really wanted was to make him happy...

It was Colin who found her after her first seizure. After having an anxiety attack at school on the morning of her 21st birthday, Laura chose to spend the evening alone at home watching bad horror films on cable. Colin arrived at her apartment with flowers and a bottle of wine around 9 o'clock. When she didn't answer, he let himself in. To his horror, he found her on the kitchen floor twitching and bleeding from the mouth.

The next year and a half was a blur of tests, research, medication trials, and, ultimately, more seizures. Laura went through three different types of medications, embarrassed herself beyond belief dozens of times, and still the doctors had no definitive prognosis.

The hardest part for Laura was adjusting her lifestyle to having to be dependent on Colin and his wonderful family. Each seizure brought a potential 6-month revocation of her driver's license until her doctors would sign off, confident that her seizures were under control. And, though she was fortunate enough to be able to afford to drive and maintain a vehicle in New York City, with the many forms of public transportation, the possible drawbacks from her handicap didn't leave her completely stranded. Of course, she was grateful for Colin's family's deep compassion and dedication to her needs, but for someone who was brought up to be independent, relying on others was more than just an inconvenience; it was emotionally crippling and deeply humiliating.

Ultimately, she received a diagnosis of having epilepsy. After doing her own research for months she knew 'epilepsy' was nothing more than a generalized term doctors used when they had no fucking idea what was causing the seizures. Her research had prepared her for the diagnosis, but it still came as a shock to her: she was an epileptic. She was *handicapped*.

Colin had been in the doctor's office with her when she got the diagnosis and didn't know what to say. They rode the elevator down to the parking garage in silence. When she and Colin finally got back to his car, she burst into tears and cried for 20 minutes on his shoulder.

The doctors told her to avoid stress, get plenty of sleep, stay away from caffeine and artificial sweeteners, take her meds on time every day, eat healthy food, stay away from alcohol... basically, turn her back on everything associated with being a modern-day millennial college student. It seemed like a monastic life-style that at first she didn't think she was capable of living. But instead of stressing herself out about changing her life all at once, she chose to take it one day at a time. At her friend Emily's suggestion, she started practicing yoga and found it helped with her stress level. She had always been slender and preferred eating organically, so that wasn't much of a challenge. And with Colin and his family's support she stayed true to her regimen of elephant tranquilizer as closely as humanly possible. As for her alcohol consumption, that was one thing she still had to come to terms with...

Laura shook her head clear of her deep musings. Sitting now on the subway, she felt the exhaustion taking over. Her nerves had been shot for the last few weeks and it had little to do with her impending audience with the thesis committee. These dreams of hers were increasingly more intense and frightening. She had gotten to the point years ago where she could ignore feelings of fear and loss, but in the recent weeks, after waking up and finding herself sobbing uncontrollably, she started remembering what fear really felt like.

And now she was in a constant state of expectation. Of what, she couldn't say. The other shoe to drop? The only thing more frightening than her own dreams was the thought of being perceived as a wounded person incapable of living with the hand life had dealt her. Her father had raised her to be independent. And that was different than just being alone.

Returning to her apartment, Laura put on some Rachmaninoff and all but collapsed on the couch. She was hungry and getting light-headed. Christ, she hated feeling so dependent and scheduled about everything in her life. Used to be, she would go for days without eating just because she forgot. Those days were long gone. As her small cadre of doctors drilled into her, any deviation in menu, stress level, or medication schedule could risk sending her into another seizure. And that was the new fear that overshadowed everything else in her life. She made a small salad, opened a tin of smoked oysters, and sat at the window in the kitchen while she ate.

Looking out from the fourth floor at the surrounding rooftops, Laura realized how much she missed living on the ranch in Far Hills. The town in northeast New Jersey had been the perfect mix of city wealth and country sensibility. Most homes had been on acres of land and many of the neighbors kept stables of horses. She remembered riding with her father every weekend in the spring as a girl. Damn, she missed him...

The shadows in her apartment were starting to lengthen. As always, she was acutely aware of the diminishing sunlight in the evenings. The night had become an adversary of sorts. And sleep was now an intimidating necessity that she rarely found comfort in. Once unconscious, sooner or later, the dreams would come and flood her with despair. While other girls her age were out thriving and taking advantage of the night, she instead withdrew and resigned herself to her new medication regime.

Two cups of chamomile tea later, Laura fell asleep on her couch while watching the streaming documentary *"F for Fake"*, totally missing her medication all together. That night, instead of phantom bathers from the past, she dreamt of a fedora'd Orson Welles, big as a house, gorging himself on platefuls of food in a café in Ibiza while a drunken Elmyr danced in his underpants painting Renoirs to the shouts and jeers of a young raver crowd. Even in sleep, she wasn't quite sure which dream was more disturbing.

At 5 AM her cell phone erupted in Bach's *'Bourrée in E Minor'*. She sat up on the couch dreading the coming day.

The morning ritual began with a sun salutation...

Four

The thesis committee meeting had been relatively painless, considering how worked up she had been. After reviewing her extensive research overview, the board accepted Laura's proposal to travel to Dallas to conduct a series of interviews to "determine the influence of geography on the origins of urban legends in modern society." She was amazed. This was to be her last major project before starting to prepare for the *colloquium* next semester, the required final oral examination to graduate from Gallatin. But she felt almost guilty for the conflict of interest. Yes, the main purpose of this trip would be to collect data for her final paper in which she would outline the themes she would discuss in the colloquium, but this trip was also a chance to find her own answers to the White Rock mystery. Perhaps she could discover what these horrible nightmares meant and, more importantly, how to make them stop. With a flawless under-graduate track record, she had convinced the committee to help her to do just that. They were giving her some major wiggle room and she suspected she knew the reason why.

Professor Carl Keyson, one of four committee members present at the inquiry, had made it well known to her last semester that he was definitely interested in more than just her scholastic career. The way his eyes lingered on her, the innocuous touch on the shoulder or small of her back for no apparent reason at the graduate social functions... All were textbook signs that he was pursuing her. He was definitely a handsome man, but at 51, was more than just a little old for her. Besides, her life was far too complicated at this point to jump into such uncharted waters. She chose to take advantage of Professor Keyson's crush and let him smooth out the committee for her. She would thank him at a later date, though not in the way he hoped.

It was amazing how many men were coming out of the woodwork now that she and Colin had separated. She had been getting a lot of unsolicited attention lately and really didn't know how to handle it. And it wasn't that she wanted to be back on the market, either. Getting hit on by strangers was both comforting and annoying at the same time. It either made her feel like a princess or a slut, there was no middle ground for her. But, regardless of the lack of intellectual depth, at least it was good for her waning self-esteem to know that strange men wanted her, unreciprocated as it may, or may not, be.

She held her breath for a moment while the realization finally sunk in. The committee has said yes; she was actually going back to Dallas. A brittle smile spread across her face. She was elated and scared half to death at the same time of her one chance to go and face this thing for real.

Her plan from the beginning had been to approach this as a documentary project, either on her own or with the support from NYU. She would take a high definition camera and a light kit and record full interviews of her contacts that she could then transcribe and edit. She would get full releases from everyone who participated and would perhaps put together a full-length documentary about the lake in a few years when she'd had time to process her findings. And just maybe she could learn how to free herself from her nocturnal visitor...

After the committee meeting, Laura went back to Reilly's office. After hearing about the committee's decision, he had offered her the use of his space while he was in back-to-back lectures. She turned on some music on his 90s-era Bang & Olufsen wall-mounted stereo, raided the tiny fridge for a lemon Perrier, and spent the rest of the afternoon on the phone making travel arrangements and scheduling interviews in Dallas.

"...Yes, my name is Laura Milton. I'm a documentarian from the Gallatin School at NYU and will be coming in to Dallas from New York next week. I would like to inquire if Mr. Stone might be available for a short interview... It's on the influence of geography on urban legends in modern society... Yes, I can hold..."

Three hours and 12 calls later Laura had the beginnings of a decent interview schedule for her three-week stay in Dallas. Her subjects were fairly diverse: an ex-city planner who claimed to know shocking details about the lake itself, a woman who professed to know the actual identity of the ghost, a software salesman who swears the ghost came to visit on Christmas Eve when he was a boy, and a female Baptist minister with some interesting insights into the underground lifestyle in Dallas in the 60's... They were all fascinating characters, each professing to have some knowledge relating in some way to the haunting White Rock Lake. She was thrilled to have the opportunity to actually meet these people in person after having cultivated relationships with most of them via social media for the past few months. In anticipation of a possible trip, she had even placed banner ads on a few related websites to get as much attention as she could in as short a time as possible. Though she was still waiting to hear back from some inquiries made months earlier, she planned her research well and felt confident there would be some good participation. There seemed to be no shortage of people willing to go on record about the city of Dallas or the ghost of White Rock Lake.

* * *

Laura stopped by her favorite grocery store on the way back to her apartment. The shop was a small health-food store, little more than a makeshift storefront crammed in a converted dry cleaners, but the prices were right and the people were friendly. She grabbed a few things, paid, stuffed them in her backpack, and walked out of the store waving to the young Hindi girl behind the counter.

"Bye, Sari. Thanks."

The girl waved back. "See you tomorrow!"

The sun cast a patchwork of colored light through the trees in the courtyard between buildings. The heat wasn't as brutal as it had been even a week ago. Fall was slowly starting to make its presence known. The thought made her smile. Being a January baby, winter would always be her favorite season.

Unknown to her, a dark figure entered the courtyard behind her. Seeing Laura across the lawn, the shadow darted behind a small cluster of trees. It watched her closely as she fiddled with her phone as a small group of children passed between them. The figure waited until everyone had left the area and she was alone. Slowly, the stranger crept up from behind.

A firm hand came down on Laura's shoulder. Instinctively, she dropped her pack, grabbed the hand and twisted it around as she side-stepped, taking the man attached to it to his knees, his arm poised to snap behind his back if he tried to struggle. It was a reflexive move and took all of two seconds to perform. The man screamed like a little girl.

"*Jesus*, Laura! I didn't mean to scare you! I called your name!"

She looked down at her ex, Colin Jonah, sitting on his knees completely helpless and at her mercy. If she hadn't been so worked up, she would have laughed out loud.

"Do. Not. Do that. Ever." She helped him to his feet.

"Don't you have a safety for that thing?" He rubbed at his right wrist.

"Sorry. But you should know better than to sneak up on me. Seriously." She picked up her pack and brushed the dirt off the side of his pants leg. They started walking.

"I'm sorry. Remind me never to throw you a surprise party." He shook his head. "I was just coming back from seeing the folks. Mom says hi."

"Tell her hi. How's your Dad?"

"Good. Stressed out."

"Business as usual, eh?"

"Yeah. I guess I should get used to it if I want that stewardship..."

"Don't do it for anyone else but yourself, Colin. It's a great job but it's the rest of your life, too."

He looked at her out of the corner of his eye. "That's kind of what I wanted to talk to you about." Her entire body tensed. "You don't think I should go through with it, do you?"

Laura dismissed the question as best she could and kept walking. "We don't want to get into this..."

He stopped her and took her by the hand, a very foreign gesture for them at this point. "No, really, tell me what you think. I trust your opinion."

She took a deep breath. Wow, it had been well over a year since he made his decision, and now he finally decides to ask her opinion. What an asshole. He knew exactly what she thought, and she had the mind to unleash all her pent up frustration on him in a barrage of expletives. But she stopped herself. Hadn't she already gotten her revenge? She wasn't a cruel person. It made her sad to know his question was just another small confirmation that she had probably made the right decision to distance herself...

Looking at him staring at her with those puppy-dog eyes, she couldn't refuse him an answer, even though she knew it would hurt him. And in a way, she was glad it would.

"I think you're doing it for the wrong reasons, Colin. You want your father to be proud of you so badly you will put your own happiness in the background to see it come true. We talked about Seattle, starting a life together. But you made the decision to stay without me." This was hurting her as much as it was obviously hurting him. "And now you ask me what I think? I love you, Colin, but I don't want to be in the middle of this. You've already made up your mind without me."

She could tell that wasn't what he wanted to hear, even though it was probably expected. She would never do anything to hurt him outright, but he knew better than to ask her something that he really didn't want to know the answer to.

"Thanks." He looked like she had just slapped him across the face.

They started walking again. After a few blocks they came to a large multi-leveled red brick building at the intersection of Peck Slip and Water Street. It was her building, the Stove Factory Lofts.

"Do you want to get some coffee or something?"

"Love to, but I've got a long night."

"So, how's the mysterious project coming along?"

She was instantly annoyed. "Anything you're not a part of is just a joke to you, isn't it?"

"I was just kidding! Jeeze, you're so touchy lately. It's just a ghost story..."

She turned around, glaring at him. "Great. Robert told you."

"No one told me anything. I figured it out from your books."

Sticking out of her shoulder pack in plain view were two hardbound books entitled *'Paranormal Research'* and *'The Road Beyond: What Ties Spirits to This World'*. Busted.

"You've been reading cemetery stats and paranormal rags for months. You didn't think I'd notice?" He laughed. "Why are you trying to hide it?"

She was embarrassed and suddenly furious. *'Why do you THINK I'm hiding it from you?'* she thought. *'You're the one who thinks everything I do is beneath me!'* But instead, her thoughts came out as, "I'm not hiding anything, Colin." Her voice was calm. "I just want to do this on my own. Please. If I need anything I promise I'll let you know."

In his ears, her tone was a soft demand for him to step down. He knew better than to push her when she was getting upset.

"Ok. I guess I'll call you later."

"I'll be at the Bobst Library till late. You're not working?"

"Not tonight." He paused. "Doesn't that place bother you? I still can't get over what happened there..."

"That was many years ago, baby."

"Still, I get the creeps every time I see that place."

"Colin, you're too logical of a person to get spooked over something like that. What happened? See a ghost?" She was totally baiting him now. He had never believed she had ever seen a ghost either.

"Being frightened and being creeped-out are two different things. Night, Laura."

He kissed her on the cheek and walked off into the evening.

She loved Colin but, Christ, he could be so frustrating at times. He wasn't even aware of his little condescending comments much less how crazy they made her. And that was the problem. One of them.

It was strange that he, of all people, would have such a strong reaction to the Bobst Library incident. What he was referring to were the suicides. In late 2003, in two separate incidents, students had jumped to their deaths from the open-air crosswalks in the atrium of the building. After the second suicide, the campus installed polycarbonate barriers on each level to keep others from attempting the same thing. Unfortunately, in 2009, a third student leaped from the tenth floor after crawling over the barricade. The campus had since replaced the poly with ornately designed perforated aluminum walls that were, for the most part, impenetrable.

The deaths were a smear on the face of the University at the time, yes, but the investigations revealed they had nothing to do with the school itself. It was the imaginations of agitated minds that ended the lives of those students. And now their restless souls were part of the library itself, just like the glass and steel of the walls, the marble of the floors, and the cement foundation, for all of eternity...

* * *

Laura took the elevator to the fourth floor of the apartment building. When the door opened, she skipped all the way to a bright orange door at the end of the hall. She unlocked the door, walked into her unit, and threw her books down on the coffee table with a deep sigh.

Grabbing a small wooden box sitting innocuously on her bookshelf, she opened it and pulled out a half-smoked joint. Fumbling with a book of matches, she finally succeeded in lighting it. Ah, one of life's little pleasures... The thing about marijuana was it was a lot less expensive than anti-depressants. And so much less dangerous when mixing it with her seizure medication...

With the joint between her lips, she continued into the hallway, reaching down to undo the button of her jeans, stepping out of them on the way to her bedroom.

Hopping up on the bed, she took a huge toke and placed the joint on a plate on the bedside table. Exhaling, she stretched out on the queen-size mattress and closed her eyes.

She was well aware that she had been isolating herself ever since her break-up with Colin. Sure, single life was lonely, but being an only-child had equipped her with the tools for dealing with isolation. Why did modern Western society condemn the single lifestyle anyway? It was the most natural thing in the world to her, to be alone with her thoughts and her work. If even just 10 percent of the world's populace could admit they felt the same way, the Earth would be a very different place.

For her, it was being around other people that was difficult. She couldn't seem to understand their motivations. Yes, she made friends easily, when she wanted to, but she constantly found herself estranged by people's need for attention and validation. She was thankful that her father weaned her from such juvenile preoccupations at a young age. Or perhaps it was the traumatic events in her life that made things like that seem so trivial.

It wasn't that she didn't want companionship; it was that she refused to sacrifice her own goals just to have it. Her few female friends in the graduate program joked that she was on the perfect path to becoming the next cat lady. So be it.

As if on cue, a small black kitten silently leaped up on the bed, staring with huge emerald eyes. Laura smiled and reached out for her. "The Evil Princess Katarina approaches..." She lay back on the bed and placed the kitten between her breasts. "How are you, my love? You don't care if I'm an old maid do you?" The kitten blinked in agreement. "I didn't think so. Let's take a little nap before the library. What do you say?"

The kitten blinked again and curled into a ball purring in her arms. Laura closed her eyes, thankful for a few minutes of peace...

* * *

...a smiling dark-haired woman, running. A 6-year-old girl at her side, a young Laura, laughing and pulling her mother to follow through the beaming sunshine... Little Laura breaks free and runs between two parked cars. She makes it to the middle of the asphalt street, stops, and turns to see a massive truck barreling straight for her. An arm appears, wraps around her little waist, and throws her back against the curb. Laura's mother falls out into the street just as the truck slams on its brakes, far too late to stop. The sound of a wet impact and Laura opens her eyes to see the body of her mother crushed and dragged for half a block under the force of the mammoth wheels. And the shrieking begins...

Laura's eyes popped open from a deep sleep, her own screams still echoing in her ears. Her heart was racing. Tears started to fill her eyes, but this time, instead of fighting it back, she surrendered to the raw, shuddering pain. It kept repeating, the scene that had haunted her for years played over and over again in her head. Christ. Losing her virginity was nothing. *This* had been the end of her innocence.

Sitting up in bed, Laura sobbed deeply in the amber light of the afternoon, embracing the sorrow. Her dear, sweet mother... The kitten Katarina snuggled up to her and gently licked her hand...

* * *

An hour later, Laura was walking through the seventh floor of the modern Bobst Library located on the NYU campus, a stack of reference books in her arms. She was a little disoriented still. The dream of her mother's death had taken her by surprise and un-centered her. It had been a long time since she last re-lived that harrowing experience, either unconsciously or otherwise. After years of therapy as a child, she finally felt like she had overcome the crushing sense of guilt over the incident and had pretty much let it go. Strange that it only took moments for her sub-conscience to bring it all back to life. God, she missed her mother so deeply...

Laura crossed in front of the cavernous atrium. Laser cut aluminum barriers the color of gold lined the open courtyard on all 12 floors of the structure, an ornate and visible deterrent to any future suicide attempts, as well as a constant reminder of the horrific events that occurred so long ago. She thought back to Colin's comment about feeling uneasy here. It was peculiar. Usually, Laura would instantly sense the presence of a wandering spirit, or rather it would sense her, and the two would be drawn together. But the only thing she had ever felt in the library was a deep sense of calm. Strange that she would feel so comfortable surrounded by the cold, angular design of Bobst, the large impersonal abundance of space framed in metal and glass and marble. Looking across the open foyer, the vast rooms behind their golden barriers seemed like geometric labyrinths that she could happily get lost in forever. If the spirits of those unfortunate students resided here, they preferred silence and space to human contact. That much, at least, she and the spirits had in common.

Perhaps Colin's feelings had more to do with the energetic history of the building itself and the spotty reputation of its namesake, the self-made pharmaceutical tycoon Elmer Holmes Bobst. Even though he came from meager beginnings to become one of the first multimillionaires without having any formal education, Bobst had been openly anti-Semitic and was accused, posthumously, by both his granddaughter and great-granddaughter, of pedophiliac rape and incest. Also, the lead architect of the library, Philip Johnson, was a known Nazi sympathizer and fascist during the reign of the Third Reich. It was no surprise that there was enough residual negative energy within these walls to ignite the disdain of even the most objective of people.

After gathering her reference materials, Laura settled into her favorite area on the sixth floor. On the north side of the building the even floors had been designed as large, double-height study rooms with floor-to-ceiling windows overlooking Washington Square Park. It was a gorgeous view during the day but was especially soothing at night.

Laura first brought up multiple screens up on her laptop, her reference tools, site links, and media bins. She then pulled up a customized timeline she had begun populating with dates and events related to White Rock and the state of Texas. She logged in to each of her reference sites. All of these elements would help in cross-referencing any piece of information she might come across, verifying the content, and helping her organize it logically.

Laura decided to start tonight with some Texas-based periodicals and newspapers to get a sense of place; D Magazine, Texas Monthly, The Dallas Observer, the Advocate, Paper City... She already had the beginnings of a hell of a dossier on Dallas but wanted to nurture a deeper connection with the city, try a different angle that might shed some light on specifics she may have missed. It wasn't brain surgery, but researching was something of a ritual to her. Opening another browser, she began dragging and dropping files into her research window.

She was perusing an on-line almanac when the name *Lester Davis* came across the screen. That was something new.

She absent-mindedly copied and pasted the entire article into her notes. A quick scan of the first page stated he was a Texas philanthropist who lived on White Rock Lake throughout the early 1950's and 60's. His family owned a number of cotton plantations in the south. Interesting. It seemed like a decent place to start gathering names to cross-reference.

She turned away from her computer for a moment and picked up one of the hardbound anthologies sitting next to her. A quick index look and she found multiple pictures of the lake in the early 1900's before and after the construction was finally completed. The bare waterline stretched out into the distance just like she remembered from her dreams. She could imagine the back of a woman's head staring out at the water, searching, yearning in vain for something that would never again return...

The night watchman stepped into the room and Laura jumped.

"Sorry, Laura-loo. Didn't mean to scare you."

"It's fine, Terry. Just a little jumpy tonight."

"I'm gonna grab a smoke on the balcony. Holler if you need me."

"Ok. Have a few drags for me..."

He smiled and walked away.

'*Why are you so jumpy?*' she asked herself, turning back to her work. She didn't have time to be overly sensitive these days. There was way too much to do. More than likely, it was the pressure of the logistics of this project. God knows, just the planning itself had been a Herculean feat of producing on her part. But something else was adding to her stress level. She was usually so calculated and exacting in her research but for the first time she really didn't know where to go next.

This investigation was a little like chasing Kilroy, the famed super G.I. from World War II who always got to the scene of the battle before anyone else but was never able to be found. He always left his calling card everywhere he went by writing the phrase "Kilroy Was Here", which would infuse the arriving soldiers with hope and a sense of pride. Little did the grunts know Kilroy was an entity created by the soldiers themselves to keep the morale of the troops high wherever in the world they might be. Kilroy never really existed. And perhaps what Laura was searching for never did either.

The emptiness of the building closed in around her like a cool blanket. Turning back to pictures of the lake, she started humming an awkward melody to herself. In the middle of the tune she stopped humming to mouth some words. Then she heard it. Somewhere in the depths of the building someone or something was humming the same eerie melody; she had subconsciously latched onto the sound and had been mimicking it.

She looked down at her right arm. All the baby-fine hair stood up on its end as a shiver ran through her. Every person had a panic reflex; this was hers. Any time it happened, she knew it was a warning to go on *'full alert'*.

'Here we go...'

She stood slowly and followed the humming out into the foyer. It seemed to be coming from the staircase that led to the floor above. She sighed heavily. Her own sense of curiosity was exhausting to her at times. She was never one to pass up a good adventure, regardless how challenging or dangerous it might be. And though, yes, her life was probably a bit more exciting than most because of that trait, it was probably the dumbest skill-set she had ever developed. *'Curiosity killed the cat,'* her mother would have said.

Yeah, well, not today. Hopefully...

Laura crept up the flight of stairs carefully so as not to allow her footfalls to frighten whomever or whatever she might find. With each step the humming grew louder, an awkward melody echoing through the ether. It was familiar in a strange way, something she remembered from her childhood perhaps. Sad and quirky, what was once nothing but a forgotten ditty had just become a tool of communication between her and something from beyond.

Turning the corner she saw a boy, probably a few years her junior, sitting on a clear bench against the golden spires of the perforated barricade. He was engrossed in something in his hand. Looking up, he smiled at her. She smiled back knowing that he was not real, only a reflection of something that was once living, a shadow cast on the ground by a soul walking into the sun.

The boy's face turned grave and he shook his head as if in answer to her thoughts. He stood and held up the object in his hand, showing it to her. It was a dead rosebud, dry and shriveled, cupped in the smooth white skin of his palm. There were waves of sadness coming from him.

The boy abruptly turned and threw himself at the barricade, his body passing through the golden security wall, which seemed to shimmer in and out of transparency. Instinctively, Laura lunged towards the barrier but there was no way to reach him in time. And even if she had been able, what she was witnessing was a ripple in the pool of Time; there was no way to prevent what had already happened years ago. She was simply watching a replay.

Still, time seemed to stop as he fell away from her, through the safety barrier, past floor after floor of glass and steel, his limp body going through a stream of motion in mid-air, a minute ballet, all the while humming the same eerie melody that she now would never forget for the rest of her life. She heard his body impact on the stereogram patterned marble floor seven stories below with a loud resounding crack.

The scream finally escaped her throat and ricocheted through the cavernous space. Below, a dark pool of blood widened and surrounded the lifeless shell of what had once been a boy.

Terry, the night watchman, appeared at the top of the stairs, gun drawn. “Laura! Are you alright?”

Her mouth open in shock, she turned back to the railing and saw the barrier was intact. The young boy’s body was nowhere to be seen.

She reeled around and pulled the hair back from her face, trying to appear calm. “It’s nothing, Terry. I thought I saw a mouse. I must be tired.”

“You’re white as a sheet, Laura-loo.”

“I’m ok, really...”

She bent down to pick up the rose bloom that lay at her feet. It crumbled into dust the instant she touched it.

Moments later, the ground-level elevator door opened and Laura stepped out. Still shivering, she passed the information desk where in her peripheral vision she couldn’t help but notice a dark figure hunched down next to the wall, its mangled face hanging from a crushed skull. As she walked through the security gates, the thing turned to watch her leave the library with a bloody eye all the while quietly humming to itself...

Five

Laura finally left her apartment building on Water Street at 9 AM. Her meds knocked her out especially hard early this morning and she ended up sleeping straight through her alarm. When she woke, she felt like she had been hit by a slow-moving train and dragged for miles. Gradually, she emerged out of the drug-induced haze and, after some yogurt and a handful of Golden Grahams, found herself in a decent mood.

Her therapist appointment was at 2 PM by Central Park West so she decided to take advantage of the free time to do a little shopping and have lunch downtown. She loved days when her schedule was free and she could take her time and just enjoy the city, which was quite a feat when you were socio-phobic in a city of 8 and a half million people. But the city of New York had always seemed so nurturing to her and she felt nothing but comfort in a metropolis that was alienating and threatening to most people.

On Peck Slip, Laura caught a cab to Greenwich Village. From there she walked to Broadway to visit the Strand Bookstore. It had been her father's favorite haunt whenever they came into the city from Far Hills. She could remember watching him reading in the aisles for hours as she did her homework at the reading tables. Just being in the building that brought him so much joy made her feel better.

She picked up a few books she had ordered on paranormal psychology, paid, and walked half a block to Starbucks. Usually, she would just purchase reading materials on-line and download them to her tablet. But these books were very rare. She had secretly been collecting everything she could find on spiritual manifestations and ghost hunting most of her life and the increased intensity of her dreams over the past few months had only amped up her obsession. Something about feeling a hard copy in her hands made the entire subject seem a little more believable.

Laura walked into the coffee shop and took her place in line.

The young woman from her nightmares was no longer just an unsettling nocturnal visitor in her life; she had *become* Laura's life to a large extent. It was because of her that Laura chose to change her major and study urban legends and sociology in the first place. This thing was holding the reins to her life and until she found out why, she would never be able to let it go. And it would never let her go, either.

When it was her turn, Laura ordered a chai latte and handed the girl her debit card. It was hard to keep this ghoulish passion a secret, especially from Colin. He was so busy all the time, she really thought he barely had time to notice *her* much less what she was working on. But apparently, that wasn't the case. Having him call her out made her feel like a functional drug addict; a productive member of society who lived a very different life behind locked doors.

Waiting for her drink, Laura observed all the patrons mulling about, reading books or checking email. Each individual person was immersed in their own world, set apart from everyone else, with their own collections of loves, hates, and tragedies playing themselves out behind their eyes and over their texts. But did any of these people harbor dark secrets like she did? Did any of them wake night after night with the image of a dead woman reverberating in their psyches, slowly sucking the sanity out of them? Probably not.

When her name was called, Laura picked up her chai and walked back out onto the street, disconnecting from the frantic human energy of the coffee shop. The day was absolutely gorgeous. Being out in the sun made her feel confident and alive. In moments like this, it was hard to believe anything dark existed anywhere in the world.

As she navigated the shuffling crowds on the streets of downtown Manhattan, something buzzed in the distance, a strange metallic hum that was continuous underneath the sounds of the traffic. She was acutely aware of the flow of cars in the street, the ornamental designs in the architecture of the buildings, the cracks in the masonry that ran 12 stories up the side of the once cutting-edge skyscraper thrusting out of the cement in front of her. Her heartbeat was like a touch; she could trace the gentle flow of blood traveling up her spine, into her limbs like a lover's caress. The hum was getting louder. The baby-fine hair on her arm was standing at attention. Something was trying to communicate with her.

And just as quickly as it came, the feeling was gone. Strange. Could this be some new seizure warning?

She walked on. As long as she was moving, she would be all right. It was when sadness and complacency took over that the attacks usually came. Stress and fear were the triggers. As long as she kept her mind and her body engaged and stayed focused, she would be fine. Hopefully.

The last few days had definitely been stressful. There was one detail she still couldn't get out of her mind; the thing in the library had called out to her. Why now? She spent most of her study time at the Bobst Library; it could have contacted her at any point over the last several years. Why did it choose this particular time to make its presence known to her? And what did the flower thing mean?

The frustrating part of all of this was that she couldn't share her thoughts with anyone. Her therapist, Colin, Reilly, not one of them actually believed she could tell a ghost from a strong gust of wind. How then could she possibly explain a complex incident like this? Not even her best friend Emily knew anything about her strange gift. Laura was completely alone in this. She took a deep breath and quickened her pace, trying to keep her mind occupied.

After window-shopping in the Village for a few hours, she took a cab to Joe's Shanghai Restaurant in Chinatown. While waiting for her crabmeat soup dumplings, the awkward feeling returned. It wasn't like a seizure warning, she just felt nervous, like someone was watching her. She kept looking over her shoulder but never saw anything out of the ordinary in the voracious lunch crowd. She ate her lunch in silence at a small table for two trying her best to relax. Perhaps it was simply a vanguard spirit tied to the building that picked up on her frequency. It was a fairly common event in her life, attracting stray souls when she ventured into their territories. Even after all these years, she had still never gotten used to it.

Laura finished her meal and decided to browse the maze of shops outside. She needed a distraction from her own mind for a while and nothing cleared her like perusing the markets. The sheer volume of merchandise was intoxicating. Sometimes she actually bought things, but what she really loved were the colors and the sounds of people haggling with the sellers for the cheapest prices. It was almost like doing battle in some medieval world.

She turned the corner and at the end of the block there was an ally with a few stalls set apart from the buildings. As she entered the first, she saw a thin wooden pulpit standing in the center of the space. There seemed to be a large copy of what could only have been a Christian Bible cracked open upon it. A man in priestly vestments stood behind it praying intensely with a young Asian woman. She was crying. Laura watched them for a long moment wondering what it was they were praying for and what was fueling the young woman's heartbreaking flow of sobs.

In the next stall, there was a woman sitting at a simple black table with deck of cards laid out in a fanned pattern. Laura looked closer and realized that the woman's eyes were grey and lifeless. She was blind.

The woman looked up in Laura's direction and startled her. "May I help you?"

"I–I was just–"

"You were watching me."

"Yes. How did you–?"

"How did I know?" The woman smiled. "I felt your sadness, dear."

"But... I'm not sad." Laura's voice sounded a little more defensive in her own ears than she meant it to.

The woman's face became grave. "You don't even know how deep in despair you really are."

"I really don't know what you're talking about–"

"She is calling to you. At night. She knows you..."

A wave of chills washed over Laura. This woman was talking about her dreams. How could she know anything about her?

"I know because I *see*..." the blind woman said, as if in answer to her.

"What? What do you see?" Laura asked.

The woman stared up at her and gasped.

"I see death..." The stranger took a deep, shuddering breath. "There is nothing I can do for you." The woman began to weep, tears flowing from the grey, unseeing marbles of her eyes as Laura watched in horror. "Go," the woman pleaded, "Please, just go..."

* * *

The waiting room of Manhattan Services was a bit more grandiose than Laura thought necessary. The view from the 35th floor overlooking Central Park West was awesome if not a little intimidating, especially for a psychologist's waiting room. On her worst days, she had imagined smashing through the glass and hurtling herself to the street below. On her best days, the view just made her feel queasy, uncomfortable, and insignificant. Today was a combination of the two.

The incident with the woman in Chinatown had put her over the edge. What the hell was going on? How could some strange blind woman possibly know about her dreams? And what she said, "*There's nothing I can do for you...*" What could that mean?

She sat down and tried to calm herself. The magazines on the glass coffee table were the usual fare of "Psychotherapy Today", "Men's and Women's Health", and the lifestyle rags like "Us", "People", and "Cosmopolitan". The first two, she could appreciate, but she couldn't understand people's fascination with the mundane, the way western society elevated such 2-dimensional characters to the status of celebrity and flaunted them as people to emulate. As far as she was concerned, the modern world was little more than an exercise in futility; a runaway train in the middle of the desert heading nowhere...

A frosted glass pane slid open in the far wall and the receptionist peered out.

"Laura?"

* * *

Adrienne Bartok was a demure woman in her late forties; calm, intelligent, and just a little too impressed with herself for Laura's liking. Even though Bartok was the first therapist to break through many of Laura's personal barriers, there was something about being in her presence that reminded Laura of sitting in a disapproving principal's office. Bartok was more than a little condescending in the way she spoke to her at times, and though Laura didn't want to seem too sensitive, she thought a therapist should have at least some sort of social skills where clients were concerned. Perhaps she thought Laura was just a spoiled girl from a privileged home. She knew everything about Laura's history, how could she make that assumption? Maybe Bartok's approach to therapy was more akin to tough love instead of compassionate support. Whatever. After all these years, Laura still couldn't tell what her therapist's motivations were. But the woman seemed to get results and that was the only thing that kept Laura coming back. And whatever her prejudices were, Bartok's job was to help Laura unravel herself, whether she liked it or not.

When they first started working together, the good doctor had even gone so far as to suggest Laura's seizures were simply dramatic episodes that Laura could control if she wanted. Damn her. How dare she imply that Laura was some kind of hypochondriac who just imagined herself into epilepsy? It was humiliating enough having to deal with the condition itself much less having to qualify everything to satisfy her therapist. Perhaps Adrienne was just another smart woman who felt she had to assert herself beyond measure to fight off some deep-seated insecurity. Laura knew all about insecurity, but she never used it as a weapon. As the years passed, Bartok had become a little more sensitive to Laura's situation, but the underlying damage to their relationship had already been done. In many ways, the two women were natural enemies.

But to look at Laura now, pale, anemic, eyes puffy from crying, no one would guess that she was the integrous one, holding herself together in the midst of extreme crises, living in the moment while her smug therapist was in fact the one living in denial and fear.

Bartok had confessed to Laura a few years ago that she was in a bitter custody battle over her infant son with her ex-husband. Over the last 12 months Laura had become painfully aware of the bitterness that had steadily grown out of that traumatic process. It had warped Bartok's effectiveness and calcified into detachment and, at times, passive unfiltered cruelty. Why she continued to come to her was a complete mystery.

As if reading the younger woman's mind, the therapist, who was wearing a short skirt, crossed her long, tanned legs, a defiant gesture flaunting her femininity and, therefore, superiority. "Tell me again, Laura, how long have you had these dreams?"

The condescension did not go unregistered. "I've already told you, they started when I was six. But the crying episodes began just a few weeks ago. "

"So, what do you think your subconscious is trying to tell you?"

Laura was suddenly overcome. Hot tears welled in her eyes. "I think something's trying to speak to me."

"Do you think these visions have something to do with your mother?"

She wiped at her face. "No, not like that. It's as if each time, each dream, more is shown to me. I see bits and pieces of someone's life, the last things they ever saw..." She felt like she was going to be sick.

"What are you afraid of, Laura?"

She could feel herself beginning to panic. She tried to calm herself by taking deep breaths. "I'm afraid of dying. I don't want to die."

"Who said you were going to die?"

"That's what I feel when I wake up. I don't want to die. I just want to go home. Please take me home..." The tears started to flow out of her again only adding to her frustration.

Bartok sat staring at her. Laura saw pity in the woman's eyes. "Laura, I think we should stop for today."

Laura snapped. "Goddamnit, I pay you a hundred and eighty-five dollars an hour! We will *not* stop!" Her voice was commanding and pleading simultaneously. "I need to know what is happening to me. *Please...*"

* * *

When Laura was finally back in her apartment two hours later, she needed to clear her head. She put on a running outfit and shoes, put her hair in a ponytail, and headed back out into the street.

She jogged to Maiden Lane and then over to Broadway. The streets were crowded as usual. She passed the subway entrance and was jogging blindly, letting her thoughts wander on their own. The Seattle band *Minus the Bear* was playing through her ear buds filling her senses as she ran through the unending waves of people. Music was her one constant escape from the world at large. It took her out of herself, consoled her, built her up, and many times gave her the strength to continue when she felt like giving up. To her, music was the great equalizer, the ultimate communicator, the ultimate intimacy. It was no wonder the spirit at the library chose to speak to her through that particular medium. She was hard-wired for it.

Laura jogged through another busy intersection glancing at the faces of the drivers sitting waiting for the light to change as she passed. What a metaphor for society...

She continued down Broadway. It felt good, the feeling of her body moving over the pavement, weaving through the crowds of people, totally into her mind and her music. It was incredibly therapeutic. While she ran, she thought about her life, mused, meditated. If she were religious, she would probably call it a form of prayer. She tried to center herself in the world as she centered her body. And today she had a lot to muse upon.

The therapist Bartok had a lot of theories, but ultimately had no idea what Laura's reoccurring dreams meant. She suggested everything from an EKG to hypnosis to consulting a battery of specialists. One thing was for sure, she thought Laura was just moments away from a nervous breakdown. Apparently, she had all the symptoms; unresolved grief, a loss of interest in other people, violent dreams, detachment... Laura thinking that she, herself, was crazy was one thing, but having her therapist agree with her was something else entirely.

Caffe Reggio is the oldest coffee shop in Greenwich Village. Having first opened in 1927, they boast about being the first *caffe* to ever have an espresso machine in America. It's an awkward, gypsy-looking establishment filled with antique chairs and couches, all wonderfully mismatched and comfortably worn.

Laura slowed to a trot and entered the funky green storefront on MacDougal Street. She loved this place. Just a few minutes from Washington Square, this century-old café had been her and Colin's favorite haunt when she first joined him at NYU. They had spent many nights together talking away the hours over French Roast and tiramisu, slowly falling in love.

It had taken a lot for Laura to finally let Colin into her heart in those days. Growing up with him from the age of 7 on, he had always occupied the space of a big brother to her, though both their thoughts went far beyond that. Garret and Grace had raised a good-natured son who was intelligent and had always been respectful of her space. Laura's father had loved him and told her more than once that they would make a great couple. In many ways, her father was the one who planted the seed. That was another reason why she couldn't seem to let Colin go.

Laura pulled her phone out of her sports bra and texted Colin. He replied almost immediately saying he was just leaving his father's New York office on 5th Avenue on the other side of Washington Square. He could meet her in ten minutes. She smiled, realizing how much she really missed him.

Laura ordered an iced decaf from the barista, walked out to the patio and took a small table. Men passed by staring at her as they always did, but she didn't let it bother her. She was excited to see Colin. Even though she desperately needed her space, some things were impossible for her to let go of, and he was at the top of that very short list.

Laura wished she could talk to him about what was happening in her life, but she knew her tales of ghosts and redemption would only fall on deaf ears, no matter how cute those ears happened to be. That was one part of her life that no one but her mother had ever understood. And therefore, instead of subjecting herself to constant criticism, she shared tales of her communications with spirits with no one. Not even her therapist.

A tall, gangly form emerged from the stream of people. She recognized Colin and waved as he crossed over to where she was sitting. Laura stood up and hugged him from the other side of the railing a little too tightly, pushing her breasts into him. He felt and smelled wonderful.

"Hi, stranger." She purred.

"What a nice surprise. You look great." He stepped over the railing, took his backpack off and sat down across the table. "How are you?"

"Good. Tired. I've been so busy, I decided to take the afternoon off for myself. I was in the area and wanted to say hi."

"I'm really glad you did."

She looked into his eyes, drinking as much of him in as quickly as she could. "I've missed you, Colin."

He sat back in his chair and smiled. She could tell he was less than thrilled with her revelation. He wanted her back, in his arms, in his bed. And she knew it. But there was something distracting him.

"Would you like something?" She was trying to start conversation but it seemed to be more difficult that she expected.

"Thanks, I'm ok. I had a late lunch."

"I know we haven't spent much time together lately, but I've been thinking a lot about you..."

His eyes didn't move. Something was obviously on his mind.

"Are you ok?" She asked.

"Reilly tells me you're leaving for Texas. Why didn't you say anything?"

Laura looked at him silently. She sensed the pain and frustration seeping out of his calm demeanor, killing her moment of joy. She didn't want to do this now. But if not now, when? She hated the thought of destroying their first nice moment together in weeks, but there was nothing else she could do except get up and run out of the building. She took a deep breath.

"I don't know how to feel better about this. I'm still really hurt, Colin. I thought I could just go and figure out a few things on my own."

"What can I do to help?"

'The eternal boy scout', she thought.

"Let me go. Just for a while. I need to do this on my own. And I need to think." She shook her head, looking away. "We want different things..."

"Different things?"

"You want a family, kids..."

He smiled. "Kids love you."

"But I don't love *them*." She suddenly realized that she snapped at him and took a deep breath. "At least, I don't want to be *forced* to. I love *you*. And that has to be enough..."

Colin saw the engagement ring he had given her still on her finger. He reached out and fingered the slim platinum band.

"I'm sorry..." She was beginning to tear up again.

"For what?"

"Everything. Changing. Leaving you at the alter... How unforgivably cliché and cruel and selfish that was..."

"We've talked about this. I don't hate you, Laura. Not in the least. And neither do my parents. You'll always be part of our family, even if you're not a part of me."

She looked at him through misty eyes. He was sitting across the table, not expecting anything, simply existing in the moment, letting this event unfurl however it was meant to. God, she was jealous of his ability to disconnect.

She reached out and touched the side of his face. "You are a wonderful, smart, compassionate, sexy man. You deserve someone who is good to you, not someone crazy like me."

He smiled one of his endearing smiles he knew she loved. "You are good to me, Laura. And you're not crazy. You just don't know what you want. And there's nothing wrong with that. Look, go and do what you need to. I'll be here when you get back. No pressure. I just want you to be happy. Really..."

She looked into his trusting brown eyes remembering why she loved him so deeply. It made keeping him at arm's-length all the more difficult. She had lost everyone she had ever loved and was scared to death she would lose him as well.

They finished their drinks and Laura excused herself to finish her run and get back to work. Colin was restless but after strolling through the Village and having a few beers at a favorite watering hole, he caught a cab back to his sublet in Gramercy.

His place was the quintessential bachelor pad. A second-story one-bedroom studio with an elevated mezzanine he used as his office. Clothing was strewn on the floor and there was very little furniture. A few empty pizza boxes were stacked on the dining table. The place didn't look like the residence of the son of the executive director of the Smithsonian Institute but rather that of a third-year game designer complete with an electric vaporizer, hidden porn collection, and shelves filled with live-action fan-boy comic characters posed and ready to rumble.

After an hour or so testing a beta for a new archeological topography program, Colin grew restless. He stretched and sat staring at the computer.

"...Damnit."

Against his better judgment, Colin opened up a Google search on White Rock Lake, Dallas, Texas. A list of links began scrolling across his screen. Easy enough. So why did he suddenly feel like he was going through his girlfriend's diary?

He browsed through the first few sites, familiarizing himself with the legend of the Lady of the Lake. He had to admit, the entire story seemed pretty creepy. It followed a pattern, though. A reoccurring theme of a similar nature had been reported all over the country, the world, even. The scenario was always the same; a hitchhiking girl in the middle of the night, soaked to the skin, asks for a ride and after being picked up, she disappears from the back of the car. Laura knew all of this from her studies. What could possibly make White Rock any different?

Laura had mentioned a 'Lester Davis'. Colin entered the name into a detailed search. A good number of references came up and he began perusing through them. The guy had an interesting background. His family owned a number of cotton farms in the surrounding counties of Houston and had old ties to oil... His father, Beau Davis, had been a prominent figure in the 1920's.

As a young man, Davis frequently appeared in the society pages, always with beautiful women on his arm. He was documented in bars and theaters, but rarely in private photographs.

Something was off. Davis didn't seem like the type of person to stay preoccupied in the family business of cotton farming. A closer look and Colin found there had been other interests; a few real estate properties and something called Davis Collectibles. Probably furniture or textiles. Colin made a note to submit Davis' name to a friend at the CIA. Google had nothing on them.

Colin knew Laura was a strong girl and could take care of herself, but she was walking blindly into this. This wasn't just some creaky old house with flickering lights and cold-spots she was investigating. No, this was an urban legend that rose out of a very tumultuous time in Dallas' history, filled with social unrest, the JFK murder conspiracies, and rampant police corruption. And from what she said, too many people were responding to her requests for interviews for this to be just a simple ghost story.

Laura would be pissed if she knew he was checking up on her, but he would rather face her wrath than simply stand by and let her walk into a dangerous situation. He would continue his own research and hopefully learn enough to keep her from doing something reckless. At least for a while...

* * *

Across the city at the Stove Factory Lofts, Laura Milton was once again twitching in her sleep. Lightning flashed behind her closed eyelids and she whimpered out loud as the visions exploded in her head.

Scores of native people darkened by the sun traveling the shallow valley that will someday become White Rock Lake... Entire families walking hundreds of miles on foot; parents holding babies, the fortunate ones on horseback, children and seniors stumbling and falling in the heat, many never to get back up... The back of an old woman's head as she stares out at the valley cursing God and crying bitter tears...

Laura opened her eyes in the dark as the images faded. She was lying on her back, which she never does when asleep. Tears were streaming down the side of her face. She forcibly ramped her breathing down until her heart rate slowed. In moments she was coherent and alert. The blades of the ceiling fan gently chopped through the shadows cast by the light from the streetlamps below.

These episodes were her deepest fears calling out from her subconscious. Each dream ripped a tiny piece of her heart out and her academic mind confirmed that these visions represented her deep sense of guilt and abandonment... The sadness that blossomed in the night was not transferred from the spirit of someone else; it belonged to her alone, for whatever reason. She was frightened, yes, but she was ready to finally face her demons...

* * *

On the morning of her departure Laura woke at 4 AM. She did 30 minutes of yoga, took a shower, and had a light breakfast. After taking her meds, she curled up on the couch to take her usual nap. She got up an hour later feeling amazingly well.

Everything had been packed two days before and Laura was proud of herself for being as organized as she was. All was as it should be.

Looking around, she realized how much she loved her apartment. There was nothing like quiet and privacy. And here, in her fourth-floor one-bedroom with a western *and* a northern view, she had plenty of both. It didn't have the warmth or the memories of the guesthouse in New Jersey, but it was fairly close to school and, for being in a new neighborhood in New York City, was pretty safe. Her father's picture had a prominent place on the main wall and she looked at it often and thanked him constantly.

The shuttle arrived at 8 AM. While the driver loaded her bags, she walked through the apartment doing a last-minute check and finishing her bloody Mary. Funny enough, the cocktail was a habit she got from her father when she was very young. At the time, he was constantly traveling for his job and would be gone 2 to 4 days a week. It was his rule to always have a Bloody Mary for luck before he got on an airplane. When he was at home, he would always make her a spicy Virgin Mary in her favorite cup so she could share that moment with him before he left. It was one of the most enduring memories she had of him as a child, sharing a drink with her beloved father. Now that she was of age, she didn't spare the Skye vodka in her own recipe. Of course, consuming alcohol raised her risk of a seizure, but as long as she imbibed in moderation, she felt confident that she could stay healthy enough to keep the fits at bay.

The only thing she really dreaded was the possibility of losing bowel and bladder control coming out of a seizure. How humiliating would that be? So far, it had never happened, thank God, but the doctors had warned her it was always a possibility. She smiled to herself. If nothing else, should something happen to the plane, at least she would go down in flames shitting her pants with a good buzz on.

Opening a jewelry box sitting on the desk, she picked out the platinum engagement ring Colin had given her and smiled sadly to herself. It always brought her comfort and for some reason, lately, she couldn't stand to be without it. Even if she didn't wear it all the time, it would definitely be making the trip with her. She slid it on her ring finger and replaced the box.

Katarina, Laura's kitten, jumped up on the counter and started rubbing against her hand.

"Now, Mrs. Pendergrass will take care of you while I'm gone, Princess." Laura petted her soft coat. "Try not to kill her before I get back, ok?"

The kitten blinked back in utter indifference and started cleaning its tiny paws.

"Miss Milton? Whenever you are..." The shuttle driver had finished loading her bags on the cart and was waiting by the door. Laura grabbed her purse, hugged the kitten, and took one last look around her apartment before closing the door behind her.

Six

At 3 hours and 43 minutes, the flight had been relatively short. Money had never been important to her, but Laura was deeply grateful to be able to afford certain luxuries. Non-stop first-class flights were definitely on the top of that list. She was free to sit back, listen to Rachmaninoff on her phone, and actually sleep. Her dreaming episodes only came when she was alone, strangely enough. After a cup of chamomile tea and a small meal, she slept like a rock and woke feeling refreshed and invigorated.

As the plane descended into Dallas/Fort Worth Airport, butterflies filled her stomach. She was mere moments away from beginning a new process of discovery, entering into an unknown world she had to open herself up to. She took a deep breath and reminded herself it was only through her own drive, determination, and sheer will that any of this was happening. Field research was nothing new to her, but she had a personal interest in this investigation that went beyond just clinical observation. Yes, there were bound to be logistical problems and obstacles that she couldn't foresee, but this was what she needed in her life, to face this dark unknown head on, to know that she was capable of opening a door and stepping through it all by herself, without anyone else's help, regardless of the outcome.

Once she was through the loading bridge, the crowded airport seemed foreign to her. The store windows were filled with Dallas Cowboys' paraphernalia and stylized faux western-wear. The blatant Texan theme was almost comical, like objects of a lost culture she had only read about in books. For a moment, she felt like she was living someone else's life, seeing fragments of their shattered existence echoing in her mind very much like the dreams that haunted her day and night.

Crossing the concourse, a quiet sadness settled over her. She had been 7 years old when she and her father moved to New Jersey, leaving Dallas and all the horrible memories behind. The only surviving relatives on her father's side had long ago disappeared. And her mother's adopted parents had died early on without siring any other children. There was literally nothing tying her to this city except the cemetery where her parents were laid to rest. Suddenly, coming here seemed like a complete mistake.

She collected her luggage, navigated her way through the airport, and rented a new black Land Rover from Hertz. In less than twenty minutes, she was pulling out onto the highway headed southeast towards downtown Dallas.

Nervous energy flowed through her. Now that she was here, she wasn't sure what to do first. Music always helped her focus so she turned on the radio. The guy at Hertz had mentioned a radio station, KXT 91.7. She found the frequency and a luscious number by Band of Horses filled the vehicle calming her down a little. Thank God for good driving music.

After navigating the long stretch of construction surrounding the airport, she passed through Las Colinas, a minor urban development that never really took off in the 1980's. On her left, the remnants of an abandoned monorail project in the form of unconnected cement towers trailed off into a passing field where it simply stopped, the monorail to nowhere.

20 minutes later, Laura passed the former location of the original Texas Stadium on her right, now nothing more than a

colossal depression in the ground at the junction of highways 183 and 114. So much for historic landmarks...

She merged left onto Carpenter Freeway and downtown Dallas appeared on the horizon with its angular spires and the recognizable ball of the Reunion Tower glinting in the distance. Disregarding all her insecure bullshit, it was now time to put up or shut up.

She had programmed her GPS to find White Rock Lake before leaving the airport. From I35 she merged onto Interstate 30. Passing close to downtown, she took note of the different periods of buildings, the blocky yellow brick of the buildings of the 30's and 40's compared to the newer skyscrapers like the 72-story Bank of America Plaza, the JP Morgan/Chase Tower, the angular Fountain Place, and the 42-story shimmering Museum Tower building. It was a gorgeous mixture of architectural styles and disciplines. A little old, a little new. Together, they made for a formidable city profile.

Minutes later, on the right she passed the State Fair grounds, the home of the Texas Star, the largest Ferris wheel in North America, and the renowned Cotton Bowl, where the famed annual Texas/OU games had been held for decades. She had been to the fair as a child, but the whole experience was nothing but a blur. All she remembered were the corny dogs and getting lost. Her mother finally found her teary-eyed at one of the many police stations in the midway eating ice cream. She remembered crying all the way home.

Laura continued up I30 and when prompted by the GPS, she exited East Grand Avenue and found herself driving through Samuel Park, an expansive wooded area that stretched out on either side of the road, part of a large inner-city golf course. The Land Rover passed under a huge canopy of trees and continued up a gentle slope.

Soon, the foliage peeled back and she drove over a bridge that led to a commercial area; a small strip mall peppered with shops and a few Mexican food restaurants. The next light was a fork where Gaston Avenue merged with East Grand to become Garland Road.

As she passed under the rail bridge, an expansive cement spillway appeared on her left framed by a wooden bridge and boardwalk. She slowed down and took a deep breath as the expanse of water revealed itself in the distance. As if out of her dreams, White Rock Lake glittered majestically in front of her.

After hours of studying survey maps, Laura knew the geography of the lake by memory. From Garland Road she turned onto Lawther Drive, the infamous lakeside road the White Rock Lady is said to favor. She wanted to see the water up close with her own eyes.

Laura pulled the Land Rover over to the right side of the street under a large oak tree and got out of the car. The lake was much larger than she remembered. The wind had picked up and the water was dark and choppy with whitecaps, almost as if her mere presence was making it angry. All the hair on Laura's arms started to tingle. Staring out even in direct sunlight she sensed something stirring there in the depths, not something created by human imagination, something real and tangible. And whatever it was, it knew she had arrived.

A tall fence ran the length of the road on the right, the barrier for the Dallas Arboretum which sat atop a hill overlooking the lake. Directly on the opposite side of the road about 15 feet from the pavement the water began. There were people in the distance bicycling at the west end of the lake but no one seemed to be in the immediate area.

Something moved in the corner of her eye, and she realized someone was sitting on a racing bicycle propped next to a tree not ten yards away. The rider was male and seemed occupied adjusting something on his gears.

When Laura approached, the bicyclist looked up and smiled.

"Hi. Looks like a great ride. How long is it?"

The man was silent for a moment. "The bike path is just over 9 miles." He kept fiddling with his gears.

"Do you come here a lot?"

The man looked up and smiled easily. "I'm always here."

"Lucky you! It's really beautiful." She looked out at the water and her body involuntarily shivered. "It kinda gives me the chills."

The man smiled back, his face calm and inquisitive.

"You're from here," he said flatly.

"Yes, but I haven't been back since I was very young. My name is Laura."

"I'm Larry."

"Well, enjoy your ride, Larry. It was nice meeting you. Be careful."

Larry smiled back at her and rode away. She noticed that his side was wet and he had marks on the back of his shirt like he had fallen and slid in water or something. Looking behind her, she saw there was no one else on the trail but the two of them. When she turned back, Larry's bicycle had already left her view. He was nowhere to be seen. He must have hurried on towards Winfry Point, a hill that lay about a quarter mile away. Strange. She had only turned around for a moment...

Laura blinked in confusion and slowly walked back to her car.

Seven

The Land Rover pulled up to the front entrance of the historic Melrose Hotel. The valet collected Laura's bags and followed her into the lobby. The interior was decorated in a modernized art deco theme populated with period furniture. An exquisite thatched pattern in the marbled floor tiles ran the length of the room. Everything was cream and mahogany, glass and stone. Very understated luxury.

She approached the front desk.

"Hi. I'm checking in. The name is Laura Milton."

"Yes, of course. We have you down for a double suite."

"That's right."

The young woman behind the counter pulled up her reservation and after checking Laura's identification handed her a card key. "Enjoy your stay with us."

Once upstairs, Laura set up her office quickly, put on her Bluetooth headset, and started dictating her opening commentary while unpacking the rest of her things.

"...This hotel served as home for many celebrities and writers through the years. I'm sure it has its own secret history waiting to be discovered. As far as I know, there have been no outstanding reports of paranormal activity... but there is something here, regardless. Strange or not, it should serve me as home base until I get my bearings. My first interview is in the morning..."

In a small anteroom adjoining her suite she set up her camera and small LED light kit in minutes. In the morning all she would have to do is aim the fixtures, mic the subject, and hit record.

After securing the interview room and grabbing a quick shower, she threw on some comfortable clothes, grabbed her tablet, and ventured down to the Library Bar on the ground floor. Stepping into the sumptuously dark lounge, she let out a sigh of relief. This wasn't your average hotel bar. Most all of the available wall space taken by deep shelves filled with vintage books giving the impression that it was a genuine turn of the century plantation library. Small couches and tables lined the room void of patrons. A black baby grand piano stood against the far wall. The bellman had told her small jazz combos performed most nights. For now, a lone pianist played a mournful rendition of "Stormy Weather". It was a perfect place to get centered.

She took a seat at the bar. In minutes she was deep into her work, a soda and lime sweating just out of her reach. She didn't notice a man in a dark suit enter the lounge behind her. The man leaned over and spoke to the hostess who, in turn, motioned towards Laura. He straightened up and approached the bar.

Laura was totally immersed in her reading and didn't notice the stranger whatsoever, even as he stood watching her for a long moment, amused. She looked like a schoolgirl engrossed in her homework.

He cleared his throat. "Enjoying yourself this evening?"

Laura looked up startled, and more than slightly embarrassed she hadn't noticed someone standing next to her. "Ah, yes, thank you."

"I'm Mallory, a managing partner here at the Melrose."

She shook his hand, felt his strong but tender grip. Her father always told her there were volumes of information you could learn about a person from their handshake. And she always took that to heart. "I'm Laura. Laura Milton." She paused for just a moment, trying not to get lost in his gaze. "This place is amazing. Haven't tried the food yet but it smells wonderful."

"Thank you." He smiled humbly. "You need to come into the Landmark Restaurant and let me take care of you." He glanced over at her open books. She noticed, closed them slowly, and changed the subject.

"I just flew in from New York this afternoon."

"I love New York. Do you live in the city?"

"Yes. I have a small place off Water Street. I love it."

"So, what brings you to our fair city?"

"I'm from here, originally. But I'm doing research. I'm a student at NYU."

"Ah, an *academic*. Excellent." He smiled.

"I'm... investigating an *urban legend...*" She was almost blushing as she whispered, "It's a ghost story."

"Really?" He leaned closer to her in confidence. "You know, every hotel has a ghost story or two. People die. That's what they do. You wouldn't believe some of the things I've had to deal with..."

Laura looked at him dryly.

"Ah, not the greatest subject for a first meeting, eh? Sorry."

Laura smiled at his candor. "No, actually it's fascinating. Just a little... sobering."

"Personally, I don't believe in ghosts."

She was about to say, *"Yeah, neither does my boyfriend,"* but thought the better of it.

Mallory changed the subject. "So, which ghost story are you researching?"

“The White Rock Lady.”

He paused for just a moment before continuing, almost seamlessly. Almost.

“I’ve heard of her. Is any of it true?”

“That’s what I’m here to find out.”

“Well, good luck,” he chuckled. “Will you be in Dallas long?”

“Three weeks doing interviews. It’s been so long since I’ve been back, everything’s changed so much.”

“Yes, it’s a very different city these days...”

A series of light chimes rang out. It was Mallory’s cell phone. He pulled the device out of his pocket and looked down at the screen, frowning.

“Excuse me, Ms. Milton. I’m sorry but I have to put out a fire.” He motioned to the bartender. “Your tab is on me tonight. Have a wonderful evening. Perhaps we can have dinner sometime during your stay.”

She looked at him, suddenly embarrassed. Was he asking her out?

Mallory saw the confusion in her face and smiled. “Here, in the restaurant, when you come down some night.” He handed her a card. “My personal number is there. If there’s anything I can do for you, please let me know.”

“Yes, of course. Thank you.” She looked at the card.

“Feel free to call me Mallory. Everyone does.”

“Just ‘*Mallory*’?” She laughed. “Like Bono and Slash?”

He smiled. “And Madonna, yes. But it’s *Mallory*.”

“That’s cute.”

He flashed a devious and wonderful grin. “Have a pleasant night, Laura...”

‘*What a great face,*’ she thought as she watched him walk off into the belly of the hotel. She hadn’t meant to flirt with him, but it had been a little difficult not to. He was an interesting guy, and extremely handsome, in a dark, mysterious 'young Christian Slater' sort of way. She couldn't tell his nationality; he could have been Italian, Middle-Eastern, Spanish, or Greek. He had no accent. And such a calm, confident air about him... Very nice. But he probably thought she was just some dumb schoolgirl on a field trip. She looked again at his card. The name on it was simply "Mallory". Interesting.

She put the card in her purse and checked the time. It was getting late. She didn't want to go to her hotel room yet for fear of what the night's dreams might show her, but she had an early morning and delaying the inevitable was worse than simply giving into it. She ordered the venison ciabatta sandwich to go and asked that it be delivered to her room. She left the bartender a twenty as a tip, collected her things, and went back upstairs to her suite.

Gramercy Park, New York, 2:23 AM

Colin spent the better part of the evening engrossed in Dallas/JFK lore. He read every conspiracy site and every blog-post he could find dealing with anything related to Dallas in the 1960's. His old roommate and CIA contact, Mackie, had come back with quite a dossier on Lester Davis. This guy was much more than he seemed. Colin kept reading till he literally passed out sitting up in bed.

After an hour or so, he began twitching in his sleep. He mumbled aloud while in his head flashes of city scenes started strobing behind his eyes.

Dark figures in a gunfight with police, people being shot randomly, muzzle flashes erupting like lightning in the dark revealing bodies exploding apart... A figure wrapped in chains, taken by strangers to a vast, dark lake... Shadows moving in the darkness, whispering... A lone man staring out at a turbulent body of water, sobbing uncontrollably, tears streaming from his dead eyes...

Colin sat up in bed suddenly awake. What the hell just happened? He had never had random nightmares before. He usually slept like a rock. Something was thumping in the distance. God, his head was pounding...

He put his hand to his face and felt the wet trails of tears streaming from his eyes. Something was rolling in his chest and he realized he wasn't breathing. The hiccupping sounds he heard so far away were actually coming from his own throat, a deep mournful sobbing that he couldn't stop. Cold waves of despair washed over him again and again, a deep sadness that threatened to drag him under and drown him...

Just like Laura had described in her nightmares.

Colin Jonah was rapidly becoming a believer.

Dallas, Texas

The next morning, Laura woke before her second alarm feeling rested and energized. She didn't have any dreams that she could remember and for the first time in weeks she had slept through the night and felt wonderful, even after taking her meds. Someone alert the media. She took a quick shower, dressed, and then bounded into the interview room to prepare the set.

Bernadette Miles, the grand-daughter of Mrs. Loretta Doyle, her contact from Twitter, arrived 10 minutes early for her interview. Miles was a soft-spoken, amicable woman in her mid thirties, very much a slightly updated version of the stereotypical southern belle. She helped herself to a cup of the coffee Laura had made and waited patiently. When Laura was ready, she positioned Ms. Miles in front of a dark patterned drape, adjusted the microphone height, focused the lights, and started recording.

"Thanks so much for taking the time to come talk to me, Ms. Miles. Just relax. Take a deep breath and whenever you're ready you can begin your story..."

"Fine," Bernadette said in a deep southern drawl. She cleared her throat and excused herself. "My grandmotha, Loretta Doyle, regrets that she can't be here. She asked me t' come in her place to answer your questions."

"I understand she's hospitalized?"

"She had a stroke last week. She's 89 years old, you know..."

"I'm so sorry. I hope she recovers quickly."

"She's a *wonderful* woman." Bernadette smiled to herself. "She was more of a mother t' me than my own mother was..." She grimaced to herself then smiled. "'Guess restlessness just runs in our family, so to speak... But *Meemaw Loretta* was always there. She taught me t' cook and sew... She used t' read t' me every night. She loved telling me stories for *hours* when I was just a baby, 'bout the family's history, our past. *Anyway*, this is one story she made me mem'rize when I got older. She won't be with us much longer and she doesn't want this t' ever be forgotten."

"Please thank her again for me."

Bernadette cleared her throat again. "Meemaw Loretta's younga sister, Louise Ford Davis, committed *suicide* in White Rock Lake in 1935."

Laura was aware of the name and the death from her research, but she didn't have any personal details. She was excited that she made a physical connection with someone directly related to a recorded incident. The confirmation was like a pat on the back.

"Loretta," Bernadette continued, "an' aunt Louise hadn't spoken in 6 years 'til that summer. Ever since she was girl, Louise had always had a *shine* for my grandfather, Frank, 'way before he and Meemaw started datin' even. Once they got together, Louise never forgave Meemaw for takin' him from her, so to speak, even though she never really had him in th' first place. In a fit of *jealousy*, Louise left th' family house early one Sunday mornin' with a suitcase 'fore anyone else was awake and *never returned*."

Bernadette's penchant for the dramatic made her story a lot more interesting than it seemed on the surface. Laura settled in for what was more than likely going to be a long session.

"Meemaw married Frank a year later and they ended up buying a house in Denton, 'bout 30 minutes north of Dallas proper. Years later, out of th' blue, Louise simply appeared one day on Meemaw's doorstep out in Denton. It'd been so long, Meemaw barely recognized her. Louise told her she'd been livin' at th' Melrose Hotel in Dallas for quite some time. Meemaw couldn't imagine how Louise could *afford* it on her own. Our family was comfortable but we weren't rich by any means. My great-grandfather had meager trust funds for all the kids in place. But when Louise left the house at 17 against his wishes, he cut her off *completely*.

"*Anyways*, 'took a few weeks, but th' two started enjoyin' each other's company again. Loretta was happy to have her sister back, but one thing bothered her to no end: Louise seemed so *sad*, as if somethin' dark and hurtful was always on her mind. She left th' family as a know-it-all child, so to speak, but returned a cautious, defensive, and quiet woman who seemed afraid of her own shadow."

Though it was a little unprofessional, Laura had to bite her lip to keep from smiling at the woman's deep Southern colloquialisms. If Bernadette said *'so to speak'* or *'anyways'* one more time, she feared she'd burst out laughing.

"*Now, Meemaw* always threw a huge Forth o' July party at their home in Denton. That year she invited her sister for th' first time. But when Louise didn't show, Meemaw became worried; in her fragile state, she thought Louise was capable of anything. *Anyways*, the next mornin', Loretta drove into Dallas in hopes of talkin' her sister into leaving the hotel and movin' in with her and my grandpa.

"When she arrived, Meemaw went straight to the front desk and asked for th' manager. She explained th' situation and told him she didn't know her sister's room number. Th' manager offered to escort her to the room."

Bernadette stopped and fanned herself with her hand.

Laura came out of her trance. "Are you comfortable? Can I get you some water?"

"Oh, no," Bernadette smiled, embarrassed. "I'm *fine*. Where was I?" She thought for a moment. "Oh, yes. Well, as I said earlier, Meemaw and her sister always had a *strained* relationship. She'd be th' first to admit that she fed a lot of Louise's dramatics when they were young. Meemaw had finally gotten to th' point where she could handle Louise's craziness. But this new, somber Louise was a complete mystery.

"*Anyways*, she and the manager took the tiny elevator up to th' 8th floor. Lookin' back, Meemaw told me that she had realized all this time Louise had been *de-pressed*. It's a common thing now, you hear ever'body talkin' 'bout it on the TV. But in th' 1930's, there was no such thing as *clinical d'pression*. They just called you crazy." She laughed nervously.

"*Anyways*, Meemaw and th' manager came to Room 815. He knocked on th' door. There was no answer..."

July 5, 1935 Melrose Hotel, Dallas, TX

"Ms. Davis? This is Damon Pernal, the hotel manager. I'm here with your sister..." The manager looks up at Loretta's puffy, determined face. The plume of the woman's summer hat hangs ridiculously low in front of her face. Her stout body is poised like a bulldog in a white polka-dotted blue dress, ready for a fight.

The manager knocks again. "Ms. Davis?" Still, they hear not a sound from inside the room.

He reaches for his keys and opens the door to a crack. "Hello? Miss Davis? Are you here?" Loretta pushes past him and storms into the suite.

All the curtains are drawn. It takes a moment for Loretta's eyes to adjust to the dark. She steps on something that crunches under foot. Looking around the room, she realizes the suite has been ransacked. Furniture is smashed and shards of glass lay like a layer of dust over everything.

In the middle of the entry way is a table with a piece of crumpled paper lying in the center covered with glass splinters and dried rose petals. It is a letter in Louise's handwriting. Picking it up, Loretta starts reading. It's a long, meandering message that makes little sense. Until the end.

Loretta drops the note in shock, turning to the manager.

"She's gone to kill herself at White Rock Lake!"

The manager picks up the phone.

"This is Pernal. Get me the police."

* * *

Officer Darryl Bryan is cruising on Buckner Boulevard on the northeast side of White Rock Lake. It's a beautiful summer afternoon. He passes Garland Road and reaches for a cigarette just as his radio squawks to life.

"10-56, Code 2. Possible Suicide in progress. The Bath House at White Rock Lake, 500 block East Lawther."

Bryan picks up his receiver.

"This is 211, Bryan. I'm at Garland Road and Lawther now. Two minutes on scene. Over."

Bryan hits the siren and speeds through a stoplight forcing the on-coming car to slam on its brakes. Once in White Rock Park, he speeds through the winding street honking his horn and flashing his lights, forcing the lake pedestrians out of the way. The cruiser squeals into the gravel parking lot of the Bath House. As he jerks to a stop he sees something bobbing in the water not ten feet off shore. It is the body of a woman lying face down.

Leaping out of his car, Bryan runs to the water and dives in headfirst. Reaching the body, he turns her over on her back, puts an arm around her waist, and gently swims her back to shore. He lifts her out of the water and lays her on her back where he begins administrating CPR. He strikes her chest and continues compression, stopping only to blow air into her mouth before continuing.

After ten minutes he gives up. She's gone. He looks down at the woman, water dripping from his face onto hers. The tawny hair frames her face like a soft glow. She is absolutely gorgeous. He brushes a strand back from her pale blue forehead.

Two more police cruisers race into the parking lot behind them as Bryan begins to cry.

Present Day. Interview room, Melrose Hotel

Bernadette wiped the tears out of the corner of her eyes. "Louise wrote th' location in th' letter so they would know where t' find her body. The *coroner* said that if the officer had been there 3 minutes earlier he would've saved her *life*..." She looks around the room nervously. "As far as I know, Louise could've stayed in this very room..."

Laura sat forward in her chair looking directly into Bernadette's puffy, mascara-streaked face. "And so you believe Louise to be the White Rock Lady?"

The woman wiped her nose and sat up straight in her chair, a haughty tone entering into her southern drawl. "Miss Milton, my grandmother has seen her sister's spirit at th' lake," she said defensively. "I think sisters would know one another even in death!" Laura sat back, not knowing quite what to say. It was an awkward moment until Ms. Miles broke the silence, her tone, once again, calm. "I have copies of some pictures we found in her apartment. You're welcome to keep 'em as long as you like."

Bernadette handed Laura a small stack yellowing photographs she had in her lap. The first was a full-length shot of a thin young woman posing in a summer dress in front of the Melrose Hotel. Louise had tawny hair, an elfin face and deep, sad, dark eyes. She was naturally beautiful. The second picture was of Louise with her arm around a very thin, handsome gentleman. He was looking into the camera like a scoundrel.

"Who is this man?"

"A *writer* who lived at th' hotel. McCoy. *Horace* McCoy. We think he might have been Louise's *lover*, so to speak. After an elongated "*friendship*" he left suddenly for Hollywood in 1933, two years before Louise killed herself. His first story sold was called "Luxury Girl". We think it was partly 'bout Louise."

"What was her full name?"

"Louise Ford Davis."

"You don't recall an uncle by the name of *Lester* Davis, do you?"

"Not that I know of. But from what Meemaw said, Aunt Louise was *very secretive*. No one ever met her first husband. Apparently, he was in the war and never returned. She kept his name and never remarried. Ford was my great-grandfather's name."

Laura looked at the photo again. Behind them there was not sky but an expanse of water. "In this picture they are by a lake or pool. Could that be White Rock?"

"I've no idea. But Meemaw found pictures and maps of th' lake in her hotel suite along with th' note that day."

"What did the suicide note say?"

Bernadette picked up her purse and turned to look directly at Laura. "That is one thing that t' this day Meemaw has *never* told me..."

* * *

After the interview, Laura left the hotel to visit the Barnes and Noble on Northwest Highway and 75 Central, across from Northpark Mall. She quickly grabbed a copy of McCoy's best-known novel and headed back to the Melrose.

Back in her suite, she sat down at her computer and went into search mode. The best thing about having a loving, attentive, doting boyfriend who's father was the director at the Smithsonian wasn't the holiday parties as much as it was the secured site passwords he shared with her. In minutes she had found and copied what she was looking for. Pulling out her digital recorder she began her commentary while scanning her notes from the interview as well as the computer screen. The Bluetooth headset sat on her head like a geeky minimalist tiara as the computer recorded her voice to text.

"...Out of the entire interview, the McCoy relationship is the most interesting..." She picked up a picture out of the small pile sitting on her desk. It was of McCoy as a young hustler in the 1930's.

"Police records show McCoy was arrested for assault while living at the Melrose Hotel in 1932. He either refused or couldn't pay the bail and decided to sit out the jail-time. Very strange, seeing as that he worked as a full-time sports editor for the Dallas Journal from 1919 to 1930. His tie to the Campisi Mafia family is vague, but apparently he had debts with unknown parties. Most likely, gambling debts...

"...In the late 1920's he started getting his short stories published in various pulp mystery magazines, but for the most part, was an unknown." She turned away from the screen to stare at the photograph. "What caused his rapid fame?"

She picked up another picture of McCoy. He was on a sound stage talking with a cameraman who was holding some equipment. A mammoth fake gorilla arm the size of a bus was lying on its side next to them.

"...In '33 he left Dallas in a hurry and resurfaced a month later in Hollywood as an un-credited script assistant for the film *'King Kong'*. He began acting, getting his first minor role in a film called *'The Hollywood Handicap'*, a minor comedy..."

Laura sat back in her chair, thinking out loud.

"What chased him out of Dallas? Was it a new connection that got his foot in the Hollywood gene pool? Could his leaving be what finally drove Louise to suicide at the lake? I guess we'll never know for sure..."

She did another quick search.

"...McCoy was an unknown when he went out there looking for fame..." She glanced at the copy of McCoy's book *'They Shoot Horses, Don't They?'* she had just thrown in her research pile. "Five years later he had his 15 minutes of fame." She turned back to the screen. "The book did poorly in the States in the 30's, but was adopted by French existentialist circles and was distributed by underground literary groups during World War II." She scrolled through a few more paragraphs. "In 1969, the novel was adapted into a film directed by Sydney Pollack and was Jane Fonda's first breakout film.

"McCoy ended up staying in L.A. and, though he never wrote any ground-breaking material, he lived comfortably writing popular but forgettable films until he died in Beverly Hills, California on December 15, 1955 from a heart attack..."

Ok, what did all this mean?

Laura turned back to her pile. The photograph Bernadette Miles had given her of Louise with McCoy caught her attention.

"...There's water in the background of the photo of McCoy with Louise. So... if they were at White Rock Lake, what did it mean, if anything? The Miles interview seemed to have created a lot more questions than it answered..."

In the photograph Louise looked so vibrant, eyes sparkling with electricity as she held onto the arm of the dapper and scandalous-looking McCoy. "Louise was so beautiful. Did she die from a broken heart? Or was it something else that drew her to end her life in the cold waters of White Rock Lake? It seems like such an odd way to kill oneself... Plus, her room had been ransacked, which would be more indicative of a homicide rather than a suicide, but there are no other statements from the police reports. The suicide note must have been enough for them..."

Laura stopped recording and saved the file. She thought for a moment. There was something else she wanted to archive. She hit the record button again.

"Off-record, the pictures of Louise Davis are not familiar to me. Certainly, her death would fit the model for a haunting, but... she doesn't look anything like the woman that keeps appearing in my dreams. For what it's worth..."

That evening Laura ordered food from the original Campisi's Egyptian Restaurant on Mockingbird Street, choosing to pick it up herself instead of having it delivered. Once inside, she took delicious pleasure in experiencing the original dining room of the now-expanded restaurant. The walls were covered in dark wood paneling and black accent paint. A long bar ran along the left side of the structure. In the center of the wall on the right, just above the black upholstered booths, was an over-sized portrait of the original proprietor, Joe Campisi himself. The spiritual residue of many long dead people lingered in the shadows like the heady aroma of garlic and old cigarette smoke. The Campisi's were widely known to have been a major mafia family in Dallas since the early 1950's, though very few people seemed to want to talk about it, even today. Laura had an entire dossier on them, but for now a sample of their famous pizza would suffice nicely.

Returning to the Melrose, she ended up succumbing to the venial sin of falling asleep watching the news and eating pizza in bed.

Eight

The next few days were filled with research and a couple of interviews that led nowhere. One man had obviously made up his story in hopes of getting his name in her book; Laura didn't have the heart to tell him she wasn't writing a book. Two interviewees were obviously high on something; one utterly incoherent and the other teetering on the edge of paranoid delusion, saying she was a *seer* and could see spirits floating in the air there in front of them. Right. If the woman only knew who she was talking to... After a great start, Laura was starting to wonder if all her amazing contacts were just a bunch of crazies who had nothing better to do than waste her time. Colin had been busy at the museum and had been persona non grata since her first night in town, but she was used to his schedule by now.

On Thursday afternoon she finished her work early and had nothing else scheduled after 2 PM. It was a gorgeous day and instead of burying her head in work, Laura decided to treat herself and go shopping at Northpark Mall to clear her mind. The expensive boutique shops were so stuffy she couldn't relax enough to find anything she liked. Instead, she hit Urban Outfitters upstairs next to the theater and found two great tops for under $20 for both. Total score.

She browsed a few other stores before succumbing to P. F. Chang's in the mall. She was sitting at the bar finishing up her lettuce wraps and rummaging through her purse when she came upon a loose business card. Turning it over, it read *Mallory*. She had been so busy she had almost forgotten about him all together. Picking up her phone, she dialed his number. A curt, very irritated-sounding voice answered almost immediately.

"Yes."

"Ah, *Mallory*? This is Laura. Milton. From the–"

"From the Melrose, of course! How are you, Laura? Are you enjoying your stay in the city?" His voice was instantly warm and inviting.

"Yes, very much, thank you. Listen, this is a strange request, but I was just looking at my schedule and noticed I had an open evening. I was wondering if you might be free to have drinks or coffee."

Silence. Not a good sign. Just as she was about to apologize for her forwardness, he surprised her.

"I'd love to. Where?"

She laughed. "Well, you're going to have to help me on that end. You tell me. But the tab's on me."

"You got it. I've got the perfect place..."

* * *

Two hours later they were sitting at the Belmont Hotel, a wonderfully restored landmark from the 1940's located just west of downtown off of Commerce and Sylvan Ave. All the rooms were bungalows designed in the old-Hollywood style, each its own individualized piece of artwork. There was a wonderful little restaurant called Smoke there as well, but the main attraction was the patio bar. The hotel sat on a hill just on the west side of the Trinity River offering a marvelous view of the city. And there Laura and Mallory sat having cocktails, the profile of downtown Dallas shimmering in the fading daylight directly behind them.

After some small talk, there was a slight lull in conversation. Laura was certain that he could tell she was a little awestruck by him and was totally embarrassed. Mallory picked up on her awkwardness and changed the subject.

"So, how's the thesis coming?" She looked into his eyes to gauge if he was simply being polite. He seemed honestly interested.

"It's really just research. The final is an oral examination. But the interviews have been fairly productive."

"So, what are you looking for exactly?"

"Eye-witness accounts, family stories, any type of supporting proof that this person may actually have lived. And died. And a possible reason why she can't break free of the lake."

He took a deep drink of his scotch.

"Do you actually have some idea of who the ghost could have been?"

"That's part of the process. I–" She stopped in mid-sentence. She was starting to embarrass herself even further. "You know, I'm sorry, I don't mean to dominate the conversation..."

"No, I'm fascinated." He smiled that deeply disarming smile of his.

"I thought you didn't believe in ghosts."

"Perception is reality, my dear. And I would love to know more about your reality. What got you interested in all this in the first place?"

She sat looking at him for a second and then thought better of starting that particular shit-storm. "It's a long story for another time. Let's talk about something else. Tell me, what's it like being a managing partner for a property like the Melrose?"

Mallory smiled. He seemed so comfortable. Laura really liked that about him. "Well, the Melrose is owned by Warwick who has properties all over the world. I don't work for the company, per se. I'm more of a... local consultant, primarily just for this property. I come in, study the business, make suggestions... It's fun and a little bit creative. I've been very fortunate." He laughed. "I always wanted to be an artist, you know? Make stuff, be different. Funny how we change. Or rather how life changes us."

"Do you paint?"

"I try." He laughed at himself easily. She liked that, too. Damnit. "I was never very good, but I love the process. Very therapeutic. But now, everything is different..."

"How so?"

He leaned forward. She could smell him, clean and masculine. She tried her best not to swoon. "A business is like a child. You constantly have to nurture it, feed it, communicate with it. It's very demanding of your time and, of course, it gets a little frustrating. Unlike children, however, it never grows up and leaves home, it never picks up after itself; its success is always dependent upon your level of involvement. And these days, everything changes so fast..."

"We live in strange times," she said, half hypnotized. *Snap out of it, Laura.* "I think we're all being tested; our faith, our resolve, desires..."

"What do you desire, Laura?"

She was startled at his sense of intimacy. Was he bating her? She looked into his eyes but saw nothing that hinted at cruelty or mockery. He was genuinely interested in her opinions. What a strange thing. She got this warm, safe feeling looking into his sable-colored eyes. They seemed so sincere, so supportive. She felt like she could tell him anything.

"I want to make a difference."

He smiled, but not in criticism. He seemed charmed. “So, you want to fix the world, eh?”

“No, I just want to influence the things I have control over. I’m no one special. But I can make a difference for the people around me.”

“And what do you want for yourself?”

It was at this point that she could imagine him reaching across the table and kissing her passionately. She took a deep breath praying that he wasn’t a mind reader.

“I just want to be happy. I want the strength to listen to my own heart.”

“That’s really beautiful, Laura...” Again, she was afraid he might be mocking her, but his smile was so genuine that her fears evaporated. She felt nothing but acceptance and gentle curiosity from him.

After dinner, Mallory wanted to take her to have drinks at a little dive in south Dallas called Lee Harvey’s. Laura wanted nothing more than to spend more time with him, but 5 AM would come early and she had to be on top of her game tomorrow.

Mallory took her back to the hotel, pulling up into the reception area. He got out of the car and opened her door himself, confounding the valet for a moment.

He took her by the hand. “Thank you for a wonderful night.”

She laughed. “Isn’t that supposed to be my line?”

“I’ll share it with you this time. I really enjoyed seeing you.”

She smiled so hard she thought her face would break. “We’ll have to do it again. Soon.”

“Definitely. Have a lovely evening, Ms. Milton.” He leaned over and gently kissed her on the lips, careful not to linger. It sent her over the edge. She felt like she was going to fall over.

"Good night..."

Falling asleep that night was difficult, but for an entirely different reason. This trip had taken quite the unexpected turn. The tall, mysterious Mallory filled her thoughts, in more ways than one. He was a charming distraction, but a distraction nonetheless. She couldn't let him preoccupy her. But spending time with him sure beat the hell out of the Cooking Channel...

She felt a twinge of guilt over enjoying the evening as much as she did, but then she reminded herself that she and Colin were not currently a couple. It was a sad thought, but she had to be willing to let it go to find what it was she really wanted in her life. And this was part of the process.

As she drifted off, she could still see Mallory's dark eyes staring at her across the table, penetrating her, melting her heart as well as other neglected body parts...

Nine

The figure of a young woman is staring out at the lake. Laura stands beside her and takes her by the hand. A bright blue sky hangs overhead, the dark water singing a low, mournful melody below. Fields of wildflowers waving in the breeze... An American Indian woman on her calloused knees crying on the banks of the lake, her tears falling into the cold, black water. A young woman's white-blonde tendrils in the waves... Rose petals swirling in the ghost-wind like languid corpuscles. Somewhere an orchestra is playing... Getting louder and louder...

Laura sat up in bed. Her Beethoven alarm was going off and the sun was blazing painfully through the open curtains. She looked at the clock and jumped out of bed. It was 7:24 AM Friday morning. She had slept through her medicine time.

"Damnit!"

In 20 minutes she had dressed and was in the interview room setting lights in place. Her only interview of the day was at 8 AM with Jules Frank, a woman who claimed to know the identity of the White Rock Lady. Laura didn't want to get her hopes up; she knew it wasn't going to be that easy to get all her questions answered in her first week of interviews. Still, she was excited to hear what this woman had to say. Just as Laura turned on the camera she heard a booming knock behind her.

"Hello? Anyone here?"

Laura turned around. A weathered, hard-looking woman in her mid-seventies stepped through the door dressed in a leather vest, jeans, and black riding boots. She looked like she had seen one too many tanning beds in her day. She entered the room, eyes darting over the lights and equipment.

"Jules Frank?" Laura asked.

The woman came towards her. Laura noticed the flesh of her face was wrinkled and the color of rust, her eyes glowing like green diamonds out of their little sagging pockets. But she was solid. This was no little ol' Texas grandmother standing in front of her.

A deep sandpaper voice cackled back, "Well, I sure the hell hope so! Ha!"

Laura extended her hand. "I'm Laura Milton. Thanks so much for coming." Her eyes scanned Laura quickly. Instead of shaking her hand, the woman materialized a pack of Pall Malls and in a single movement put one in her mouth, lit it, and exhaled a huge cloud of smoke into the air.

"Ah, you know," Laura started timidly, "I'm not sure they allow smoking indoors here..."

"Ah, they'll never know," the woman croaked. "Where do you want me?"

Laura didn't really mind her smoking during the interview, she just didn't like the smell. Making the best of the situation, she repositioned the lights and got an interesting look accentuating the haze. It would end up being a great editorial visual. Besides, anything that helped make the interviewee more pliant and trusting was a plus. She placed a demitasse plate on the table next to the chair as a makeshift ashtray, cracked a window open, and left it at that.

She positioned Ms. Frank in front of the lights and then took her place on a chair in front and to the left side of the camera. Through the viewfinder she saw that the woman was illuminated by a dramatic three-point lighting configuration, the smoke from her cigarette swirling around her like a fiery phantom vapor. Perfect. Laura placed her headphones on and smiled.

"Could you say something in your normal speaking voice so I can get a level on you?"

"Ah, ok. *Hello...*" The burley woman shifted in her seat. "Ah, one, two, three. Check. *Sibilance, Sibilance...* Ha!"

Laura smiled. At least the old girl was having some fun with it. She got her audio levels within a good range, reached over and hit the record button on the camera.

"Alright, Ms. Frank. Just look directly at me and, if you could, try to answer the questions in complete sentences. Take a deep breath and when you're ready, tell me what you remember about the White Rock Lady."

Frank cleared her throat. "You know, what I remember most about the White Rock Lady was–she was no fucking *lady*!" Frank laughed and then erupted in a coughing fit. She took out a red handkerchief from her back pocket, wiped the phlegm from her mouth, and continued.

"I was just a young girl when we lived next to the Davises on the West bank of White Rock Lake..."

Laura caught her breath at the mention of the name Davis. It was too much to be coincidental.

"...This would be in 1945, the year World War II ended. I remember the date because that year my daddy helped liberate the first Nazi death camp Ohrdruf in Germany. Our house was next door to the Davis house. A large field separated our homes but the way the lake is set up, we might as well have been 10 feet away. We could hear everything that went on in that place. And it wasn't pretty."

Frank pulled out the handkerchief, blew her nose, and put it back in her pocket. For a moment Laura wondered if it was the same handkerchief from a moment ago.

"I remember one day my mama was bathing us in the upstairs bathroom. She was telling us that daddy would be coming home from the war soon. We were all so happy... The next thing, I hear this inhuman scream coming from outside. It was the most horrible thing I had ever heard. Sissy and I were so scared we burst into tears. Mama looked out the window and that crazy woman was running through the lawn like a lunatic shrieking at the top of her lungs. Things like that were always happening..."

Laura wanted a concrete statement. "For the record, Ms. Frank, you are stating that the legend of the White Rock Lady is actually based on a real woman who lived next to your family in the 1940's, is that correct?"

"Yup."

"What about the sightings previous to your birth? Accounts of the ghost go back as early as 1933..."

"I don't know about all of that. All I know is my sister and I had nightmares for years because of that raging bitch. And that was just the beginning..."

White Rock Lake, July 12, 1945.

It is a sweltering summer night. The water on the lake is like black glass. A car sits parked in a dark lot facing the water. 17-year-old Robby Bolin and his girlfriend Christine are sitting in the front seat making out while the radio plays "I'm Making Believe" by the Ink Spots. Robby starts to get a little aggressive. He puts Christine's hand in his lap and she feels his hardness through his jeans.

"Robby, don't!"

"But I love you, Chris. Please, baby. Just touch it."

"No–what if somebody sees us?"

"Ain't nobody on this side of the lake 'cept old people. Come on, baby. I'll pull out this time, I promise..." He pulls her close and kisses her deeply.

"Robby..."

He smothers her with kisses, his young hands wandering all over her body. He holds her close and starts trying to undo her bra. She moans and he can tell she's starting to enjoy herself.

"Oh, Robby..."

She puts her head on his shoulder and lets him have his way. He fumbles with her bra strap and grunts in frustration. She pulls away from him, reaches behind and undoes the clasp herself, and puts her arms around him again.

"Oh, baby..." He kisses her neck with wild abandon. She remembers the pack of rubbers she has in her purse. This is going to be so good...

The young girl opens her eyes and sees the stark-white figure of a woman, naked, staring at them through the car window, a coil of black matted hair framing a horrendously grinning face.

Christine's screams echo through the White Rock valley.

Across the cove, Officer Wally Brighton and his partner Jed Donnelly are parked in front of the marina sitting in their police cruiser when they hear the screams.

"What the hell?"

The cruiser comes to life and speeds towards a parking lot around the next bend. There they see two teenagers leaning against a car. The young girl is visibly shaken and is still crying when the officers walk up.

"There's some mad woman walking around here *nekkid!*" Christine screams.

Officer Brighton looks at his partner and sighs.

“I chased her off,” Robbie says, pointing into the trees. “She ran into the woods, there...”

“Thanks. You kids get on home, now. We’ll take care of it.”

“But–”

“Robbie. Don’t make me call your father.”

“Yessir...”

Brighton waits for the two get in their car and drive off. The officers then pull out their flashlights and head into the tangle of brush.

For 10 minutes they search the deep brush and find nothing. The woods run for miles around the lake and it would be easy for someone to hide in the lowlands indefinitely if they wanted to. Just as the officers are about to head back, Donnelly hears a shout. He draws his gun and turns back towards the lake as Brighton follows him.

Walking out of the trees, they see a nude woman, pale and hunched over, standing on the shore screaming out at the water.

Donnelly can’t believe his eyes. “My God, is that–?”

“It sure is.” Wally Brighton sighs. “Donnelly, you’re no longer a rookie. I’d like to introduce you to Chesapeake Davis. In the flesh.”

The woman crouches down and starts sniffing the air like a dog.

“This is the woman who has been terrorizing the kids out here?”

“Yep. Poor thing. She gets liquored up and can’t control herself.”

The woman turns and sees them in an instant.

“Fuck you, you sissy liberal motherfuckers! You are the *scourge*–” She slips and falls into the mud. The woman starts shrieking and tearing at her hair.

"Poor thing, my ass, Wally. Look at her. That woman's fucking crazy!"

It takes more than a little diplomacy for the two officers to get the inebriated Mrs. Lester Davis to calm down enough to cover herself with a blanket and get in the cruiser.

Brighton calls the dispatcher and tells her they are taking Mrs. Davis back to her home on the west side of the lake.

As Brighton pulls up to the Davis residence, he sees two back-up squad cars already in the circular drive, their red and blue lights spinning in the night.

In the house next door, a 4-year-old Julie Frank gets out of her bed and walks over to the window. There are three police cars pulled up in the front of the Davis house next door. The red and blue lights flash into her bedroom lighting it up like Christmas as the small group talks in hushed whispers outside. Julie Frank's eyes are big as saucers as she watches.

Outside, Lester Davis is beside himself with embarrassment.

"I don't know how to thank you, Wally. I feel just awful. I can't apologize enough for this."

"Nothin' to 'pologize for, Lester," the trooper said. "I just wanted t' make sure she got home safe. But this *is* the second time this month..."

"I understand. I'll keep a good eye on her. I promise. Thanks again, Wally."

"Fuck you, Wally!" Chesapeake always chooses the perfect moment to speak. She throws off the blanket and slowly walks into her home in all her naked glory. She has a decent body for a crazy woman. Donnelly snickers out loud before calming himself. Wally pats Lester on the shoulder.

"Good night, guys."

Present Day. Interview Room, Melrose Hotel

Jules Frank sat back in her chair and put out her 4th cigarette.

"...Chesapeake Davis wasn't a ghost from beyond, she was just some crazy, lonely woman who wanted attention. Somehow, everybody turned it into a ghost story."

Laura felt a little nauseous. This couldn't be right, could it? Was all her research ending here, as it begins, with the ranting of one bitter old woman? Surely not...

"Personally, I just felt sorry for the daughter."

Laura snapped to attention. "She had a *daughter*?"

"Yeah, poor thing. She had to have been a few years younger than my sister. She was just a baby back then, not more than 1 or 2-years-old. I remember seeing a colored nursemaid taking care of her during the day."

Frank paused for a moment to cough up a big phlegm ball and spit in the red handkerchief. It made Laura spit up a little in her own mouth thinking how many different body fluids were comingling in that one piece of cloth.

Jules Frank continued. "That girl must have gone through the shitter with that banshee for a mother."

This new thread was intriguing. What kind of woman had that little girl grown into? Laura wanted to know more.

"You wouldn't by any chance remember the girl's name, would you?"

"Christ, lady, that was a billion years ago." She stared at the ceiling for a moment, searching. "Some flower... Violet? Daisy? No... Rose. That was it. Rose. Ha! I can't believe I fucking remember that. She had yellow hair. I remember thinking that was so weird with a name like Rose..."

Ten

1962 Davis home, White Rock Lake

The Davis house is a classic split-level encased in mossy white stone that is the lake's namesake. The structure faces the western shore of the lake in a small cul-de-sac off the main road. In the living room there is an altar with a morbidly graphic statue of a crucified Jesus surrounded by a dozen or so glass cylinders of garish holy candles burning night and day. The furniture is all dark wood, over-stuffed couches, polished hand-carved tables, and vintage finery. Knick-knacks and objects-de-art are everywhere. A parade of porcelain figurines dominates the low cabinets running along one side of the living room. The shutters on the windows are all closed and the faded pink curtains drawn. Only a faint wash of sunlight penetrates the layers of moth-eaten cloth.

Upstairs in her room, 18-year-old Rose Davis is lying on her bed reading a Hollywood gossip magazine. Her only window is open and the afternoon sunlight is streaking in. She is mesmerized by page after page of pictures of famous film stars and their glamorous lives. The doo-wop song "Tears on My Pillow" by Little Anthony and the Imperials drifts out of the radio sitting on the windowsill. Rose hums along, turning pages and dreaming.

The singer is telling the object of his affections that love is not a gadget, nor is it a toy, for, apparently, when you find the one you love, he or she won't hurt you but rather will fill your heart with joy... that sounds so romantic...

'Tears on my pillow...'

She rolls off her bed and poses in front of the full-length mirror on the wall. She brushes her long, white-blonde hair back from her face and arches her back in perfect posture. Closing her eyes, she pretends to be a princess holding her hand out to be kissed by some handsome, scandalous man. Any moment, a big strong prince will climb through the window, take her into his arms and whisk her away from White Rock Lake, far away from the Texas summer heat, far away from her mother...

Rose grabs the magazine again. She can see herself on the arm of Tony Curtis as they walk into the Twenty-One Club for a late dinner. Or perhaps she is sitting by the pool with Janet Leigh and Nanette Fabray having cocktails waiting for her best friend Tuesday Weld to arrive.

"Rose! Where are you, demon child?"

Rose jerks her head up just as her mother throws the door open. She barely has the time to hide the magazine behind her back before her mother bounds into the room with a wild look in her eyes, a look Rose knows only too well.

Chesapeake Davis stands in the center of the room, a porcelain-white demon draped in a matronly black dress, dark hair pulled back into a tight ponytail that sweeps down her back. Her black eyes dart around the room and she starts sniffing the air like a dog.

"What are you reading? Give it to me!"

She snatches the magazine from behind Rose's back and looks at the cover. Chesapeake rips the periodical in half, raises her right hand over her left shoulder and slaps Rose hard across the face.

“Get that hellish fountain of sin out of your hands this instant!”

Rose stares at her mother with absolute hate but keeps her tongue. She turns her gaze down to the floor.

“Yes, ma’am. I’m sorry.”

“You make me sick with your stupid dreams!” Her southern drawl descends into a hiss. “You ain’t nothin’ but *white trash* and you’ll never be anything else! ‘You hear me?”

“Yes, ma’am.”

“Now clean up this mess and get ready for bed!” Chesapeake storms out of the room.

Rose puts her hand up to her cheek and rubs where the sting is beginning to throb. Tears well in the corner of her eyes but she holds them back, refusing to cry because of that crazy woman who dares to calls herself her mother.

She starts to pick up her torn magazine when she hears her mother scream from across the house. Without hesitation, she runs out across the mezzanine hallway to her mother’s room and finds Chesapeake standing in her bathroom paralyzed. Looking down she sees the reason. Chesapeake has lost control of her bowels and is standing in a puddle of her own filth on the white tiled floor. She looks up at Rose and starts to cry. Rose goes to her and puts her arm around her.

“We’ll get you cleaned up in a sec, mama...”

She starts filling the tub and helps the woman off with her dress. Standing there naked in front of her, Rose can’t believe her mother is only 32-years-old. Not really overweight, her pallid skin still hangs off her body like wet rags on a wire frame. Eczema covers the backs of her arms and legs, running even between her pendulous breasts. Long scabbed welts crisscross her wrists from constantly scratching herself. Her course black hair is peppered with premature grey streaks. She smells like shit, whiskey, and cigarette smoke.

Moments later, Chesapeake is sitting in her claw-footed tub hugging her knees while Rose sits on the floor next to her with a sponge gently squeezing warm water over her.

"I'm sorry, Rose..."

The girl sighs. "It's ok, mama."

"No. I'm the reason everyone is so unhappy. I'm *horrible!*" She starts sobbing silently.

Rose has heard it all before. After a bad episode, Chesapeake always has these momentary sparks of realization and apologizes for being the person she is. It changes nothing. If anything, these episodes only prove that her mother is in full possession of her faculties and chooses to be this way. Chesapeake is a cruel, bitter woman, and that is that. As her father would have said, "A cat can't change its stripes..." Fuck her.

Rose runs her hand through Chesapeake's tangled hair. There is no way out from this situation. She has two choices: either learn to deal with the stress of having a maniac for a mother or fall apart, just like her mother did so very long ago. And Rose was damned if she was going to let that happen.

She looks at her mother curled up in the soapy water like a frightened child.

"Don't you never mind, mama. I'm here and everything's gonna be fine."

Eleven

Present Day. Dallas, Texas

After the Jules Frank interview, Laura decided to visit the Hall of Records downtown. She grabbed the phone and called for the Land Rover.

From the Melrose, she took Cedar Springs to Stemmons Freeway and went south. Soon, the gleaming downtown buildings appeared on her left, almost close enough to touch from the highway overpass. The profile of downtown was beautiful, even more so with all the construction going on. She knew all about it from her research. The stately One Arts Plaza, the red swipe of color that was the Winspear Opera House, the abstraction of the elemental cube of the Wyly Theatre and the cubist Perot Museum; all the new buildings in the arts district were so stunning. And a whole new center of development was flourishing just inside the McKinney Avenue belt, the area where the Ritz-Carlton Hotel was located all the way over to Harry Hines behind the Stoneleigh Hotel. There were at least five buildings in that area alone that were in the process of being completed, not including the new Omni Convention Center Hotel located on the other side of downtown next to the WFAA studios. She didn't remember the city being anywhere near this grand when she was young.

From Stemmons, she exited Commerce Street and decided to continue through the city for a bit. With her phone's GPS, navigating the streets wasn't as difficult as she had expected. Construction sites were everywhere, but the drive was fairly straightforward. Strange, it was as if the entire city was infused with growth at every turn she made. This wasn't how she remembered the city at all.

She had been a high school senior when she came to Dallas with the Jonah family to bury her father after his sudden heart attack. That was when the historic Deep Ellum arts district had begun to die, taking with it the only real artistic history the city had ever really owned. It was in this old factory sector of the city that the seminal jazz and blues artists of the south such as Blind Lemmon Jefferson, Robert Johnson, and Bessie Smith would play dive clubs like The Harlem and The Palace back in the 20's and 30's. As time went on, the district became a hotbed for alternative music and nightclubs, and in the mid-90's it reached its pinnacle. On the weekends, Deep Ellum looked like New Orleans with all the people on the street, filling the clubs and making a statement in the artist community. Unfortunately, the growing crowds eventually led to vandalism and gang violence. Coupled with a few questionable police beatings and zoning problems, the area was all but abandoned and forgotten for the last decade. But after a long period of complacency, Deep Ellum and Dallas proper was once again growing, even as the rest of the country struggled to dig itself out of the first major economic catastrophe of the century. Someone in Texas was definitely making money.

Laura parked across the street from the Old Red Courthouse on Houston Street. Once the seat of local government, the southern Gothic-style red brick building had been restored and was now a historic museum commemorating everything Texan. The Records Building was right across the street.

Laura found the front the building easily enough and entered the yellow stone structure through a guarded entrance. After going through two security checks, she descended into the belly of the information center. As she followed the archivist through the labyrinth of media she realized how deep this project was taking her. It was almost as if her search for the identity of the White Rock Lady was directing *her* now, forcing her to ask questions that she wouldn't normally think to ask. The entire investigation was taking on a life all its own, almost as if something external was giving it the inertia it needed to thrive and survive. She now had a point of reference that she felt strongly about. This woman Chesapeake Davis was the key. There was no way the reoccurring name was just a coincidence.

Two hours later, Laura was deep in the trenches of research. The microfiche viewers proved to be a little cumbersome but yielded some good information. She sat at a table surrounded by aged hard-back volumes of community records and was going back through the pages of notes she had taken on her laptop.

It seemed like Chesapeake appeared out of nowhere in Lester Davis' timeline. There were no records of a public courtship, no ceremony, nothing. Very strange for the children of two wealthy families... There was a single three-sentence blurb in the Dallas Times Herald, a now-defunct newspaper that was once the city's informational mainstay until the 1960's. It seemed the unlikely couple married in a private ceremony the week after she first appeared in print associated with Davis.

'Strange also,' Laura thought, *'that Chesapeake was never mentioned in the Dallas or Houston society columns, either before or after her marriage to Davis. And why were there no public announcements about the birth of their daughter, Rose? They would have been a high enough profile couple to warrant some sort of coverage...'*

Laura found a series of pictures of Rose Davis at her high school graduation from Ursuline Academy in 1961 and clicked through them. The girl was beautiful. Blonde with big blue eyes, or so the papers noted. The photos were all black and white.

'Strange that her parents were both brunettes', she thought. Staring at Rose's face, a quiver ran through Laura's spine from the base of her skull to her extremities. There was something about this girl... Her eyes seemed to call out in quiet supplication, even through a tiny computer screen.

One of the pictures dated 1967 showed a gorgeous dark-haired woman standing next to Rose in a newspaper article entitled "Life of the Party". The caption under the photo said "Rose Marie Davis and Kendall Reece at the Mockingbird, Hilton". Laura spent another half hour looking for more pictures or articles mentioning Rose but could find nothing; no marriage license or announcement, no birth announcements, and especially no obituary. It was as if after 1967 the young girl simply disappeared off the face of the earth.

Another shiver ran through Laura. She was starting to feel a little light-headed. It was five in the afternoon and she hadn't eaten since room service brought her bagels at 6 AM. She knew she was stressing her body out and that was a sure-fire way trigger a seizure. She was furious at how helpless her situation made her feel. She felt her heart rate starting to increase and took three slow, deep breaths to calm herself.

There was something about this woman, Reece. She would be another point of interest. But for now food and rest were calling. Laura shut off the viewer, collected her things, and left the building.

1967 Davis home, White Rock Lake

Rose Davis pushes open the screen door with her shoulder and walks out onto the porch. The heat of the day is finally dying down as the sun sinks behind the tree line. Across the yard, under a large oak tree where she's been for hours, Chesapeake is propped up on an aluminum folding chair staring out at the lake. Rose feels a stab of pity shoot through her at the sight, but she quickly numbs herself and brambles down the steps towards her mother.

"Mama? Time to come in."

Chesapeake's gaze never leaves the water. "It's there," her mother hisses. "In the water. It's waiting for you, too, Rose."

"Mama, I told you 'thousand times, ain't nothin' in that ol' lake but fish n' ducks. Now, you need to come in 'for you catch your death." Her foot hits something in the grass next to the chair. It's an empty bottle of whiskey.

"It's callin' t' me, Rose. It sings t' me in my sleep..." Rose turns away, getting a scent of her mother's flammable breath.

"It can sing you t' sleep t'night, too, mama."

"Don't mock me! Don't you mock me, child! The things I've seen would turn your hair white!"

"My hair's yellow now so 'guess I'm half-way there already. Come on, mama..."

She pulls Chesapeake up on her feet and helps her across the lawn towards the house as the woman mumbles to herself like she always does. At times, it is just gibberish but more and more her incoherent ramblings are directed at the lake. Sometimes under her breath she confesses it's her lover, sometimes she screams and calls it Satan himself. Whatever Chesapeake imagines to be in the water, Rose can tell it both calms and agitates her equally in some strange way.

Once inside, getting Chesapeake up the stairwell is always an exercise in restraint. The woman's health has not completely deteriorated, but she acts so infirm most of the time that the family needs someone to look after her, if just to keep her from wandering off on her own. For a time, Lester had hired a private nurse until Chesapeake attacked the poor girl one morning with a fistful of feces. Instead of horrifying more young nurses, Rose decided to put off college for a few years and care for Chesapeake herself.

And every day since then she has regretted her decision.

As soon as Rose puts Chesapeake in bed, the woman passes out right away. Rose takes off her worn slippers, pulls the covers over her, and kisses her sweaty forehead. Chesapeake is already snoring and panting like a hound-dog. Regardless how much torment she suffers from her, Rose can't help but look down at her mother's drooling face and feel pity for her. But it isn't some endearing act of affection; it is pure pity and disgust for the waste of life that her mother has allowed herself to become.

Rose never goes into her parents' room unless she has to put Chesapeake to bed, which is starting to happen more and more frequently. This room is the source of the musky stench of roses and dust that permeates everything in the house. Rose smells it every time she passes the doorway in the hall and it is nauseating to the degree that she can barely stand to breathe around Chesapeake. Now, standing at the foot of her mother's bed, she looks around room in morbid disbelief.

There is a small bric-a-brac menagerie collecting dust on her dressing room chest of drawers. In her youth, her mother had been a collector of antiques that now stand like museum pieces around the parlor, tiny souvenirs of a life long past. Porcelain figurines of women in hoop skirts and petticoats, posing dogs and cats, giraffes, tigers, great apes, clowns and dancing girls leading proud horses, all marching in a procession like a sad, pale pink circus. Charms and bracelets from another time are stacked in crevices, green and tarnished with age. Rose can still remember going with her mother to the grand antique shows as a child. That was the only time she can actually remember enjoying being with her...

A line of photographs sits on a torn lace runner on the dresser. Rose picks one up and stares at it. It is a shot of Chesapeake when she was a child in Houston. The young girl in the photo is 10 or 12-years-old, beautiful and confident, a smile beaming off her face. Rose puts the picture down. Sadly, that person no longer exists.

Framing the single window in the room are grimy lace curtains, streaks of brown soot running down the folds. The fading pink paint of the walls, the dusty canopy drooping over the bed, the worn slippers on the floor deformed and soiled grey from years of use... Rose is disgusted. This place is nothing but a mausoleum, a collection of dead dreams and fading memories rotting like corpses in a tattered lace grave. How can her father bear to sleep in here? So much grief in this room... as well as everywhere else in the lives of the Davis family, for that matter. What could possibly have happened to destroy her mother's sense of self so completely? Rose couldn't imagine. As a child at Ursuline Academy, the nuns had taught Rose that good people always prosper and every story has a happy ending. Now that she was older, what a very different place the real world had proven itself to be.

Rose walks out of the room, quietly closing the door behind her. It is like coming up for air from deep, cold water. She leans against the doorframe for a moment, dreaming of some other life a million miles away... A life free of the smell of sickness, the stench of whiskey and urine and roses.

Downstairs the television is on. From the banister she can see her father Lester sitting in his E-Z Boy recliner reading the newspaper under the orange light from a crooked standing lamp. How miserable he must be...

She continues down the stairs and stands next to his chair.

"Daddy, I'm goin' for a walk, 'kay?"

The newspaper drops and he looks out over the sports page. "Your mama might wake up with you gone. I'll never hear the end of it, Rosalee."

"Mama's passed out. I just put her to bed. I just wanna get some air. I'll be back soon. Promise."

He looks up at her with the same deep sadness in his eyes that she always sees on his face. So much pain...

"Ok, pumpkin. Be careful."

"I will." She leans over, kisses him on top of his balding head, and walks out of the room.

Pushing the screen door open, Rose escapes to the porch with a heavy sigh. It's a warm summer evening. The sun has dissolved into a low wall of blue-gray clouds stretching from one end of the horizon to the other. Only a smear of bright purple sky remains, slowly melting into a velvet blanket of night. A ripe full moon hangs low over the black water making the lake seem like a bottomless pit in the earth.

Faint sounds of laughter echo across the lake. Rose walks off the porch and past a small line of trees that runs beside the house. On the far east side of the lake she sees the beach in front of the Bath House is lit up with hanging lanterns. Music is drifting across the water. They must be having a party.

She looks down at her dress and brushes some lint off with her hand. It would be so nice to go, just for a little while. There would probably be people her own age there. She thinks for a moment, looks back only once to make sure her father isn't watching, and then takes off in the direction of the Bath House

***

The White Rock Bath House is an all-purpose community building built in a cove on the east side of the lake. The common area in and around the structure is often rented for private functions. There is a man-made beach leading into a small cove where people used to swim in the 30's. But now there's a strong undertow in deeper parts of the lake and they have banned swimming altogether.

Tonight dozens of couples are slow dancing on a parquet floor set up right on the beach. Strings of Chinese lanterns hang over the makeshift dance-floor illuminating the scene in red and purple and green. There are Tiki torches burning on the beach as well. A small stage is set up against the Bath House for the band.

Rose Davis looks across the dance-floor and standing there in a form-fitting polka dot dress is a tall, voluptuous girl with raven hair. Her skin is the color of milk. She is sipping a can of cola through a straw and watching the dancers with a slight mischievous look in her eye. All the young men stare at her but none have the courage to ask her to dance. Instead they gawk lecherously at her bright red lips as she sips from her red and white striped straw as if they've never seen a woman sipping soda before.

Rose is impressed. This girl has it down, the feminine allure that she's always dreamt of having. She watches with jealous fascination how the men, even the women, react to this woman's blatant femininity. She looks like a bathing beauty or maybe Miss America.

Abruptly, the girl looks up and meets Rose's gaze. The woman smiles large and warm. Rose can't help but smile back. She feels herself blush and she turns away. What a strange feeling to get worked up from looking at another woman...

The band tears into a fast song. Without warning, the brunette runs over and grabs Rose by the hand, dragging her onto the dance floor. All of the couples turn to stare at them in disbelief as the two women dance with complete abandon, swinging one another around and around to the music. The men are fascinated and the women glare at the girls with open jealously as the two dance oblivious to anyone else.

The raven-haired girl spins Rose around and takes her in for a dip that makes all the men shout excitedly. She hovers over her close enough to kiss her on the lips. Pulling Rose back to her feet, they swing to the center of the floor, jamming hard to the music.

The song ends and the entire crowd erupts in applause for the two girls. They both break out in laughter. The stranger takes Rose by the hand and they run off the floor.

Rose is panting. "Oh, my God, that was the funnest thing I've ever done!"

"You're pretty good, sweets," the stranger says in a northern accent. "I didn't think you'd keep up. *They* sure liked it though."

The girl nods towards a group of young men who have been watching them like hungry wolves. Rose is a little embarrassed by the attention but loves it.

"I'm Kendall Reece." The brunette extends her hand in mock formality.

Rose takes her hand and shakes it. "I'm Rose. Rose Davis."

"I think we're gonna get along just fine, Rose Davis." The dark-haired beauty leans over and kisses Rose on the cheek. Rose blushes again.

The girls grab a drink from the makeshift bar and retreat to a table beside the dance floor.

Rose was curious. "So, how did you find this place?"

"Eh, I get around!" Kendall laughed heartily and slapped Rose on the back. "Actually, a friend of mine sponsored the party and invited me out. I didn't think a walk in the country would be this much fun." Her eyes never leave Rose.

"I'm usually not so much of a dancer. But you're a great lead!" Rose was smiling so hard Kendall was afraid she'd hurt herself. "Do you live in the city, Kendall?"

"I grew up in Chicago but I've been in California for the last couple years."

"I love California!"

"Yeah? Where you been?"

"Well, I haven't actually *been* there, but I read all the magazines and it looks wonderful!"

Kendall smirks. "You are the cutest thing. You know, there's a whole world out there, Rose, just waitin' for ya."

Rose looks up and realizes that scores of young men have been walking past checking the two of them out all night. Kendall is acutely aware of each pair of leering eyes and feigns disinterest.

Rose watches the way Kendall holds her head. She is like a princess holding court. The woman looks like a porcelain doll. Not one to be played with by children but rather by men...

Rose reaches for her cocktail and sees the face of her watch.

"Oh, Lord, I've been gone almost two hours! I have to go. I'm surprised my father doesn't have the police out looking for me by now."

"Do you need a ride?"

"Thank you, no. I walked."

Kendall frowned. "You live close by?"

"Just on the other side of that tree line," Rose points across the cove. "The big house, facing the lake."

Kendall gets suddenly excited. "I gotta great idea; let's have a sleep-over! I can get a bottle or two to take with us–"

Rose reluctantly interrupts her. "I'd love to, but–I can't. Not tonight. My mother is ill and I just put her to bed a little while ago. But we can do it some other time, though. I promise."

Kendall smirks, amused and surprised by the young girl's sincerity. "Ok, another time, sugar. I'll take a rain-check."

"I'm really glad we met, Kendall. I'd love for us to be friends."

Kendall throws her bag over her shoulder. "Sure thing, sweets. I'll see you around then."

"But–how will I find you?"

"Don't worry, sugar. I'll find *you*..."

Twelve

Present Day. White Rock Lake, Dallas

Most of the neighborhoods surrounding White Rock Lake were built in intricate veins of charming avenues and quaint little cul-de-sacs huddled up against the lake shoreline. The houses were small but well built and full of personality. There was an exclusive neighborhood on the west bank where many of the homes sat on sprawling lots and were owned for generations by old Texas money families. This was where the former home of Lester Davis was located.

Laura drove down Mockingbird Lane to Dalewood. It was a beautiful residential community and a gorgeous drive. From there she turned left on Kimberly Lane, which led directly to the water. There, West Lawther continued hugging the edge of the lake along the cove between Green Heron Park and Tilly's Point, two landmarks in the lake's geography. Driving, she could see the diminutive whitewashed walls of the Bath House far across the lake. She passed a tall line of fir trees and there on a gentle slope facing the water was a house that literally took her breath away.

Pulling into the long gravel driveway, she parked and got out of the car. She pulled out her phone and took a picture of the residence for her notes.

Mammoth sheets of glass had replaced the entire front of the structure revealing an open California-style design. You could literally see straight through the house to the back yard. The place was very different from the aging structure Laura had seen in photographs during her research. The view of the lake was magnificent from the porch. And in the lawn stood a behemoth oak tree, probably 80-feet tall, where undoubtedly Chesapeake Davis would have sat staring out at the water day after day waiting for something that would never come.

Right after the Jules Frank interview, Laura had researched the property and contacted the current owners, Dr. Paul Marshall and his wife Greta. Mrs. Marshall had been charming and extremely accommodating. After Lester Davis' death in 1983, the residence had stood vacant until the couple purchased and wholly redesigned the residence in 1992.

Laura pushed the doorbell. She heard the tone of a low gong ring once, twice, three times. What a soothing ringer, she thought. The tangerine door opened and a young girl who looked barely 18 stood in front of her. "Yes?"

"Hello, I'm Laura Milton. I'm here to meet Greta Marshall."

"I'm Greta Marshall!" The woman smiled, obviously proud of the fact that most people probably mistook her for being her own daughter. "Come in!"

The house was now a glass and metal homage to contemporary minimalism, very tasteful and comfortable. Bamboo slat floors ran the length of the first level. The expansive living room was sunken and lined with citrus-colored couches and chairs. Walking through the home, Laura felt none of the latent aggression she had expected to linger from the Davis family. There was nothing but sunlight and warmth radiating throughout the home.

Greta was a gracious hostess. She offered Laura some tea and they sat in the kitchen against another glass wall and started talking. She was from a prominent Dallas real estate family, had graduated pre-med from Baylor University, and met and married her husband right out of college. She got pregnant a month later and gave up the hope for a career in medicine to have her first child.

The couple loved the house and had never had any ill feeling in the 17-plus years they've lived there. The rural atmosphere was a perfect environment in which to raise their two children. And neither one had ever encountered the White Rock Lady.

When Laura pulled out of the driveway, she was more confused than ever. This wasn't a dead-end necessarily, but the Marshall home was anything but a haunted house. It made her question whether Chesapeake and Lester Davis had anything to do with the White Rock legend whatsoever. Maybe this was just another dead end. There was no smoking gun, no physical evidence that proved any of these events actually occurred, nothing to substantiate a haunting whatsoever.

Laura drove back to the hotel in frustrated silence. She was checking out of the Melrose tonight to relocate to the Fairmont Hotel on Akard Street in the Arts District downtown. It would be a different perspective for her and she wanted to see the Venetian Room, the infamous nightclub that had been a hotbed of underground activity in the late sixties and early seventies.

Her phone rang bringing her back to the present. She checked the display. It was Colin. Finally. She let it ring twice more before she answered.

"Hi, stranger."

"Hey, sorry, this week has been a real killer. I had a second and wanted to check on you. How's it going down there?"

"It's pretty intense. I've been following the Davis trail but it's come to a dead end. I'm moving to the Fairmont Hotel tonight for a change of scenery."

As always, Colin was in front of his computer.

"I see you guys are in for some storms for the next week or so. At least you're out of the heat for a while. Thank God for global warming, right?"

"Colin, I–"

"Look, I don't want to keep you. I just wanted to hear your voice."

Damn, he always knew how to defuse her. She smiled, in spite of herself. "How are things there?"

"Good. I drove to DC yesterday and I'm here at the museum. It'll be another late night." He paused. "I miss you, Laura."

It really tore her apart when he was so sentimental. It was true, he was a part of her life that she could never imagine living without, regardless of her present frame of mind. But people changed constantly. It was the healthiest thing a person could ever do. And she had changed drastically in the past few months, she just didn't know what into.

"I miss you, too. I really do." And she couldn't have been more sincere.

"Remember that thought. And be safe tonight. I gotta run, but I'll talk to you soon."

"Kay. Bye."

She hung up the phone, totally frustrated with herself. As sweet as he was, if she really loved Colin, talking to him wouldn't be so exhausting. Things weren't supposed to be this difficult. Love was not something that you hid and made excuses to be absent from. She wished they had just gone through with it, moved to Portland, and started their own consulting company like they had talked about. At least their relationship would still be intact. But when Colin decided to accept the offer from his father and the Smithsonian without consulting her, he thoroughly destroyed her trust. And, regardless of her love for him, that was one thing that was irreparable.

The worst part of it was she knew he probably did it for a good reason. Most likely, he wanted to secure a good career that could afford the two of them a comfortable life together. And for that, she was grateful. But, then again, he knew she had her own money. There was no reason not to tell her the truth. Besides, Colin knew how paranoid she has always been of being disregarded and lied to after the tragedies in her life. There was no way he could have forgotten how hard it was to earn her trust in the first place.

Dealing with her father's death had been incredibly difficult. When he died, Laura slammed the gates of her heart shut and lived a quiet, monastic life. The sheer weight of her sorrow isolated her further from not only Colin but from the world at large. During this period, the ferocity of her dreams became unbearable, feeding thoughts of suicide. Through it all, Colin stayed close, giving her the space she needed to grieve on her own but being a constant, albeit passive, positive source of encouragement. Even though they shared a mutual desire, he never once pushed a physical relationship with her at any point and was respectful of her boundaries. Even if sometimes she was not.

It took months of extensive therapy with Adrienne Bartok before she finally got to the point where she felt strong enough to even think of supporting a relationship. When she finally allowed herself to fall into Colin's arms, she collapsed and cried for hours.

Except for one boyfriend in her sophomore year in high school, Colin was the only man she had ever been with. He was smart, funny, sensitive; all the things a woman could hope for in a lover. So why was she pushing him away now, allowing Mallory's advances? Why didn't she just marry Colin when she had the chance, instead of leaving him and his entire family waiting at the church in the worst form of rejection conceivable? You didn't do that to people you were supposedly in love with. Or did you? One thing was certain; she didn't want to hurt him any longer with her confusion. He was a wonderful guy and she wanted him to be happy, with or without her.

The truth was, with the advent of her epilepsy, Laura's entire outlook on life had changed. She was simply a different person, with a different set of needs and priorities altogether. Now that life had reminded her of just how fragile we are as organisms, there were more important things than simply having a mate, no matter how perfect he happened to be. There was no such thing as security, only security blankets. If she couldn't find a way to deal with her issues and be happy on her own, no outside force would ever be able to do it for her.

Most of all, she didn't want Colin to be a collateral victim of her pain and confusion. He had a chance to live a life devoid of all of her darkness. And whether he knew it or not, allowing him that chance was the greatest gift she could ever give him.

Laura pulled the Land Rover up to the valet desk in front of the Melrose Hotel. She had checked out earlier in the morning before leaving to meet Greta Marshall. She gave the porter her ticket and he ran to retrieve her luggage. While she waited, she watched a steady stream of new guests arrive at the hotel. A small family pulled up in an SUV and got out of the vehicle. The father looked barely over 20, the mother, even younger. They had a little daughter who must have been all of 15 months old. The child teetered on her tiny legs, still unsure of how to make them work while holding onto her mother's hand.

The valet returned. Laura popped the back hatch and he started loading her things into the back of the Land Rover.

What was the fascination with children in the first place? She couldn't understand the attraction for young couples. The thought of giving up her freedom and independence was abhorrent. And for what? And as far as she was concerned, infants had no personalities. They were basically eating-machines for the first two years. Not to mention, children were such bad business models. She wanted to be more than just another active uterus in the world. She was an academic, for God's sake. She wanted to help humanity, not add to an already-oversaturated gene pool.

'And that will happen,' she thought, *'long before I give up my identity to some black-hole of a child that will swallow every ounce of matter and light that surrounds it.'*

There was something behind Laura's intense dislike for motherhood, a fear that churned in the pit of her stomach every time the thought entered her mind. Her greatest fear was not so much the level of responsibility, but rather the chance of passing her emotional and physical baggage along to a fledgling organism. To give birth knowing the risk of infecting her child with possible epilepsy would be the cruelest and most selfish thing she could ever conceive of doing. It didn't seem like a problem for the rest of the world, however. Every day, thousands of people birthed children indiscriminately with little or no concern of the atmosphere or temperament said child is being brought into. She didn't want to be guilty of making that mistake as well.

The porter finished loading her bags and closed the hatch. Laura tipped him, wiped the tears straining in the corner of her eyes, and drove out of the parkway towards the next leg of her adventure.

Thirteen

The Fairmont Hotel opened in Dallas on May 7, 1969 and, at the time, was touted as the finest luxury hotel in the city. Located on the west side of downtown in the Arts District, the hotel catered to the upper-echelon of art patrons and executive travelers from all over the world. Even today, the quiet understated elegance insures their guests a different experience than the more modern hotels in the city.

Laura took her key cards from the smiling desk clerk and continued through the crowd. There were members of a wedding party standing, with gifts in hand, in the center of the lobby. An older couple sipped cocktails on a couch, a few prom couples stood around laughing in their rented tuxedos and colorful dresses with matched-dyed shoes. Laura shook her head smiling as she stepped into the elevator.

After securing her equipment and taking a quick shower, she was again sitting alone taking notes, this time in a strangely empty and luxurious Pyramid Room restaurant. Dinner was excellent. The coriander-rubbed red snapper with early fall vegetables hit the spot and was definitely more than she had eaten in one sitting in a while.

One of the things she hated most about epilepsy was having to be so mindful of everything she did, especially watching everything she ingested. Once more, against doctor's advice, she ordered a glass of cabernet with dinner. The truth was no matter how mindful you were, anything could kill you, be it bubblegum, milkshakes, or car wrecks. So why not just minimize your risks, enjoy yourself in moderation, and hope for the best? It seemed the best approach. God knows, worrying only made everything worse. In her case, there were almost always warning signs in advance before a seizure hit. She told herself as long as she listened to her body and had time to settle herself when the symptoms came, she would be all right. She hoped.

After dinner, she ordered a cup of chamomile tea and read through some notes on her laptop as she waited for her dessert. In a few moments, the waiter brought out a baked Dutch apple tart with cinnamon ice cream and sat it in front of her.

"Thank you."

Laura felt the slightest twinge of guilt until she took the first bite. Ahhh... Life is just too short to say no all the time. She took a sip of her tea and continued reading about Lester Davis' wife, Chesapeake. There was something about this woman that was compelling, regardless of the fact that there was hardly any information available about her whatsoever. What she could find had huge holes in the timeline. Again, none of it made much sense.

Her family was from Houston, Texas. Her father, Warren Millstone, was the third son in an old oil family. Her mother, Rosalyn Mable Millstone, died giving birth to her in 1931.

'Well, at least we have something in common,' Laura thought.

Rosalyn's maiden name *Clement* was something new. Laura did a quick search. It seemed there was a history of mental illness in the Clement family; Chesapeake's grandmother Beatrice Clement died in an asylum in 1911. Chesapeake herself had three separate stays at the St. Paul Hospital's psychiatric ward in Dallas between '59 and '61.

Which brought up two questions: who had her committed and why?

The next thing Laura could find was an obituary dated November 1, 1968, in the Dallas Times Herald. No cause, no location. She was survived by husband Lester and daughter Rose Marie Davis. And that was it. Funny, Laura thought. That happened to be the same year the Vietnam War began. Strange, how history overlaps itself...

There were so many unanswered questions, the first being, why was the wife of a wealthy philanthropist never seen at any social functions or benefits? Wasn't that part of the arrangement when you married money, socializing? And what were the circumstances surrounding her hospital stays? One thing was certain; the story of Chesapeake Davis was getting stranger and stranger by the minute.

She finished her desert and the waiter brought her check. Laura signed the tab and went back to her room to work on the itinerary for the rest of the week before reluctantly taking her meds and going to bed.

November 1, 1968, Davis home, White Rock Lake

The smell of fried chicken fills the house. In the kitchen, Rose pulls a pan of roasted corn-on-the-cob out of the oven and sets it on the stove. She scoops the mashed potatoes from a deep pan into a ceramic bowl. With two potholders, she grabs a dish in each hand and walks into the next room, setting them in the center of the dining room table. Lester is planted in front of the grainy television as usual.

"Daddy, dinner's ready!"

"Smells great, Rosalee!"

"I'm gonna grab momma."

Wiping her hands on her apron, Rose walks out onto the porch. In the distance, her mother is where she always is during the day: sitting in that aluminum chair under the giant oak tree staring out at the lake. Rose takes off her apron and walks out into the yard.

“Momma, time to come in!”

Chesapeake doesn’t respond.

A shiver runs though Rose. She nervously glances out at the lake and then back to Chesapeake. “I know you hear me, Momma. Time for supper.”

The woman still doesn’t respond. Walking quickly up behind her, Rose puts her hand on her mother’s shoulder.

“Momma?” She freezes in her steps. The shoulder is stiff and cool to the touch. Rose holds her breath. She slowly turns to face the woman.

Chesapeake is dead. Crimson spittle runs down the side of her chin; her wet eyes, covered by a thin white film, are still open, staring out at the lake forever. Rose sighs with a strange mix of sadness and relief. What a horrible waste of life, dying alone, staring out at the lake, tormented by her own delusions. Having thought repeatedly about this day had not prepared Rose for the reality of losing her only mother in such a way. She crouches down in front of the corpse and gazes at her mother’s panic-stricken face, not knowing what to feel other than shock and emptiness. But one thing is certain, at least now she is free.

* * *

Located adjacent to White Rock Lake, Cox Cemetery is the oldest recorded cemetery in Texas. An overwhelming percentage of the graves belong to freedom fighters from the Texas Revolution era. The Davis family has had a family plot there for generations. It has always been a prestigious honor to be laid to rest in Cox Cemetery. But then again, Rose believes once you are dead, why the hell does it matter where you are buried anyway?

Except for the rhythmic slap of the windshield wipers, Lester Davis drives his car in absolute silence. Rose and Kendall are in the back seat staring out at the rain falling in large droplets. Rose is almost catatonic.

The car stops and the three step out into the rain. The girls lead Davis slowly across the cemetery lawn to the gravesite. A small canopy has been erected for the service in the middle of the garden of headstones. The funeral party is waiting for them, a small cluster of mourners all dressed in black. Rose recognizes the faces of Officers Brighton and Donnelly. Davis' lawyer, the tall, gangly Daniel Morrow, stands stoically in the shadows behind the funeral party.

Rose takes her place next to the open grave. She is wearing all black; a simple sleeveless dress, elbow-high gloves, and a dark veil over a pillbox hat. Lester stands on her left in a wrinkled black suit, still in a state of shock. Kendall is on her right wearing a skin-tight dark green linen dress and black satin gloves. After a few moments of silence, the priest stands and begins the service.

"In the name of the Father, the Son, and the Holy Spirit..."

The prayers become an unintelligible din drowning in the soft white noise of the rainfall. Rose is numb, unable to cry. She had often thought how she would feel when her mother passed away, had always suspected it would be a clash of conflicting emotions, but she never thought she would be frozen in shock.

While the ceremony continues, Kendall carefully looks behind her and catches the eye of the lawyer, Morrow, who has been watching her intently since she arrived. She smiles like a Siamese cat and turns back to the procession.

Finally, the priest blesses the coffin and turns to the family. Rose walks up and places a large red rose on top of the casket. Davis is next. He places a bouquet of wild flowers on the mahogany wood of the coffin and breaks down sobbing. The priest puts his arm around him and gently leads him off.

After the service, the small crowd slowly disperses into the rainy afternoon.

Rose stays close to the plot, watching the workers lower the casket into the ground. Kendall stands behind her hiding under an oversized black umbrella trying desperately not to complain. Eventually, two men in overalls come and remove the canopy, all the chairs and flower arrangements. Slowly, Rose turns and walks away from the grave. Kendall follows her, reaches over and takes her by the hand.

The girls wander through the tombstone garden in silence as the rain falls gently around them. The sound of the droplets is like thousands of little voices all whispering at once.

Kendall breaks the silence. "Do you miss her?"

"I–I don't know... Can you miss someone you hate? I think I need some time to adjust to the thought of being free..."

"You know what I think, sugarbear? I think you need to get the hell out of here. Seriously. Why don't we get a place together? You need a change. And so do I."

Rose is shocked. She has never lived away from home. The idea of it is exciting and terrifying at the same time.

"I could never leave daddy," she says cautiously.

"Oh, *please*. Your father's a good-looking man. He's probably dying to get back into the swing of things and have a life. Maybe even be happy with someone new for a few years."

"I don't even have a job, Kendall..."

"Quit making excuses. I can handle the bills for a while. And besides, I might be able to get you a job at Neiman-Marcus department store..."

A huge smile erupts on Rose's face. "Oh, my God, I *love* that place!"

"I know *all* the boys there. They'll love you! Not to mention you get 20% discount as an employee." She winks.

Rose looks at her, tears cresting in her blue eyes. "You would do that for me?"

"Sure I would. You always wanted to be in the thick of it, Goldilocks. Nothing's standing in your way now..."

Rose decides to take a few weeks to bring the matter up with her father; she doesn't want him feeling like she is abandoning him. She will stay and help him with all the post-funeral business, help him remove the mountains of junk Chesapeake has piled all over the house, and make sure he is healthy. And then her life will begin. Finally.

She takes a deep breath. Standing there in that old graveyard, surrounded by thousands of corpses, she has never been happier in her life...

Fourteen

A few days after the funeral, Lester and Rose begin the arduous task of packing all of Chesapeake's furniture and collectables. Some will be stored in Davis' warehouse; others are to be taken directly to a consignment store run by one of Lester's business partners, Chel Sheldon. Sheldon is a mover and shaker in the antiques business and assures Davis that he can broker the sale of the small fortune of collectibles Chesapeake has amassed over the years.

Over the next week, Davis hires a couple of SMU students to assist them in cataloguing the vast collection of antiques. They spend days going through the house, tagging and pricing everything in silence, the quiet drone of the radio the only sound echoing through the house. Davis refuses to keep any emotional reminders of his deceased wife, and whatever isn't tagged for storage or sale ends up in a large refuse pile in the front yard. He strips the musty curtains from all the windows, has the carpet ripped up from the living room, and lets the light stream in the house for the first time in decades.

Even though he has always been slightly detached, Lester has consistently been ten times the parent to Rose than Chesapeake ever could have been. And now that his wife is gone, the deep cloud of sadness over him is slowly dissipating and Rose can see a lightness behind her father's eyes.

That following week, Davis hires Sheldon's crew to come in and remove anything with a tag. Ornate desks and armoires are pulled out of the garage, dozens of boxes full of glass and ceramic knick-knacks are loaded shoulder-high in the back of a large moving truck along with racks full of clothing, over 30 hatboxes, and God-only-knows how many boxes of shoes. Rose can't believe the staggering amount of stuff they find in the recesses of the house. It's no wonder she felt so claustrophobic all the time, surrounded by this morbid, depressing collection of dead things from a dead era.

On the third and last day of moving, the crew arrives early. They clear Chesapeake's bedroom of the canopy bed and the chests of drawers before noon and attack the stack of boxes in the corner of the room. Only the contents of Chesapeake's private office are left to load and then the process will be complete.

Rose unlocks the door to her mother's office, a small room at the far end of the upstairs hallway. Pushing the creaking door open, the scent of the room assails her, stale and musty. The office has been shut for years. She walks into what feels like a tomb. The windows are covered with dusty lace curtains. A single dead rose sits in a glass vase on the windowsill, a spider web elegantly draped between the glass and the sill.

When she had been a small child Rose remembers her mother spending hours at time in this dark, stuffy room. But as her mother's demeanor grew more and more unpredictable, this strange sanctuary of hers was all but boarded up and forgotten. Rose couldn't recall when she last saw the door open, much less heard the tapping of her mother's fingers on her ancient Smith-Corona typewriter that sits still covered by a dusty cloth on the desk.

Davis had come in earlier in the week. The books, files, and financial records had all been boxed up and stacked against the wall ready for the movers. The more intricate retrieval of personals items would have to be done by hand.

Rose slowly takes a seat at her mother's ornate wooden desk. As a child, she had always been forbidden to enter the room, which served no purpose other than help Rose cultivate a deep hatred for anything Chesapeake cared about. The desk is the last large piece of her mother's belongings left to remove, like a last bit of cancer to be torn from raw flesh. Rose does her best to disregard her disgust and gets to work. The faster she finishes, the quicker she will be rid of any evidence of Chesapeake's existence whatsoever.

She pulls out all the side drawers and empties their contents into either boxes or the trash. In one drawer there are stacks of unopened letters bound with twine from people she's never heard of. In a hand-carved wooden cup, she finds a collection of antique fountain pens in a gorgeous array of colors. Strange, discovering things her mother had affection for... when she clearly had no affection for her only daughter...

The center drawer is the last to be checked. Rose pulls on the handle and finds the drawer stuck partially open. She tries to close the drawer but the side hangs up on the edge of the opening. She yanks hard on the handle and the entire drawer comes out in her lap. It is empty but there is a small compartment hidden in the back of the drawer, a rectangular box the width of the drawer itself, a fake back. She knocks on the rectangular block and it seems hollow. She pulls the panel out and reaches in. At first she feels nothing, but just as she pulls her hand out it brushes against something solid. She extracts a small brass key. It is tarnished and crusted with green oxidation. She looks around the room but sees nothing with a lock on it. The key could be to almost anything.

The movers walk in the room and Rose slips the key in her sweater pocket.

"Miss Davis? We're almost done. Should we start with this room?"

"Yes. Please, don't let me get in the way. You can get the boxes first, if you like."

"Yes, ma'am."

The movers carry out two large stacks of boxes on tilt dollies. Rose turns back to the task at hand. The quicker this is done, the better.

She kicks something with her right foot. There is an object wedged between the desk and the wall. Rose reaches down and pulls it out with a yank. It is a worn leather satchel covered in dust. There is a latch that keeps the hood in place. On the latch is a small keyhole.

Rose pulls the key from her pocket. It is the right size. But why would Chesapeake hide a key to something so insignificant? But then again her mother was never one to do anything logically. It was just like her to create melodrama, even from the grave itself.

Rose feels suddenly anxious, like she is being watched. She turns around and confirms she is by herself in the room. Turning back to the satchel, she slowly puts the key in the latch. It fits perfectly. She gently turns the lock and feels a click. Taking a deep breath, she opens the top flap at the hinge.

The satchel contains a single hand-bound book and nothing else. What a disappointment. Chesapeake could have left something of value behind, but no. Just some dusty book of God-knows-what. But what did she really expect to find? Did she hope that Chesapeake, in a moment of clarity, had left a precious heirloom of some sort for her only daughter? Or perhaps a letter to her child begging forgiveness for a lifetime of cruelty, a last word of sanity before she went insane? Right...

Angry at her own naïveté, Rose turns the object over in her hands. She opens the book and sees it is a diary. The first entry was September 12, 1941.

'...I miss my mother, but not the place. Quaker life is not for me. I don't believe in fellowship. I don't believe in Man- I only believe in God. And never the twain shall meet...'

She recognizes the writing as Chesapeake's. It is a childish scrawl, the handwriting big and obvious with large loops and dramatic tails on the end of words. They were written when her mother was just a child. It seems Chesapeake's penchant for the dramatic started at young age.

Rose sighs aloud. Now, just as she has managed to escape her mother's suffocating grasp, here are Chesapeake's most intimate thoughts, waiting to infect her all over again.

Though her curiosity is killing her, Rose can't allow herself to be pulled into her mother's demented life again. Hot tears crest in her blue eyes. How dare that bitch reach out to her from the grave like this.

'Just die, Chesapeake. For God's sake, just die!'

Rose closes the satchel and sets it next to a box filled with disintegrating paperbacks. Whatever rantings her mother entertained herself with, she was welcome to take them to the grave with her. Finally, when the movers come back, they take everything to the truck to be deposited God-knows-where. Including the satchel.

'Goodbye, Chesapeake.' Rose thinks to herself. *'I hope you rot in Hell...'*

* * *

While Rose deals with her mother's estate and all that entails, Kendall Reece has been busy looking for an apartment for the two of them. She has been sleeping with Lester Davis' lawyer since Chesapeake's funeral, a married young man by the name of Daniel Morrow. Morrow owns a second office perched dramatically on the top of the historic Wilson Building overlooking Main Street in downtown Dallas. The 1,500 square foot suite on the twelfth floor has been converted into a lush living space for his international clients but is rarely used. When Kendall tells him about needing a place for her and Rose, to her surprise, he offers the space to the girls.

After hearing the good news from Kendall, Rose waits another week before telling her father about her and Kendall's plans. The last thing she wants is for him to have to deal with yet another loss so quickly. When she finally breaks the news to him, he cries like a child at the thought of her leaving. But inside, he knows Rose deserves to be free to go and live her own life. Davis gives her $2,000 cash and hires a company to move her things.

The girls' first week in the building is a sensory overload. It takes some time for Rose to get used to the private parking garage and elevators. And living in a building that shuts down for the night and on the weekends is more than a little strange. But after befriending the two night security guards, the girls start to adjust to the glamour of their new home. Even though the closest grocery store is a few miles away, how many girls their age could hope to live alone in a place like this? It is like a dream come true. Every morning Rose wakes up to the sun streaming through the 8-foot windows in their living room. Outside, the majestic Dallas skyscrapers stretch to the heavens while the rhythm of the world continues 12 stories below. It is what she imagines living in New York must be like.

And, of course, directly across Main Street facing her side of the building, the Neiman-Marcus department store glitters and sparkles in all its alluring glory. Every afternoon she crosses the street and stands in front of the display windows staring at all the beautiful clothes. There on display is a gorgeous powder-blue gown she has been coveting for the last week. But without a job, she can only look and dream, like Audrey Hepburn's character in "Breakfast at Tiffany's".

On her third Sunday morning at the Wilson residence, Rose wakes up at dawn, dresses, and walks 8 blocks to attend the 7:30 AM service at the Sacred Heart Cathedral Church located on Ross Avenue. For some reason, attending church makes her feel like she is paying respect to Chesapeake in some way, though God knows that woman didn't have a Christian bone in her body.

There, kneeling in the cavernous Cathedral surrounded by candles and statues of saints, Rose feels next to nothing. Even with the new novelty of having the mass said in English instead of Latin, she is stoic. She goes through the motions but her heart is vacant. Looking at the few people in the pews she wonders how many of them feel the same emptiness in their hearts. How many of them are there not to glorify God but in a desperate attempt to curb the deep loneliness of their lives?

After mass, Rose returns to the Wilson Building. She walks through the empty private parking garage and takes the elevator up to the top floor. The entire place is eerily quiet at 9 AM on Sunday morning.

She quietly unlocks the door and steps into the apartment. *Her apartment.* She has always dreamt of living in a place like this ever since she was a child. And now it is her reality.

Chesapeake, the emotional despot, is gone, gone like the Wicked Witch of the West in the Wizard of Oz, melted away by the water from that cursed lake she loved and feared so much. Rose is free. And the rest of her life stretches out in front of her like a highway into the unknown. She isn't sad and doesn't feel remorse. But, shouldn't she feel something, anything at all? Instead, she feels like she's made of stone. Why is it that, in the quietest of moments, when she listens to her heart she hears nothing but utter silence?

There is a deep window seat in the living room. Rose sits in the alcove in silence, staring out at the coming morning.

The door in the hall opens and Kendall slinks out of her bedroom like a sleepy cat, the thin silk of her Japanese robe hanging off her lithe body. After a late night, she is moving slowly. She finds Rose sitting in the window seat staring out at the city below and sits across from her in the alcove. The morning sun streams in filling the room with bright white light.

"Chicago is just like this. We all live in the city," Kendall purrs, staring out the window.

"It's beautiful..." Rose stares out at the buildings dreamily. A few cars crawl across Main Street like tiny beetles far below.

"How was church?"

"Fine. There aren't many people at the 7:30 mass."

Kendall looks at her roommate's sullen face. She touches the palm of her hand to her cheek. "Are you happy, Rose?"

Rose nods slowly. "Kendall, meeting you has changed my life. I don't know how to thank you..." Her voice sounds a million miles away.

"I just want to make sure you don't regret your decision."

"No, not at all. I've just never lived away from home. It's a bit of culture shock I think. Everything has changed so fast..."

Kendall smiles. She gets up, picks up a rectangular box sitting on the couch in the living room, and returns to the window seat. Dust particles are floating in the amber beam of sunlight streaming in the window like minute jellyfish swimming in the thick air.

"Look, I know this was a big leap for you. I wanted to get you something special to celebrate." She hands Rose a large box with Neiman-Marcus stamped on it.

"Kendall, you didn't have to get me anything! And from Neiman's..." Her blue eyes are huge and starting to tear up.

"I meant to give it to you last night, but my date ran late."

Rose opens the box and pulls out a gorgeous powder-blue silk dress with thin spaghetti straps. It is the same dress Rose has been staring at in the window of Neiman's for weeks. "Oh, my God!" Rose holds it up and looks at herself in the mirror on the parlor wall. It is so beautiful she starts to cry.

"Hey, now, don't go and get all blubbery on me. You're a new woman, Rose. Time to look the part. It's a little much for Sunday morning, but I thought you needed something nice."

"Thank you so much! And I can't believe you got me an interview at Neiman-Marcus. I'm so scared..."

"You'll be fine, sweets. They'll love you. Now wadda ya say we get out of here and grab some grub?"

The girls dress and have a late breakfast at HL Green's around the corner from their building. Afterwards, they sit at the counter and Kendall lights a cigarette as they watch the sparse Sunday traffic crawl by.

"Let's go out." Kendall is getting antsy.

"On Sunday afternoon? I'm a little tired. Besides, I have my interview tomorrow and I want to be fresh."

"Oh, you're fresh, all right," Kendall sneers. "Come on, sleepy. Sunday afternoon is prime time at this dance club. Besides, I need to see a guy. You'll have a blast! Am I ever wrong?"

Kendall finally talks Rose into going. They jump in Rose's Chevelle and head over to Lou-Ann's Bar on Greenville Avenue and Lovers Lane. To Rose's surprise, the parking lot is full. When they get out of the car they can hear the thump of the band in the building.

Rose is curious. "I've never been here."

"Are you sure you're from Dallas, chickie?"

"I don't get out much."

"Well, that's about to change. C'mon."

Kendall takes Rose by the hand and the two girls walk into the crowded bar. The dance-floor is packed. On the stage a young band is rocking out. Rose recognizes the song as "Wooly Bully" by Sam the Sham and the Pharoahs. The two girls walk in front of the bandstand and Sam winks at them from the stage. "Hey-y, baby!"

The girls work their way up to the bar and the bartender yells out to Kendall. "Hey, baby-cakes!" Kendall stands on the rail and gives the big sweaty guy a hug across the bar.

"Good crowd today, Dill!"

"It is now that you're here!" The bartender puts two shots down on the bar in front of the girls. "Fasten your seat belts!"

"Here we go..." Kendall takes the drinks in her hands.

Rose looks at the red liquid in the shot glass. "What is that?"

"It's *free.*" Kendall hands her one and Rose reluctantly accepts.

"What do I do?"

"Slam it. Ready?" Rose nods, reluctantly. Kendall's eyes go wide. "See ya!"

They both slam the alcohol down at the same time. Rose starts coughing and red liquor runs down the side of her chin. Kendall reaches over and licks the side of Rose's face and kisses her on the lips to the shouts of the men surrounding them.

A random guy walks out of the crowd and whispers in Kendall's ear. He turns to look Rose in the eye. Kendall laughs and shakes her head. "*No!*" She playfully smacks him on the shoulder. She whispers something to him. He nods back.

Kendall grabs her purse. "Be right back, princess."

"Sure..."

Kendall follows the stranger into the throng leaving Rose alone in the middle of the chaos. The kids around her are all dancing close. Liquor has been flowing and even though it's the middle of the afternoon, people are intoxicated and swaying to the music. She ventures out on the floor and starts dancing by herself. The crowd is a mix of bobby-socksers and hip greasers with ducktails and packs of cigarettes rolled in the shoulder of their t-shirts. Many of the girls are still dressed in ponytails and large skirts that twirl as they dance across the floor next to other girls sporting slacks and pantsuits. She didn't see any beatniks or hippies. Maybe they never come to the dancehalls...

A tall, skinny guy slinks next to Rose and starts dancing with her. He's cute but he gets so close that he starts pressing up against her. She can smell the musk of him. It's more than over-powering. She feels him rubbing against her in the stifling crowd. She tries to step back from him but there is a wall of people dancing around her, pressing in from every side. It's hard to breathe. The tall guy puts his arm around her and grabs her ass. Rose feels faint, like she's about to pass out. She starts to panic.

A ripple opens up in the crowd and Rose rushes off the dance floor. She's sweating. Looking around, she sees a group of girls headed towards the back of the club and follows them. There in the back corner of the building is the ladies room.

Walking in, there is a line of women primping in the counter mirror, brushing hair, fixing their bras. One girl is doing cocaine right off the counter.

Rose passes them and goes into a stall, pulls her panties down, and hovers over the commode as she pees. She hears a man's voice coming from the next stall. He grunts and a girl's voice sighs loudly as the metal wall starts shaking back and forth. They are obviously having sex in the stall next to her. Rose flushes, fixes herself, and walks straight back out into the club, mortified.

Kendall is waiting outside the door.

"There you are. Come on!"

She grabs Rose by the hand and they start towards the very back of the building.

"I didn't know where you were. Some guy started rubbing on me on the dance floor, and..." Kendall let her talk, dragging her towards the exit.

"Where are we going?"

Kendall pushes the double-doors open as they exit the back of the building. Two young men are sitting in the front seat of a candy-apple red Chevrolet Impala convertible waiting for them. They are both extremely handsome, in a dangerous sort of way. Rose recognizes the driver as Kendall's friend from earlier.

"We're going to a party, Doll-face," the driver says.

Kendall opens the car door and pushes Rose in the back seat, climbing in behind her.

"Now? In the middle of the afternoon?"

"Don't worry, little girl," Kendall's friend says. "Where we're going, the party never ends..."

They drive down Greenville Avenue to a building next to the Granada Theater. It's a boarded up grey building that looks deserted. They park in the back and get out.

Kendall is hanging all over her 'friend' while the other guy is quiet and stays to himself. Rose thinks he looks like he's on something.

The four of them enter through a non-descript back door and start down a dirty hallway. At the end of the hall, there is a single steel door. Next to it sits a large black man in a leather coat. The boys stay behind as the girls walk up. The man looks up from his newspaper and licks his lips.

"'Afternoon, ladies... and gentlemen."

Kendall knocks on the door and a small slide opens. Someone looks at them through the opening. The slide closes, something clicks, and the steel door swings open.

Kendall grabs Rose's hand and the girls step through the threshold with the boys in tow.

The warehouse is dark but filled with movement. To the right, a large group of people is crowded around a craps table. On the left, a man in black spins a roulette wheel to the amusement of an eagerly watching audience. In the center of the space, rows of black jack stations are buzzing, each filled to capacity. Girls in skimpy costumes are everywhere, serving drinks to the players as music and cigarette smoke waft through the air.

Rose is in awe. "Where are we?"

"This is what's *really* going on in Dallas, baby. 'Not what the Bureau of Tourism would have you believe, is it?"

Rose looks over at the roulette table as they walk past. There is a man in a dark blue jumpsuit. He has big hair with long sideburns. On his face sit large dark sunglasses with rhinestones embedded in the frame. He laughs and throws the dice, "Come on, baby. Gimme some *love!*"

Rose whispers excitedly to Kendall, "Was that *Elvis*?"

"Could be, sweetness. Sammy Davis, Jr. hit on me here last week. Bob Hope the week before. Go figure. This town is Disneyland for adults and nobody outside of this circle knows anything about it."

Rose can't believe this is happening. "I'm not comfortable with all this. Couldn't we be arrested for just being here?"

Kendall turns to her and laughs. "Don't crap out on me now, little one! We're just getting started..."

Fifteen

Present Day. Dallas, TX

Wednesday morning came early. Laura Milton was up at 5 AM for her routine: yoga, breakfast, meds, and then settled in for her post-medication nap. She woke up an hour later, cranky with a splitting headache. Other than a few random texts, she hadn't heard from Colin in 4 days. He was probably just giving her the space he knew she needed, but still, it wasn't like him to respect her privacy–at least, not 4 days in a row. At the moment, it was just another point of aggravation.

Laura got dressed and called for her car. She grabbed her equipment bags, still packed, and all her notes. By the time she was in the lobby, the Land Rover was waiting for her.

Bethany Nursing home was located in far North Dallas. Laura took 75 Central Expressway up through Richardson to the suburb of Plano and exited Legacy Drive. It took all of 40 minutes with light traffic, but the drive gave her time to listen to some music and get in the frame of mind to work. Right after exiting the highway, Laura noted the artistic detail in the median landscaping. It meant that this community was obviously well-funded; the entire Legacy strip looked like a country club.

Two minutes later, a low modern structure appeared on the right side of the road. Laura checked the address and turned onto the property. She pulled up to a small valet stand next to the front entrance and parked. Valets seemed to be everywhere in Texas. She got out, took her ticket from the young man, and he helped her pull out her equipment from the back of the Land Rover.

She extended the handles on her two bags and walked into a beautiful garden atrium. The 30-foot ceiling was made of glass, bathing the room in gold and bronze light. It looked more like the entrance to a posh upper-Eastside New York mansion instead of a nursing home. In the center of the pathway sat a dark marble information desk.

"Hello, my name is Laura Milton. I'm here to see Vera Kessler." Laura showed the woman her driver's license.

The attendant smiled genuinely, checked the picture, and looked at a chart on the desk in front of her. "Yes, she's expecting you. Room 227."

"Thank you."

Laura turned to the chrome and glass elevators behind her.

The doors opened on the second floor. The cream-colored hallway was beautifully decorated with pastel pieces of abstract art on the walls. Laura checked the signs and started down the hallway towards Ms. Kessler' room.

As she passed room after room, she wondered what her life would be like in old age. Would she be here, or somewhere like this, alone waiting for Death to finally come and introduce himself to her? Or would she have children who would take care of her? Or would she succumb to Alzheimer's or Parkinson's and be a shell of a human with no memory of her life whatsoever? So much uncertainty everywhere... She felt her pulse begin to quicken at the thought and started taking deep breaths. Calm down. She couldn't wig herself out right before an interview.

She came to room 227. The door was ajar. Laura knocked and pushed the door in.

"Hello?"

The space was lavishly decorated with screens and drapes creating separate sectors in the large open room. Flowers filled multi-colored vases and antiques peppered the walls in intervals. At a desk against the far wall next to the bed Vera Kessler sat in a wheelchair, a very refined and demure woman playing solitaire on her laptop.

"Ms. Milton? Come in."

It took about 10 minutes for Laura to set up the camera. She was using the natural light of the big bay window to light her subject. When everything was in place she checked focus and started recording.

"Ms. Kessler, thank you for making time to speak with me. As you know, I'm researching the story behind the legend of the ghost White Rock Lake. In your email you mentioned you were born and raised in Dallas and worked at Neiman Marcus..."

Vera Kessler cleared her throat. "Yes, my first job was as a seamstress in alterations when I was in my 20's. After moving to intimate apparel, I was promoted and served as manager for the bridal shop at Neiman-Marcus for 42 years. I retired in 2008. I worked for the company my entire life. Almost." She smiled. "The culture they create there is so warm and inspiring. Those people were more like my family than my actual family was..." She smiled to herself, musing. "I am happy to have given the best years of my life to the company."

"It sounds like a fascinating culture to have been a part of. So, how does this relate to the White Rock story?"

"Well, I had two associates at the store, Guy and Josephine Malloy. They were a husband and wife team who were the primary directors of display for the store in the late 40's. One night we met for drinks at a downtown bar and I noticed Josephine looked a little sullen, definitely not her usual jovial self. I asked her what was wrong and they proceeded to tell me a story of picking up a woman one night down by White Rock Lake..."

"They were out at a dinner party at a friend's home and were driving by the lake on the way home. They came upon a young girl soaked to the bone standing on the side of the road. They picked her up and took her to somewhere on Gaston in the nearby Lakewood area. Their story was similar to others I had heard except that Josephine distinctly remembered the girl to be wearing a dress from Niemen's."

Laura wasn't sure she heard her correctly. "Josephine believed the ghost to be wearing a dress from the store?"

"Both she and her husband knew the inventory by heart. They had been with the store for years and were intimately involved with the merchandise. Personally, I've never seen the ghost myself, but I think if I saw someone or something wearing one of our gowns I'd know it."

On a hunch, Laura asked, "You don't happen to remember a young woman by the name of Rose Davis working at Neiman's in 1968-69?"

"Yes, I think I remember her name. Skinny slip of a thing, worked in intimate apparel. I recall she was very pretty but so naïve..." Laura couldn't believe what she was hearing. Could there actually be a connection here? "I remember her first day," Kessler continued. "It was something right out of a Sandra Dee movie." She laughed to herself. "The gorgeous air-head knocking over displays and having all the men fall all over themselves to help her. She was friendly, though. All the boys liked her. Poor thing. She had the looks to make it, but she seemed too... *nice*. She was one of those girls who you couldn't tell if she was really that green or was just playing the act of the ditsy hot girl just to get her way.

"She wasn't with us for long, maybe a year. I believe she did some personal shopping for some notable clients. Did pretty well, too, from what I remember. One day she just didn't show up. No one ever heard from her again. What does she have to do with all of this?"

Laura smiled nervously. "I'm not sure. It's just a name that keeps coming up..."

Wednesday May 7, 1969, Neiman-Marcus, Dallas, TX

Rose is fitting a woman, Mrs. Dawn Crane, in the dressing room. The woman is in her early 40's, has a sublime body, and is trying on a bustier and garters. She admires herself in the full-length mirror as Rose pretends not to watch.

"What do you think, toots? Will my lover's eyes fall out?"

Rose tried her best not to stare at the woman's generous cleavage. "I think it's very flattering, Mrs. Crane. Any man would be crazy not to desire you."

The woman gently put her hand against the side of Rose's face. "You are a cute young thing, aren't you?"

Rose could feel herself beginning to blush. She had been feeling a little warm today and thought she might have a fever. But this was a little different. "Thank you, ma'am." She doesn't know how to respond. "If I may ask, does your husband know you have a lover?"

It takes barely 30 seconds for Mrs. Crane to storm out of the fitting room in nothing but a bustier, garters, and heels, walk across the sales floor, and start screaming at the top of her lungs to the floor manager. She is furious. The manager immediately pulls Rose from the floor and reluctantly sends her home in hopes of settling Mrs. Crane down.

As Rose sulks out of the employee entrance completely mortified, she bursts into tears. At that moment, Kendall walks around the corner.

"Just the girl I wanna see! Put on your dancing shoes, kitten. We have a party to go to!"

"I'm not going anywhere."

Kendall realizes Rose is crying. "Why the long face, doll?"

"These people hate me."

"Aw, toots... What happened?"

"In not so many words I called the DA's wife a whore."

Kendall cackled out a laugh. "Oh, my God! I would *love* to have seen that! I guess she had no sense of humor, eh? You ok?"

"My stomach hurts."

"Ha ha!" she laughs. "That's what Charlie Brown says." Rose can't help but smile. She loves Charlie Brown. Kendall snickers. "Come on. I know exactly how to make you feel better..."

The girls walk across the street to their apartment at the Wilson Building. Once upstairs, Kendall forces Rose to put on one of her sexiest gowns, helps her slap on some make-up, and drags her back out into the night.

The girls climb in Rose's Chevelle and drive to Ross Avenue on the northern edge of downtown. They park on the street half a block down from the Fairmont Hotel. They turn the corner and see scores of cars waiting in line for the valet. Photographers and newspaper people are congregated on the red carpet waiting for some unseen celebrity. Rose and Kendall stand across the street watching the mass of people.

"How are we going to get through *that*?" Rose is openly frustrated.

"C'mon." Kendall pulls up her dress, grabs Rose by the hand, and drags her across the street to the rear of the hotel, both of them almost falling over in their heels. They come to a plain metal door in the concrete wall on the side of the building. Kendall knocks in a pattern. No answer. She repeats it louder. Still nothing. Rose looks at her, disappointed.

Just as they are about to walk off, the door swings open and a sweaty, gruff-looking Mexican cook with a cleaver in his hand is standing in front of them.

Kendall sticks her chest out and smiles. "Hi! I'm Jack's friend. We're here for the party."

The cook looks them over disgustedly, grunts, and lets them in.

The girls find themselves in the middle of the hotel kitchen. It is a vast tiled space with rooms and tunnels running like tendrils throughout the ground level of the hotel. Waiters in black jackets and white aprons are everywhere carrying large trays of food and buckets filled with ice and bottles of champagne.

Kendall pulls Rose along and they carefully maneuver through the wet tiled spaces where multitudes of chefs and waiters are rushing around in organized chaos.

In the center of the throng, an aging rotund man in a tuxedo is screaming while the catering captain nods his head nervously taking notes. The screamer sees Kendall and shoos the man off impatiently. He runs over and gleefully throws his arms around the brunette.

"Well, if it isn't my favorite bitch! Looking the nines tonight, sugar!" He grabs her breasts with both hands and adjusts her while Rose watches, smirking. "*There* you are," he says, looking her over, "perfection on two legs!" He notices Rose standing off to the side. Leaning over, he whispers to Kendall, "Who's the cute friend?"

"Jack Montana, this is my new protégé, Rose Davis."

"Protégé, eh? Well... *Enchanté*, mademoiselle Rose." He bends and kisses her hand in a dramatic gesture. Rose giggles like a schoolgirl.

"Jack is one of my oldest girlfriends..."

"She means 'closest' girlfriends, you catty cunt," Jack interjects.

Kendall ignores him. "He's the Maître-D for the Venetian Room." Rose looks confused.

Jack rolls his eyes and groans. "For Pete's sake, it's only going to be the hottest club in the city, girlie, and your future destination! You bitches are late for the party. Come on, now. The first set is almost over."

He grabs Kendall by the hand, she grabs Rose, and the small train starts off through the tiled corridors. Everywhere, scores of chefs are preparing meals for ballrooms full of guests. The waiters stare at them as they pass by.

The three come to a little service door where the tunnel dead-ends.

"Gotta run, divas, but have a blast!" He looks directly at Kendall. "Tell Reuben, the captain, you're *my* bitch. And tell Bobby I said hi!" He turns and disappears into the kitchen maelstrom.

Rose looks at Kendall. "Who's Bobby?"

Kendall pulls the door open and they are struck by a wall of sound. Rose looks confused but the two stumble excitedly into the dark throng.

The Venetian Room is the newest premiere nightclub in Dallas in 1969. Gold paint covers the walls, empire-backed booths in black and gold leather frame the room, and a plush red velvet curtain lines the stage where a big band is currently playing. Banquet tables fill the open area and are filled with handsome men in tuxedos and their beautiful dates draped in gorgeous evening gowns. Leggy girls in fishnet stockings and heels carry cigarette boxes around their necks vending to the crowd. People are drinking, smoking and having a wonderful time.

"This is more like it!" Kendall screams to Rose above the din.

Rose looks over at a table next to them. There is a man with a silver Zippo lighter in his hand staring straight at her. He keeps lighting the mechanism and putting it out over and over, the glare casting sinister shadows over his angular face. Sitting at the same table is the District Attorney Darryl Crane and his sensuous wife Dawn, who Rose embarrassed herself in front of earlier at Neiman-Marcus. Two other couples are with them.

The Lighter Man keeps staring at Rose. He catches her eye but she quickly looks away. Kendall recognizes a man at the next table. He smiles and waves the two girls over. Kendall slinks up next to him and starts talking to him.

Rose looks up on the stage. The famous singer Bobby Darin is belting out his hit, "Mack the Knife". There is a 16-piece big band accompanying him and they are rocking the room. The small dance floor is packed.

Kendall leans over and shouts in Rose's ear. "This is Murdock! He's a Hollywood producer. Very big!"

Rose shakes Murdock's hand just as the band finishes the song. The crowd erupts in applause. Bobby takes a bow, jumps off the stage and heads straight through the crowd to Murdock's table. Murdock keeps clapping as the young man approaches. "Amazing, Bobby! You are hot tonight!"

Darin is dressed in a dark blue sharkskin tuxedo. The collar of his shirt is undone, his bow tie hanging untied around his neck. He looks at Rose. "Coming from you, Murdock, that's quite a compliment." He can't take his eyes off of her. "You seem to be keeping wonderful company lately. How do you do it?"

“It’s all in the wrist, my boy.” Murdock smiles a wide Texas grin. “Rose Davis, I want to introduce you to Mr. Bobby Darin.”

Darin takes Rose’s hand, leans over and kisses her on the cheek. He then whispers in her ear.

“I have to make the rounds but stick around for the next set. I’ll be looking for you.” Rose nods and Darin walks off into the crowd.

At the table next to them, The Lighter Man watches Darin and Rose together. He pulls the cigarette out of his mouth and stamps it out in the ashtray violently. A waiter comes by and the man hands him a card and motions to Rose. The waiter takes the card and walks away.

Wandering away from the table, Rose strolls through the crowd, eyes as big as saucers. The people are all very glamorous and fun-loving, definitely the upper echelon of the city all dressed up and letting themselves go wild. Handsome men and women are everywhere.

Towards the back of the room, the scene is a little different. She notices a window cut into the golden wall 20 feet up where the spotlight shines from. There was a room there. She could feel eyes, staring down at her from the window. What could be going on up there?

To her right, a beautiful young girl is being coerced behind a curtain by her companion. In one of the empire booths against the wall three men are kissing on a very drunk woman. She looks to be unconscious.

A hand abruptly comes down on her shoulder, startling her. Rose turns around and a waiter hands her a card.

“You have been invited,” he says to her and walks away. Holding it up to the light, Rose sees the card says ‘The Jewel Club’. The number 825 is hand-written on the back. Rose looks around but sees no one who could have sent it. It must be a party. She smiles to herself.

She feels so thankful to have a good job at a wonderful store, and she is starting to attract very eligible men. Things are certainly looking up compared to what her life was like only a few months ago. Gone are the days sitting in that God-forsaken house on the lake longing for deliverance or death, whichever came first. She can barely even remember the thick, sickly sweet musky scent of roses and sweat. Surrounding her, scores of beautiful people are dancing and enjoying themselves. This is the beginning of a new life for her. Her heart is filled with excitement over what the future holds.

And from a hidden alcove, the Lighter Man watches her greedily from the shadows...

Present Day, Fairmont Hotel, Dallas

It was late in the afternoon when Laura Milton found herself staring at the ornate arched doors leading to the Venetian Room. Large chains looping through the serpentine handles held them in place. A sign stood on a stand that stated "Closed: Renovations in Progress". From what she could gather, the hotel hadn't used the venue regularly for years, perhaps only for private functions, and kept it closed most of the time for insurance purposes. She found a banquet server in the service hall and slipped him a twenty to let her in. In ten minutes he returned with the keys and opened the double doors for her.

Laura stepped in and surveyed the auditorium.

Crews had already brought in most of the scaffolding and drywall supplies, which were stacked on a large pallet towards the back wall. One third of the open space had already been taped and prepped for painting. Even though clean white tarps and plastic sheeting covered everything, she could still smell decades worth of nicotine from cigarette smoke saturated in the carpet and the ceiling tiles. The gold-painted walls were dingy and almost green with age. The workers had removed most of the molding and had already begun sanding in preparation for a complete renovation.

The only furniture in the room were two banquet tables set on the floor in front of the stage. Without crisp white linen on top, they were nothing more than naked circular wooden slabs set on slim aluminum legs. The once-beige carpet they were standing on was stained grey and black with grime.

The stage was a black gouge in the gold wall framed in faded red velvet curtains.

The Venetian Room was a mere shadow of its former self, even in the early stages of repair. But Laura could feel the residual energy of the room, the footprint of its history, buzzing like a distant vibratory hum that lay just outside of the range of human hearing. She could imagine the tens of thousands of different people and personalities that had come through those doors over the decades leaving little particle resonances of themselves behind; in the walls, in the ceiling tiles, in the faded red velvet curtains that hung from the rafters framing the dead stage. What strange forces would lie dormant in a place like this waiting for the right catalyst to awaken them? No renovation in the world could ever fix the karmic DNA of the place. Laura shivered and hugged herself at the thought.

Silently, the doors opened behind her and Mallory entered the room. She turned and smiled. He walked up and put his arm around her waist.

He looked around the room and said with a sneer, "I see what you mean about this place. Anything could have happened here..." Looking at the stage, he said, "You know, I remember hearing my father talk about this place when I was a kid. I think he saw Sinatra here in the early 70's. Wow. What a time that must have been..."

"I was thinking the exact same thing." She smiled and sank into to him. "Let's go."

* * *

The drive through the Turtle Creek district was soothing. Minutes from downtown, this was basically the Manhattan of Dallas. Wonderful late-60's high-rise apartment buildings framed the serpentine creek that wound through the center of some of the most prime real estate in the city. The top was down on Mallory's Mercedes and the air was cool from a day of scattered showers.

Nick and Sam's has been one of the premiere restaurants in the city for the past decade, a very up-scale steak and chophouse. They pulled up to the valet, Mallory took the ticket, and they stepped into the building.

There were a few small groups waiting to be seated. The young hostess was buried in her reservations book. When she looked up and saw Mallory standing in front of the hostess stand she beamed.

"Mr. Mallory, it's wonderful seeing you this evening!" Her eyes glittered on him for just a second too long for Laura's taste. "Everyone's waiting. Let me take you to the table..."

"It's ok, Megan. We'll find them. Thank you." He took Laura by the hand and led her through the bar.

"On first-name basis with the beautiful hostess?" Laura teased, "I see how you operate."

"Occupational hazard, my dear." He smiled that wonderfully disarming smile that she was beginning to love. He was a cool one, this Mallory...

The dining room was full of guests eating and drinking. The aroma of prime rib and venison filled the air. Against the farthest wall there was a large banquet table surrounded by a group of 20 people, wine glasses in hand, chatting among themselves. Mallory took Laura's hand and led her through the maze of tables towards their party. He gently prepared her as they walked.

"So, these are some special friends of mine. Business associates. They are kind of old school but I think you'll like them. I'm giving you fair warning, though; they can be a little *rambunctious...*"

She laughed. "I think I'll be ok. Besides, I have you to protect me." She smiled and squeezed his arm as they reached the dining table.

Laura noticed that the men were all mostly in their 50's or older. Each had a very attractive woman at his side, most of which were easily 10 years younger than their dates. The waiters were pouring wine as everyone mingled. A white-haired gentleman at the far end of the black glass table cleared his throat and was about to speak when he saw Mallory and Laura walk up out of the corner of his eye.

"Well, if it isn't the prodigal son! You grace us with your presence, Mr. Mallory..."

The group laughed and raised their glasses. A few men shook hands with Mallory. He introduced Laura casually to a few people. A waiter handed them both baubles of luscious red wine.

The host turned to Laura. "And you bring us such a beautiful guest. Welcome, my dear. You're just in time." Laura smiled, slightly embarrassed.

"As I was about to say," the host continued, "here's to the friends who couldn't be with us tonight; we are who we are because of them. And to *new* friends; we welcome you with open arms..." He motioned to Laura who blushed and raised her glass. "Salute."

"*Salute!*" The crowd toasted and cheered heartily.

The servers descended on the table, dropping an array of mouth-watering appetizers. A few more people introduced themselves, but when the host made his way over to Mallory and Laura the crowd parted and made room for him. Mallory put his arms around the older man and kissed him on the cheek lovingly.

"Laura, I'd like you to meet my good friend and mentor Daniele Cinno. And friends." A few people laughed and raised their glasses again.

Cinno took Laura's hand and bent down and kissed it gently.

"I am honored to be in the presence of such beauty." The intensity in the old man's dark eyes startled her and for just a moment Laura felt almost naked in front of him. She shook it off and surrendered to the formality of it all.

"The honor is all mine." She gave him a slight bow, never breaking eye contact.

He smiled. "I like her," he said to Mallory, his eyes never leaving her. "You know, if you two don't work out, I'd love to talk to you about–"

"Let me screw it up for myself, Cinno, please."

"Ah, Mallory, my boy," Cinno laughed, "you are the son I never had. And a wonderful friend." His grey eyes shifted over the both of them. "You kids make a cute couple." Looking up, he clapped his hands. "Here, everyone!" Cinno raised his glass once more. "To the son I never had... and his lovely guest, Laura Milton."

The guests all raised their glasses again and toasted the couple. People cheered gratuitously. All of the guests were very gracious and welcoming.

Except something was wrong. Laura didn't remember telling Cinno her last name. Did Mallory tell him in advance? She was about to ask just as a small group of men pulled her date into a conversation. A few women surrounded Laura and led her away, segregating them. Mallory smiled back at her. This appeared to be the norm.

When she had turned away, Cinno caught Mallory's eye. He bowed discreetly to the older gentleman and continued his conversation with two other guests.

Another group of women greeted Laura and began asking a myriad of questions until she felt herself almost dizzy from the constant banter. Just when she thought she would have to sit, Mallory appeared next to her, pulling her close.

"I'm starving," he said, his eyes traveling over her.

"Shall we?"

He took her by the hand and they took their seats at the table surrounded by the noisy crowd.

The remaining guests eventually sat and began to leisurely order dinner as wine and conversation flowed copiously around the table. All the guests were extremely interesting, telling entertaining tales of everything from Wall Street disasters to new film reviews. Everyone laughed and drank and openly enjoyed themselves.

As the salads were delivered, Mallory reached down and took Laura's hand under the table. She leaned into him.

"Thank you."

"I should be thanking *you*. Cinno is always bitching about me coming alone and screwing up the table count. You took the heat off me for a while." He leaned over and gently kissed her on the cheek.

After dinner, they had tawny port wine and dessert, a perfect ending to a perfect meal. The crowd said their goodbyes quickly. By the time Mallory and Laura were back at the valet it was close to midnight. Laura was well aware of the time and felt a little lightheaded from the small amount of wine she allowed herself. She hoped and prayed that her luck would hold out for the rest of the night. The last thing she wanted was to ruin an amazing night by having a seizure.

They jumped into Mallory's car and took off through the quiet Oak Lawn neighborhood. Mammoth oak and elm trees lined the road, looming beneath the streetlights and casting animated shadows on the asphalt. The illuminated Merchantile Bank Building rose out of a cluster of downtown buildings that seemed only blocks away.

"Your friends were wonderful," Laura said leaning against his shoulder.

"They liked you. Especially Cinno. Gotta keep my eye on that one..."

She smiled. "And how do you know him again?"

"When I first moved to Dallas ten years ago Cinno took me under his wing, helped me get on my feet. He connected me with people associated with the Melrose and trained me to be a competent businessman."

"He loves you very much."

"He's a little weepy. From the old country. But I owe him everything."

The night was perfectly gorgeous. A quiet breeze started blowing as they drove through the winding streets of Turtle Creek. A few of the buildings south of Lemmon Avenue were the first high-rises in the city and reminded Laura of Frank Lloyd Wright and the modernist movement in the 40's.

Actually, located on the opposite side of the creek sat the demure Kalita Humphreys Theater, the stylish home to the Dallas Theater Center, which had been designed by Wright himself.

The creek itself was hidden in the darkness, but Laura could smell the water in the air. And in the center of the creek, an illuminated waterfall glowed like pale fire flickering in a blanket of night.

With the wind blowing in her hair, Laura felt like she was a princess in a dream. Everything was so perfect, she couldn't have imagined a better evening. And she couldn't keep her eyes off of Mallory. His easy, confident manner was endearing, from the way he held himself at the party to his expert touch as he directed his car through the winding roads. She felt safe with him. And he was a total gentleman. She secretly hoped that part would change later in the evening, but she was grateful knowing that he could behave himself. Not like so many of the male students at NYU. Most of the boys there were smart but coming from wealthy families had totally ruined them, giving them an air of entitlement. Except for Colin, that is. He was the one exception.

She quickly turned her thoughts to the present and decided to enjoy the moment as best she could. *'You only live once, Laura. Make it a good one.'*

Mallory sensed her rolling thoughts. "How about a night-cap? The guy in my building makes a wonderful chocolate martini that you have to try."

"Sounds terrific." She took his arm instinctively. "Where do you live?"

"Right here..." He pulled up to the valet at the ultra-modern W Hotel in Victory Park, an exclusive residential district on the southwest edge of downtown. The residences were on the upper floors of the hotel and gave an unparalleled view of the city.

"Mr. Mallory, good evening..." The young valet took his keys.

"Hey, Dex."

Everyone seemed to know him. It wasn't anything flashy, but it said a lot about him. At least people weren't rolling their eyes and excusing themselves when he walked into a room.

They took the resident elevator to the 16th floor.

"So, do all consultants live in ritzy high-rise apartments in the center of the city?"

He smiled easily. "Actually, I got an amazing deal on this place. When the market tanked in 2009, they couldn't keep them occupied. I made a deal with the owner and signed a 10-year lease for peanuts."

"Smart and frugal. Impressive, Mr. Mallory."

"Do I pass the test?"

"With flying colors." She smiled. God he was adorable.

The elevator opened to a wide hallway lined with fine art and tasteful minimalist sconces. His was the second door on the right; a beautifully carved slab of dark wood stained a deep translucent blue. A stylized aluminum relief set chest-high in the doorjamb said '#1620'.

Mallory unlocked the door and let her walk in first.

"After you..."

Laura had seen a lot of nice flats, but this one was breathtaking. Bamboo floors, deep area rugs, thick, generous couches and loungers in a very tasteful arrangement around the generous living room. In the far corner was a black Baby Grand piano facing out into the room. Everything was glass and steel and dark wood with subtle color accents in the lighting and furnishings. The effect was a deep three-dimensional space accented by the most magnificent view of downtown Dallas she had ever seen.

Mallory went to the bar. Laura was drawn to the bank of windows facing downtown. She opened the sliding glass door and stepped out onto the balcony. There were two illuminated plastic cubes sitting against the barrier casting a pale glow on the dark railing. Facing her was the brilliance of downtown Dallas shimmering in the night.

"I gotta hand it to you, Mallory. You sure know how to treat a girl."

Mallory stepped out on the balcony and handed her a martini glass filled with a viscous dark brown liquid. She took a sip. It was a delicious chocolate martini.

"From my days as a bartender. A million years ago..."

"It's wonderful. But I think I'm a little toasty already." She put the glass down next to her.

Low music began to waft out of the hidden speakers. It was an old Do-Wop crooner, lush and fluid. She immediately recognized the melody from somewhere...

'You don't remember me, but I remember you...'

The music was arresting, so honest and genuine that it almost brought tears to her eyes just listening to it...

'Tears on my pillow, pain in my heart caused by you'

Laura was suddenly back at the Bobst Library in New York humming at the table by herself...

"That song. What is it?"

Mallory changed his voice to a fairly realistic impersonation of Casey Kasem. "That was the debut single by Little Anthony and The Imperials, '*Tears on My Pillow*', written by Sylvester Bradford and Al Lewis in 1958..."

Laura is staring inward, watching the young ghost there in the library, singing to her, calling her to come and see...

"I can change it if you don't like it..."

"No, no..."

Laura shook her head and came back into her own body. She stared into Mallory's brown eyes trying to reconnect with him. How could he possibly know this song?

As if reading her mind, Mallory spoke. "It's the first song my father ever sang to me as a kid. He was a real Dap-king. A sax player back in the day. Anyway, it means a lot to me. I have a thing for music..."

"Me too..." She felt more than a little light-headed.

"Are you ok?"

"Just a little dizzy. I'll be fine." She leaned against the railing to steady herself. Maybe this wasn't such a good idea after all. *'Please, God, don't let me have a seizure...'*

He handed her his glass of water.

"Thanks." She took a sip and sat trying to catch her breath.

"Is there anything I can do?"

"No, I'll be alright. Just give me a sec."

She started breathing evenly. "I'm so sorry. I hate it when that happens."

He chuckled to himself. "It's fine. I just wanted to make sure you were alright."

"I guess it's a little past my bed-time. I don't want to be a burden..."

"Don't even think of it. You are anything but a burden. I was just concerned." He put his hand on hers.

"Thank you."

Laura gazed out at downtown Dallas glistening in the night. The view was breathtaking.

"I really had a wonderful time tonight. Everyone was so nice."

"Well, after digging in the past for so long, I thought you'd enjoy a taste of what Dallas is like today."

He looked at her casually, but the touch of his eyes burned into her. He was in total command of himself, but not in a guarded way. She knew in the back of her mind that she needed to slow down, but everything about this Mallory melted her, in more ways than one.

She gripped the handrail on the glass barrier. From his balcony, the buildings of downtown seemed close enough to reach out and touch. "It's so beautiful. Thank you for making me feel so welcome." She looked at him, treasuring the excitement of the moment.

Mallory leaned over and gently kissed her on the mouth. It was like a spark sending shocks through her. She was cautious at first, not wanting to seem overly eager. But he tasted so good. His hands softly caressed her back sending chills down her spine and straight to her loins. He pressed against her and she could feel him growing hard in his pants. His entire body was ridged and warm.

She gently coaxed his tongue into her mouth, sucking on him. He ground his pelvis into her as she reached down and slowly stroked him through his pants. He moaned, making her even hotter.

Mallory grabbed her by the wrist. His face had changed. In the shadows of the night, he now looked menacing, almost dangerous.

He turned her around and bent her forcefully over the balcony rail. His hands were rough, squeezing her breasts as he ground his pelvis against her ass. He put his arm around her neck and held her so tightly against him that she couldn't breathe.

"You are so gorgeous, Laura. Little Laura..." He whispered hotly into her ear as he ground against her. It was exciting and frightening at the same time. He was manhandling her, digging his fingers into her soft flesh as she pressed her entire body weight against the barrier. It would only take a single push to send her over the railing to fall 16 floors to the street below.

Just when she knew she was about to pass out, Mallory let go of her neck, picked her up, and carried her into the apartment. She climbed up into his arms, pulling him to her, kissing him hard, even though she was frightened out of her mind.

He carried her to the bedroom and threw her onto the bed. Standing over her, his body looked like a black demon framed by the light shining from outside the window. She recoiled, truly not knowing whether he was going to make love to her or strangle her to death.

Mallory seemed to relax when he saw the fear in her eyes. He came to the bed and silently sat next to her. Putting an arm gently around her, he held her close.

She leaned into him and silently began to cry...

* * *

At 4:30 AM Laura was already dressed and putting on her shoes. Mallory lay asleep in his king-sized bed oblivious of her. Before leaving, she wrote a note thanking him and left it on the bedside table. On the elevator ride to the lobby she fought back the impulse to reprimand herself for engaging in the walk of shame. This was her life and no one was going to criticize her decisions, not even herself. As the elevator doors opened, she saw that her ride was already waiting outside. With her head held high, she hopped in the back seat and headed back to her hotel.

She had a big day ahead of her...

Sixteen

Later in the morning, Laura met with an old college friend Kenneth Dolan who had moved to Texas a few years earlier and worked for the Dallas Business Journal. Over coffee, Laura told him the complicated story of White Rock and how the urban legend had ingrained itself in her life. Though he was intrigued by the implications, he had nothing in the way of information for her. He had not even heard of the White Rock ghost before their meeting. Dolan offered her access to his extensive archive of business records if she needed any particular information, but otherwise there was nothing else he felt he could contribute to her search. She left their meeting knowing at least there was one more resource she could eventually draw from if need be.

She returned to the Fairmont and spent a few listless hours cataloguing data. It was frustrating trying to communicate with people who were convinced the White Rock urban legend had no credibility. For every rock-star eyewitness, there were five utter disappointments.

She was restless. Try as she might, she couldn't get the night before out of her mind. Dinner with Mallory had been more than wonderful. But what the hell happened after that? His aggression back at his apartment had taken her by surprise. And she had made an idiot of herself by bursting into tears in his bed. His demeanor changed when he realized she was frightened and had held her until she calmed down.

Then, after he apologized, they made love in his bed for the rest of the night. But what a strange courtship ritual it had been. Was this what single life was all about? Surely not.

The reality was she barely knew anything about Mallory at all. Yes, the encounter had been exciting in a way, but domination and humiliation had never been her particular kink. She didn't believe women should allow themselves to be abused whatsoever by a man, in the heat of passion or otherwise. Call her old-fashioned, but objectification was one thing; disrespectful humiliation was quite another. It was as if Mallory had become a different person altogether...

Even though she and Colin were technically separated, her embarrassment made her feel that much more guilty for betraying him. She couldn't change the past, however. All she could do was move on and try to understand what was complicating her heart and mind.

She was tired. She ordered a salad from room service and ate to keep her stamina up. At 1 PM she turned off her notebook and gathered her things for her afternoon meeting. She wasn't sure what an aging Hungarian man would know about the White Rock Lady, but she was looking forward to finding out.

* * *

The Lakewood Landing bar was located in an old building that had defied time itself. Originally built as the first Goff's Hamburgers in Dallas in the 1940's, the building has stood literally unchanged for the last 80 years. It was one of the original watering holes in the Lakewood area of east Dallas.

Laura pulled into the front parking space off of Gaston Avenue. There were only three other cars in the lot. The building was pretty non-descript; a whitewashed exterior with no windows and a simple utilitarian patio to the left of the front door made out of painted cinder blocks. On the opposite side of the entrance was a faded blue and purple mural of what seemed to be a mermaid staring out at a body of water. A light shiver ran through her.

Even though the weather was cloudy, as soon as Laura entered the building she was blinded by the darkness of the room. It took a few moments for her eyes to adjust. Soon, she was able to make out tables on the main floor and a row of black booths sitting in the shadows against the right side of the room.

The bar stretched the entire left side of the building and was dimly lit in an amber glow. A couple of old-timers sat sipping their draft beers at a table, a small group of college kids sat next to them getting an early start to the evening.

Nowadays, the Landing was no more than a popular watering hole for older patrons and the young hipster crowd alike, but she could easily imagine nameless people meeting here, decades past, talking in the dark over cocktails about unspeakable things.

An older man was sitting at the far end of the bar reading the newspaper with the aid of a pocket light. Laura approached him.

"Andrásné Szabó?"

"Ms. Milton? So nice to meet you." He extended a thin, strong hand. "We can sit in the back where we can be by ourselves, if you like."

Against her better judgment, Laura ordered herself a Sam Adams and the two retreated to one of the booths in a dark corner of the room. Szabó was a gentle, polite man in his late 60's, though he looked young for his age. Tall and very thin, he appeared almost frail, but by his handshake Laura could tell he was strong and steady. His wire-framed bifocals and black cardigan sweater over a white shirt gave him a European peasant look, but his eyes were intelligent and clear as if they held volumes of information.

"I appreciate you meeting me, sir."

"Ms. Milton, you are doing me a great service allowing me to clear my conscience after all these years. Believe me, ours is a symbiotic relationship."

She pulled the digital recorder out of her purse and set it on the table between them.

"If I may ask, how did you hear about my research?"

"To be honest, my grandson saw your post on Facebook and told me you were seeking people who knew history of the city. He knows nothing of what I have to tell you, nor does my wife. Until now, I have never told anyone any of this."

Laura activated the recorder.

"I'm all ears."

He took a deep drink of his beer and settled back in the booth.

"The 1960's were very tumultuous for immigrants in Dallas," he began. He spoke with a pronounced Hungarian accent but, though he spoke slowly, it was with excellent syntax. "Aside from the Afro-Americans and the Hispanics, there was also a large group of Hungarian nationalists who relocated here in the 50's after the war. Very few people know that. It wasn't advertised to the local workers because to them we were just another racial group coming in to take up all the jobs. But we were smart, intelligent. And we were willing at first to work long hours for less pay. We became the industrial workforce, the *skilled* factory workers, regardless that some of us had the equivalent of PhD's in our native country. Local workers couldn't engineer, couldn't theorize. We could do it all.

"And because of that, socially, we were ostracized and, at times, demonized. It's amazing how people want to destroy what they don't understand. As a group, we stayed to ourselves, mostly, but in many instances that wasn't enough. Our young men and women were getting lynched all the time for simply existing in a society that didn't readily accept foreigners. We had to be careful and keep our heads down, not draw attention to ourselves.

"We began learning to use the system, even while the system turned its back on us. We weren't considered citizens then, so many people disregarded us as a whole. I mean, we were immigrants and couldn't understand the language anyway, right?" He laughed. "It gave us leverage in the community. When people think you are an idiot you are free to truly pay attention."

Laura was fascinated. "On the phone you mentioned that you worked for Jack Ruby at one time."

"Yes, I worked for Ruby. At the Carousel Club as a bar-back in 1961. He was a very strange man. Very fair and protective one minute, and a raving lunatic the next. I saw him literally beat someone almost to death and then apologize, buy him dinner, and offer him a job. Very schizophrenic. And he didn't care that I saw this brutality. This is something you Americans wouldn't see. But these men were not afraid to be themselves in front of us. We weren't even citizens to them. And Ruby's own mother was a Russian immigrant. Amazing. The bartender at the Carousel, Andy Armstrong, was colored and was the only one who consistently treated me with respect. He was Ruby's right-hand man.

"Though history has painted him as a dangerous element, Ruby was small-time. But he knew everybody. And sometimes his acquaintances led to opportunity. I assume he was probably manic-depressive before the term ever existed. That and a megalomaniac. He always wanted to be perceived as a big shot but he was just, as they say, a *name-dropper*. And I'm confident that he was an informant for the police. They were always at the club, bringing him gifts and partying with the girls. He'd end up comping huge tabs for them. Something was going on there, surely."

Laura was so fascinated by his story, she could barely remember her questions. "You mentioned something about a club..."

He took a sip of his beer. "Yes. I suppose the whole thing began in 1962. Apparently, as a favor to friends, Ruby's Club Vegas was rented out for a very elite small party. Ruby was asked to provide some new girls, those who did more than simply strip. I understand from Andy that by 2 AM the entire club had become an orgy." He chuckled to himself. "Ruby went over and told Andy to keep his head down and not look at the white women. Can you imagine?

"Well, when the word got out to some of Ruby's wealthier friends, they were very interested in the whole idea. Jack talked them into dropping 5 grand a night plus 'entertainer fees' for a party that he would set up. He supplied the place and the alcohol and found the girls who would entertain these men. That was the beginning of his stag parties. He wanted to call it something special. One late night after closing, he came up with the name, *'The Jewel Club'*.

"You have to remember, Ruby was in the stripper and bar business. He knew a lot of people, but in that atmosphere most of them were dirty in one way or another. It's not a judgment call, it was simply a lifestyle choice.

"Anyway, all hell broke loose when Kennedy was shot in '63. Ruby went into a rage, ranting and cursing up a storm in the middle of the club. He wanted to avenge the president. He was ranting about elevating the Jews by doing something so noble, or something. Of course, Ruby ended up killing Lee Harvey Oswald in a rage. Heck, everybody wanted Oswald dead. I'm only surprised that the police didn't kill him themselves.

"Ruby went on to become the first in a long line of witnesses who were inflicted with an aggressive form of cancer that took them quickly. But that's another story all together..."

Laura had so many questions, she could barely think. She tried to calm herself down. “So, how did the Oswald killing affect Dallas?”

“Ruby died in jail from cancer in 1967 waiting for a re-trial. After that, the conservatives took a stronger hold on the city than they already had. The police started cracking down on gambling, prostitution, everything. The element didn’t disappear, mind you, it just went deeper underground.

“In ‘67 the Hilton Inn, Mockingbird opened at Mockingbird Lane and Central Expressway. It was a big, modern building that brought a lot of influential people into the city. It became the epicenter of the mafia presence in Dallas. And though Ruby was gone, the concept of the Jewel Club lived on there.”

Laura remembered seeing a photo of Rose with Kendal Reece at the Mockingbird, Hilton. “Sir, do you recall ever meeting a girl named Rose? Rose Davis? Young, blonde. She disappeared in 1969. She would have been probably around 25...”

Szabó thought for a moment and smiled. “There was a girl. I remember the name. She was with Neiman-Marcus, the high-end department store downtown, for a while. I remember because she was a personal buyer for Mr. Forester, the manager of the hotel for a time. She was very pretty, blonde, with big blue eyes... Many of the young men were taken with her.”

“Was she in any way involved in these parties that you know of?”

“I don’t think at first she had it in her to be a courtesan. But it was so easy for a young girl to get caught up in the excitement, the money. And I remember: someone wanted her, a doctor who officed across from Southern Methodist University in Highland Park. I cannot remember his name. He, Joe Civello, Joe Campisi, Carlos Marcello from Louisiana, and a few others ruled Dallas then. This man wanted her. And, believe me, those men always found a way of getting what they wanted.

"A large group of them would congregate a few times a month at the Hilton for their events. Some of these parties involved The Jewel Club. This was 1969, two years after the hotel first opened. A lot of very bad things happened in that place during that time."

"How do you know so much about the Jewel Club?"

"I know because I worked there."

The bartender came over to their table. "Would you like another, Andi?"

"Please. And one for my friend."

"Thank you." Laura didn't want another drink, but accepted graciously.

Szabó waited until the bartender left and continued in a whispered voice. "I was there one night and I barely made it out with my life."

"What happened?" Laura was entranced.

"At the time I was working part-time as a banquet bartender for the hotel. I picked up a shift from a gentleman I didn't know very well, a man named Bora. It was all very secretive. I remember meeting him behind the hotel in a service parking lot. He handed me a nametag with his name on it and swore me to secrecy. He said it was to be a *VIP party*. His daughter was getting married and the hotel wouldn't let him off work. He told me all I had to do was wear his nametag and speak to no one. He said the money would be great and in cash at the end of the night. So, I agreed..."

June 1969, Dallas Hilton, Mockingbird 1:32 AM

The entrance to the back corridor of the opulent Hilton, Mockingbird Hotel is barricaded and guarded by men in plain clothes who are obviously not policemen. The only way into the series of private suites is through a single door at the back of the hotel facing the railroad tracks. A group of A-List gentlemen sit at cocktail tables in the courtyard next to the pool smoking cigarettes and awaiting admission while scantily dressed cocktail waitresses serve them. An unseasonal chill is in the air tonight.

Within the suite there is a private hidden room. A beautiful blonde European woman puts a handful of cash into a lock-box, places it in the safe in the wall, and closes the hatch. She knocks in a pattern on the metal door and it opens allowing her out of the room. A tall young Italian boy hands her the keys, admiring her with dark lustful eyes. She locks the door behind her then slowly pulls back her dress at the slit. He watches her high-heeled foot rise up on the top of stool he'd been occupying, the milk-white skin of her muscular thigh taunt in pale nylons. She attaches the keys to her garter and lowers her leg staring past him, feigning indifference.

There is a patterned knock on the door across the hall. The blonde woman answers and Rose Davis saunters in wearing a sheer gown with a black bustier underneath, silk stockings and garters. The room is dark and smoky; people are everywhere languishing in the haze. The older woman smiles and closes the door behind her. She hugs little Rose in the shadows and slips a pill in her hand.

"What is this, Belle?" Rose looks at the white pill in her palm.

"It's called 'Quaalude'," the woman purrs in a thick Scandinavian accent. "It will help, believe me. Don't be afraid. These men are all VIP's, very wealthy. They will take care of you. Just be your beautiful self..."

She leans over and kisses the side of Roses' face, a little too tenderly. Rose turns towards the din. Belle pats her on the ass and gently pushes her into the thick of the crowd.

Men and women are everywhere in various states of undress, touching, breathing, watching everyone and themselves. She wonders how long it will take for the pill to take effect. Rose grabs a glass of champagne off the waiter's tray as he passes by, a skittish skinny man whose name tag says BORA.

She continues slowly through the adjoining rooms watching the spectacle. She recognizes Isaac Hayes' music playing over the stereo and notices the couples dancing close together in the shadows. A few feet away, a group of men surround a single girl on her knees. They start unzipping their pants.

The entire suite is writhing. A group of young men masturbate each other on the white leather L-shaped couch. Women are servicing men in all manners all around her. She can feel the drug seeping through her body like serum now, hot and syrupy. She stares into the mist, remembering the house on the lake and all it has taken from her...

Rose pulls a cigarette out of her robe. Just as she's about to light it, a hand appears out of the dark and strikes a silver lighter. It's flame is high and bright orange.

"Thank you."

She knows who he is immediately. She carefully lights her cigarette and checks the man out. He is tall and lanky, in a grey suit, and smells like Aqua Velva. His hair looks like it has shoe polish in it. He is the guy from the Venetian Room the night of the Bobby Darin show. He had been staring a hole through her all night long, flicking that God-forsaken lighter. Still, he seemed harmless enough. Besides, his money was just as good anyone else's. And she so wanted Belle to be proud of her...

Rose slinks next to him. She can feel his muscles under his coat and can tell he's strong. He bends down and kisses her, hard. She pulls away, coy.

"I'm Rose. I recognize you from the Fairmont. What's your name?"

"It's none of your fucking business, *cunt*."

Rose isn't certain she heard him correctly. Surely, he didn't say what she thought she heard. *"Excuse me?"*

The stranger takes one massive arm and shoves her up against the wall by the throat, his other hand grabbing her breasts. Rose can't breathe, she can't even scream. She starts to panic because she realizes that in the dark no one can see she is in danger.

She thrashes under the force of his arm. Her right leg comes up and she rams her knee into the soft center of his groin. He screams and doubles over, letting her go as he instinctively grabs himself. She falls to the floor gasping for breath and crawls away from him through the legs of the people standing around them. Lighter Man straightens up and pushes his way through the crowd towards the entrance, knocking other patrons over in his haste to get out the door.

Rose runs to the back of the farthest room and finds Madame Belle talking to a guest. She runs to her side and cowers behind her like a frightened child.

"Belle, I can't do it! He tried to strangle me. Help me!"

"Baby..."

Belle puts her arm around the shivering girl just as the security man Burke walks up and grabs Rose by the wrist. She screams and pulls away.

“She’s just a kid, Burke, for Heaven’s sake!”

“Whatever. Tonight she’s an entertainer. And everybody here has to be *entertained*. At least once.”

“Let me fix her up. She’ll be along.”

Belle shoos him and Burke reluctantly walks away. She pulls out a wad of bills from her robe pocket and hands it to Rose.

“Here. Take it, little one. And go. This place is not for you.”

“I–don’t understand...”

“Go. And don’t come back. Do you hear me?”

Rose looks at Belle’s beautiful face. She takes the wad of bills from her hand, and nods her head. “Thank you.” She kisses the side of the older woman’s face, wipes her eyes, and stumbles out the service entrance. Belle locks the door behind her and glances at the watch on her wrist.

In minutes, Burke bounds up to the door and knocks. Belle cracks the door and he kicks it open.

“Where’s the princess?”

“She’s sick. I let her go. I can’t have the newbies throwing up on our customers.”

“Goddamnit, Belle. Where do you find these idiot kids?”

“You take care of your end, I take care of mine, thank you.”

“You shouldn’t take such a *personal interest* in the help, Belle.” He smiles a toothy, disgusting grin. “It will get you in trouble...”

Belle squeezes out her most insincere smile and watches him walk away.

A moment later, Belle is in the suite talking to a small group of girls. She looks down at her watch nervously. It is 1:58 AM. The suite is beginning to fill with men. Wealthy men. She takes out a cigarette, puts it on her extender. One of the waiters leans over and lights it for her. She takes a deep drag and exhales into the air. She can feel the warmth of the drugs working their magic inside of her and she smiles to herself in the dark. She wants to be as numb as possible for the rest of the night.

A cold shiver runs through her and she turns around in time to see two men in trench coats enter the suite. They approach Burke at the front check-in as she excuses herself from the group.

"Good evening, gentlemen." Burk says to the new gentlemen. "Welcome to the Jewel Club. How many?"

"Just the two of us."

Burke tries to look into the eyes of the man speaking, but the shadows are too dark under his hat.

"Fifty dollars cash, please. Each."

A knife flashes in the dark before one of the men buries it deep in Burke's stomach. Burke's enormous bulk doubles over and falls to the floor. In the dark, no one notices the skirmish but Belle. Turning into the hallway, she quickly opens the hidden room and steps in, locking the thick metal door behind her. She leans against the cold steel waiting for the inevitable.

In the main room, the two men walk forward in the darkness and stand like demons silhouetted against an illuminated wall of glass. In a single motion they both pull out shotguns from under their trench coats.

The guests don't even realize their fate until the executioners start firing into the crowd. Screams erupt in the darkness. The room is black except for the rapid pulse of alternating muzzle flashes that reveal, for that one fraction of a second, bodies exploding apart in all directions. The killers walk through the connecting suites side by side, sparing no one, stopping only to reload. Blood seeps into the white shag carpet, turning their footprints black with the blood of their victims.

In the hidden room, Belle stands with her back against the security door listening to the screams and shrieks from the guests, a cacophony of despair raging behind the booms from the firearms. People are pounding their fists trying to get out of the suite and escape the execution, but the exits have all been barricaded from outside. Belle takes a deep drag from her cigarette and blows a thin stream of smoke into the air even as blood seeps underneath the security door wetting the soles of her brocade shoes.

Andrásné Szabó is carrying a box of wine back to the suite when he comes to the end of the service hall. Police lights are flashing in the distance and people are running past the door in a panic. An officer runs past shouting at someone and Szabó pulls back into the shadows, watching the madness. Another officer walks up and starts taking names of anyone in the area. Szabó backs into the hall quietly. He sees an emergency exit behind him, gently opens the door, and runs out into the night...

Present Day, Lakewood Landing, Dallas

Andrásné Szabó took another sip of his beer and wiped his mouth.

"By the time I returned, it had already happened and the police had taped off the scene. Officers were beginning to take names so I ran. I didn't want to be incriminated in something so horrible just for being a server for those cretins.

"The next day there was no mention of any of it in the papers, the news, nothing. When I returned for my next shift two days later, all the staff had been changed. Everyone who knew about the Jewel Club had either been shot to death in that room that night or let go. I'm sure I would have been one of them if they had known my real name..."

Laura sat looking at him with her mouth open, stunned.

"That hotel has absorbed all the anger and fear and woe that has transpired behind its walls through the decades," he continued. "If you want to find something frightening, that's the place you should go. It's now a boutique hotel called the Highland Dallas. Very modern. Just down Mockingbird from the Campisi's restaurant. It's a perfect place for the ghosts of the past to feed off the lives of the present..."

He pulled out a manila envelope from beneath his coat.

"I have collected some photographs over the years that might be of some use to you. They are nothing special, just of the hotel and some events. Personally, I want to get rid of everything that reminds me of that time."

Laura took the envelope and sat back almost in shock. This is not what she expected to hear from this interview. What the hell has she stumbled on to?

"I can't thank you enough, Mr. Szabó. This is startling stuff." She pulled out a few photos and glanced at them. There was one of Szabó in a waiter's uniform serving wine to some women in lavish gowns. Another of the hotel lobby filled with patrons, probably New Years Eve.

"With respect, I know all of this happened decades ago, but please be careful, Ms. Milton. These people were never to be toyed with. And I fear, though many are now gone, there is still a presence that, more than likely, holds the same sentiment. I couldn't forgive myself if my testimony put you in danger in any way."

She almost laughed out loud, but looking into his eyes, she could see that he was completely serious.

"Thank you..."

Laura was numb as she pulled out of the parking lot onto Gaston. Half a mile from the bar, she pulled the car over, opened the door, and threw up in the street.

Seventeen

In the late 80's, the Hilton family formally relinquished their ties with the Mockingbird Hotel. In the years following, the 5-acre property changed hands a number of times, first quickly becoming the Hiltop Inn for a few years, then the ill-fated Hotel Santa Fe. After falling into disrepair in the mid- 90's, it was purchased by the Realty America Group in association with Behringer Heritage Funds in 2004 and redesigned into the 4-star luxury Hotel Palomar. The 80 million dollar project included an accompanying 10-story condo tower, 25,000 square feet of lower-level retail space, and a state of the art health spa. However, despite the boutique hotel's popularity, in 2014 the property was again purchased by Annapolis, Maryland-based Thayer Lodging Group and is now called the Highland Dallas, soon to be the flagship hotel of their Curio Group of hotels within the city.

Laura knew the history well from her immersive research the night before. Standing at the valet, she admired the face of the Highland Hotel. A 40-ft glass wall over-looking Central Expressway framed by neutral brick pillars added to the majestic entrance to the property. Directly to the right of the front entrance area was the Exhale Spa, a gorgeous modern structure that connected the hotel with the residence tower.

She followed the porter through the 10-foot glass doors. Long sheer curtains hung the height of the ceiling and added texture to a minimalist modern twist on an Asian theme still left over from the Palomar days. An open aquarium filled with bright orange and white koi lay beneath the angular, cherrywood stairway that led to the mezzanine level overlooking an occupied reception area. Small signs of renovation were perceptible, but for the most part the property was near flawless. An odd crowd of people were strewn across the geometric dark wooden floor; an older gay couple, both in velveteen warm-ups, stood arguing with a bell captain, each holding a tiny shitsu with bows in their fur; a small group of Asian businessmen, all dressed in identical suits, were politely waiting for a shuttle; and a young transvestite wearing sunglasses, wading boots and a fake-fur coat was desperately looking for the ladies room.

Laura checked in at the front desk, got her key and then went to the brushed aluminum elevator doors. Stepping inside, she breathed deeply, consciously opening her mind to the possible detection of entities. There was a very faint white noise, like a radio receiver with multiple voices whispering over one another, reverberating from somewhere. Just as that thought came to her, she felt a wave of chills rush through her body.

Here we go...

The elevator door opened on the 6th floor and Laura stared out into the hallway before exiting. The modern decor and the low level light were tasteful but added to an ominous feeling in the pit of her stomach. She took a deep breath and stepped out into the hall.

She was slightly dizzy as she slowly made her way down the plush walkway, passing door after stylized door, huge mahogany slabs that for some reason seemed to be holding back terrible forces. There were muffled voices coming from a few of the rooms, but nothing intelligible. And there still was that hissing sound that kept its dissonant note singing through her consciousness. And above the white noise, a faint sound persisted, something like a far away bell or maybe a distant scream.

Finally, she came to the door numbered 627. Waving the cardkey, the green LED lit and the lock clicked open. She pushed the door inward and quickly stepped into the luxury room, letting the door close behind her.

The room was quite elegant, an understated décor done in pastels and dark wood. A small bouquet of bright red calla lilies sprouted from a black glass vase on a circular table in the center of the room.

A chill passed through her. Something was here, watching her. She held her breath and listened intently. Just behind the hum of the air conditioner there was that strange hissing sound, again like a murmuring of voices...

And it was suddenly gone.

Laura dropped her bags, sat on the leather chair in the middle of the room, and called Colin. He picked up on the second ring.

"I was just thinking about you," he said. "How's it going?"

She felt like she was shrinking, like in her dreams from her childhood. Something pressed in at her from all sides.

"Well, I'm here. And I'm not alone."

Laura was usually a pretty balanced, logical woman, far beyond Colin's own capacity for rationale at times. But at this moment, he could feel her anxiety, even across the ether of satellite phone connections.

"You need to protect yourself. Listen Laura, you know I'm naturally skeptical about all of this, right? Well, I've started having dreams myself lately. I think something is up."

"Really? Thanks for the tip."

"I'm serious. And I think somebody's been following me."

"What are you talking about?"

"I started having processor issues ever since I started checking your research last week..."

"You've been checking my research?" She was instantly furious.

"Laura, I found a key-logger on my machine. Someone is keeping an eye on me."

"You've been checking my research?" '*You little mother–*'

"Laura, listen to me. I've found something. This Davis guy was not just some southern gentleman. He's tied to Jack Ruby back in the day as a muscleman. And he seemed to have pissed off some influential people. Mackie tells me he was blackballed from everything and everyone for some unknown reason. I'm sending an encrypted folder from another computer in a few minutes."

She was angry but understood what he was saying. Her project was under attack. "What should I do?"

"Just decide how much this really means to you."

"I really want this, Colin. I *need* this."

"I'm not trying to take anything from you, Laura, but you have to be careful."

"Colin... I've had everything that I've ever loved taken from me. Please." Angry tears crested in her eyes even as she fought them back. "You above anyone else should know what it's done to me..."

"I understand. Just please take care of yourself."

When she heard the sincerity in his voice, she realized his concern. She held her anger back.

"I will."

* * *

That evening she decided to escape the oppressive feeling of the hotel and get food somewhere nearby. She wanted to be around regular people who knew nothing about dead debutantes or mass murders or mafia kingpins. She asked the concierge and he recommended a pub called the Old Monk one exit South towards downtown off Central Expressway.

She put the windows down in the Land Rover and drove with the wind in her hair. The air felt cooler this evening. Regardless of the time of year, in Texas it could start snowing, pouring rain, or there could be a heat wave any second. She was thankful for a few days of mild weather.

The dark English-style pub was set in a small neighborhood restaurant district just a block off the highway. She miraculously found an empty space, parked, and stepped into the crisp night air. Couples were walking holding hands between the different shops and bars in the area. She wished Colin were here with her.

The entrance was a multi-colored brick arch leading through the patio. The tables were filled with patrons drinking and laughing in the night air. She decided to check out the interior and opened the giant wooden doors.

Inside, the building was a single open space lined with wood and stone, mandatory HD televisions hanging everywhere showing sports replays. The place was packed. She squeezed her way through the crowd and found a lone seat towards the back of the room against the wall rail. A passing waitress with brightly colored tattoos on her arms and shoulders came over and Laura ordered a Strongbow cider.

She sat back and actually allowed herself to rest for a moment. It felt good just sitting there with her back against the wall, watching the crowd, totally anonymous. A few minutes without the ghost of a Texas debutante overshadowing her every thought were welcomed.

The waitress brought her drink and Laura handed her cash. She took a deep draught of the ice-cold cider, relishing the flavor.

There were so many beautiful people in Dallas, male and female, and both groups were amply represented this evening. It reminded her of California in a way, sans the ocean and earthquakes, that is. Everyone was tanned and animated and gave the impression of being wealthy. Beautiful women and men with tattoos were lined up at the bar, drinking, living their lives without care. Their preoccupations went far beyond seeing ghosts and having nervous breakdowns. These people were vital and young and *alive*.

What was fuck was wrong with her?

Laura felt completely alone and very old in the loud throng of people. She would never be this carefree, this blithe. It just wasn't part of her personality. Perhaps it had never been. She would forever be an outsider in her own life looking in. Goddamnit.

Having lost her appetite, she finished her cider, walked out to the Land Rover, and drove back to the Highland Hotel in silence.

Eighteen

Laura left the Highland at 8:30 AM and drove through the Lower Greenville area into Lakewood towards Garland Road, which ran along the eastern shore of White Rock Lake. To the east lay the historic neighborhood of Little Forest Hills, her early morning destination

In the morning light, the area was lush and gorgeous. She drove down the serpentine Garland Road heading north past the shimmering waters of White Rock, past East Lawther. The next light was Lakeland Drive, which branched off to the east across the street from the Dallas Arboretum, a 66-acre botanical garden located on the southeastern shore of the lake. She turned right at the light and entered the subdivision.

When her interviewee suggested a breakfast meeting, Laura expected a quickie at some greasy spoon diner off the interstate. Instead, he offered to make a special brunch for the two of them at his home in the quaint historic district. She happily agreed.

Jaoul Merrick was once the executive chef at the Hilton Inn, Mockingbird hotel in Dallas in the early '70's that was now the Highland Hotel. She had found his name through searching the public records of the Hilton. Unlike many leads she found, Merrick was still alive and had been more than willing to talk to her.

He had set a quaint table for two on the back porch of his modest mid-century home. A lush backyard sprawled in front of her as Merrick prepared their plates at the outdoor range.

"You have a beautiful home, Mr. Merrick."

"All my friends just call me Merrick. Yeah, I love this place. My wife and I bought it in 1974 and lived a happy life here. When she passed in the early 90's I just couldn't part with it. Too many good memories here to just throw away. I hope you're hungry," he said, smiling a toothy grin.

"You didn't have to go through all this trouble."

"No trouble a'tall. To be honest, I feel more like myself when I'm taking care of someone else than when I'm not." He had prepared hot beignets, fresh ground coffee with chicory, and mini eggs Benedicts with grilled roma tomato and spinach hollandaise. He placed a plate in front of her dressed with roasted rosemary potatoes. It looked almost too good to eat. Laura picked up her fork and took a bite. It was heavenly.

"Mmmm... It's wonderful!"

Merrick smiled from ear to ear, satisfied.

"Cooking is my passion, Laura. You know, when I started out I was working in diners and greasy spoons making next to nothing. But I loved cooking. I put my heart and soul into every patty melt I grilled." Laura smiled. "I made the most amazing corned-beef hash you've ever put in your mouth. I knew the key was taking pride in your work and being consistent. Finally, I saved enough to send myself to a proper cooking school.

"One thing led to another, and in less than 24 months, I made head chef at a place called Renfro's in East Dallas. I helped make that place into a great restaurant. That next year, I got an offer to open the old Hilton Mockingbird for some big money starting in '67. When we opened, we were the talk of the town, yes sir-ee. I had stayed true to my calling, and I was blessed by the Lord." He took a seat next to her and sipped his coffee.

"Yeah, the Hilton is now called the Highland. They made it into a luxury bow-*tique* hotel called the Palomar in the early oughts and it just recently changed hands. But back in the day, 'used to be where all the Hollywood celebrities would stay. Elvis, Sammy Davis Jr., Lawrence Olivier, Dean Martin, Sinatra, Richard Nixon, Jane Fonda... I fed some of the most famous and notorious people in the world in that place."

"Sounds like it was a fantastic time."

"It was great. Hell, Bob Hope was a benefactor for SMU and had a private penthouse suite. Parties were going on all the time. He had a weakness for the Braniff stewardesses out of Love Field..." He laughed. "But who didn't? He would keep the private club Harper's Corner open all night for his guests. We always knew when Bob was in town because we couldn't keep champagne in stock. And he didn't even drink!" Merrick laughed heartily.

"Did you ever feel there was an underground element at the hotel? Like criminal activity?"

Merrick's smile faded into a scowl. "There were a lot of VIP events. Some people say the Mafia was involved. I saw a lot of people during those years come and go. A lot of things were happening, that's for sure. To be honest, Ms. Milton, I just kept my head down. You don't get to be 78 years old by getting into other people's business, that much I do know.

"The place fell into disrepair in the 80's and finally got cut from the Hilton name in 1990. That's when I left.

"A few years later, the Maharishi Yogi, who was the spiritual guru to the Beatles in the 60's, bought the place to create a combination hotel/meditation center chain that he was trying to start. It never took off, though. They began renting the first 5 floors as apartments. I heard from some of my friends who stayed that they started leasing to prostitutes and drug-dealers. Very bad shit going on, pardon my French. People started doing strange things in the residence floors, things I don't ever want to know about. Personally, I think that place was just born bad, no two ways about it."

"Have you been back since the remodel?"

"No, I can't say I have. I don't want to go back. Too many good memories gone bad. Besides, I hear that place is haunted like the dickens."

"Thank you, Mr. Merrick. I'll keep that in mind..."

Laura left Merrick's home just before 11 AM. She drove down Garland Road past White Rock Lake on the way back to the hotel. The lake shimmered in the sun like liquid gold. Again, in the warm sunlight it was hard to imagine that evil existed anywhere in the world. But the truth was, behind every gorgeous façade, there was always a darker, more unbelievable world lurking underneath...

* * *

Laura stopped at a Central Market on Greenville and bought five dozen roses on her way back to the Highland. She took them to her room and, while watching CNN, took a pair of scissors and cut the tops of all the flowers off. She collected the petals into a towel, humming to herself mindlessly while her hands worked.

She packed the towel in her backpack and called back downstairs for the Land Rover. In minutes she was back on the road. A blanket of clouds had rolled in and the smell of rain was in the air. Turning on her headlights, she drove on into the grey afternoon.

Calvary Hill Cemetery was on the other side the city. Laura didn't know her way around Dallas very well and got lost in the Bachman Lake/Love Field Airport area. She knew she could use her GPS, but this was something she felt she had to discover on her own. So many landmarks ignited memories from her past. But most of the places she remembered from her childhood were simply gone. The old Shakey's Pizza parlor and Tupinamba's on Northwest Highway were nowhere to be seen. And the bowing alley across from Bachmann Lake she had loved as a child had been replaced by a modern Sam's Club Warehouse.

Further down Walnut Hill Extension, the neighborhood had become like little Mexico. The supermarket in the strip mall she remembered was now a thriving Fiesta Mart. Street vendors were on the sidewalks selling frozen fruit pops and tacos out of chests secured to tricycles. All the shops were now geared towards bilingual business. Not that it was a bad thing, necessarily; it was just different from the early seventies when this was more of an exclusive singles area of apartment clusters. Man, how things had changed...

Walnut Hill veered off the to the west and became Lombardy Lane. A quarter mile down at 3235 she passed the length of 10-foot barrier fence for the Calvary Hill property. Laura drove through the gates and pulled over to check the map of the plots she had downloaded.

She had no trouble finding the right road leading through the acres of low graves. The surrounding grounds were peppered with pastel flower arrangements and wreathes. In moments, the Land Rover rolled up to a familiar large group of trees and stopped. This was the place. Grabbing the bunched up towel in the passenger seat, she got out of the car.

It started sprinkling lightly. A few yards away, an older man stood holding a little girl by the hand. The two were staring at a very ornate headstone. The girl's head turned slowly, watching Laura pass.

As she continued through the city of graves, gray figures began appearing out of the shadows, some perched on headstones, watching her curiously as she continued through their home, the cemetery. They would seem normal at first glance, but if Laura looked closer she could notice the pallor of the skin, the sunken eyes, the open wounds that would never heal...

Ignoring the inquisitive spirits, she walked into a small clearing. There was a pair of headstones sitting under the arms of a large oak tree. One headstone read “Theresa Birch-Milton”, the next one “Nathan Kyle Milton”. Her beloved parents.

The shock of seeing their graves after so many years was both comforting and unsettling. Laura ran her hand over the cold stone marker, wishing so badly that she could sense her parents’ presence. But aside from calm feelings, she had never seen or heard either one of them after they died. In a way, she was thankful for being spared the shock of having to look into her mother’s long-dead face. The shock would probably be too much to handle. But inside, she wished she could just sit with her, like she did with the little dead boy in their old house, and read to her, just be next to her again... And to be able to tell her father how much she loved him one last time... Tears welled up in her eyes. Instead of fighting them back, she let them fall in a torrent down her face.

Laura released the towel in her hands and a shower of blood-red rose petals fell out over her parents’ graves floating like corpuscles in the breeze. A small group of spirits hovered close by watching, amused by the bright red dots of color floating in the wind.

Turning, she was startled by the spirit of a man standing directly in front of her. Half of his blue face was gone leaving a large area of exposed flesh and bone. He looked hideous but she could sense his gentle nature. He slowly leaned his head to one side in a very human gesture of curiosity. He was being sweet.

“Please, let me be. Just for a while.” Laura spoke gently and directly to him.

The spirit smiled sadly at her with half a face and gently melted into the shadows.

She took a seat on the bench next to the headstones and closed her eyes. She had not been back to see her father since his death so many years ago. What a horrible morning that had been. She had cried like a child in Colin's arms. And his poor family had done all they could to help her get through the funeral. She was so upset she couldn't even speak on her father's behalf.

Afterwards, she was almost catatonic, unable to face the fact that her father was gone. She let Colin drag her around the city trying to preoccupy her, but she was broken. The two people she loved most in the world had been taken from her... How could she ever hope to go on?

Laura shuddered at the thought of what her life would have become had it not been for Colin. She would surely have committed suicide during the period when she had been on anti-depressives right after the funeral. She owed her life to him. In a way, she felt like her father had unconsciously handpicked him to be her protector. Even though her father had never believed in the '*gift*' she shared with her mother, he seemed to glimmer with it himself occasionally, probably without ever realizing it.

Even though she was crying, a deep joy filled Laura's soul just being there in the gentle rain, together, a family once again. Her mother had always told her there was nothing more important in life than family; it was a bond that no man, no disaster, not even Death itself could ever break. And she felt that bond with her now, stronger than ever.

She sat there in the rain alone riding waves of grief for a long time. Eventually, she looked up.

Surrounding her were dozens of gentle spirits, watching. They hovered everywhere, their rotted and contorted faces staring with sensitive eyes that peered inside her soul. She could feel their compassion radiating out, touching her like a comforting breeze.

But there was something else...

Even through the waves of support coming from the dead surrounding her, Laura sensed something watching her. A sea of graves stretched out under a dark sky in every direction. But whatever watched her was *living*. She could feel it breathing, could feel the expectation, the thrill of the hunt it was experiencing. Christ, she hated having this sensitivity. Was it her imagination or her intuition? And how easy would it be to make a fatal flaw one day mistaking one for the other? Whatever it was, she had felt its presence ever since she arrived in Dallas, following her everywhere.

Driving back from the cemetery, she decided to take the long way back and go through the White Rock area. She entered White Rock Park from the west entrance, on the far side of the spillway. There by a bridge was an old whitewashed boathouse.

At the entrance of the lot there was a fire-truck, a water utilities truck, and a handful of men who were trying to quell a substantial water-main break. The water had been contained to a dramatic geyser shooting in the sky. The few people present were being forced back by firemen who were trying to get the situation under control.

While she sat there watching the commotion, a young woman approached Laura's car holding her purse over her head. She was dressed in a soaking wet dark sweater and a form-fitting skirt. She waved and Laura lowered the window. The woman was a very pretty redhead. She smiled, a little embarrassed.

"I'm sorry to bother you! There's been an accident..."

There was a geyser of water spewing from the street. A dark car was only feet away from the pillar of water and was caught in the deluge. The passenger door was open and water was filling the vehicle.

"Oh! Please get in!"

The woman was very grateful. "Thank you so much! I would hate to ruin your front seat. I'll get in back."

The woman reached out with a wet hand for the door handle and let herself in car.

"Sure. Here's a towel." Laura pitched the towel that she used to hold the rose petals in the back for her. The woman caught it and started drying her hair as Laura drove through the lot and back onto Lawther Drive.

"Thank you so much."

"I'm glad I could help. Do you come to the lake often?"

"It's one of my favorite places. I don't ever want to leave here..."

Laura watched her in the rear-view mirror. The girl was pretty. She had a 50's-style coif and a knockout figure. She looked like a pin-up girl out of a calendar. "Are you from around here?"

"No, I'm from Mansfield, originally. But I have family in Ft. Worth."

"What happened back there?"

"I'm not sure..."

Laura thought that was strange, her being caught in an accident and not knowing what caused it. "It looked like a water main burst to me," Laura said, not knowing why. "So... where are we going?"

"Just up on Gaston Avenue. It's not far..."

Laura instantly recognized those words from the numerous accounts of Lady of the Lake sightings. She looked down at her arm and all the hair suddenly stood on end.

'Damnit...'

Laura slowly looked up into the rearview mirror. The young woman was drying her auburn hair with the towel. She stopped for a second and smiled warmly at Laura in the mirror. Laura casually turned around and looked behind her.

The woman was gone. The wet towel was laying on the back seat of the car in a puddle of water.

Laura slammed on her brakes and started screaming.

* * *

Laura didn't remember the drive back to the hotel. But she was back in her room, on the phone, pacing.

"It was *her*, Colin, I swear it. I turned around and she was *gone!*"

"You're over-worked, Laura. I think you're putting too much into this–"

"Goddamnit, I am *not* over-worked! I saw her with my own eyes!" She took a deep breath and tried to calm herself. "It's not so much that I saw a ghost. It's that she was in my car, we smiled at each other; I was having a pleasant conversation with someone who was *dead!* And I couldn't tell the difference!"

"That's it. I'm flying down tonight."

She took a deep breath. "No, don't. I'm ok. I know you're busy. I just had to speak to somebody."

"Laura, you're in over your head. If what you say is true, I think you might be in danger."

"She doesn't want to hurt me, Colin."

"I'm not talking about the ghost. There's no reason to be afraid of the dead, Laura–be afraid of the living. They're the ones who can hurt you. This isn't just a ghost story you're investigating; it's the entire fucking history of Dallas itself. And everyone in it."

"I'll be careful. I promise. Listen, I want to send you copies of what I have so far. Just in case."

'Just in case of what?' he thought. But instead, he was as supportive as he could be in his panicked state. "Sure, send everything to my personal email. And, you might want to make hard copies of all your media and send them as well. Send those to my office. You don't want to take any chances, Laura. Please be careful..."

After Laura hung up the phone, she jumped on her computer and started scurrying through websites. On the site *whiterocklake.org* she found the details on the second suicide at White Rock Lake and started reading.

'On November 24, 1942, another distraught woman, 35-year-old Rose Stone of Mansfield, Texas, also committed suicide by drowning herself in the lake. Her body, dressed in sweater and skirt, was discovered in eight feet of water near the municipal boathouse...'

Her first name was Rose, but she wasn't the same woman. One thing screamed out in her brain: *'It wasn't her!'*

Laura could see flashes of her dreams, hair the color of white gold, the bracelet of red flowers on a delicate wrist, the cobalt blue eyes that seemed to stare into eternity...

She breathed a sigh of relief that escaped her lips as words.

"It wasn't you."

* * *

That afternoon, Laura drove to Fry's Electronics across town and purchased four small terabyte storage drives, a handful of high-capacity flash drives, and some assorted accessories. When she returned to the hotel she ordered room service and ate while she began backing up all her interview footage. She also made multiple hard copies of every digital link, voice note, email, and text related to the White Rock Lady project. She filled two small FedEx boxes she had gotten from the concierge with identical copies of the same disks, addressed one to herself and the other to Colin's New York office and set them aside while the footage copied from her laptop to the new storage devices.

While waiting, she did some yoga in her hotel room and meditated for about an hour. Afterwards, she showered and put on some sleeping pants and a tee shirt. By then, all her footage had been copied. Laura wrapped the redundant drives in bubble-wrap, placed one in each FedEx box, sealed them, and placed the packages by the door to take to the post office first thing in the morning. As crucial as this content was, she didn't want to trust the hotel to mail it.

Lying in bed, she fought the urge to call Mallory. He would be working late anyway, but her body yearned to be touched again. *'Can't spend all your time playing footsie,'* she told herself. She turned over restlessly. At least it would take her mind off of this afternoon's episode. Visions of Rose Stone sitting in her car drying her auburn hair were playing over and over in her head. It all seemed so fantastic. Laura wasn't even certain that any of it really happened and wasn't just some hallucination.

She reached over to the nightstand, took her pill, turned out the lights, and forced herself to sleep.

That night she slept soundly without dreaming.

***

In Gramercy Park, New York, Colin Jonah was watching found footage of the White Rock Lake project starting from 1900. Photographs of the building crew, testimonies from the original workers about the site... there was so much to absorb.

Could the legend be true? Was there actually a spirit haunting White Rock Lake? God, there were so many crazy things going on in the world at any time. But ghosts? Really? He couldn't understand how someone as smart as Laura could be sucked into all this ridiculousness. Yes, the nightmares he started having were harrowing, but they proved nothing. Perhaps he was just being influenced by her obsession. Hell, it might as well be a vampire Laura was chasing...

Something slammed in the kitchen downstairs bringing him back to the present. Colin got up and slowly crept down the stairwell.

"Hello?" His heart was pounding. Turning the corner, he saw the light in the kitchen was on. He couldn't remember leaving the light on. What the hell was going on? He heard something shuffling against the linoleum floor.

"*Hello*?"

Walking into the kitchen he saw 3 bodies lying face down on the floor. The backs of their heads had been blown away. They lay in a crimson lake of blood that slowly pooled out underneath them.

Voices were whispering in the next room.

Colin turned and found himself outdoors under a dark cluster of trees. There was a man standing with his back to him, facing out at the black, turbulent waters of a lake. The sky was dark and wind whipped wildly around them. He could hear the man sobbing uncontrollably. As he walked a few more paces forward, the figure slowly turned around to face him. Colin saw his own face staring back at him with dark hollow pits where his eyes once were, now eaten out of his waterlogged skull.

Colin sat up, suddenly wide-awake in bed. His head was swimming. He put his hand to his face and felt the hot tears still streaming out of his eyes.

"*Fuck...*"

* * *

Early that next morning Laura went to the post office on Oak Lawn Avenue, just down the street from the Melrose Hotel. She paid the postage for the boxes and handed them to the attendant with a relieved sigh. She needed to get in the habit of doing this after every interview. God forbid, but if something went horribly wrong, at least her work would be preserved and, if need be, there would be an evidence trail.

She picked up some bagels at Einstein's then went back to the hotel and waited for her 9 AM interview.

At 8:50 Damon Young arrived looking very dapper in navy blue suit and a white open-collared shirt. Laura thought the man looked amazingly youthful for being in his late-50's. She guided him to the interview seat and applied a little translucent powder to take the shine off of his nose.

He sat back in his chair, staring at the equipment set up. He seemed a little uncertain, as if the new technology of this age had left him behind.

"Are you comfortable, Mr. Young?"

"Yes, thank you."

"Thanks for coming so early. I hope I didn't ruin your morning."

He shifted in his seat. "No, not at all. I'm always up early." He stared at the camera while she finished setting up. "How long have you been doing documentary work?"

Laura smirked. "Since high-school, really. I was an English major taking journalism and acting and was writing the great American novel in my spare time." She laughed, only because it was true. "I think documentary filmmaking is the only option I really had."

"It seems interesting."

She looked at her view screen to focus on his face. "It is the most fascinating thing I could ever imagine doing. Meeting different people, learning about their personal lives, their dreams and goals... It's a very personal form of art that is different from journalism in that it exists solely for the glorification of its subjects."

She found her focus, hit record, and settled into her chair.

"Unfortunately, it didn't translate into my plans for college. Oh, well... But it's become an invaluable skill. Especially for this project. Ok, sir. When you're ready take a deep breath, give me your name, tell me where you're from, and then in detail tell me about the night of your encounter."

"Of course. Should I look at–?"

"Just look directly at me. Whenever you're ready."

"Ok. I, ah, I'm Damon Young from Dallas, Texas. I must have been four or five years old when this happened. It was Christmas, 1962. I remember because it was pretty cold that year. We have a lot of 80 degree Christmases in Dallas now, but then we still had winter." He laughed nervously. "Anyway, we had a wonderful dinner that night. My mother was a great cook...

"Afterwards, our family gathered around the Christmas tree to hand out presents. My mother had just brought out my gift, a beautiful Basset hound puppy." Young smiled deeply at the memory with a faint glistening in his eyes. "She was the most beautiful little thing I had ever seen. I was playing with her as my father put another log on the fire. My mom and older brother were sorting presents and talking.

"We were getting ready to open another round of presents. It was probably 12:30 AM. Ah, I guess I should tell you we were Catholic, so, after going to late mass, my family usually stayed up all night on Christmas Eve opening gifts. My father could never wait till Christmas morning...

"He had just picked up a package and handed it to me when the doorbell rang. It was late, but being Christmas Eve it could easily have been any one of a number of relatives coming by for some Christmas cheer and a slice of my mother's cherry cheesecake.

"My father got up and went to the door with martini in hand and opened it. Halfway through saying "Merry Christmas!" he saw there was no one on the porch. He shrugged, closed the door and came back to the celebration.

"A few moments later my brother was opening a box and the doorbell rang again. My father got up a little annoyed and went to the door but again no one was there. He closed the door a bit more firmly and headed back to the dining room. As soon as he turned his back on the door the bell rang a third time. This time I hopped off the couch and followed my father to the door, curious as we all were to see who would be playing pranks on Christmas Eve.

"The bell rang again. I was next to my father when he swung the door open.

"A young blonde girl was standing on the porch in a soaking wet dress. Her face was turned sideways. As the door opened she turned towards us and her jaw seems to unhinge itself. Her little mouth stretched down to her chest and she shrieked out hideously in an unearthly banshee voice. I covered my ears, it was so loud and frightening. My father slammed the door shut in panic. When he yanked it open again there was nothing but a puddle of water covering the welcome mat.

"As long as I live, I will never forget that night. Not ever..."

* * *

After Damon Young's interview, Laura had the afternoon free so she decided to follow a hunch. She called for her car and got on the highway. There was a company she wanted to check out on the other side of town. She had found their ad in a tattoo magazine she was reading at the spa and saved their information. Even though it was probably a long shot, she had to start thinking out of the box about this case. There was simply too much to do on her own.

It was still fairly early but it was already promising to be a warm day. The rainfall overnight made it humid as a rainforest. It would surely be almost unbearable by noon.

Laura exited Interstate 30 at Sylvan Ave. Oak Cliff was one of the oldest suburbs of Dallas that had been the latest area to be revitalized. Trendy restaurants and art shops popped up everywhere taking the place of decades-old community buildings, adding to the artistic flair of the historic neighborhood but also homogenizing the original flavor of the area. Modernization was definitely a bittersweet process.

At Bishop, she turned left and took the first right. A block down she turned left into a cul-de-sac. Over-sized oak trees framed the only house on the circle making it seem dark even though the structure was painted brilliant white and lemon yellow. She pulled up in front and checked the address. There was a large sign on the side of the house with a stylized death's head caricature. Underneath, were the capital letters MGH, the acronym for the Metroplex Ghost Hunters. The graphic was compelling, but looked more like ingenious graffiti or tattoo art rather than the logo of a business that took itself and its clients seriously.

Laura got out of the car. It was as if she stepped into a sauna. The humidity was stifling.

Walking to the house she noticed intricate designs and symbols painted on the 8-foot fence, like medieval runes or incantations. Some of them looked authentic but she didn't know enough to decipher what they said. It could have been anything.

She climbed the steps to the door and thought, '*What the hell am I doing?*'

Laura took a deep breath and knocked. She was a little embarrassed, like the time she ran into another teaching assistant while picking up a video for her and Colin at an adult bookstore. Awkward. But this was something different, entirely. This was just plain silly.

Just as she was about to turn and walk away, a lanky young man in his mid twenties answered the door. He had on a pair of thick-rimmed glasses and with his scruffy beard he looked a little like a younger version of her advisor, Robert Reilly. She was a little cautious until she got a good look at him. He had a lollipop in his mouth.

"Don't be scared. We don't bite. Hard."

Wrong thing to say. "Ah, I think this might be a bad idea..." Laura was halfway down the stairs when he called out to her.

"Hey, I'm sorry, that was a bad stab at humor. I'm Samuel. I *am* Metroplex Ghost Hunters. I mean, I started it."

She looked him over with a cynical eye. He seemed pretty normal considering he just delivered what was probably the worst opening line she had ever heard in her life. He pushed his glasses up on his nose, looking at her, waiting for some hint at his fate. The gesture made him look 12 years old. She smirked, walked up, and offered her hand.

"Hi. Laura Milton."

They shook hands and he held onto her for a moment too long. There was a moment of awkward silence as they silently summed one another up. He was obviously attracted to her. And she thought he was cute, in a frumpy, emo sort of way. Finally, breaking the silence, Samuel pulled the lollipop out of his mouth.

"Frozen Charms pop?"

...

The interior of the house was very pleasant; open spaces, not a lot of clutter everywhere. Laura gave him 10 points for decorating. After getting her a raspberry lollipop out of the freezer, he sat down across the coffee table from her.

"So you're interested in ghosts?"

Coming out of a stranger's mouth, those words sounded a little ridiculous, even to her. She chose to be prudent so as not to seem too in love with the romanticism of it all. "I'm in Dallas researching an urban legend."

"Really?" His curiosity was sparked. "Is it the *black fog* that haunts the abandoned house on Dowdy-Ferry Road? Or maybe the Granada Theater ghost on Greenville Avenue?"

"Actually, it's the White Rock Lady."

Samuel hesitated for a split second and then continued. "The Lady of the Lake. It's a well-known haunt. And super well-documented. Why the interest in her?" Something changed in his demeanor, but she couldn't tell exactly what. His eyes opened like windows as he waited to hear her story. And she could tell he was not just being Texas-polite, his interest was sincere. She didn't feel like an idiot talking about the most intimate facet of her life. She sat back in the couch and got comfortable.

"When I was young my mother and I were very close. She was always... a little more sensitive than most people. When I was a kid she always knew what I was up to. Not just mother's intuition, she knew things I never told anyone else."

Samuel was attentive, nodding and smiling as if she were sharing intimate knowledge about something he absolutely agreed with.

"Well, when I was four I started having really horrible nightmares. I would wake up screaming five nights out of seven. My mother would rush in my room and try to wake me up. The dreams were so vivid. It was like I was being suffocated; everything around me was breaking apart, cellular walls shot to the sky as I was shrunk to the size of an atom... It's a little hard to describe, especially when you are a kid and don't have the knowledge nor the vocabulary to communicate what you're seeing correctly. I guess it was around that time that I started seeing things that may or may not have been there..."

"Like *what*?" Samuel was hanging on her every word.

She smiled. "Well, the first time I ever remember thinking that something in me had changed was when a plumber came to our home to fix a leak under the house. I was young, maybe 5 years old. The only way to the crawlspace was through a trap door in the closet in my bedroom. He was down there working one afternoon. Mother had told me to stay out until he was done, but I was curious. I wanted to see. I walked over and looked down into the hole.

"A pale little boy was sitting there on the dirt staring up at me. It didn't occur to me that he could have been a ghost. I was just curious of how this little boy got into our house. After that, I started seeing him in different places all over the house. I remember telling my father who, at the time, wrote it off to my imagination. But my mother had a very different opinion about it. She said to make friends with him, talk to him. He wasn't here to hurt anyone. From then on, when I'd see him around the house, maybe sitting on the couch by himself, I would tell him hello and he would smile. I'd look away and he'd be gone, but it became sort of a game between us. Sometimes he'd appear next to me while I was reading and I would read to him. It would make him so happy..."

"*Wow...*"

"Yeah. Well, when I was in high school, I did some research and found out in the 50's a little boy died a very slow death by cancer in my room."

"*Intense...*"

"Totally. Anyway, as I got older I realized I was able to see spirits or whatever you want to call them. Especially after my mother died, I saw them everywhere, always watching me. And to answer your question, finally, the reason I'm interested in the Lady of the Lake is because I saw her when I was very young. My childhood nightmares never stopped, but since that night they have all been about her."

He was addicted. "Tell me all about it."

Looking in his eyes, she knew Samuel was different than everyone else. He didn't just act like he believed; he *knew* she was telling the truth. And she wanted him to know.

"One Christmas, we were visiting a friend of my father's who lived on a house right on the lake. It was Christmas Eve 1988 or maybe 1989... It was actually very cold and I remember seeing colored lights up in all the houses we passed along the way. I was in the back seat of the car staring out the window.

"We were on the way back from the party very late. As I said, it was cold and the roads were icy. My father took a wrong turn and came to a sign that said 'No Cars Beyond this Point'. He cursed under his breath and turned back under an old bridge that dead-ended to an old boathouse right on the water.

"I looked out the back window trying to see the water. And there, just outside of the car, a beautiful blonde woman walked out of the mist. She approached the rear of the car and looked straight at me through the back windshield. That's when I noticed she was wet from head to toe.

"I called out, 'Look, Daddy! It's a lady!' but my parents were arguing about how to get back to the main road and didn't hear me. The woman seemed to float towards the car and held her hand out to me. She was like an angel. Her face looked so sad but she smiled at me. My father drove away and I watched her as long as I could until she disappeared into the mist. And she's been in my dreams ever since... I know it sounds silly, but–"

"Not at all." He was being sincere. "That's why I do this, Laura. I try to find out why these souls can't rest and help them find a resolution, if I can. Everyone is searching for something, even after they're dead. There's a force that binds these souls to the Earth. Until they can reconcile their problems, they are unable to go to the next plane. Sometimes it's an unresolved issue; sometimes it's fear or shock in death that fuses a person's soul to a geographical location. Every situation is different."

"I saw one. Yesterday at the lake."

"*What?*"

"In broad daylight. I swear. A woman got into my car. We spoke, I handed her a towel. She was nice. I was going to ask her to grab a drink sometime. When I turned back she was gone."

"Wait, you made contact with the Lady?"

"I saw someone. But I don't think it was the Lady. Her hair was different in my dreams."

"Hold on. You traveled 1,300 miles from New York to pick up a hitchhiking ghost but it wasn't the one you're looking for? What makes you think there's another?"

"I just know." She could tell by the look on his face how lame that excuse sounded. If she was going to get him to help her, she should be as honest as she could without getting him too involved. "The woman in my dreams has flowing blonde hair. On her wrist I see a bracelet or something made of tiny flowers carved out of red stone. The woman I met yesterday had red hair and no bracelet. What I need is evidence if this ghost is real..."

At that moment a dark-haired, slightly Goth-looking ghost hunter came in the room reading a book.

"Rachel," Samuel said, "this is Laura. She's looking for the White Rock Lady."

Rachel smiled, turning towards their guest. “Well, you’ve come to the right place...”

* * *

Laura returned from Oak Cliff in the early evening. She changed clothes and decided to jog across 75 Central Expressway to the SMU campus to clear her mind. Running past the university buildings on the lavish campus grounds, she couldn’t help but think about her home and NYU. Dallas had its charms, but it was still a foreign world to her. She couldn’t wait to be back in her apartment surrounded by her things. She missed the noise of the city, the *real* city. It was a comfort she couldn’t find here.

What had she gotten herself into anyway? Without physical evidence of a haunting, this entire investigation was nothing but conjecture. And now, she had made the decision to outsource a company to help her find some shred of proof to help substantiate her research. Everything seemed like such a Herculean feat. She wanted to cry. But cowardly tears were a luxury she could no longer afford.

‘Buck up, Pumpkin...’

Returning back to the hotel, Laura took a shower, popped her dreaded medication, and fell into a black, dreamless sleep.

* * *

Sunday morning Mallory picked her up and took her to the Modern Art Museum in Fort Worth. Designed by the Japanese architect Tadao Ando, the building itself was an amazing mechanism of concrete, glass and steel suspended over an immense pebble-lined meditation pool. Her first thought was that Colin would surely love this place. She felt a twinge of guilt being with another man in a museum, a place where Colin belonged.

Mallory must have sensed her distance. He tenderly took her by the hand and talked quietly as they perused the exhibits, bringing her back to the present. When they found themselves standing in a glass alcove looking out over the expansive water garden, he leaned over and kissed her gently. Later, they had lunch at a café called the Flying Saucer in Sundance Square in downtown and then browsed the many souvenir shops on the surrounding blocks.

When they made it back to Dallas, it was almost 7 PM. Laura had really enjoyed the time with Mallory, but when he asked her to spend the evening with him, she politely declined. She was definitely tempted, however, there was a lot of preparation to do for the coming week, not to mention a hefty portion of guilt she was still chewing on. Besides, though she knew putting all her surplus energy into Mallory would be easy to do, it ultimately stole her attention from her goal. Of course, Mallory was a complete gentleman and understood. He dropped her off at the hotel, kissed her goodbye, and drove off into the night...

Nineteen

Monday was, as always, a slow start. Laura's medication made her especially groggy so after her morning nap she took her time getting up and did some busy work from bed.

Before leaving New York, she had attempted to schedule an interview with Amber Campisi, the youngest daughter of the famed Dallas Mafia family, but none of her calls had been returned. She wasn't surprised. The family, though having successfully turned their main interest from book-making in the 60's and 70's to expanding their restaurant empire, seemed to be stricken by the modern plague of privilege and complacency. Of course, Amber herself had been a prominent party girl who graced reality television as well as the pages of Playboy Magazine as Miss February in the early oughts. And one of the twin elder daughters Gina Marie Campisi, the 26-year-old proprietor of her own restaurant called Fedora located downtown at One Arts Plaza, was found dead of an apparent suicide in 2010. It was sad that being gorgeous and wealthy didn't seem to be enough for some people. Oh, well. Though Laura didn't expect to hear back, from beneath a luxurious down duvet she called and left her name and number once more at the Campisi's business office. You never know, today might be her lucky day...

Leaving the hotel, Laura decided on a late lunch at Mi Cosina in Highland Park Village and then drove through Highland Park proper, the most affluent neighborhood in

Dallas. The neighborhood was actually its own municipality within Dallas County and even had its own police force. Most of the homes within the township borders were worth a million dollars and up. With a population of just over 9 thousand in an area encompassing only 2.2 square miles, Highland Park was the 3rd wealthiest location in Texas per capita income and 40th wealthiest city in the nation. Funny, Laura thought, that back in the 60's there was an actual upscale brothel, Madame De Luce's, which operated in the Turtle Creek area of Highland Park.

After learning so much about the city through her initial research, it was a treat to actually drive through the neighborhoods, explore the beautiful Turtle Creek area as well as the rest of University Park, the area surrounding Southern Methodist University. So much history resided there. The amount of money that had been invested into the design and the reputation of the city itself was probably staggering. And it was awesome to witness it all first-hand. Texas pride was definitely alive and well in Dallas.

Laura had also taken the time to research some of the darker events in Highland Park history. Over the years, there had been a number of shocking murders committed in this community, many of which were covered up, and a few that made national headlines. Almost all of these crimes had been committed by wealthy men against their wives and children. These were cases in which privilege and wealth, in her estimation, superseded justice.

After a while of sightseeing, Laura's morbid sense of curiosity eventually got the best of her. She drove to the 4200 block of Colgate Avenue in University Park where in 1999 Patrick Timothy Richardson, a doting father of three, murdered his heiress wife in a sudden crime of passion. Investigators determined that, after enduring a prolonged period of condescension from her, he cracked when she ordered him to leave their home. He almost completely beheaded her in front of their children with a pair of scissors.

Laura drove slowly down the street not knowing the exact address of the incident. She stopped at an intersection and then started to cross when a black cat appeared out of nowhere and darted in front of the car. She felt something strike the bottom of the floorboard. Slamming on her brakes, she stopped abruptly and got out of the car. There was nothing in street.

Getting back into the vehicle, she drove slowly half way down the block and realized that there were no people visible on the residential street whatsoever, no children playing, no one mowing the lawns, nothing. The entire lane was deserted. It was then that she noticed a figure standing in the shadows on the porch of a grey stone bi-level home on her right. The woman held a wine glass in her hand and intently watched the Land Rover roll by. She had a multicolored scarf around her neck that seemed to have stains on it. The woman's eyes were black as coal. A shiver ran through her and Laura had no doubt that the figure was that of the deceased Mary Williams Richardson, glass in hand, getting ready to leave for a night at Junior League that she would never attend...

The sighting left Laura more than a little disturbed. She decided to go back to the hotel and take a catnap. An hour later she woke feeling much better. It was going to be a busy evening.

* * *

At 6 PM the sun was still visible in the evening sky. Laura left the hotel and drove out to meet 77-year-old ex-assistant city planner Clate Wilkinson at the lodge located at the top of Winfry Point, the highest hill overlooking White Rock Lake. The white stone structure on top of the hill was built in 1947 and had once been an Officers' Club and recreation building when the Army Air Corps were stationed at White Rock Lake during the Second World War. The lodge, made from the famous white Austin chalk and slate the lake itself was named after, was now a vaulted and dramatic venue rented out for parties and fundraisers. From the front of the house where they were standing, there was a panoramic view of the lake and surrounding land in 360 degrees with downtown Dallas glowing in the early evening light 6 miles away.

"It is gorgeous here." Laura was taken back by the sheer acreage visible from the hill. The sun was in the west blazing blood-orange in the lower third of the sky.

Wilkinson pointed across the lake. "When the bathing beach opened in the summer of 1930, the mayor of Dallas at the time, J. Waddy Tate, had the city streetcar line extended to the western shore of the lake. A boathouse there held a fleet of speedboats that would ferry visitors to the park from one end of the lake to the other. You could never get away with that today, even with millions of dollars of insurance. The boathouse still stands and is leased by a rowing club now, I believe." Wilkinson was obviously a fountain of information.

"Why is Lawther Drive blocked in so many places?"

"Well, you used to be able to drive around the entire lake. Lawther was a popular 'cruising' lane with the teenagers in the 60's and 70's. The Bath House parking lot was a big hangout. Fights would break out constantly. In 1977, a huge riot erupted and 49 people were arrested. Two years later, the city divided East Lawther Drive into four sections to discourage loitering. And it actually worked."

"You mentioned some problems associated with the lake itself..."

"Yes. Well, man-made lakes like this are prone to accumulating sediment over the years from their tributaries. Periodically, maintenance crews need to go in and dredge out the sediment otherwise it would build up and eventually fill in the lake.

“The first dredging was in 1974, but by the mid 80’s it was filled again with silt and sediment. The place was a marsh. You could almost walk across the lake at certain points. In ’87 a bill was passed to the tune of $12.3 million dollars that would pay not only for a list of renovations to the park but also for the long-overdue de-silting of the lake. The work began in 1996 and took the better part of three years to complete.

“They brought barges fitted with cranes and lines of dump trucks to haul the sediment out. There were multiple teams working different parts of the lake simultaneously. It was tremendously hard work, controlling machinery half-submerged in water for 8 to 10 hours a day in the Texas heat. I felt sorry for the crew, poor guys. The contractors ended up pulling in 40 Mexican nationals as a labor force. They taught them to run the cranes and let them loose with a couple of crew bosses and barge captains.

“In late February of ‘97, I got a call. They found something. I came in to help identify a strange elevated landmass 30 yards off shore.

“Now, I have to tell you first about some local lore. There has always been a legend of a place called Bonnie Belle Island, supposedly a small island somewhere in the middle of the lake that was occasionally visible. Since the 1930’s, there have been all kinds of strange stories of fires seen burning out on the lake and strange sounds coming from the water in the middle of the night.

“Well, we found it.” He pointed out across the water to the west side of the shore. “Just west of the Jackson Point cape close to the shore, a small raised area, approximately 1,000 square feet, sitting on a lone limestone shelf just 5 to 6 feet below normal water level.

"The strange thing wasn't that this was an elevated area. What was strange was there were remnants of stone pillars built into it that looked like some kind of markers in rows of ten, fifteen feet apart.

"When I arrived that Saturday afternoon, I met Alan Feefer, the crew foreman at the location. He was in charge of a small team working an area about 5000 square feet 30 yards offshore in what was almost the center of the lake. He told me they had two barges, one that held the clam, the digging apparatus, and one for tools and supplies. Supposedly, they were out dredging and ran up on a landmass that wasn't silt. It was hard limestone. And from what Feefer told me, there were indications of possible artifacts buried in the surrounding bed. Basically, I had been called out to document the find, describe the geographical details of the area, take samples of the sediment, and submit a hypothesis. Same old shit."

Laura smiled a wide grin. He told an interesting and fun story. She was thoroughly enjoying this.

"There were eight men on Feefer's crew; two skippering the barges, one operating the crane, an electrician, a spotter, a diver, and two runners in outboard rafts. The spotter was the first to view the clam as it came out of the water in case we accidentally snagged a power cable or anything. They had been working for about four hours. On the third load, the first thing the spotter saw half-buried in a mound of silt was a partial human skull. He whistled to the operator who then called me over on the walkie. I remember the men gathering around us.

"It was in the deepest part of the lake, then only 15 feet at most, that we found a huge pocket of human remains. There were six or seven layers of bones piled upon one another. It was insane. No one could believe it. Some of the first skeletons found were wrapped in chains, some even had blocks of cement around their ankles. And I believe there were a large number of smaller skeletons as well, obviously children.

"I had all crews stop working and called it in immediately. It took only about 20 minutes for a huge number of police to descend upon the area. The officers detained and interviewed us all. No one got to see much, there just wasn't time, but the officials were paranoid the find would leak out to the media and they'd have to make a statement. A diving team was brought in within the hour and a blockade set up to keep anyone from leaving the scene."

Laura was in awe. "While all this was going on around you, did you ever feel in danger?"

"Of course I did. I knew the situation could turn bad at any second. And no one but the company knew where we were. Working for the city all my life, I knew things could be fabricated. We could all have just disappeared in a tragic 'train disaster', anything that could go on record accounting for the tightening of a loose thread.

"Obviously, it never worked out that way, thank God, but still, the find was never released to the media and none of us ever received an official apology for being detained. And they wouldn't tell any of us how many bodies they recovered. But that in itself said something..."

"How could they have kept this quiet?" She was appalled.

He shook his head. "I know for certain there are three distinct regions that are ceremonial Native American Indian burial grounds in the surrounding area. One is that island we found in the lake. Even though there were decades worth of other bodies piled on top, that place has all the markings of a historical cemetery. The other two sights are in the marshlands, the area called Bear Hollow, across Northwest Highway and Buckner Boulevard. There the lake turns into a sediment-choked marshland and goes on for miles. It's like a swamp with indigenous wildlife, though I've never heard of bears reported." He chuckled, to Laura's amusement. "But God only knows what's out there... I've seen markers left by the tribes themselves. I've even registered some, but they have never appeared on an official census."

"Why hasn't the state attempted preservation of any of these burial sites if they know they exist?"

"Your guess is as good as mine. I had one man visit me the day after all this happened who introduced himself as an executive with the 'holding company', whatever that meant. He told me I was never to discuss the remains *or* the burial grounds with anyone outside of the company. I would lose my job and he implied that they could take legal action." Wilkinson laughed nervously. "They didn't want anyone to know. Probably still don't. When I saw your request for an interview online, I thought it had been so long since I retired that I could finally help in some way..."

He paused and sighed, his eyes clouded over with sentiment. When he spoke again his voice was constricted with emotion. "I've felt so guilty about all of this ever since. I've had dreams about it over and over for years. A figure, staring out at the lake, crying. An entire family, cast into the water..."

'Dreams. He's had dreams about this place!' Laura's heart began racing. She desperately wanted to ask him about his dreams in detail, hear everything he had to say. But she was here to get the facts only. And she could see by the way he stared out at the vast expanse of water that he was telling the truth. She kept it to herself.

"You had nothing to do with the cover-up, Mr. Wilkinson. Don't burden yourself."

"You're right. I just wish I knew the truth. How much is being kept from us everyday, all of us?" He shook his head as if to rid himself of the memory. "I'm sorry..."

"Don't apologize. There should be more men like you." She quickly changed the subject to keep him going. "Now, you were telling me about the area. What do you know about the Mt. Vernon replica H.L. Hunt had built on the lake?"

"Well, the story is that Hunt purchased the house around 1938 from a cotton merchant for $69,000. He seemed to have had a strong urge to live on the lake. And he always admired Washington in some obsessive way, enough to have his home modified to resemble the original Mt. Vernon and be displayed on a public lake site. Kind of crazy, if you ask me, but I suppose he had his reasons. That's really all I know."

"Thank you, sir, for your time. This really helps."

Wilkinson stretched silently. He looked at his shoes and tried to be unassuming. "If you don't mind me asking, Ms. Milton, what are you looking for?"

She hesitated for just a moment. "The ghost."

"I figured." Wilkinson looked up and stared out at the majestic view of the lake with a sigh. "Well, for what it's worth, if it's a ghost you're looking for, I think you're in the right place..."

* * *

Laura sat on the hood of her car for an hour after Wilkinson had left watching the sun descend. It blazed a brilliant orange and purple behind a grey band of clouds, slowly burning itself up like a red celestial ember dying in the sky. Staring into the sunset, she thought of the visions that have haunted her dreams throughout the years, the deep sadness she felt upon waking. How long have these visions been a part of her life? Did it start when she first saw that floating woman in the haze so long ago, or had she always dreamt of her? Laura couldn't remember a time when the Lady of the Lake hadn't been part of her life...

The sun was only a dark blue smear in the violet clouds by the time the Metroplex Ghost Hunters van pulled up next to the Land Rover. A stylized Death's Head logo was skinned on the side of the van with the initials MGH underneath. Laura smiled to herself. Whatever possessed her to go this route, she'd never know. But it was too late to change her mind now.

The side door of the van slid open and two of the crew jumped out and started removing equipment, ignoring her. Everyone was dressed in black shirts and jeans, Doc Martens or some other utility boots, field gear hanging off of utility belts, and night-vision goggles hanging around their necks. To Laura they looked like homemade terrorists. Or the Ghostbusters, sans the portable nuclear-powered proton packs.

Samuel was the last out of the van. He took one look at Laura and was concerned. Her eyes were blood-shot and she was pale white.

"You alright?"

"It's been a long afternoon, but yeah, thanks."

Samuel could see that she was exhausted. But instead of sabotaging the moment and saying something, he decided to support her in any way possible. She was a big girl. If she needed his help, hopefully she would ask for it. If not, he would be here to catch her if she fell. Happily.

"You remember Rachel. And this is Danny." The two ghost hunters gestured politely and continued prepping the equipment. They were both vaguely Goth and each had multiple visible tattoos running up their arms.

"Hi." Laura waved.

"The other guys are at Point B checking data loggers."

"What's a 'data logger'?"

Samuel pulled a thin metal spike from his pocket. It looked like a large golfing tee.

"It's a small USB device that can be programmed how often to record temperature, humidity and dew point. You plant it in the location you want to monitor, leave it, and collect the data later. Standard-issue ghost hunting paraphernalia."

Rachel started taking photographs of the area, two cameras hanging around her neck. She shot details of the geography, different perspectives of the focal points, with high-speed color and infrared film. It would soon be too dark for conventional digital photography. Danny continued checking the electronic gear.

Laura sighed. She couldn't believe that she was here with a crew of ghost hunters searching for *her* ghost. She felt a sense of possession, of ownership of the Lady of the Lake. Staring out at the water, she felt a connection she couldn't deny.

There was a click behind her and turning she saw Rachel looking at her camera. She leaned over and showed Laura the photograph. It was the exact scene from Laura's dreams, except that *Laura* was the one staring out at the expansive body of water. Which only made it that more creepy. Chills shot up her spine in waves. This was already promising to be one hell of a night.

Samuel plucked the walkie-talkie from his belt. "Lizard-brain? This is Thorhammer. We are at the Fortress of Solitude, come-back."

A voice crackled through the speaker. "I read you loud and clear, Thorhammer. Over."

Laura looked at Rachel with a smirk. The gothic ghost hunter rolled her eyes and walked on. Laura tried not to laugh out loud at how incredibly geeky this all was.

Samuel continued. "Start a large-scale EMF sweep of the perimeter from H12 through 15. Stay in front of the tree line.

We'll shoot some infrared and then head down Lawther to Garland Road and meet you at Checkpoint B in 20. Over."

Sam turned back to Laura and motioned around him. "There are burial grounds all over this marshland. It's not a wonder your little girl is drawn to stay here. She probably has a lot of company." He threw a light backpack over his shoulder.

"Are we ready, ladies? Time to pick us up a ghost."

The group climbed into the van and headed out towards the second East Lawther entrance off Buckner Boulevard. Samuel drove the van slowly down the deserted street. "We know our little lady likes to hitchhike and this is her preferred route. Let's see if we can find her."

Danny held the EMF device out the window.

Laura looked at him and snorted. "You really think you can find her with that, out the window?"

"Ms. Milt'n," Danny slurred in a thick East-Texas accent, "ghost huntin's 15% technology and 85% luck. And I happen to be *very* lucky."

A light started blinking on the EMF device.

"Woah! And it looks like I'm battin' a thousand... Heavy spike, Sammy, right in the range! Gotta be twenty yards or less. Slow 'er down."

Laura leaned over and whispered to Rachel, "Do these guys *really* know what they're doing?"

"Sad but true, these guys are the best."

Danny shouted out. "Hold it! Dead cold. *Nothin'*."

Samuel cursed between his teeth. "Goddamnit."

"She ain't gonna make it *that* easy." Danny was really starting to enjoy this. "It's ok, honey, we're *friends*," he cooed. "We ain't gonna hurt chew..."

The van was starting to get a little claustrophobic for Laura's taste. She turned to Rachel to get her mind off her nerves.

"Do ghosts have personalities?"

"I've seen apparitions take on full personality traits. Playfulness, defensiveness, even spite and revenge. They seem to be totally mindful and volitional, when they want to be."

"Kinda like people?" The women smiled at one another.

Samuel turned into a park down closer to the lake. Just as they entered the lot the EMF spiked.

"*Bingo!*"

The van rolled to a stop. Everyone looked out the windows simultaneously towards the center of the park. There was a single dead tree standing ominously in the clearing like a monolith shooting into the night sky with the black tree line behind it. Something was there. All the hair stood up on Laura's neck as her whole body shivered.

"*They're here...*" Danny said in a child's voice.

Samuel looked around, suddenly aware that something was very different. "What the fuck?"

"Does anyone else feel that?" Rachel asked.

"I do." Laura hugged herself.

Danny looked at one of his instruments. "The temperature just dropped 10 degrees. Instantly."

Samuel reached for the EMF. "Gimme."

Danny handed Samuel the unit as he and Laura jumped out of the van and slowly approached the tree. He could feel something watching him from all sides. As soon as he got within 10 feet of the huge black trunk, the EMF went wild.

"Danny, come look at this! It's off the map!"

Standing next to him, Laura could almost see something rising from the ground with the mist. Something pressed against her, caressing her. The sensation was hypnotic and sensual, almost like a lover's touch. A faint smell of perfume filled the air for just a moment. Then it was gone almost as quickly as it had appeared.

Danny walked up to Samuel and the EMF blinked at a different frequency.

"Wait. It's gone." He looked around pointing the device and went slowly to the left.

The presence let Laura go. She jerked back and realized what had just happened. Samuel was looking past her.

"What is it?"

"It's moving." He swept the device around and grabbed the walkie from his belt with his other hand.

"Lizard-brain, do you copy? We have a strong reading here at Point B. Comeback."

The walkie spit and chattered. "We're on our way."

Samuel put his hand on Laura's shoulder.

"You ok?"

Tears were coming from Laura's eyes. "Yeah," she nodded her head slowly. "She's so *sad*..."

Samuel turned the device back around behind them and walked a few paces forward.

"She's heading back towards the road."

"Not good," Danny said. "Power lines. We'll lose 'er."

"She's going..." Samuel was almost shaking. "Damnit, babe, we were just getting started..." He searched around a little more. Nothing.

"Man, she was right here..." He lowered the device and tried to get a clear perspective of what was happening. "What is she doing? We didn't scare her..."

Rachel agreed, "No, we didn't."

"She was waiting for us..." Samuel turned to look at Laura, his brain deciphering the last few moments. She felt his gaze and slowly turned towards him. "She was waiting for *you*, Laura."

Samuel kept on formulating. He motioned behind her to the van still sitting on the street. "She saw us get out of the van," he continued, "and saw..." He was thinking. What would he do if he were the ghost? The van was open and filled with equipment. It suddenly hit him.

"She saw we didn't have room for her... She's headed back to the lake to look for another ride!"

He spoke into the walkie. "Lizard-brain, we're headed back to the Fortress. She's backtracking."

He turned to the small group of ghost hunters. "We have to get back to the lake."

* * *

The group ran through the black tangle of trees, hearts pounding in rhythm to their steps. At one point, Laura heard strange noises crashing in the trees beside them and was certain someone or something was running along side them.

Finally they came to a clearing. Laura recognized the pale open shell of the boathouse sitting about 100 meters away at the base of Teepee Hill. It had 36 bays, and the windows and doors had long since been removed. The building stood like a bleached skeleton washed up on the shore.

"This is where I saw the ghost as a child."

Danny stepped into the structure holding the EMF. "I'm gettin' all kinds of readings here, Sam. Everywhere."

Rachel was taking infrared photos of the exterior. "He's right. There is something here. All over the place."

Laura closed her eyes. She felt something pressing against her once again, like cold hands running up her thighs, traveling over her breasts, over her pubic mound, pressing into her through the thin fabric of her clothes.

At that moment two men leapt out of the darkness, running towards the group. Laura screamed as they dashed out of the trees.

Samuel jumped in. "Laura, this is Vic and Garry. They're the guys we've been waiting for. Thanks for joining us, gentlemen." Samuel's tone did not go un-noticed. He was pissed.

"It's my fault," Vic said. "We had a spike and I made the call to follow. We lost it on the other side of the Bath House."

"It was really moving," Garry said.

Samuel looked at Rachel. "How'd you do?"

"I'm golden."

"Good girl." He ran his fingers through his hair.

"Killas, I think we're done for the night. Nice work everyone. I want to check the film and the new data loggers at Lawther. I'm sure they'll prove it."

"Prove what?" Laura asked.

"That we just met your girl tonight. Face to face."

Twenty

After her eventful evening with the Metroplex Ghost Hunters, Laura was equally energized and exhausted. She returned to the hotel, took a shower, and started decompressing. After scrolling through Netflix and indulging in some mindless Internet surfing, she was officially restless.

Reaching for her laptop, she began reading about the Hilton Hotel in the late 1980's. This was the place to be back in the day. So much to read and index... The task seemed to have no end. The clock on her taskbar said 12:38 AM. She had taken half of a muscle relaxer earlier and it had had an interesting, if not annoying, side effect. And she didn't quite know what to do about it.

It had been months since she had been with Colin. And though she hated to admit it, she missed his touch. And she so wanted to be touched. Even though they weren't together, she always knew she could call him if she were lonely. If he were anywhere in the same city, he would come to her. The trip to Texas was a great experience, but she was more than cognizant of the fact that she was entirely alone here.

Except for Mallory, that is. What a serendipitous event meeting him turned out to be; he was completely hot, the sex was amazing, if a little alarming, he let her have her space, *and* he lived in another city. He was almost perfect. She was certain that it was only a matter of time before she'd do something to screw that up as well...

Sounds started coming from the wall behind her headboard. They sounded like muffled gasps. Laura laughed to herself. The thought of some timid little couple having a rambunctious second honeymoon on the other side of the wall was extremely hot. Good for them. At least someone was having fun in this chamber of horrors. And by the woman's groans, it sounded like quality playtime.

After a night like this, she was far too antsy to just sit and listen to her neighbors pound one another into oblivion. Laura closed her laptop, reached for the remote, and turned the television on for distraction. A couple appeared on the screen naked and embracing. Laura stared at the soft porn for a moment in disbelief and then flipped the set off. That wasn't helping her situation. She picked up a magazine and the cover article was "The Most Amazing Sex of Your Life". She sighed heavily and threw it down. On the wall, she noticed, was a headless female nude on silkscreen. On the table, a miniature of Michelangelo's David stood naked as the day is long, his fig leaf jutting out prominently.

'Ok, this is getting ridiculous...' She knew she could just masturbate, but in her state it would only fuel the fire.

She stood up and looked at herself in the full-length mirror. Laura had always been a bit of a gym-rat so for the most part she was in decent shape. Good legs and arms, flat tummy. But she didn't consider herself attractive. Her face was pretty and men seemed to gravitate towards her, but they did that to every girl with such little discrimination that it almost meant nothing to her. It wasn't that she didn't want attention, she just didn't want to have to advertise to get it.

Laura lifted her shirt to look at her belly. She was tanned and had the makings of a six-pack. Actually, it was more like two 40-ouncers, she once joked to a friend. She turned sideways and sucked in her gut all the way till she could see her ribs. She could never fit the stereotype of the anorexic waif. Not with *her* hips. She then pushed her stomach out in a pooch till she looked almost pregnant. Ugh. So not a good look. Who the hell would ever find *that* sexy?

She dropped her shirt and grabbed her breasts, weighing them in her hands. Though pert and natural, their size was less than impressive.

Turning around, she looked over her shoulder at her ass in her cotton shorts in the mirror. She clenched her butt-cheeks and released. Again. She bounced up and down, jiggling her cheeks and watching it in the mirror for a moment. She smacked herself on the hip, and smiled. Yep. Definitely her best feature.

The moaning began again behind her headboard and she sighed in frustration. It would be great to have some company tonight. Especially, some intimate company. For a second, she thought of Colin...

She picked up her phone and, though it was late, she dialed Mallory's number. After 3 rings there was no answer. She hung up before it went to voicemail, disappointed. She knew she had no business falling for the stereotypical stranger in another city, but he seemed genuinely interested in her. Besides, the sex the other night had been intense. That was by far the most spontaneous tryst that she had ever engaged in. She was almost embarrassed by how little restraint she showed with him. And when he let her come first, it was all over - the gates had been opened and she became shamelessly vulnerable to him. She needed to feel him against her, to feel his desire for her pushing him further and further into darkness. She wanted more of it. The thought of it set her on fire.

'If he only knew what he was missing tonight...'

She decided to get off her ass and have a cocktail downstairs to cool off. In 10 minutes she had thrown on a pair of jeans and a tee shirt, pulled her hair back in a ponytail, and headed out the door.

She walked out of the room and instantly felt a change in the atmosphere, like a barometric shift in air pressure. The hallway was empty but she felt claustrophobic, like something was hovering next to her, following her every move as she walked to the elevators.

It was dark. The lights seemed dimmer in the hallway than she remembered. She heard a door open behind her. Turning around, she saw she was alone. She kept walking. It seemed like the corridor went on forever. Was this just the muscle relaxer taking hold or was it something else?

Finally, she came to the inlet for the elevators. The doors were made of shiny brushed chrome. She pushed the button and the doors slid open. She stepped inside and exhaled, feeling a little safer in the confines of the car. She pushed the button for the lobby. The doors didn't move. She pushed the button again. Still, they were frozen open. A wave of chills washed over her. She imagined some unseen force holding the doors open, waiting. But for what?

Laura mashed the button with all her might before the doors finally closed and the elevator descended to the lobby with a gentle lurch. The sudden rush sent her heart racing. She took a moment to regulate her breathing, slowly, in and out, until she felt stable. The last thing she wanted was a seizure now. She steadied herself as the doors opened on the lobby floor.

The Highland's bar and dining room was called Knife. The décor was modern and minimalist and seemed like a welcome retreat for Laura. It reminded her a lot of Bobst Library with its high ceilings and walls of windows. Nothing like cold, detached open spaces to make her feel right at home.

There were small groups of people scattered throughout the bar. Not many people out on a Monday night. Good. Even though some company would be nice, the last thing she wanted was to be groped in a crowd of strangers. And for some reason, that didn't seem like such a stretch for some of the people who were mulling about.

Laura took a seat at the illuminated glass bar and ordered a cocktail from the handsome male bartender. Christ, she was still so worked up. If only Mallory could miraculously appear, make love to her, and then get the hell out she would be eternally grateful. Unfortunately, it just wasn't in the cards.

Across the room two young businessmen were drinking and talking to one another. One of them noticed Laura across the room sitting alone. He looked at his partner, nodded in her direction, and they both walked to the bar.

The taller of the two turned to her. "Can I get you something?"

At that moment the bartender placed a club soda with lime in front of her.

"Just ordered. Thanks. Maybe later."

"I'm Josh. My friend and I were just discussing the–"

Her phone rang. She looked down and saw it was Mallory calling.

"Excuse me, I've been waiting for this."

She turned away from them and answered the phone. The guy and his friend made a face and continued talking to each other in hushed voices.

"Hey. Thanks for the save," Laura purred into the receiver.

"The *save*?"

"Long story. Come meet me at the Highland."

While she was preoccupied on the phone, one of the men leaned over and dropped a small pill in Laura's glass and silently walked back to the other side of the bar.

Laura was struggling to hear Mallory over the dull roar behind his voice. "I'd love to," he was saying, "but there's no way. We're slammed. I won't be out of here at least till 2. Sorry."

"Not a problem. We can do it some other time." She was surprised at how disappointed she was. Not a good sign.

"You bet. Hey, I've been thinking about you. A lot. I'll call you tomorrow."

"Kay. Have a good night..." *Click.*

She sat back, annoyed at herself. *'There is no reason to feel so rejected,'* she told herself. She was pouting like a schoolgirl and was embarrassed about it.

Laura picked up her glass and drank half of it in one swallow. She tasted something bitter and put it down without finishing it. The young business guy had come up behind her and was ordering another round from the bartender and pointed to Laura.

"One more here, too. On my tab."

"No, I think I'm ok... Thank you." God, but she hated pushy men. No one ever bothered her in Manhattan or even when she visited friends in Los Angeles.

A small group of people had entered the dining room. Apparently, a show had just let out at the Winspear or the Wyly Theatre, or maybe something at SMU. The patrons were dressed in formal regalia; the men, in handsome dark fitted suits and the women, in black floor-length gowns accessorized with opulent jewelry and ravishing hair and make-up styles. It was a refined crowd that appeared more discerning than most. She absently wondered how many of these people knew anything about the atrocities that had occurred behind these walls decades ago...

Laura felt a shiver run through her and turned around in her chair. A beautiful, statuesque woman was staring at her across the populated room. Even in the distance the woman's eyes glittered like emeralds set in her ashen face. She was a platinum blonde, very slender and tall. Her style was timeless but with a modern flair that made her seem European. Laura caught herself staring back before even realizing what was happening. The woman caught Laura returning her look and smiled warmly. The annoying business guy next to Laura touched her arm and distracted her for just a second. When Laura turned back the woman was gone.

"Sure I can't get you another?"

* * *

Back upstairs, Laura carefully put her cardkey in the reader and stumbled into her hotel room. She didn't have any alcohol, there was no way she could be so inebriated. The asshole at the bar must have slipped her something. *Damnit!*

She shuffled over to the wall and leaned on her shoulder in an attempt to take her shoe off. She slipped and almost fell over.

She kicked them off and fell into the bathroom. The light came on automatically and she almost jumped out of her skin.

"*Crap!*"

Seeing the motion sensor on the light-switch, she relaxed. Until she looked in the mirror. She looked like she had been smoking crack all week.

"Would I like another drink... Ugh. Damned date raper..."

Laura splashed water on her face, stripped to her panties, made her way into the bedroom and fell face-first onto the bed. In seconds, she was passed out on her stomach snoring lightly.

In the haze of the drug, she started lucid dreaming. Her sight was not her own. Her height, her muscle-mass, even the deep rumbling of her breath felt foreign to her. She felt herself walking out of an elevator. The thing that was not her crept forward, its heart pounding rapidly. She felt her legs tense and she started dashing down the hallway. There was a sense of urgency, a maliciousness coming from this thing that she had become. She was the beast, the anger was radiating from her.

She moved quickly through the hall, passing room after room until she came to #627. She felt herself go under the door and materialize on the other side. Across the room, she saw herself sprawled on the bed sleeping. She bounded across the room in a single step and towered over the foot of the bed staring down at herself.

Laura sat up, suddenly awake, and turned on the light. The thing was gone. She was back in her own body. The dream had let her go.

She sensed movement, something passing beside the bed. Turning around, she saw nothing but her own reflection in the glass windows behind her. Even in the dark, she could feel all her baby-fine hair on her arms standing on end.

"Jesus, can a girl catch a fucking break here?"

Something started moaning in the dark, and this time it sounded like it was under her bed. She listened for a moment to make sure it wasn't the neighbors. This was not the sound of people making love, it was the sound of something dying. Or about to attack.

Laura shook her head trying to focus. Something was here in the room with her! She grabbed the robe lying next to her and leaped off the bed. Grabbing the handle, she threw the door open and fell out letting it slam shut behind her.

She struggled to her feet in the deserted hallway. Staying close to the wall she started down the corridor. Where to, she didn't know. Anywhere to get away from the surprise visitor in her room...

Slowly, she made her way to the elevators just as a drunken couple stumbled out of the car, laughing and hobbling past her. Their voices stopped and when Laura looked back, the couple had disappeared. Another wave of chills washed over her and her mouth filled with bile. Swallowing hard, she shook it off and continued on down the hall to the other side of the building. She was under attack and had to get some distance from here, quickly.

Toward the end of the hallway, there was an indentation in the wall next to a swath of fabric hanging from the ceiling. She pulled back the curtain and there was a sharp turn where the hallway continued to the left.

She rounded the hidden corner and continued on, realizing the walls seemed different in this part of the hotel, more classic in design, a different texture to the plaster. The carpet felt different on her bare feet as well.

Turning another corner, she saw there was a single elevator entrance at the far end of a narrow hallway. Large black planters sat on either side, each overflowing with colorful and exotic flowers. The door was obsidian black.

Laura stepped slowly forward, acutely aware that this level of curiosity was totally out of character, even for her. Danger was radiating like mad from this place, but instead of listening to her intuition, she was enthralled by the chills coursing through her limbs. Something was interrupting her logic; pulling her forward, beckoning her to ignore her fear, and making her hungry to see what was beyond the curtain separating reality from the unknown. Faint whispers were seeping from the walls in muted supplications, keeping her putting one foot in front of the other until she was standing directly in front of the elevator door, mesmerized. Sighing loudly, she fought to regain mental clarity. She had allowed herself to come this far. It was enough. Now was the time to simply turn around, go back to her room, and forget this place altogether.

Instead, she reached out and pushed the green call button on the wall. The black door slid back revealing an elegant brushed chrome interior. Without thinking she stepped inside. The doors slid shut and she felt movement. There was no music, just a quiet far away hum and the sensation of rising.

In moments the car stopped and the door opened automatically revealing yet another narrow hallway that ran for about 50 feet in front of her. There was another black door with no markings at the far end. By the strip of flickering amber light cast into the hall floor, she could tell the door was open.

Laura slowly crept out of the elevator and started down the hall. Her entire body was buzzing with warning signs, but she wasn't sure if it was the drug racing in her veins or just her nerves.

She came to the door and quietly pushed it open, stepping into an expansive private suite that seemed to encompass the entire penthouse level of the building. The wall facing her was a bank of windows displaying a breath-taking view of downtown Dallas in the distance. Plush couches and chairs filled the space. There was a sunken living area with a floating aluminum fireplace in the center, ignited and inviting.

Laura sensed someone watching her. She turned around just as a silhouette emerged from the shadows. A train of blonde hair glowed like a pale flame as the figure passed into the light. Laura's heartbeat quickened. The European woman from the bar was standing in a cobalt blue silk robe across the room intently watching her.

"I'm so sorry," Laura stammered, "I don't even know where I am. I'm trespassing. I–"

The woman spoke slowly. "It's alright. No one ever comes up here so I leave the door open. It's my fault. Don't be embarrassed." Her accent was thick, not Hungarian but perhaps Russian or Slovakian. But her English was excellent.

"You're the woman from the bar," Laura said.

The woman stepped forward and smiled warmly. "I'm Eva. I hope you didn't mind me staring. You are so beautiful."

Laura blushed at the comment. "I live on the premises and usually know everyone and everything that happens here."

"You live here in the hotel? Not in the apartments next door?"

"They have trouble leasing certain spaces in the hotel. Some people are superstitious and feel... uncomfortable in parts of the building. Nothing bothers me." She stopped directly in front of Laura.

"Uncomfortable? What do you mean?"

Eva paused, obviously searching for the right words to explain. "The state of this property is not something that is advertised much. Places have memory, just like we do. This hotel has seen its share of things..."

"Do you live alone?"

"By myself, yes... but I'm far from alone." Eva smiled the smile of an angel. She was the most beautiful woman Laura had ever seen. So demure, so gentle, so desirable...

Eva put a cool palm to the side of Laura's face.

"You remind me of someone I knew a long time ago." She gazed into Laura's eyes. Laura had never felt such a strong connection with another woman. It was like electricity. "Would you like a drink?" Eva asked.

Laura laughed. "Ah, no, thank you. I've had enough tonight already. I'm Laura, by the way." She extended her hand. The woman did not reach for it.

"What are you searching for, Laura?"

Laura felt very small, as if she had never really thought about her goal. And in a flash of introspection, she found herself afraid and ashamed. "I'm not sure..." Tears welled up in the corners of her brown eyes.

Eva reached out and placed the silken palm of her hand between Laura's breasts and sighed deeply.

"I feel such loss in you..."

Laura couldn't take any more. Sleep deprived, ill, and frightened, the tears began to flow in front of this beautiful stranger.

"I'm so tired..." She all but collapsed in Eva's arms.

Eva helped Laura to the couch. "Sit. Rest. You are in a safe place." They sat next to one another. Eva took Laura's hand in a natural gesture. Her touch was gentle and cool, Laura thought, like water. "I understand searching. I never knew my parents. And though I have had many wonderful loves and experiences in my life, my heart has been forever empty..."

Laura looked up through her tears. Eva's green eyes caressed her, holding her in their compassionate gaze. The woman was ravishing. She looked like a porcelain statue; Aphrodite carved from Nordic bone and flesh.

Eva leaned over and kissed Laura gently on the lips. Laura was mesmerized. She didn't have the time to protest or think, her body simply reacted to the touch. Her heart was hammering in her chest. She couldn't believe herself. Her tears of humiliation were barely drying on her cheek and here she was allowing this woman to touch her. Her head was swimming. What was happening?

"Such sadness..." Eva's voice was like velvet. "What can I do for you?"

She gently pulled Laura's robe off her shoulders revealing her naked chest underneath. Laura closed her eyes as the woman put a cold hand on her breast, gently rolling the nipple between her icy fingers as she leaned into Laura lightly kissing her on the lips. It felt like the wings of a frozen butterfly. The woman's mouth grazed her shoulder, sending shockwaves through her unlike any she had ever felt before. Gently working her way between Laura's breasts, Eva took a nipple between her cold lips. Laura gasped, pulling the woman closer to her, holding her in place. She never wanted it to end.

The woman pulled away gently and laid Laura onto her back. She continued kissing her trembling body, holding the younger woman's arms down gently but firmly against the couch. Laura lifted her head, watching Eva's every move.

Down Eva's mouth went, slowly and passionately, her lips caressing Laura's taut stomach, her icy tongue leaving a trail inching towards the younger woman's hot center. So lovely, so comforting... Closing her eyes, Laura gave into the ecstasy as the night wrapped around them like a blanket...

* * *

Shivering, woke Laura from a deep sleep. Slowly opening her eyes, she immediately knew something was terribly wrong.

'Oh, my God!'

She had been sleeping on a tall pallet of vinyl flooring covered with newspaper in the empty, unfinished penthouse spanning the entire top floor of the Highland hotel. There was no furniture, no sheetrock, no walls; only naked columns and a cement slab for a floor surrounded by a continuous wall of glass. And most of all, there was no *Eva*. The early morning sun was barely cresting over the downtown skyscrapers bathing her in crimson light.

She wrapped her robe around her and gingerly jumped off the pallet of material, landing on her bare feet on the cold, grimy cement floor. Tears fell in hot rivers down her face as she threw open the fire door and stumbled back to her room.

* * *

The hotel room curtains were shut, blocking out the morning sun. Laura sat on the floor in the walk-in closet holding her phone to her head. Her eyes were swollen with tears. Colin was on the line. His silence was lingering.

"...I'm in the middle of this installation now. But I'll be there Saturday," he said, finally.

"No, don't do this–"

"Laura..." His voice was patient but she could hear his frustration. "I'm not going to let you stay there by yourself. I'm coming to bring you home. You're in danger." His voice was getting louder. "You don't know any of these people. I can't believe you..."

"Not now. You're right, but please, just not now..." She started crying again.

He sighed loudly on the other end of the phone. "I might have to fly stand-by. I'll let you know when I find out."

"'Kay..."

"Stay away from strangers."

"I will."

"I'll be there soon. Don't worry."

"Thank you–"

The line went dead. Colin sounded furious but she knew he was frightened as well. She could hear it in his voice. And she couldn't blame him.

She had told him about the guy at the bar who drugged her and about waking up in some forgotten part of the hotel, but she didn't have the courage to tell him about Eva. Not only would he refuse to believe it, but he also might start wondering about her orientation, and with everything else going on with them, that was the *last* thing she needed to worry about. There was no way she could have explained the sequence of events to him. Hell, she couldn't even explain it to herself.

There was a common probability theory called "Ockham's Razor" that came to her mind, something she had learned in her first year of college. It was a basic precept relating to the scientific method of gathering data. The theory states, basically, that all things being equal, the least-complex solution is usually the correct one. So the question was: did she actually have a nocturnal liaison with a spectral lover from beyond the grave who had the power to project a complex illusion in which to rape her? Or had she simply been a victim of her own imagination? Delirious from the effects of the drugs and excitable from the events at the lake, did she in fact create the entire episode in her mind? It seemed the scientific method was making mincemeat of her defense.

She was dizzy. She had missed two of her medication doses in the last 36 hours. That, on top of the muscle relaxer and the roofie that guy at the bar slipped her, was more than enough to induce a seizure. She felt sick and needed some sleep, black, dreamless sleep; sleep that could wipe out the last 12 hours; sleep that could erase all the guilt and fear and need she's harbored for the last 24 years of her pathetic life...

She needed the sleep of the dead.

* * *

Laura was tossing and turning in bed when Bach's *'Bourrée in E Minor'* began erupting from her phone. The room was pitch black. She reached out and groped for the pulsing phone in the dark and miraculously found it, answering with her eyes still closed.

"*What?*"

"Are you asleep?" She recognized Samuel's voice.

"Oh my God, what time is it?"

"Ah, it's 3 in the afternoon, killa. Time to get serious." Laura leapt out of bed. "Listen, I got the results back from the data loggers. There was definitely something there with us last night at the lake. The numbers are off the wall. And I'm convinced it was there to see you. I'm emailing you a picture Rachel got at the boathouse now. And a close-up detail..."

"Hold on."

She went to the desk and flipped up the screen on her laptop. It came out of stand-by mode and a notice appeared from Samuel in her mail. Opening it, she saw a dark picture, but there was something visible, transparent, like mist, only it was in a serpentine shape, not dispersed. It looked like an arm. On the 'wrist' of the translucent 'hand' was what seems to be a sparkling bracelet. On the edge of the photo, there were wisps of what appeared to be blonde hair from off-camera. It was Rose Davis. She knew it.

"Thank you, Sam. For everything..."

Laura hung up the phone as he was saying goodbye. She was sure Samuel had seen the blonde hair and that alone was supporting proof of a connection with the woman in Laura's dreams, but what stood out to her was the bracelet with the tiny red flowers. She zoomed in and stared at it closely as all the hair on her arms slowly stood on end.

The flowers were roses.

Twenty One

Laura spent the rest of the day and most of the next morning in bed. She had set her alarm to wake her only to take her meds, which she did and then passed back out. When she woke up from her morning nap at noon on Wednesday, she felt like hell. It took a big breakfast to settle her stomach enough to even think about working. By 2 PM, she put on a pair of over-sized sunglasses and forced herself out into the afternoon sun.

Her second visit to the downtown Records Building was a little less hectic than before. On her previous visit she had made friends with the two archivists and today they were being overly helpful. One woman, Ruby, brought Laura a black and white photographic journal from 1962 that she had created for some personal research on JFK. Seeing that she had lost a full day yesterday, Laura was thankful for the help, but she wasn't about to get on the conspiracy bandwagon. Yes, the assassination undoubtedly shook the entire world, much less this city, to its foundation. But what Laura was seeking was just a minute detail of that entire macrocosm of corruption and speculation. It was difficult to shut that entire episode out of her research, but she had to keep focus on her goal of finding Rose Davis.

Even with all the statistical inconsistencies, Rose had long ago become the focal point of this investigation. In the back of her mind Laura could already hear Colin lecturing her in his holier-than-thou pious tone: “Laura,” he’d say as if talking to a three-year-old, “what you are investigating is a *modern crime*, not a historic murder that is responsible for a haunting.” And that was when she would punch him square in the face.

Yes, there were a million facets to this White Rock story, conflicting accounts and probable identities of the ‘ghost’, none of which were verifiable. But what Laura lacked in hard and fast evidence was more than made up for with intuitive deduction; she knew in her heart that it was the spirit of Rose Davis that restlessly haunted White Rock Lake. And for some reason, this long-dead woman was reaching out to her. Perhaps it was simply the lure of Laura’s radiant gift of empathy that attracted Rose’s spirit, like all the other entities she’d experienced over the years. But perhaps it was something more...

Laura knew if she told any of this to Colin, he would have called her crazy. No surprise there. But his skepticism wasn’t about to make her second-guess herself. Not this time.

Laura had multiple windows open on her laptop. Checking email, she saw she had received a reply from the head of Human Resources at Neiman-Marcus. There had definitely been a woman named Rose Marie Davis on the employee records from October 1968 till June 1969. That was a huge score for the home team. At least now she had one piece of *factual* evidence verifying a part of the puzzle that wasn’t an eyewitness or simply hearsay.

Laura turned back to her open tabs. Rose Marie *Millstone* was born at Rickland Memorial Hospital on January 9, 1944, in Houston, Texas. Her mother was Chesapeake Lyra Millstone; no father was listed on any document. On the birth certificate, the second signature belonged to Warren Millstone, Chesapeake’s father. Laura thought for a moment. Millstone had obviously been there to verify the birth because of Chesapeake’s age. She had just turned 13 years old only two months before Rose was born.

Laura sat back in her chair, totally shocked and confused. What could possibly account for Chesapeake, a debutante from a wealthy, high-profile Texas family, getting pregnant at such a young age? The 40's weren't colonial times, for Christsake. It seemed so out of character for a family of their stature. And to have no account of the identity of the father...

Who fathered Rose Marie? Laura wrote the question down in her notebook in large print and under-lined it. Staring at the words, she realized she had found an important element to this entire story: discovering the identity of Rose's father would answer so many things. Still, the *real* question was: if Rose Davis was indeed the White Rock Lady, how did she die and why?

OK, one thing at a time...

Laura turned back to her screen and continued reading. In 1945, a year and a half after Rose's birth, Chesapeake Millstone and her daughter moved to Dallas to live with Lester Davis at his inherited home on White Rock Lake. The couple was married 3 months later, in September, and Davis legally adopted Rose. The girl was only 21 months old. Strange. Why would Chesapeake move here, away from her only family? And what was the connection with Davis? He was so much older than she. How did they first meet?

Laura changed her focus. She wanted to know more about Chesapeake's background, where her family originated. She logged onto two of Colin's subscription record sites and did multiple searches. In moments she was staring at pages of reference links.

"Talk to me..."

Laura opened four different articles on her screen and began reading, cutting and pasting headlines and paragraphs into a master document as she went.

Chesapeake's family lineage went back to before the Civil War. Her great-grandparents had been founding settlers of

Friendswood, Texas, a quiet Quaker-established community that became a thriving settlement just outside of Houston.

Chesapeake's grandmother, Beatrice Anne Lytle, had been raised by very strict Quaker parents until she ran away in 1909 and married Earl Clement, Jr. at the age of 14. Clement, only 21, had been a soldier in the Spanish/American War and had just returned to the States as a war hero. A year later, Beatrice gave birth to her only daughter, Rosalyn Mable.

Beatrice contracted syphilis somehow. From the atmosphere at the time, Laura speculated Lytle probably brought it back from the war. Either that, or he had a taste for prostitutes, brought the venereal disease home, and infected his wife. Either way, Beatrice died in an insane asylum at the age of 22 in 1911.

Clement married his cousin Cynthia Grettle, herself a cattle heiress, two years later and they raised Rosalyn as their own.

The Clements, for the most part stayed out of the public eye until a 1930 wedding announcement in the Houston Chronicle for Rosalyn Mable Clement to Warren Millhouse, the son of an oil family.

Laura thought for a moment. That was the year after the Great Stock Market Crash of '29. To the citizens living in that era the crash must have seemed like the end of the world. They sure as hell didn't have bailouts back then. She squirmed in her chair and kept reading. This was getting good.

Millhouse inherited a huge farmhouse from his family located in the countryside just outside of Houston, Texas. He took his young bride there and... The next two things Laura could find were a birth announcement and an obituary, both with the same date, November 12, 1931.

Chesapeake Lyra was born to Rosalyn and Warren Millhouse in 1931. A diabetic who was also suffering from acute anemia brought on by her pregnancy, Rosalyn Clement, only 21-years-old, died during childbirth at the family home, leaving Chesapeake to her father, Warren. *'How incredibly sad'*, Laura thought. She could identify with the loss, but she couldn't imagine what it would be like to never actually know your mother.

She remembered the Millhouse family from some earlier research. Warren had been the only son of Jackson Tanner Millhouse, an ex-grocery storeowner who had been a silent partner in Spindletop, the first great oil field found in 1901 in Beaumont, Texas. Even with his meager initial investment, Millhouse, Sr. became one of the first oil tycoons in America. That was the beginning of the oil boom. That one event changed the world's economic structure forever.

Laura read on. Warren, fully supported by his father, lived the life of an aristocrat and had been setting the scene to go into politics when he met his bride in 1930. After his wife's death, it seemed Millhouse became a recluse and was rarely seen until his death in 1984.

Wow, this was better than television, Laura thought. These people could easily have been the first reality family series. The Kardashians had *nothing* on them...

Either out of spite or out of convenience, Millhouse stayed single for the rest of his life. He became an intensely private man, shunning out most people except for a few close friends and business partners. He seemed to have hired nursemaids to care for Chesapeake around the clock. Laura found a Christmas picture from 1932 of 5 women posing with the infant.

Millhouse enrolled Chesapeake at St. Agnes Academy in Houston, an all-girls Catholic preparatory school, when she was four-years-old. The nuns there took Chesapeake in as their youngest boarder.

Her scholastic records at St. Agnes showed that Chesapeake was a happy child and excelled in her studies. She was on the honor roll three years in a row, excelling in her art and reading classes. By 6th grade she had won two regional poetry contests and was the darling of the English department.

In 7th grade, at the age of 12, Millhouse pulled her out of the school two weeks before summer commencement for unspecified health reasons. Nine months later, on the 9th of January, Rose Marie was born.

The next thing Laura could find was a short exposé on Chesapeake in a 1951 article on antiques. That was the year Davis opened a collector's warehouse for her, Davis Collectibles, near downtown Dallas. Evidently, over the years Chesapeake had become quite a collector of sorts. The article stated that she had upwards of tens of thousands of dollars invested in pre-civil war artifacts and clothing.

'She was trying to start her own business,' Laura thought. *'Good for her.'* Which proved that Chesapeake hadn't always been a raging lunatic. Something traumatic must have happened in her life to slowly unravel her through the years. She had spent time in St. Paul's Hospital's psychiatric ward in '59 and '61, which was noted. After that, there was no mention of Chesapeake having anything to do with the company whatsoever. Perhaps the business venture was more of an effort to keep her occupied than an actual testament to her mental stability. Again, finding the father of her daughter would answer so many questions...

Laura read on. After Chesapeake's death in 1968, Davis Collectibles all but completely disappeared from view. The Davis Collection itself was mentioned in numerous articles up to the present day, but just the artifacts as a compendium, nothing about the company itself. Laura cross-referenced her searches over and over but could find no other mention of the actual company Davis Collectibles after 1968. Very strange.

Laura made a note to research antique dealers in the area. If Chesapeake Davis had truly been that well known, someone would remember her and be able to answer some questions.

Well, one thing was certain: the women of the Clement family had made a habit out of dying tragically. It was almost as if the family was cursed. That had to have had some sort of effect on surviving relatives. God knows, living in the shadow of death had changed Laura in the deepest way possible.

Laura pushed that thought out of her head and went on to the next point of interest relating to Rose Davis: Kendall Reece. In 1966, Reece had been quoted in the Dallas Times Herald saying she was originally from Chicago, but Laura could find nothing to substantiate her claim; not a driver's license, a birth certificate, nothing. Aside from a modeling job for the 1967 Sears catalogue in Dallas, very little could be found about her at all. The surname '*Reece*' was probably an alias, Laura thought. The woman showed up in a few photographs from some private functions, benefits and galas in Dallas, at the Neiman-Marcus department store, but not much more.

In 1969, Reece's name had been transferred onto the lease of the Wilson Building apartment. A young lawyer by the name of Daniel Morrow owned the unit.

Laura remembered one interesting fact: Morrow was also Lester Davis' lawyer. '*What a tangled web...*'

She read on. Morrow was in a freak head-on collision with a bridge support later that same year. The car burst into flames and... Laura recoiled when she read the next sentence. He burned to death in his car. There were no other details on the death and the case was considered a traffic fatality.

There had to be more to this woman. Laura did another search and came upon a digital archive of men's magazines in Texas from the 1960's and 70's. How strange that there would even be such a thing, seeing as that Texas was such a conservative state.

Laura began clicking through an issue of something called Lost Girls, August 1968. There were pictorials of young women in various states of undress, light editorials about private sex parties, and interviews with strippers from the famed Jack Ruby clubs. Even though the photographs were nothing like modern pornography, they were pretty racy for the time. Some S&M, light bondage, spanking, but nothing like actual penetration. The women then were voluptuous and curvy, not the skinny sundried Barbie dolls of today. They were all woman, and damned proud of it.

On the next page, Laura found an interview with a raven-haired dancer by the name of Reece Carrie. Clad in black lace and stiletto heels, Laura recognized the stunning woman immediately. It was Kendall Reece in all her alluring glory. The pictures showed her on a stage surrounded by shadowed figures, grimacing like a conquering princess under the glaring spotlights for all to see. Another picture had her kissing another woman, which was pretty risqué for 1968. No doubt about it, it was Kendall Reece in the flesh. This made a lot of sense.

God knows what kind of things Reece may have had introduced Rose Davis to. What strange hold did this woman have on her? And why would someone like Reece befriend such an unassuming young girl in the first place? Again, nothing made much sense.

Reece was probably a transient who was one of three things: independently wealthy, a kept woman, or a sex worker. She was obviously caught up in the striptease nightlife of Dallas, which, at the time, was a booming business. That was the first and only pictorial Laura found of Kendall in Lost Girls but it was enough. She returned to her other research sites. By January of 1970, Reece had forfeited on the lease of the suite at the Wilson Building and simply disappeared off the grid. Along with Rose Davis. What a crazy story this was turning out to be.

Laura stretched and yawned. She had been staring at her computer screen for hours and fatigue was starting to set in. She stood up from the desk and walked around the viewing room to get the blood pumping back in her legs.

Her shoulder pack was sitting on the table next to her and she noticed the corner of a manila folder stuck out of the pack. She walked over and pulled the folder out. It was the collection of photographs that Andrásné Szabó had given her at the end of his interview. She poured the contents on the table in front of her.

She started browsing through them again slowly. The first one was an exterior shot of the Hilton Inn, Mockingbird. There was no date on it. The next one was a black and white photograph of a line of workers in a mill. The next, a shot of a large dining room filled with waiters in white waistcoats, probably taken in the Hilton, Mockingbird during its heyday. She dug through the pile. A certain photograph caught her attention. It was yellowed with age but there was something strange about it. Pulling it out of the pile, she stared closely at it. It was a head and shoulders shot of a man and a woman. The woman looked all too familiar to her. She was a beautiful European-looking blonde, her arm resting on a young Andrásné' Szabó's shoulder, a soft yet determined look of independence on her face. Laura looked at the date. It said 9/68.

Chills shot through her as she made the connection.

"Oh, my God..."

She gazed at the photograph in total disbelief. Staring back at her was Eva, the woman she had the encounter with at the Hotel Highland a few nights ago.

Her heart was racing but she couldn't look away from the piercing eyes staring out at her from the photo. She had to be hallucinating. Laura shook her head and looked again. The platinum blonde hair, the eyes, that mouth... She remembered the icy touch of those pale lips all over her body. And Eva hadn't been a day older than the woman in the photo. There was no doubt in Laura's mind that this was the same woman.

Laura's head was swimming. She had crossed a barrier of some sort. No longer were spirits simply moaning from closets and passively brushing against her in the dark. No, these entities were reaching out, grabbing hold of her with both hands, and shaking her in front of everyone. And in broad daylight. For her sanity's sake she had to find some way to protect herself from this intrusion into her life. She couldn't go on being a passive antenna for any aberrant life-echo that randomly decided to land on her frequency. Regardless what they had to tell her, these fucking things were *dead*, whether they knew it or not. And as far as Laura Milton was concerned, life was hard enough without having to worry about the dead rising up and screwing with you 24/7.

She had until Monday night. Then, whether the key to her mystery had been found or not, a ticket back to New York was waiting for her at the airport. That is unless Colin dragged her back before then. She could kick herself for wasting an entire day recovering from her little roofie episode, but there was nothing she could do about it now. She was determined to cram every bit she could into the next five days to make this happen. She didn't come all this way to leave empty-handed.

It was after 5 PM and she knew the archivists were waiting for her to finish so they could leave for the day. She would grab some food and spend some time pouring over her notes before crashing early. She needed a good night's rest so she could hit the ground running first thing in the morning.

God knows she had her work cut out for her...

Twenty Two

Thursday morning Laura left the hotel at 7 AM. Her destination was the Cathedral of Hope Christian church off of Inwood Road and Lemmon Avenue. Located between Love Field Airport and the Oak Lawn district, COH was an "LGBTQ Liberal" church, catering primarily to the lesbian/gay/bi/and transgendered populace. Being close to Cedar Springs, the main gay strip in Dallas, the church boasted a hearty congregation of LGBTQ patrons from all walks of life.

Laura had first been contacted by Reverend Valerie Bellman almost a year before she ever thought of coming to Dallas. Ms. Bellman had apparently heard of Laura's interest in Texas folklore from a guest-blogger entry Laura had written for a documentary film blog they both subscribed to. The Reverend had recently become computer-literate and had immersed herself in the cyber world, literally devouring everything she could get her hands on. She had read Laura's post and had felt a 'kinship', as she described it, with the writer. She prayed about it and felt God was telling her to keep in contact with Laura. She sent a series of emails Laura had happily answered and the two women became Internet pals. When it was finally time for Laura to schedule interviews to research the history of Dallas, because of her past, Valerie was the first person Laura approached. Bellman agreed happily to be involved.

Laura came to the address she had on her GPS and slowed down. The church was hidden behind side-by-side car dealerships that ran along Inwood Road, about a mile away from Love Field Airport. The main entrance to the church parking lot was a narrow alley that ran snuggly between two of the car lots. Strange that such a majestic building was placed on a random piece of land. To Laura, it just illustrated how skewed this country's priorities were.

She pulled the Land Rover into the alley slowly. An angular spire shot into the sky from behind the wall of dealerships banners. When she entered the lot on the other side, she saw the expansive super-white Cathedral of Hope and next to it, the new addition, the ultra-modern structure of the Interfaith Peace Chapel. The manicured landscape was strangely devoid of people. The parking lot was empty except for a white cargo van parked next to the sidewalk. Granted, it was 7:30 AM, but still...

Laura parked the car next to the van, unloaded her things, and wheeled the cases up to the wall of glass doors leading into the main building. She pulled on the handle and found it locked. She tried the one next to it and again it, too, was secured. She cupped her hands and put her face against the glass, peering into the dark space. To the left, there was a vast open room, probably the main cathedral itself. To the right was what looked like a gift store and a line of offices of some sort. A shadowed expanse of hallway stretched out in front of her that disappeared into the darkness of the building's interior.

As Laura peered in, a rotund but visibly bouncy woman appeared around the corner of the office. She was dressed in dark blue priestly robes and shuffled quickly towards Laura. She came to the secured glass doors, a genuine smile beaming off her face, black vintage cat-eye glasses sitting on the bridge of a button nose.

"Laura?" she called through the glass.

"Yes. Valerie?"

The woman unlocked the door and threw it open.

"I'm so sorry! We have to keep these locked to stop the homeless from wandering through the building. It's so nice to meet you finally face to face!" Laura reached out to shake the Reverend's hand. Bellman surprised her by pulling her close and giving her a big bear hug that left Laura almost out of breath. "Don't be silly! I feel like I've known you forever!" They both laughed. "Here, let me help you!"

After pulling the equipment through the threshold, the Reverend locked the doors behind them.

"This building is incredible..." Laura stared into the dark cathedral, its vaulted ceiling accented by shafts of pale sunlight shooting through the stained glass creating a majestic kaleidoscopic glare in the vast space.

"Thank you! We are so very blessed. And proud of the new addition."

"I saw the chapel coming in. It's amazing. Do you think we can possibly shoot there?"

"Oh, of course! We need to go back the way we came, but it's not a problem." She unlocked the doors and soon they were walking across the circular courtyard joining the two buildings.

"Tell me a little about Cathedral of Hope, Valerie."

The Reverend stopped between the buildings for a moment. "Well, the church was founded in 1970 by a group of 12 friends to provide a place of worship and healing for the lesbian, gay, and trans-gendered community. The church celebrated its 40th anniversary on July 24, 2010. But when we first began, it was dangerous to be openly gay in Dallas, much less to be *Christian* and gay. Society has changed a lot now, thank the Lord. We're even seeing more and more straight families coming to our services, those who feel the importance of nurturing tolerance and acceptance as part of their children's education..."

The Reverend continued on about the history of the church in a flood of information as they slowly approached the chapel. Laura wished she had her hands free so she could take notes, but she knew the Reverend would send her anything she needed electronically. It was her favorite way to communicate, second to speaking.

Reverend Valerie had a very easy way about her, almost childlike. Her personality made you feel like you were talking to your best friend. As she continued, the Reverend seemed amused by her own anecdotes, enjoying the process of communicating as much as the information she was imparting. It was almost like she was intimating something very personal and binding with you in every sentence. Laura listened trying to absorb the flood of information. Not that Laura was by any means judgmental, and certainly not of a person's inherent right to choose their own sexual preference, surely, but she found it hard to fathom that the Reverend was indeed a lesbian. Valerie seemed so far from the stereotypical candidate. Laura reminded herself that she had no right to question anything after her experience at the Highland this week, but really, she knew far too little about the lifestyle to voice an accurate opinion. She was suddenly embarrassed about the depth of her own naïveté.

"And here we are."

Laura was in awe. They stood before the ultra-modern building. It was an asymmetric 3-tiered white structure that seemed to sprout out of the very ground itself. The doors and windows were all organic shapes that brought to mind dancing Pentecostal flames.

The Reverend unlocked the thick Kona wood doors and stepped aside.

"Welcome to the Interfaith Chapel."

Laura stepped into a vast crème-colored space devoid of superficial ornament. The pearl-white walls were approximately 50 feet high and slightly tapered inward creating a dramatic horizon line. At the far end was an expanse of stone that was more reminiscent of an operatic stage than a traditional church altar.

While Laura acclimated herself to the space, Valerie Bellman continued talking like a tour guide. "The chapel was designed by the award-winning and world-renowned Dean of American Architecture, Philip Johnson. It seats up to 175 people currently, but phase two will be permanent seating that will hold 75 more. The opening celebration was held on November 8, 2010. This is the jewel of our church."

The space was breathtaking and a little intimidating. Even with the natural wash of diffused light coming from the windows, Laura thought it would be a logistical nightmare to shoot the Reverend's interview in the cavernous space. But after a quick 10-minute set-up she looked through the viewfinder and saw it worked on camera surprisingly well.

The Reverend Bellman took a seat in her chair and shifted in her robes slightly, her infectious smile beaming.

Laura checked her audio levels and cued her.

"Anytime you're ready, Valerie." The woman cleared her throat gently and smiled.

"Hello. My name is Reverend Valerie Bellman. I have been an ordained Baptist minister for the last 15 years, praise God. But I took a roundabout way of reaching the Lord, that's for sure. In my younger days I was a bit of a work in progress, spiritually. Before I met the Lord. And the love of my life, Delphina."

Laura chimed in. "We've known one another through the Internet for some time, Valerie. At one point, you mentioned that you worked for Jack Ruby..."

"Well, I used to dance when I was under-age at Amateur Night at Jack Ruby's Carousel Club. It wasn't a paid job, other than the tips you walked with, but it was the greatest thing I had ever done up to that point.

"It was 1962. Back in the day, if you were married in Texas you could do anything your husband said was ok. I married the first time when I was 16. I remember, it was at the Justice of the Peace. My husband Carl was 22. Afterwards, we went to the Carousel Club and had a crazy night. I told him I wanted to be a famous burlesque dancer like Candy Barr, the greatest of Jack Ruby's Girls. They were all so glamorous and classy, like movie stars..."

"That's quite a different lifestyle than where you are now."

"I can't lie and say that I didn't enjoy it! The first time I stripped I was scared as monkey-poo, but I totally loved it!" The Reverend got a far-away look in her eyes as she spoke. Laura could detect a slight shift in the woman's accent, as if she were reliving the moment to a greater or lesser degree. "And the crowd loved me! My husband was so proud. I started doing it twice a week just for fun."

"Do you know if any other of the original girls are still in Texas?"

"Oh, you won't find any Ruby's girls left. A stripper's career is 10 years, if she's lucky. And the ones who survive have to be strong enough to pull their lives together. Most of Ruby's girls weren't that strong."

"Can you give me some examples?"

"Sure. Baby LeGrand hung herself by her toreador pants in an Oklahoma jail while she was in overnight for prostitution charges. She was a tough cookie, too. When we heard about it, none of us girls could imagine what could make her take her own life, much less turn tricks on the side. Somebody set her up. She wasn't that kind of girl.

"Also Tuesday Night killed herself. Poor thing. She was a wreck. And Marilyn Walle, who went by the name 'Delilah', left Dallas when the Carousel finally closed. She was found dead in a hotel room in Omaha in September of 1966. I'm pretty sure it was because she was planning to write a book on the Kennedy assassination. The things we saw in that club were unbelievable..."

"So, you actually stuck around the Carousel for a while then after your initial debut?"

"Yeah, Carl, my husband at the time, liked hanging out there. And that's where I first realized that I was attracted to women. Carl and I took one of the younger girls, Jackie Snow, as a lover, for threesomes, but we didn't let anyone know what we were up to. Ruby was a terror. God only knows what he would have done had he found out. We called him 'Sparky' because of his quick temper." She laughed out loud.

"Can you tell me a little about the atmosphere at the Carousel Club?"

"I sure can. Well, the club was in the Southwestern Bell Building, across the street from the Adolphus Hotel at 1312 ½ Commerce Street. It was on the second floor above a delicatessen. Outside, the walls of the club were covered with photos of the dancers posing in costume, to lure customers in. I thought they were great at the time.

"The interior was basically a square, barn-like room with thick red carpet and a hideous gold boomerang-shaped bar. And cheap-looking gold curtains." She cackled again. "The only other decoration in the club was a huge gold painting of a stallion rearing up on its hind legs. Jack really loved that ugly thing. He always said it was 'real class'. What a joke."

Laura thought for a moment. "Tell me about the scene off-stage. What was really going on?"

"Well, I don't know about some of the other girls, but after I got off the stage I'd put on a sheer blouse and go to the bar. Men would come up and buy me drinks and tip me well to do private dances. That's where we made our real money, the 'dog and pony show' I called it!" Valerie giggled like a little girl. "Carl liked to watch it from afar, so he would let me even though I wasn't a real stripper.

"Most of the guys were swell. Real respectful, you know? Regular guys out having some laughs. They tipped well and treated you like a lady. But there were always creepy friends of Ruby's who hung around. They made passes at the girls, grabbing them, and refusing to tip. It caused a lot of the younger dancers to leave. Ruby wouldn't let anyone cause any real trouble but some of his friends could literally do almost whatever they wanted.

"I know some of the other girls were hooking on the side. I could never understand that. To me it was just show business. But in the dressing room we heard everything. I was just in it for the thrill.

"Jack, of course, shot Lee Harvey Oswald, who every one of us had seen at the club. Only we decided as a group not to admit it to anyone. We knew they would whack anyone who said anything about anything. Jack died of cancer in January of '67 waiting for a retrial. I remember because a few of us wanted to stop by and wish him a happy new year...

"The club closed and all of the girls had to leave and find work. Two of Ruby's ex-dancers Diane Hunter and Alice Anderson ended up writing a book called 'Ruby's Girls'. It tells the story of two strippers after the doors of the Carousel closed forever. Their characters try to get hired at an upscale bordello in Turtle Creek called Madame De Luce's, which was a real place. But the proprietress refused to hire them because she believed Ruby ruined women. After working for him, they were, as she put it, 'all tease and no fuck'. That was the ironic stigma of being a Ruby Girl. And, for the most part, it was true."

"Do you stay in touch with any of the other girls?"

"For the first few years I kept in touch with a couple. Most of them were taken by their own vices. After Ruby died they all scattered. I just thank the Lord God my savior for delivering me from that sinner's lifestyle. Praise be to God!"

Laura smiled, realizing that the interview had just ended.

June 1969, The Colony Club, Dallas, TX

On November 24, 1963, on live television, Jack Ruby fatally shot Lee Harvey Oswald, a 24-year-old warehouse worker who was in police custody after being charged with the assassination of President John F. Kennedy two days earlier. Ruby claimed he had acted out of grief and denied any involvement in a conspiracy. A Dallas jury found Ruby guilty of murder and sentenced him to death. He appealed the conviction and eventually it was finally overturned on October 5, 1966. But while awaiting a new trial, Ruby died in jail of a pulmonary embolism due to an aggressive form of cancer that had quickly spread to his liver, lungs, and brain.

The week after Ruby's Carousel Club closed its doors, the best of Jack's girls were hired by Abe Weinstein to dance at the Colony Club, a competing establishment that sat literally next door to the strip joint.

Now, five years later, The Carousel is just a bad dream in many people's opinion. But the Colony Club is lit like a beacon shining in the night, a thriving organism pulsing in the heart of downtown Dallas.

Instead of driving the Chevelle, Rose Davis decides to walk though the bustling downtown streets to the club on a clear night. It's only 6 blocks from the downtown apartment and the weather is warm and inviting.

In twenty minutes, she turns the corner and sees the Colony Club glittering across the street. There is a small group of people in line to get in. She takes her place behind them but unlike the others waiting, she is not in a jovial mood.

The doorman recognizes her and lets her enter with a smile.

Once inside, Rose scans the crowded room. Kendall is on the far stage performing her routine. Groups of men are going crazy watching her dance. Rose stares at her with a hint of jealously. Her body is perfect. Kendall spots her roommate from the stage and blows her a kiss to the shouts of the men throwing dollar bills on the stage.

When the song ends, Kendall jumps off the stage and hugs Rose tightly. Her breath reeks of alcohol.

"Rose! My darling little sister. What brings you out into the wilderness, sugar-bear?"

"I haven't seen you for weeks. Why don't you come home?"

"Aww, baby..." She scrunched up her face. "Do you miss your mama?"

"Don't say that."

Kendall throws her head back and laughs. "Just a figure of speech, little one!"

"I need to talk to you."

"Talk away, honey-pie!"

A man reaches between the two girls and hands Kendall a shot. Kendall takes it and slams it in a single gulp. Rose watches her, disgusted.

Rose grabs her by the arm.

"If you need money we can think of better things for you to do other than this." Kendall takes her free hand and gently pulls Rose's fingers off of her arm with a disarming smile on her face.

"I told you, baby, I don't need the money. I do this for fun."

"It's not right!" She pushes Kendall away from her causing the leggy brunette to stumble into the wall.

Kendall looks up with fury in her eyes. Reaching out, she aggressively pulls the younger girl to her, so close that their lips are almost touching. Staring into Rose's frightened eyes, she holds her tightly in a mock embrace. The men surrounding them start chanting, "Kiss her, kiss her!"

"How dare you, you self-righteous little bitch..." Kendall's voice is a vicious hiss tearing through the air between them. "You're no saint, petunia. Hell, if it wasn't for me you'd still be too shy to hold hands with a virgin farm boy much less do your trip with the Jewel Girls." Rose tries to jerk herself free but Kendall tightens her grip. Her voice becomes a white hiss. "Oh, yeah. I know all about it, you little slut. You're my greatest success, Rose. You just can't get over the guilt of enjoying it so much, can you?"

Rose screams, yanks herself free, and runs out of the club in tears. Kendall laughs hysterically as she turns back to the bar...

Present Day. The Men's Club, Dallas, TX

The Men's Club was one of the premiere men's clubs in the country. They had luxurious high-end clubs in Houston, Raleigh, Mexico City, Guadalajara, and, of course, in fabulous Dallas, Texas. Laura Milton walked into the plush lounge area through a sea of men and women and took a seat at one of the bars by herself.

The music was pumping. On stage, a beautiful young woman was gyrating as the crowd watched hungrily. She looked to be all of maybe 22 years old. What a body... The dancer looked up straight at her and smiled. Laura turned away quickly, slightly embarrassed.

Across the room she saw Samuel standing at the bar and waved to him. He waved back and crossed the dining room filled with crowded tables.

Standing up, she hugged him, pressing her body into his. “Thanks for meeting me!”

“Sure! When you asked me to help you with a little research, I expected Google and Starbucks, not shots and strippers. You’re my kind of girl, Laura Milton.”

She smiled. The music stopped and a voice came over the sound system.

“Ladies and gentlemen, give a warm welcome to Miss Virginia Scene!”

Another incredible woman strutted onto the stage. The music began thumping and they were both mesmerized by the gorgeous specimen in front of them showing every crevice of her immaculate body. The dancer was not just some skinny speed freak; she was all muscle, probably 2% body fat, and built for speed. Laura could tell by her moves that the woman studied yoga. Her somersaults were flawless. She did a handstand and spread her legs parallel with the floor as if she were a gymnast. She was good. Laura couldn’t take her eyes off of her.

Samuel leaned close to her and managed to make a full sentence. “So, what are we looking for again?”

“I don’t know. Motivation?”

The woman on stage collapsed into a back-bend, the fabric of her g-string barely covering her pubic mound. Laura could feel herself begin to sweat.

“I don’t know about you,” Samuel stammered, “but I’m feeling pretty motivated myself right about now.” He squirmed in his chair. “Do you think Rose was a stripper?”

"I'm not sure. But Kendall Reece definitely was. I'm just going on a hunch..." The woman was on all fours in the center of the stage whipping her hair around in a frenzy. Seconds later, she had jumped up, climbed the brass dancers' pole, and was hanging in mid-air supported only by lean, muscular legs, her head draped down all the way to the floor.

Laura snapped out of the trance for a moment. "I mean, what would make a smart girl turn to a life of stripping?"

Samuel leaned towards her. "That's easy. The attention. The admiration of thousands of men lusting after you every day, wanting you. What girl doesn't secretly fantasize about that? Not to mention, the money."

"The money would be a major factor, I can understand that." She watched the woman on stage do a double back flip, a wide grin across her face as the crowd applauded. "Unless, of course, the girl wasn't in it for the cash and was simply an exhibitionist who did it for the thrill..."

"And that would be a good reason to be here. An exhibitionist without a voyeur or a voyeur without an exhibitionist is a lonely existence. They need each other."

"One good man would be enough for me," she said under her breath.

"Really? Most young girls love sparkly shiny things. They just want to feel special. Even if they're not."

"I think that goes for all of us..."

They finished their drinks, Laura paid the bartender, and they walked out the door. The valet took their tickets and ran towards the parking lot.

"Can I interest you in dessert and coffee, Ms. Milton?"

"I'd love to. But I have an early morning. Thanks again for coming out." She smiled and kissed Samuel on the cheek.

"Sure. Strip clubs with a beautiful woman who picks up the tab? Any time you need a friend, I'm there."

She smiled. They stood looking at each other for a long moment.

Laura was the one to ruin it. “It’s getting late...”

“Oh, sure, yeah. Have a good night. If you need anything you can call me any–”

“Anytime. Yeah, I got it.” She was making fun of him but smiled genuinely. “Thanks again, Sam. I had a lot of fun.”

”So, what’s next in your research?”

“I really don’t know yet. Let me sleep on it.”

“I want to help, if I can. I’m a great back-up.”

“Thanks. I think I’ll probably need it.”

“I’ll call you tomorrow and we’ll sit down and make a plan.”

“You got it.” A shiver ran through her, unexpectedly. She looked up at him trying to shake it off. “Be careful, Sam.”

The valet pulled up with his hybrid and got out, waiting for him to finish.

“You got it. See you tomorrow...”

He handed the valet a few bills and got in his car.

The Land Rover pulled up next and the valet jumped out. Laura slipped the guy a ten and climbed in. *‘Sam’s nice,’* she thought, *‘but you cannot complicate your life any further, no matter how cute he is. Time to focus. Seriously, Laura...’* Putting on some music, Laura pulled out of the parking lot and got on the freeway heading toward downtown Dallas.

Samuel waited until Laura’s car took off and then pulled out of the Men’s Club parking lot taking Northwest Highway to I35. He was content after spending a surprisingly fun night with a woman that had surprisingly captured his attention. What a smoking-hot girl Laura was... And to be there, surrounded by the top strippers in the city with her at his side? It was like a ghost-nerd’s wet dream. She probably had no interest in him whatsoever, but whatever time he could manage to spend with her was worth every ounce of shame he could muster.

Interstate 30 went past downtown towards Arlington and Fort Worth. Samuel exited at Sylvan Avenue in Oak Cliff. The Kessler Park area was dark except for a single car that pulled onto the street behind his little hybrid as it climbed through the hills. Samuel looked up in his rearview mirror, noticing the car behind him. He slowed down and the car sped up quickly, passing him closely in the dark. It disappeared around the corner and was gone.

"Asshole..."

There were no streetlights on the road and no traffic. Handsome mid-century homes lined both sides of the street and stood with black windows surrounded by the silhouettes of gargantuan 60-foot trees.

Samuel stopped at the red light at the next intersection. A Lincoln Town Car suddenly roared up the hill behind him, slowed just a little, and then sped through the intersection, hip-hop music blaring from the open windows.

Samuel watched the car speed away and shook his head. People seemed to always be trying to get away with something these days. It was asinine.

Just then, the interior of the car filled with light and Samuel looked up in his rear view mirror. Above the glaring headlights, a set of red and blue LED strobes started flashing as the car pulled up and stopped behind him.

"Shit." Samuel put the hybrid in park and hoped he didn't smell like alcohol.

He watched a dark hulking shadow emerge from the car and slowly approach in his side-view mirror. The figure came along the driver's side door and shined a bright flashlight down in his face. Samuel looked up into the glaring light.

"May I help you, officer?"

It was the last thing he would ever say.

Twenty Three

Laura found herself unable to sleep, her mind consumed by countless questions. By 4:30 AM she finally gave up and got out of bed an hour and a half before her first morning alarm. She popped her horse tranquilizer and logged on to a few of Colin's subscription databases, determined to fight the Topamax side effects with the help of green tea and some old 80's hair metal. She had a compulsive need to see the details on the report of Rose's disappearance.

She searched for a police report filed on January 13, 1970. After a few moments, the document appeared on the screen. Davis himself had called it in. It was 4 days after Rose's birthday when the police finally went to the apartment in the Wilson Building. Kudos to Colin's research sites once again. Laura was truly amazed by the scope of information a museum curator had access to.

The police had searched her bedroom thoroughly and the list of evidence was pretty extensive. She had kept a lot of souvenirs from the places she went, each one a potential lead to follow. One of the items on the list was a piece of paper with a local telephone number.

Laura did a double take. Why is there a list of evidence on a report like this in the first place?

Laura did some backtracking and found an archive of phone listings in the Dallas area and found that the number belonged to a defunct company called Highland Village Clinical Services. It had been the office of a group of general practitioners. So what does the medical community have to do with any of this? Questions within questions... One thing was for sure; Laura had a lot of ground to cover in a very short amount of time.

June 1969 Neiman-Marcus Department Store, Dallas, Texas

At 7:40 AM Rose walks into the store hiding behind a pair of Dior sunglasses, her long blonde hair pulled back in a multi-colored silk scarf. She takes the ornate elevator to the second floor to her department. Exiting, she walks through the displays of mannequins dressed in stockings, garters and lacy bras and heads to the back room. There she puts her things under the counter and takes her hair down.

Rose takes a deep breath. She is shaky and puts her hand out to steady herself. She abruptly puts a hand to her stomach and runs to the trash bin, throwing up her morning breakfast in a heaving fit.

She lifts up her head and wipes the spittle from the edge of her mouth. Closing her eyes, she starts crying silently...

Present Day, Dallas, Texas

Laura met her interviewee, Carolyn Rush, later that morning at her dance studio on Lower Greenville Avenue. Rush had been teaching tango and ballroom dancing for the last 20 years. The woman was tall and thin, a wondrous head of silver hair flowing in wide curls to her shoulders. She only had 30 minutes between classes to fit an impromptu interview in, but was extremely gracious.

She led Laura into the studio and watched her set up the camera and a single key light in a matter of minutes. When Laura was ready for her, she took her seat and calmly began to speak.

"The story I want to tell you is probably not what you want to hear, Ms. Milton," she began, "but it's something that has stayed with me all my life. You told me in your emails that you were looking for something otherworldly and this is the most harrowing thing I've ever experienced in this or any other city. It was 1970 I was just 19 years old. I had been cheating on my new husband with his best friend. He had been cheating on me, too. Anyway, after a few months, I got pregnant. Of course, not wanting to face the consequences of my actions, I decided to do something about it. A friend of mine told me about a 'Doctor Fowler' who had a clinic on McFarlin, across Hillcrest from Southern Methodist University in Highland Park. She said he'd been there for 15 years. Abortions were difficult to come by then, but he had an underground business going after hours at the clinic for years. I know so many girls who went to him..."

Laura saw the tears cresting in her eyes. The woman was visibly upset. "What happened to you, Carolyn?"

She wiped off the tears swelling under her eyelashes, careful not to smudge her make-up.

"You know, I'm sure I'm not the only one it's happened to. When I finally told my friend Betty, she said other women had told her about similar experiences. God damn him..." Tears were flowing freely from her now. "But, at the time, there was no other choice. I still can't believe it happened to me..."

June 1969, Highland Park Pharmacy, Dallas, TX

Rose and Kendall are sitting in a booth facing the soda fountain in the Highland Park Pharmacy. They are quietly nursing tall root-beer floats. Rose looks up at Kendall and they stare at each other awkwardly. Kendall slides a slip of paper across the table to her.

"This is the number for Dr. Fowler. He's the one who can help you."

Fowler. Rose has heard the name before.

"He's the only man in the state who will give you the abortion." A woman two booths over looks up from her hot fudge sundae. Kendall lowers her voice a fraction. "I'm sorry. There's no other choice." Kendall looks like she hasn't slept in days.

Rose is sullen, her eyes swollen from crying. She hates having to listen to Kendall go on like this, so coldly.

"Don't look so sad. If it wasn't for him, you'd have to go to Mexico to get it done."

"What is up with you, Kendall?" Rose finally had to stop her. "Where have you been all this time?"

"I'm in love..." She holds up her hand and waves a big diamond ring in Rose's face. Something was horribly wrong.

"What about Daniel Morrow?"

"Who?"

Rose frowns. Kendall seems to be high on something. She takes the slip of paper and puts it in her purse. Kendall might as well be a complete stranger. Tears threaten to come but she fights them back.

"I'm really sorry, Rose. I wish I could do more..." Kendall's voice is far away. She reaches into her purse, pulls out a hundred dollar bill, and flings it on the table between them. "Listen, I have to go. I'll call and check on you later in the week." She stands to leave.

"You won't be home?"

"If you need me, leave a message at the club."

With that, Kendall grabs her things and walks out of the pharmacy leaving Rose sitting in the giant red booth all alone.

* * *

Rose drives back to their apartment in the heart of downtown Dallas in silence. Once upstairs, she pulls the slip of paper out of her purse and sits down in front of the telephone. God, the last thing in the world she wants to do is to make this call. She can't let herself think of the consequences. Closing her eyes, she reaches for the receiver. She dials the number and waits, wishing in the back of her mind that the number is wrong or the line has been disconnected. The phone rings once, twice, three times. Rose is about to gladly hang up when a strange voice sounds over the receiver.

"Yes..."

"Hello. M-my name is Rose Davis. I got your number from Kendall Reece..."

"...I see. How far along are you?"

"Not long, six weeks, maybe..."

He paused. She could hear him breathing.

"*Hello*?"

"Come to the clinic after 4 PM Thursday. On McFarlin. Off of Hillcrest, across from the SMU campus. Everyone will be gone by then. Bring $1,200 and come alone."

"*What*?"

"This is non-negotiable, Ms. Davis. Or you can just choose to have your baby and live with the stigma of having a bastard child for the rest of your life. Of course, you could always go to Mexico to have your procedure done..."

$1,200 is almost half as much as her car is worth. She can't afford this. Still, there is no other choice. The thought of aborting her child has given her nightmares for weeks, but she is terrified of the prospect of being a single mother and having to raise a child alone. And what would her father say? He would call her a whore and probably disown her. And at any moment, Kendall could disappear and she would be forced out of her amazing apartment. The dream life is rapidly falling down around her ears. A stream of tears silently runs down the side of her cheek.

"No, I'll be there. McFarlin. Across from SMU..."

Fowler hangs up on her.

* * *

Rose calls in at Neiman's on Wednesday afternoon and takes Thursday off as a sick day. It was very unlike her to take off work for any reason and Mrs. Shapiro, the head of Human Resources, seems genuinely concerned about her. Hating having to lie, Rose hangs up the phone relieved that Shapiro didn't grill her for more information.

Thursday morning comes silently. Kendall has been persona non grata for the last few weeks and Rose is thankful that she doesn't have to deal with her profane indifference this morning. She crawls deeper under the covers wishing she wasn't alone and goes back to sleep.

She wakes at 10:20, opening her eyes to a roomful of sunlight. The irony of the beauty of the morning compared to her dark mood is unsettling. She lies there knowing after today her life will never be the same. She has never been the kind of girl to fantasize about having children. But now, feeling the change deep inside her body, knowing a life is gestating there, she is devastated about having to get rid of her baby. Why is this happening? Her tears soak the goose-down pillow her head is lying on.

Rose decides to go to the noon mass. She dresses in complete silence and leaves the building without even saying hello to the doorman, to his surprise. As she walks through the busy downtown streets she is filled with deep shame and regret for how her life has turned out. All the energy she put into the last few years, wasted on some silly, darkened lifestyle that has brought her to where she is now...

When she finally enters the church she blesses herself and takes a seat in the very back pew. Her eyes travel all over the cathedral, picking out details of the building she has never noticed before, all a simple distraction to keep her from thinking. But regardless how she tries to ignore it, she is painfully aware of the new life forming within her. Halfway through the mass, she starts crying uncontrollably and silently walks out of the service during the Transubstantiation.

After a listless afternoon of window-shopping, she finally drives her green Chevelle across town and parks in front of a small freestanding building on McFarlin Drive in Highland Park. The lot is deserted. Directly across Hillcrest Avenue stand the buildings of the prestigious Southern Methodist University. Her father had always wanted her to enroll there, be a successful businesswoman, and make something of herself outside the circle of the family's wealth. It is another in a long list of things she hasn't accomplished in her life...

Checking her face in the mirror, she sees how puffy and red her eyes are. She reaches into her purse and puts on a pair of large dark glasses to hide her face and gets out of the car.

The sign on the front door says the clinic hours are 7 AM to 3 PM. Her watch says 4:20 PM. She takes a deep breath, opens the door and walks in.

All the lights are off. The clinic is dark and filled with shadows. She sees movement in the far corner of the room. A tall man in a white coat is in the corner closing the blinds. He looks up calmly through thick bifocals.

“Miss Davis...”

“Yes.”

Fowler walks up to her and steps into the light. His elongated face is pockmarked and sullen, the skin, pale and moist. Beads of sweat are forming on his brow. She smells the thick aroma of Aqua Velva and Brylcreem in the air around him. She immediately recognizes him from the Hilton Hotel massacre. He is the man who almost strangled her at the Jewel Club.

She looks at his hands and remembers the powerful and bony fingers flicking that silver lighter, remembers the feeling of them wrapped around her neck. He doesn’t seem to recognize her. But there is no way she can go through with this. She starts to panic.

He pauses for a moment then turns and locks the door.

“You brought the money?”

Mechanically, she hands him an envelope with $1,200 cash inside. He hastily opens the envelope, counts the bills, and then stuffs it into his pocket. All she wants to do is run for the door, get away from this madman. But then where would she go? She feels like she’s going to pass out.

Fowler motions to an adjustable examination table in the corner of the room. A large light illuminates the shameful device from overhead, making it look even more ominous. A paper gown is draped across the chair next to her.

“Disrobe, put on the gown, and lie on the table.”

She begins undoing her shirt, a little apprehensive because he is only a few feet away in the room, watching her. She turns her back towards him and continues undressing.

She feels dizzy and is afraid she might pass out. Then she'd have no defense against him.

"I'll administer a general anesthetic. When you're under I will conduct the procedure. It will take only a half-hour or so. You'll need to rest for a while afterwards..."

Rose finishes changing, feeling the cold tile floor under her bare feet. She climbs up on the table, only the coarse green paper gown covering her shivering body. The opposite end of the padded surface has been raised into a reclining position. She leans back, the leather cushion freezing on her naked skin.

"Put your feet in the stirrups."

She does so, trying not to be self-conscious. She quickly makes the sign of the cross while the doctor's back is turned.

'Please, just get me though this...'

Fowler takes a large hypodermic needle and draws a clear liquid from a vile. He places the needle against the skin of her arm and penetrates her. She winces, digging the nails of her free hand against side of the table. Blood flows quickly into the chamber before he pushes the plunger and sends the liquid slowly into her bloodstream. She is acutely aware of the scent of bleach and lye in her nostrils. She begins to feel very warm.

"Relax. It will all be over in few minutes..."

Fowler's speckled eyes travel over her young body, her erect nipples under the paper gown, her strong, slender legs, her crotch. Rose can barely keep her eyes open and starts to nod.

'God, help me...'

She passes out in seconds.

Fowler looks down at her beautiful young sleeping face and smiles.

"That's a girl..."

* * *

Deep, cold blackness... Groans echoing in the dark, something wet and slithering, pressure, then release... Flashes of blood, pressure, hands on her thighs...

Rose is lying on her back, just teetering on the edge of consciousness. She can hear Fowler working, wet sounds and the distant feeling of being filled. Her legs are spread apart and shaking with his efforts. She stirs ever so slightly, forces her eyes open to mere slits. It's a huge effort for her to open them at all. She struggles to lift her head only a few inches and looks down at her crotch.

Fowler is crouched between her legs, his face blocked by her pelvis. He is making strange noises. She tries to stay still so as not to let him know she's conscious. Without warning, he lifts his head looking off to the side. And she sees the horror.

The bottom of his face and mouth are smeared with dark red blood. He wipes his mouth with his sleeve and stands. His pants are undone and his cock is erect. He puts his bloodied hands on her knees and she feels him slide inside of her. He starts thrusting against her viciously. He slaps her hard across the face. It takes every ounce of willpower for Rose to keep her eyes closed and lay still.

Somewhere, a phone rings in the distance. He keeps panting on top of her, squeezing her breasts, pumping inside of her faster and faster. Again, the ringing...

"Goddamnit!" He stands up and pulls out of her. Grabbing a towel, he wipes himself off, pulls his trousers up and waddles into the office to pick up the phone.

"*What?* I can't talk now!" She can hear him arguing with someone. He sounds so far away...

Rose is petrified. The room is spinning. She turns her head and sees what looks like her clothes and valuables lying on the chair next to her. The sky is starting to turn a light purple between the slits of the blinds on the windows. Fowler is cursing into the phone in the other room. *Fowler!* God, she remembers his face, the abomination he has been performing on her.

'Oh, my God, this is real!'

The anesthesia is still impairing her. She grabs onto the handrail and slowly pulls herself into a sitting position. Her legs feel like rubber. She shakes her head back and forth trying desperately to snap out of her drug-induced haze. She pushes herself up with her hands and onto her feet. Standing, she aims her body for the chair next to her and falls into it. She grabs her things in a bundle and forces herself to stand again. She can hear Fowler slam down the phone in the next room. She panics and shuffles quickly to the door, unlocks it, and stumbles out of the clinic wearing only her paper gown.

She runs wildly into the parking lot, almost falling over herself. She makes it to her car and fumbles to unlock the door, her vision blurring uncontrollably. Finally, the key finds the hole and she throws the door open. She falls into the driver's seat, slamming the door shut behind her. Starting the car, she roars out of the parking lot, bottoming out on the curb in her panic to escape the clinic. Looking in her rear-view mirror, she sees that no one is chasing after her.

She speeds through the next red light and heads into the thick of Highland Park. Blocks away, she pulls over to the side of Hillcrest Road and starts screaming hysterically...

Twenty Four

Present Day. Dallas, Texas

The interview with Carolyn Rush was still running through Laura's mind hours later. What a horrific tale. And if that poor woman had gone through something like that in the center of one of the most cosmopolitan cities in the south and stayed quiet, how many other women had done the same thing? And with Rose having had information about the same location, could she, too, have been pregnant and perhaps been another victim of this lunatic's mad hunger? Laura's flesh crawled with the memory of Carolyn's description of her ordeal. The name Fowler would forever be etched in her mind. She was sure of one thing, the horror from beyond the grave was nothing in comparison to the horror of the living.

She grabbed a smoothie at Central Market and then ran across the street to the post office on Greenville Avenue and mailed copies of her most recent interviews to Colin's office in New York. She immediately felt better knowing that the last few days' worth of notes and footage were safely on their way.

Afterward, she returned to the hotel and did a little research on local antiques dealers in Dallas. There were clusters of shops located fairly close to her, on the northwest side of downtown in the Design District. Laura entered the address into her GPS and then took off into the grey afternoon.

Laura drove around the district locating the galleries and showrooms for a while before deciding on starting with one of the more prominent establishments. Feinstein's Collectibles was located off of Stemmons Freeway and Oak Lawn Avenue. It was in a large stone building that had been converted into a showroom. She wanted to ask some detailed questions and hopefully any reputable dealer in the city could provide her with at least some of the answers she needed.

The building was a vast warehouse, much larger than it looked from the street. Antiques were laid meticulously out on rows of pristine tables. Several customers leisurely browsed the aisles and chatted with dealers.

There was so much merchandise in the building, Laura felt a little overwhelmed. As she walked, she could feel some of the items resonating with past energy.

She came to a large stained-glass window from a southern cathedral somewhere in east Texas. It was almost vibrating with the amount of spiritual energy it held. She felt a sense of hope in its waves, strength and even deep fear. God only knows what horrors and miracles that glass had seen... Some of the pieces seemed to reach out and catch her attention. A life-size porcelain doll sat in a corner by itself dressed in dusty blue velvet. Laura stared at the frozen child's face, the marbled eyes that stared at everything and nothing... She could feel the essence of the young girl it once belonged to, almost hear the girl's laughter on a mild spring day over a century ago...

Off to the left was an information table. A young, slightly rotund woman sat there with eyeglasses on immersed in a paperback. It was one of those torrid paranormal romance novels that Laura couldn't imagine wasting her time on. In an attempt to look journalistic, she put on her glasses and pulled her notebook and a favorite pen out of her shoulder bag and held them in view. Laura approached the desk. She stood there astonished for a long moment just watching the woman read. What the heck was wrong with people? Laura cleared her throat.

The woman looked up, a little annoyed. “Yes?”

“Hello. This is a strange request, but I’m looking for antiques from a certain estate. Is that even possible?”

The woman sighed, as if a child had asked her a stupid question. The gesture reminded her a little too much of Colin. “Well, depending on the size and relevancy of the estate, they are either sold piecemeal at public auctions or bought by collectors outright. Depending on the circumstances, sometimes items are donated to charities...”

This wasn’t what Laura wanted to hear. She didn’t know enough about the industry to ask the right questions. Time to try another angle.

“I’m actually looking for some pieces from the Davis Collection, Chesapeake and Lester Davis. Have you heard of them?”

The girl almost rolled her eyes. If she had, Laura felt sure she would have reached out and slapped her across her chubby face. The woman commenced to speak in a cadenced, bored voice that dripped with condescension. “The *Davis Collection* was one of the most inclusive collections of pre- and post-Civil War memorabilia in existence. There are still small groups of artifacts that tour museums across the country all year long, but they belong to the Raulston House now. Most of the more valuable pieces were destroyed by fire in 1969. Horrible loss.” She turned back to her book.

‘*Well, of course it was 1969. That was the pattern,*’ Laura thought. So many events occurred in ’69 in this case. Way too many to just be coincidence...

“What happened? Do you know the story?”

The girl looked Laura over and wrinkled her nose. "I'm very busy, Miss. If you'd like to submit a written–"

Laura immediately changed her attitude again. "I really appreciate you taking the time. My name is... *Kendall Reece.* I'm a writer from AntiqueTrader.com and I just hoped you could help me with some information. I'd be happy to give you a mention in the article..."

The girl sat up immediately and smiled. "Well, in that case, I would love to help in any way I can. My name is Kris Jentzen. That's Kris with a K, one S, J-E-N-T-Z-E-N..."

Laura pretended to write her name down in her notebook, but instead wrote the word "CATTLEPROD" and underlined it.

"It was in 1969, at a storage facility somewhere here in Dallas. They say someone broke in and set fire to millions of dollars worth of merchandise and collectibles."

"What a shame."

"But that's not all..." The girl looked around her as if checking for spies. "They found human remains burnt beyond recognition there, too."

Chills rushed up her arms. This was definitely something worth checking out.

"You don't know if the location is still standing, do you?"

"Sorry, I'm not originally from here. So, what is your article about?"

"Excuse me, Ms. Jentzen. I need to make a call..." Laura walked away and pretended to enter something into her phone. Why didn't the warehouse fire come up in her search for Davis? She must have missed something. Damnit. It was another fork in the road that led seemingly nowhere.

Just then, she felt a tap on her shoulder. Turning around, she saw a young, shaggy-haired hipster with a shoulder pack standing in front of her.

"Ms. Milton?"

"Yes?"

"For you." He handed her a sealed envelope and turned to leave.

"Excuse me. Who sent this?"

The boy turned around his. "Lady, I'm just a courier. I was told to look for the pretty brunette. That's all I know." He turned around and left the building.

Laura turned the envelope over in her hands. How archaic, she thought. In this day and age, to receive a handwritten letter was almost unheard of. But it was untraceable, unlike email or texting. There was a charming old-school quality to it. That is, once you got beyond the whole stalker thing.

Opening the parcel, all she found was a single slip of heavyweight paper stock the size of a business card. There were no words printed on it whatsoever, just a series of handwritten numbers:

32.761292, -96.782996

N32° 45.6775', W096° 46.9798'

She recognized them immediately as GPS coordinates, entered them into her phone, and an address popped up immediately.

2714 Parnell Dallas, TX 75215. Bingo. God bless technology.

Laura looked up, cautiously scanning the surrounding area. If someone were watching her, they would have seen her interact with the courier and would know she was now in possession of the message. This could easily be a trap, but the only other option was to go back to the hotel empty handed. This was the only real lead she had.

Resigning herself to the task ahead, she turned towards the exit. Behind her, the antique girl was calling after her, "Miss Reece? Don't you want to know about my background?"

Once in the car, she set off in the light rain toward old east Dallas. It was 5:53 PM. At least she had a modicum of light in the sky for another hour or so. She had no idea what she would find at this address, if anything at all. But one thing was certain; someone had sent that message to her and it wasn't a ghost. She had told no one she was going to the antique gallery, not even Colin. And she made no calls or texts during her trip. Someone was definitely watching her. And the fact that he or she had followed her to the showroom meant they probably knew Laura was headed in the right direction. But was this a warning or was it just bait, something to pull her off track?

Her father's voice echoed from years ago in her ear. He had always been one to randomly say the strangest things to her as a child. It wasn't until she was 14 or so that she realized these cryptic sayings of his were film quotes.

'Knowing of a trap is half-way to avoiding it...' She couldn't remember if that one was from an old martial arts film or the Dune Trilogy. She smiled to herself. Words of wisdom, nonetheless...

She opened her glove box. There was a large black metal Maglite flashlight lying there. It wasn't a gun but at 14 inches long it weighed probably a good 3 and a half pounds. If nothing else, she could use it as a club if need be.

'All right,' she told herself, *'now you're starting to sound like Colin. Chill out.'*

The thought of Colin brought her back to her wits. What the fuck was wrong with her? She was being *followed!*

'Christ, Laura, this isn't some fucking game you're playing. These are real people out there–and they are watching you.' She felt herself switch from an excited dopamine high to

something more akin to real fear. Perhaps the tragedies in her life had succeeded in making her a little too detached, too confident in tense situations. But those coping mechanisms, though helpful, were far from actual courage. *'Best to err on the side of caution than the side of stupid,'* her father would have said. Gee, thanks, Dad.

She pulled the car over and texted Colin. 'GOING TO CHECK A TIP. 2714 PARNELL, DALLAS 75215. THINK I'M BEING FOLLOWED. WILL CALL ASAFP. <3'. At least now someone knew where she was going. Even if she didn't.

She pulled away from the curb and continued on. As she drove further southeast from downtown, she entered an area where most of the buildings seemed to have been cleared out for future development, except for a couple of scattered houses. The empty structures left standing were covered with graffiti and were slowly disintegrating in disrepair.

She parked on the corner of a street called Park Row, a block over from her destination. Just in case, if someone went so far as to confront her, she wanted to give herself an escape route that wasn't easily cut off. She locked her car and walked out in the misting rain.

The next street over was Parnell. There was a single brick building standing in the center of a cleared field. The sign above the entrance said 2714.

As Laura came closer, she saw the building was all but falling apart. The few windows, though covered with wire mesh, had most of the glass missing; only jagged fragments were left hanging from the frames like razor-sharp teeth in sleepy, gaping mouths. There were warning signs to keep out posted everywhere.

Laura looked up and down the street. There was no one in sight. She took her phone out of her pocket and saw it was 6:31 in the evening. Even though Grand Avenue, a fairly busy street, was a few blocks up, the immediate area was deserted at this time of the day, a little more so than she would have preferred. There weren't even street people mulling about.

'Nerves of steel, Pumpkin...'

An ancient security gate framed the front door of the building. The lock appeared to be rusted shut and reinforced by thick linked chain that circled the metal doorframe and the jam. The lock holding it in place was covered in grime. Obviously, no one had been here for years.

What was this place? Could this be Davis' long-lost warehouse? And if so, did she really want to know what was inside? Really? Well, whatever she was going to do, she had to do it quickly. The shadows were growing long and within the hour she'd be in total darkness.

She walked around to the back of the building and from an empty window she could see ambient light inside the structure. It appeared that part of the roof had caved in at some point.

At ground level, there was a ramp that led to a single metal door on the far corner of the building, but the door had been welded shut long ago. Other than four small exhaust windows the size of cinder blocks along the topmost edge of the back of the building, there seemed to be no other visible way into the structure.

She took a little comfort in the fact that if someone *were* inside waiting for her, he or she would either have had to climb up the side of the building and rappel down the hole in the ceiling or walk through the cement wall. That was in her favor; people, by nature, were both lazy and bound to the current laws of physics.

A corroded dumpster sat on thick, greasy rubber wheels next to the building. Something scuttered behind the iron box and she realized there was a small space between it and the wall. She pressed her face close to the wall and saw that behind the receptacle was a dark rectangle that looked like a small door of some sort embedded into the structure.

She pulled on the edge of the container and to her surprise managed to move it a few feet, enough for her to wiggle behind it.

She was right. There was a small steel door covered in grime about three feet off the ground built directly into the brick wall. By the look of it, it appeared to be a waste door to a furnace or something. The square plate was made of black corrugated steel and had no exterior handle. It sat sunken into its frame, but she could see there was a small margin of space on the opposite side of its spring hinge.

She walked back to the Land Rover and grabbed the Maglite. She also found a tire iron in a compartment by the back hatch that could be used to pry the metal door open. Her heart was pounding in her ears but she moved mechanically, trying not to let fear affect her efficiency. The rain fell in a steady mist about her and sounded like whispering voices. She closed the hatch as silently as she could and headed back to the warehouse.

Chills shot up her spine as she turned the corner and saw the dumpster again. Taking a deep breath, she put the Maglite on the ground and moved in to inspect the grimy object more closely. *'Four years of college and two of grad school,'* she thought. *'All for this...'*

She put her hand against the metal container and felt decades worth of muck slick the face of her palm. Disgusting. Well, this wasn't the time to start being overly girly. Disregarding the filth, she pulled on the corner of the dumpster with all her might and moved it enough to give her some working room. She checked the street to make sure she wasn't being watched. There was no one visible anywhere.

Working the flat tip of the crowbar into the crevice, she forced the metal door open to a crack. Leaving the bar in place, she searched the ground for something to prop it open further. She found half of a brick under the rusted dumpster and fit it in the opening. Now there was just enough room to fit the bar in the door at a better angle. She put her entire weight against the bar and the door sprang open.

A dark portal gaped open before her. Inside, all she could see was black nothingness. The stale smell of burnt metal and acetylene jumped out at her.

She picked up the Maglite and bent down, peering cautiously into the entrance. It seemed to open into a large cylindrical metal chamber, maybe 15 feet across. There were mounds of burned debris on the sunken floor. It looked like there was another door on the opposite side of the chamber. Turning off the flashlight she could see a faint glow through the cracks on the sides of the door. Hopefully it was unlocked. The walls of the chamber were black with soot. She looked down at her clothes and sighed. So much for her new Sketchers...

Bending forward, she put her foot against the dumpster, and pushed herself through the opening. As her body slid through, she was assaulted again by the smell of burnt metal. The thick scent was choking her. She put one hand out to steady herself and tried to keep the flashlight pointed ahead.

She slid face forward into a deep mound of ashes. Ugh. She pulled the rest of her body through the door and crawled into the corner with her back against the wall, afraid to look too closely at the pool of debris surrounding her.

Her heart started pounding. She took a deep breath to try and calm down but almost vomited from the thick, oily scent of the furnace. She shut her eyes tightly and forced herself to regulate her breathing. In her mind, she could hear the voice of her father lovingly urging her on.

'In and out, steady... That's it, Pumpkin. You're all right. Breathe steady, through your mouth so you don't have to smell it. Don't give in to fear, Laura. You are OK. Breathe...'

After a few moments, she finally felt calm enough to open her eyes. Thick black shapes jumped out at her from the ink-like darkness. She could hear the pattern of rain softly beating against the metal frame of the cylinder. Drips echoed from somewhere deep within the structure. She turned the light up and saw she was buried to the knees in ashes. Above her, a large section flanged out from the ceiling, possibly the feed from the gas lines that powered the furnace. What was this place?

Laura worked her way to the opposite opening. She pushed against the door but it wouldn't budge. It looked like there was a security bolt on the outside, but it didn't look locked. Years of rust and neglect kept the door stuck in place.

She leaned back and kicked as hard as she could against the metal door. A resounding boom echoed through the furnace startling her. If someone were in the building waiting for her, they now knew exactly where she was. And it would be so easy to simply lock her in the furnace and turn it on... She began to panic.

She kicked at the door, again and again, the booms reverberating in her ears, her only thought, to escape the furnace before the flames incinerated her.... Finally, the door started to move on its hinge ever so slightly. She knelt in the ashes and put her shoulder to the door, pushing with all her weight. Her foot slipped and again she slid into the waves of stinking soot. She regained her footing and pushed again, harder. The door began to creak and shudder, barely squeaking open enough for her to squeeze through.

She fell out of the furnace and landed in a dirty heap on wet cement. She was free. Raising her head, she put her hands in a puddle of water to wash the soot and grime from between her fingers as she tried to calm herself. Her heart was still pounding. She looked around the open space and as far as she could tell she was alone. Cautiously, she pushed herself to her feet.

The flashlight revealed piles of rags lying on dilapidated wooden tables surrounding her. She grabbed the first piece of cloth and wiped the thick black dirt off of her face and hands. She realized the cloth was once a beautiful silk blouse, now ruined by mold and moth holes. It also reeked of smoke. And she knew where there was smoke, there once was fire...

Water fell from the hole in the roof in a thin stream. She stood under it and let the cold water hit her full in the face, washing the ashes off of her. She let it run through her hair and could feel it seeping through her soiled clothes. She squeezed the excess water out of her hair and pulled it back from her face. Calmer now, she took her first complete survey of her surroundings.

The building was a single open space separated into zones by metal screens. The charred ceiling was a good 40 feet up, allowing for a mezzanine level that was stacked with crumbling boxes. On metal braces, gargantuan spools of what looked like rotting cloth hung from the ceiling. The place appeared to be a long-abandoned textile factory.

In the center of the warehouse, under a gaping hole in the roof, was a large pile of debris; charred slabs of wood, pieces of concrete, and burnt roofing. There were black swirls toward the top of the cement walls where they touched the ceiling that looked to be scorch marks, proof of a fire here long ago.

She was acutely aware of everything around her; the sound of the rain falling just a little harder on the roof, the smell of old gasoline, the cold trail left by a drop of water rolling down between her breasts... All her senses were alive and tingling.

Surrounding her were piles of blackened refuse that smelled like charcoal. Closing her eyes, she could hear nothing but falling droplets of water and the light breeze that blew the mist down from the massive hole in the ceiling. There was no one in the charred shell of a building, at least no one alive. But Laura knew she was being watched, nonetheless. She could sense panic, despair, and confusion coming from different points in the building. She didn't need to look at her arm to know that her hair was standing on end. People died here. Horribly. And they were still here, watching her. Not making contact, not even stirring in the shadows. But simply watching.

Turning back to the center of the room, she was drawn towards one of the rusted gates that led into a small alcove off to her right. There was something there, a deep sadness radiating from the shadows themselves. Stepping over a mound of splintering boards, she pushed the gate open and stopped. Directly in front of her was a table piled high with decaying fabric. As she approached, she saw something buried in the stinking folds of linen. The edge of a large purse of some sort jutted out from the debris. Approaching the table, she carefully pulled the object out from under the fabric. It was a small leather-clad satchel warped from water damage. And the latch was open.

Laura pulled the top open and let it fall backwards. Inside, there were the brittle remains of a once-waterlogged book, the edges curled up and frayed. The cover of cloth-covered cardboard was warped and ripped away in multiple places. The sight of the bound pages forced a deep shudder through her. There was obviously something here waiting to be found.

She hesitated for a second. This seemed too easy, as if this book had been planted here in plain sight. Or was it her intuition that was revealing all of this in real time? Her surge of adrenalin made it almost impossible to tell the difference.

Opening the book, there were clumps of pages stuck together with decades worth of mold. The few she could safely turn were faded and barely legible, the ink having all but bled and faded away long ago.

There was a section halfway through where the pages were loose enough to open without tearing. Laura pulled the pages back gently and saw the faint handwriting clearly. It was in a very deliberate style, full of large loops and dramatic indentions. It looked like a child's diary of some sort. And as she read, though the handwriting had a youthful look to it, the words seemed to leap from the page in a very mature voice.

'...the smell of alcohol on his breath. I was so frightened. What stared out at me from those eyes was not human. It was made of flesh but the heart was demonic...'

Was it a story? Laura didn't understand. But in her hands, the book was almost vibrating with energy.

The rest of the page was missing. She turned to the next readable section. The date *July 8, 1945* was at the top of the page. There was a dramatic indention, and then the child-like script continued.

'...He despises me. He hates the fact that I am intelligent. I am a monster to him...' The next paragraph was smeared and indecipherable. 'All I want is to be left alone. I feel like Shelley's creation, a composition of parts of dead things, something created and then cast aside...'

From the handwriting she guessed the author to be in her early teens. But the words, they were far beyond that age in weight and portent. She felt a connection with the kind of alienation the writer felt. Intelligent, she was seemingly ostracized by those closest to her. Laura felt a profound empathy for this girl resonating in her own heart deeper than she dared to admit. She read on.

'...They came to the house to see Father. That night everything changed. I fell asleep a child, and woke up a woman...'

Laura turned the remains of the book over in her hand. Inside the back cover, the initials CLM were written in that same dramatic scrawl.

Laura directed the Maglite to search the dark corners of the room. Piles of dilapidated file boxes and bolts of cloth were strewn everywhere. The fire had been bad enough to destroy a large section of the roof. The water damage to the remaining merchandise must have been from exposure to the elements over the years. After the fire, it seemed the place had simply been sealed up and left to rot.

There was the silhouette in the fading light of something hiding in a far corner. The smell of mold was almost overpowering. Gingerly, she worked her way through the maze of debris in that direction.

On her left were the remnants of what was once a child's basinet. The sheets and pillows had long ago mildewed and rotted into a wet mass. Behind the decaying piece of furniture lay a strange bulk hiding in the shadows. Laura stepped over the piles of trash and shined the light into the darkness.

A queen-sized carved four-post wooden bed sat constructed against the far wall. The soiled pink canopy sagged, its dripping center partially filled with sour black water and leaves. The mattress underneath was soiled, covered in mold from rain and baking in the summer heat for years. But for the most part, it looked like the bed had been made and left there long before the fire. Tiny pillows were piled against the soiled headboard, the dirty lace hanging in tatters from their edges.

Laura backed up into something and jumped. Startled, she turned around quickly. Tall wooden cabinets loomed over her, their surfaces covered in black soot. She cautiously took her hand and brushed off the fine layer of black ash and grime that covered one of the glass panes. Within, she saw shelves of glass holding scores of tiny porcelain figurines and assorted bric-a-brac. She reached for a piece of cloth lying on the floor and wiped the entire face of the display case. Hundreds of individual pieces were laid out on multiple shelves in painstaking detail. It was a menagerie of tiny poodles, dolphins, mermaids, sailors, sea otters, clowns of all descriptions, horses, giraffes, lions, elephants, and children, all marching on parade in a cupboard lost in time.

On the center shelf, there were probably twenty framed pictures set staring out of the glass doors into the warehouse. Each was a different picture of the same young woman. She was a brunette in her early teens, a thick mane of hair falling over her squared shoulders.

Laura felt wave after wave of chills rush through her body as her fight or flight instinct kicked into overdrive. She recognized the woman staring out from the photographs. The self-assured look on the angular face, the milk-white skin, the dark, intelligent eyes that stared out with pure confidence...

The pictures were of a young Chesapeake Millhouse.

She suddenly remembered the initials CLM. Chesapeake Lrya Millhouse. Laura felt faint. She picked up the fragmented journal and stared in amazement.

These were Chesapeake's words.

She grabbed a piece of tattered fabric lying on the table next to her and wrapped it around the book. She slid in inside her jacket and held it close to her heart.

It was now completely dark. The bright beam penetrated the gloom as she continued through the structure. Light fell upon the brick wall in front of her and she almost squealed. Stenciled in fading yellow and black paint was an enormous logo, probably 20 feet across, which read 'Sheldon Antiques' set in an elongated oval. Beneath the logo the words 'A Richter/Sheldon Company' stood out prominently. She pulled out her phone and took a few pictures. Colin was never going to believe this...

Laura climbed out of the building the same way she climbed in. When she slithered out of the furnace her entire body was black from all the ash and soot. Returning to the car, she pulled out a towel under the back seat and grabbed a piece of old cardboard to place on the driver's seat. Taking off her caked jacket, she climbed into the Land Rover trying her best not to touch anything, started the car, and sped away.

When the Land Rover pulled up to the hotel, the valet almost fell over when Laura emerged from the car crusted in black soot, her hair a wet, tangled mess. She acted like everything was normal. The grandmother with her two daughters probably didn't appreciate her much on the elevator ride up to her floor, though.

Back in her room, she stripped and got in the shower. The hot water felt heavenly against her skin, washing the layers of grime away. Her mind was swirling. She could still see herself inside the warehouse surrounded by those macabre artifacts while the eyes of the dead watched and silently encouraged her.

Laura stepped out of the shower and wrapped herself in a towel. For the first time all day she felt human. At that moment, her phone rang. It was Colin. She answered immediately.

"Oh, my God, I'm so glad you called. Where are you?"

"I'm at the airport trying to get on a flight. Everything's booked up and I'm flying stand-by. What the fuck are *you* doing? I just got your text."

"I'm doing what I have to, Colin."

"You need to just lay low until I get there. Who the hell is following you?"

"I don't know, but I just found some major shit!"

Colin swallowed hard trying not to scream through the phone. "Laura, you need to wait for me behind locked doors. You're not safe."

"I think I just found the name of Davis' partner. I have to follow this up."

Colin decided having a coronary on the phone wasn't worth it. He was at her mercy. "I can't stop you, damn it." He sighed. "Just keep me informed. Let me know where you are."

"I can do that."

"I love you, Laura."

"I love you, too. Talk to you soon..."

Le Guardia Airport, New York, New York

Colin Jonah hung up the phone, totally exasperated. Laura was the most intelligent and capable person he knew, but she was being thoughtlessly reckless. And it was only frustrating him more knowing there was absolutely not a damned thing he could do to help her.

The airport was packed with people. Of course, it had been impossible to book a non-stop flight to Dallas at the last minute and he had no other choice than to travel stand-by. It would more than likely take multiple layovers and plane changes, but at least he knew he would be in Dallas within 24 hours. Give or take.

With a little persistence, he got a seat to Colorado on the first plane he tried, but the departure was delayed from La Guardia by a line of thunderstorms. He decided to wait instead of searching for a different route. A couple of beers and an hour later, Colin was in his window seat staring out at the black of the tarmac waiting to take off. The air in the cabin had that stale smell of human cattle making him feel slightly claustrophobic. He was only traveling with his backpack so at least he didn't have to worry about losing his luggage.

Because of the storms, he had not been able to get through to Laura to tell her he made the flight. He covertly activated his phone and texted her, hoping it would reach her.

The plane finally started inching towards the runway and within 20 minutes they were airborne. Colin ordered a coffee and sat staring out at the pitch-black sky. God, he hated traveling. This was all such a pain in the ass, having to drop everything and go rescue his girlfriend from her own self-made menace. But she was well worth it, a thousand times over. He settled back in his seat and closed his eyes, his irritation finally starting to dissipate. In a few short hours, they would be together again.

And that was all that mattered...

Twenty Five

Dallas, Texas

The next morning Laura woke from her morning nap and took the Land Rover to be cleaned and detailed at a carwash off Greenville Avenue. There was a Starbucks across the street and the thought of a ventè no-whip white chocolate mocha was a little too much to pass up. While there, she got on-line and emailed her contact Kenneth Dolan at the Dallas Business Journal. Three minutes later, he sent a reply.

According to his records, James Richter, the Floridian investor whose name she found on the wall of the warehouse, died in March 1987. Kenneth also confirmed the name of his partner *Chel Sheldon* and gave her a business address and phone number to reach him. Sheldon was a Jewish antiques dealer who had retired in the mid 90's. He now owned a small tavern in Oak Cliff off of West Davis called the Lion's Den. Laura thanked him immensely.

It was just after 10 AM, but surely someone would be at the pub getting ready to open. She dialed the number and after a few rings a gruff voice answered. She introduced herself as a journalism major from NYU trying to find some information about the Davis Collection. The man paused noticeably but cleared his throat and admitted to being Sheldon. He agreed to meet her at noon as long as it would be quick and he wouldn't have to go on camera. She agreed and hung up the phone very excited.

This was kind of break she had been looking for. But even with that thought, she admitted to herself that this search for the White Rock ghost had morphed into something entirely different from what she first expected. She was no investigator. It wasn't her place to go around digging into people's lives and history. For what? Just to prove that some young woman died decades ago and that her spirit just happened to be bound to a body of water in Dallas Texas? And what if she actually found the answer she was looking for? Then what? Would she go to the police and try to convince them? It seemed a far-fetched concept that offered no reward whatsoever. But one thing was for sure; she had come too far to simply turn back now.

By the time Laura returned to the car wash, there was a small mob of Hispanic men wiping the vehicle down, white rags flailing in their hands. The interior had been cleaned and all the soot stains removed. She even had a little new-car smell infused just for grins.

Once she was back on the road, she entered the address for the Lion's Den into her GPS and headed south.

She exited 8th Avenue off of Interstate 30, just south of downtown. The serpentine street wound through an industrial district that gave way to an old residential neighborhood that was constructed in the early 40's. About a mile down, 8th became West Davis.

Here the buildings were decidedly more modern and inviting. This was Oak Cliff's Bishop Arts District; a charming area full of bars, restaurants, and art galleries nestled between the aging neighborhoods. The Metroplex Ghost Hunters were located right off of Bishop Street, the main artery of activity. Laura thought she would enjoy perusing the shops and galleries at some point but knew her schedule wouldn't allow it, at least not on this trip.

A quarter mile down, she came to a home-style diner called Norma's Café and parked on the street. Sheldon's pub was located two blocks down on the same side of the block, catty-corner to the restored Kessler Theater on the 1200 block of Davis. She would walk and leave the Land Rover out in the open in case she had to make a hasty exit.

She grabbed her notebook and organizer to look as official as possible, locked the car, and walked towards the whitewashed strip mall. The Lion's Den was the third space down next to a tattoo parlor. Laura pulled open the door and stepped into the bowels of the lounge.

Inside, the place was fashioned after an Irish-style pub, but dank and a little more seedy, probably by design. She could smell the sour odor of rancid beer coming from the drink wells. There was an older man sitting at the bar reading the sports pages. She approached him.

"Mr. Sheldon?"

The man turned around in his seat. He was tall, probably close to 6 feet, but his back was hunched severely as if by palsy or perhaps osteoporosis. A black-streaked wave of greasy white hair was swept back from his face.

"Ms. Milton? It's a pleasure." Quickly shaking her hand, she noticed his grip was weak and clammy like a dead fish. "Can I get you something?"

"Maybe a water? Thanks."

Moments later, they had moved to an isolated table in the back of the main room. When they had made themselves comfortable, Sheldon was the first to speak.

"Now, what can I do for you, Ms. Milton?"

She had already decided she would use the direct approach. "I'm researching the origin of the Davis Collection. The daughter of the proprietor disappeared sometime in 1970. I'm trying to find out what may have happened to her."

Sheldon sat back in his chair. "It's an interesting story. How can I help?"

"First of all, I'm looking for someone who knew Lester Davis of Dallas." Though Sheldon sat perfectly still, Laura felt him stiffen ever so slightly in his chair. His eyes didn't flinch. Laura continued. "His family was in cotton, originally from Houston. He lived at White Rock Lake until his death in the mid 80's."

Sheldon shifted in his seat.

"Yeah, I knew Davis."

"May I ask how?"

He hesitated for a nanosecond.

"Davis was a character. Everyone knew him, at least in certain circles." Sheldon never broke Laura's gaze. He was evidently very practiced in this game. "Mainly through his handyman, a guy named Ketter Naples. He knew everything about the family."

"And how did you know Naples?"

"He worked for some associates of mine. Ketter took a job on Davis' estate at White Rock Lake until he and Davis had a falling out."

"What was their fight over?"

"I have no idea."

"Did Naples have ties to Jack Ruby?"

Sheldon shrugged. "Naples had ties to everybody. Ruby? Yeah, he started working for Jack right after he left Davis' place. But Ruby was small-time, a *nobody*. Naples had his hands into a lot of things back then. He once told me about being a cleaner for some shady guys from Louisiana. He wouldn't do the jobs, but he would take care of the scene. Clean up, you know?"

"You mean, clean up crime scenes?"

"Whatever. When I met Naples he was just a kid running bets for Ruby, back when Ruby was still known as Rubenstein, a Russian immigrant who just moved to town from Chicago in '45. I came into his first joint, the Silver Spur, in the late 50's and he took to me, probably because I was in television at the time. Ruby always wanted to be famous so he surrounded himself with people who were in the industry. Anyway, Naples would do jobs for him."

"Was Ruby that powerful?"

"Like I said, Ruby was a nobody. He put his nose into other people's business and that's what got him killed. He wanted to be a hero. It's a wonder nobody took him out earlier. He was a real wise guy. When Ruby went to jail, Naples traveled around, spent some time in Houston and Texas City. Then, in the late 60's he went out to Tyler and took over his father's slaughterhouse. Perfect job for him, if you ask me."

"I've come across references to the oil tycoon H.L. Hunt in my research. Is there anything connecting these men?"

Chel sat back in his chair and wiped a thin layer of sweat that had slowly accumulated on his brow. The bartender came over and placed a shot and a beer in front of him and left.

"Ms. Milton, you're venturing into dangerous waters. Hunt may have had questionable judgment, but he was one of the richest men ever to walk the earth. He was the first real oil billionaire in Texas. Hell, his grandchildren are in litigation over their trust funds right now that still amount to billions."

"I know who Mr. Hunt is, Mr. Sheldon. I don't care about his transgressions other than how they apply to Lester Davis."

"I shouldn't even be talking about any of this."

"Why not, Mr. Sheldon?"

He laughed nervously. "People have a short shelf life when they talk, little girl."

"You're the second person this week to tell me that. Did you know Davis' wife, Chesapeake?"

Chel looked at her and took a sip off the shot in front of him.

"You cannot use my name whatsoever. You understand?"

She became a little more compassionate. "I promise you, this will be completely confidential. This is for school. All I want is the truth."

Chel wiped at his lips. Sweat dripped down the side of his face. "You will never find evidence to prove any of what I'm about to tell you. It's all been destroyed or the people have either died or been snubbed. But I was there. I saw it all. I'm probably the only living man left who could ever testify to any of it. I'm trusting you with my life, little girl..."

"I understand, sir."

"Lester Davis was a quiet, mousey guy, but he was a brawler back in the day. And he had a passion for guns. He ran around with H.L. in the 30's and 40's, not sure how they met. Probably through the military.

"Now, you need to know the background of Hunt himself. This was a fascinating guy. I mean, here was a guy who left home at 16, who believed in asserting his genetic superiority over the rest of the world, and worked a slew of blue-collar jobs until he began capitalizing on his knack for mathematics. He then became a professional gambler and bought his first famous oil fields with money made at the tables. Of course, some say he is supposed to have had funded the JFK assassination. I'm not sure about all that, but personally, I believe if someone stood between H.L. and something he desired, he would do whatever was needed to get it.

"And that boy could talk any woman into bed. It's not that he was handsome or witty or anything, he was a regular guy. But he had this strange light in his eyes. He was just so *sincere...* No one could resist him. Plus, I'm sure the money helped.

"Regardless that he was a Bible-thumper, that man ended up having 14 children with four different women, three of which he married. He was an aristocrat, a polygamist, a thief, an opportunist, a genius, and a womanizer. And not necessarily in that order."

Laura was almost blinded by the fountain of information. Sheldon obviously wanted to get this off his chest.

Sheldon slammed down the rest of the shot, chased it with a swig of beer, and continued.

"Ok, the story is H.L. met Davis' first wife at a charity fundraiser one night in the early '30's and became obsessed with her. He ended up giving Davis a huge wad of cash just so he could fuck her a few times." Sheldon didn't excuse himself for his language. He didn't seem like the kind of guy who made excuses for anything. "He made it look all proper, like he was courting her. But H.L. knew he would never marry her."

"What was the woman's name?"

"Louise Davis."

Instant clarity. So, Louise Davis *had* been a part of this after all.

Sheldon continued. "Anyway, Lester just let him have his way. Even though Davis was a dangerous guy on his own, he was loyal. He wouldn't dream of telling H.L. no.

"When H.L. lost interest, Louise fell into a deep depression and started seeing some writer who lived next door to her at the Melrose Hotel, which Hunt was paying for."

"McCoy."

"Yeah. Horace McCoy. Well, it ended up that Hunt didn't want Louise for himself, but he sure didn't want anyone else to have her either. H.L. paid off McCoy's gambling debts, gave him a stack of hundreds, a list of contacts, and a one-way plane ticket to Hollywood just to get the hell out of town and never come back. McCoy left Dallas that same night, forgetting Louise in an instant. After pining over him for months, the poor thing committed suicide that next year in the lake. Damn shame. She was gorgeous..."

"Yes, I know." All of Laura's leads were being confirmed. Though kind of a slime-ball, this guy Sheldon was golden. "What can you tell me about Davis' second wife, Chesapeake?"

Sheldon again sat back in his chair and frowned to himself.

"I can't believe I'm telling you any of this. I must be fucking crazy."

"Again, this will never be released to the public, Mr. Sheldon. I promise."

He looked into her eyes and sighed.

"One weekend H.L., Davis, and a creepy guy named Fowler came in to Houston to see my friend, Warren Millhouse. Millhouse was an oilman that H.L. was trying to get to invest in his next venture. I had been invited to come stay for a few days to ride horses and get away from the city. I definitely chose the wrong weekend to come down...

"Anyway, Millhouse had a young daughter named Chesapeake. She was home for a few days before the summer session began. That weekend, in a drunken rage, one of those men raped that poor girl. For God's sake, she was only 12 years old..."

"Did you witness it?"

"God, no! I passed out early. Millhouse had some emergency and had to leave. He left her there alone with the four of us... Damned fool...

"The girl ended up pregnant and kept the child. I think H.L. gave her a wad of cash out of pity, but that was it. When

Chesapeake moved to Dallas with the child to get away from the public, Davis proposed and married her. And she proceeded to drive him crazy for the rest of his life."

Her eyes didn't flinch off of him.

"Look, you don't have to believe anything I say, Ms. Milton. There's one person who knows the truth of what happened that weekend. Ketter Naples. He was there."

"Where can I find him?"

"His family owned a farm in Tyler somewhere. That's all I know."

"So, why did Hunt build a house on White Rock Lake?"

Sheldon took another swig of beer. "He didn't build it. He bought it in '38 from a cotton merchant and had it modified to resemble Washington's Mt. Vernon. Crazy old man."

"Is there anything else you can tell me, Mr. Sheldon?"

Sheldon sighed loudly. His eyes darted around the room in case someone was listening. Sweat stains had begun to spread on the back of his shirt collar and under his arms.

"Look, Davis was no saint, alright? He got mixed up with some people out of Louisiana and made a fortune over dumping rights in the lake."

Now we were getting somewhere. "What lake? What do you mean?" *Say it, Goddamnit. Say it.*

"White Rock."

It was as if the heavens opened up and a choir of angels erupted in song. She was right again.

"Davis was the liaison between the mob and the city," Sheldon continued. "He distributed the payola that kept the police from investigating any... *usage* of the lake. A large sum of money was supposed to be in-transit to the bigwigs one night at a big party, but there was an incident where gunmen came in and killed everyone in the suite. It was a massacre at the Hilton on Mockingbird in '69. During the chaos, someone took the cash. Everyone thought Davis was behind it, but no one could prove it. The transport guys were found garroted outside the hotel when the police arrived. Everything else was hushed up and never made the papers. And Davis left a fortune when he died that no one has ever claimed. *Tens of millions*."

Laura couldn't believe it. This was so much more than just a ghost story she has been following.

"Did he do it?"

Sheldon stared at her for a moment. "If so, he never admitted it to me."

Wow. Her mind was officially blown. She sat for a second collecting her thoughts. This was huge. She didn't want to fuck this up.

"So, was Hunt involved in all this?"

"Honey, Hunt was involved in everything. He was a silent partner on both sides. He kept Davis close, though. He bought the White Rock house to keep an eye on everyone, decades earlier. He was planning. For JFK, White Rock, *everything*. I'm telling you, the guy was a genius."

Something didn't fit. Why was H.L. Hunt slumming around with these people in the first place? Had Lester Davis actually been capable of planning and executing a plan like Sheldon described by himself? And if so, why? He had his own money. What was his motivation? Was he in financial trouble?

It was time to drop the bomb.

"Mr. Sheldon, what would you say if I told you I had visited 2714 Parnell?"

The blood visibly drained from Sheldon's face.

"I–I don't know what you mean–"

"You don't remember that rotting shell of a warehouse you own in east Dallas, Mr. Sheldon?" She looked him dead in the eye. "Now, would you like to tell me again about your relationship with Lester Davis?"

Sheldon wiped at his mouth, his eyes like black lifeless stones. He was visibly sweating. He answered in a low growl.

"I don't have to tell you anything, *bitch*."

He had her there. "True. I can't force you to tell me anything. But I *can* go public with this story and implicate your name in the details."

Sheldon's eyes went wide with fear. She had found his weakness: the need for anonymity.

"Ok. So, I worked with Davis for a while. No big deal." He was still tight-lipped.

"And?"

He sighed deeply. "I was his partner in the original Davis Group. After Chesapeake went crazy, I took over the antique business, ran it for him. We made a lot of money in those days."

"Why don't you want anyone to know you were associated with him?"

"Little girl, after the massacre, Davis had a price on his head bigger than the polar ice cap. Everyone knew if you helped him you were taking your life in your own hands. He was a fucker, yes, but he was my friend..." A certain tenderness passed over Sheldon's craggy features for just a moment and then it was gone. "It's a secret I've kept for fifty some-odd years and I'd like it to stay that way."

Laura nodded. "Fair enough. So why couldn't I find anything connecting Chesapeake to Davis Collectibles after 1961?"

Sheldon sighed deeply. "It was Chesapeake's second stay in the loony bin and Davis had to get her out of public view. He came to me and asked me to buy the company, change the name, and sit on the inventory for a few years. He would give me the money to purchase it in cash from his holding company and I would be paid by him directly to keep an eye on the merchandise while the Davis Group 'restructured' itself. We would reopen in a few years after things had settled down and make a fortune."

Laura stared at him incredulously.

"Don't hate me, little girl. It was easy money. We literally had hundreds of thousands of dollars worth of merchandise stockpiled in a secure climate-controlled warehouse. Until they found the place."

"Who is '*they*'?"

"That's something I don't even want to know. *Cosa Nostra,* most likely."

Laura knew the old Italian term. Translated literally, it meant "our thing" but was a phrase that referred to an organized crime syndicate related to the Sicilian Mafia. This story was bigger than she had ever imagined.

Sheldon's voice got very low. "They were coming for Davis. Men had already visited him, threatened to bring his life down around his ears and make him live to see it. Eventually, they even threatened his adopted daughter..."

"Rose," Laura said. This was starting to make some sense, finally.

Sheldon continued. "Davis was into a lot of shit I knew nothing about. But I could tell he was in fear for his life. And his daughter's."

Laura paused for a moment to let Sheldon's words sink in. She watched him closely. The old man's watery eyes were downcast and blood-shot. His gaze darted about the room nervously. And then it came to her. The people who killed Rose Davis could still be alive. And Sheldon was obviously petrified of being discovered.

"Why was the bedroom set up in the warehouse, Mr. Sheldon?"

"After Chesapeake died, Davis went crazy. He'd go and spend days there, arranging Chesapeake's things, playing music... I couldn't keep him away. Guilt drove him mad."

"Guilt about what, Mr. Sheldon?"

"I don't know."

"Are you lying to me, Mr. Sheldon?"

"Goddamnit, lady, I've told you enough!" He slammed his fist down on the table, looking her straight in the eye, his voice becoming a venomous hiss. "I'm not risking my neck for you and your little *bullshit* school project. If you want to know something, go find Naples. He was there. I think it's time you left, Ms. Milton." He stood up and shuffled away, leaving her alone at the table.

Colorado International Airport, Colorado.

When the Boeing MD80 finally landed at Colorado International, Colin Jonah took the time to find the john and grab a quick bite and a beer at a restaurant in the airport. He had a short hour wait to see if he could get on an express flight to Dallas/Fort Worth. As far as he was concerned, modern air travel was a complete pain in the ass; even though his family had money, for him the concept of flying was only for the filthy rich or the easily impressed. And he was neither.

He tried Laura a few times but the calls wouldn't go through. Goddamn this fucking weather. Well, she was a big girl and one thing was for sure, she could take care of herself. Still, this ordeal was bigger than either of them had ever guessed. Whoever these people were, they were persistent. And that meant this was no longer a support trip...

This was a rescue mission.

Dallas, Texas

Back in her car, Laura opened her phone browser and searched for slaughterhouses in Tyler. She found two, one of which was called Naples Meat Processing. Bingo. Since she was already in Oak Cliff, she decided to call Samuel. Even though he had a bit of a crush on her, he was the only male in the city that she trusted to back her up. There was no answer so she let it go to voicemail.

"Hey, it's me. I've found something. I'm driving out to Tyler, Texas today to try and find a guy who might have some answers. Wish you could go with. Call me when you get this." She entered Tyler, Texas into her GPS and took off on the next leg of her adventure...

Just as she was about to charge her phone, she got a text from Colin. He was in Colorado waiting for a flight into D/FW Airport. She really wished he could be here, but this was something that couldn't wait. Come hell or high water, she was going to try to find Ketter Naples. She didn't want to worry Colin any further by telling him her plans, and she felt bad about outright lying to him. Instead, she chose to feign ignorance and simply not return the text.

From I-30 she took the US 80 exit merging with I-20. It was roughly 99 miles to Tyler but pretty much a straight shot. A behemoth thunderhead was boiling straight ahead in what was otherwise a lightly clouded sky. Laura turned on some good driving music as she drove straight into the on-coming rainstorm.

Traffic was light headed out of town. After about 20 minutes, she had gotten beyond the Dallas city limits and was on the open road. Small droplets of rain patted against the windshield intermittently but for the most part the path was clear.

She was nervous about confronting this guy Naples, but at least it was still daylight and whatever was waiting for her in Tyler would be out in the open. The players in this little Texan soap opera were like roaches; they only came out in the dark and ran hiding from the light. As long as things didn't change, it would work in her favor.

The landscape of southeast Texas was flat and featureless for hundreds of miles. Laura tried to imagine what the first settlers in the state had seen traveling through these flatlands for the first time. Then, there had been no highways, no fences, no homes, no boundaries whatsoever. It had been a beautiful wilderness waiting for the cunning and destructive hand of the white man to come through and build his empire. Laura smiled to herself at her ability to ruin just about anything, even a nice drive in the country.

90 minutes into the trip, she merged onto Interstate 64. About 5 miles up on the right side of the road a small farm popped out of nowhere and stretched out across what looked like dozens of acres. As the Land Rover passed, a crimson blur smeared across the horizon. Instead of corn, soybeans or wheat, giant rose bushes grew in great scarlet rows that ran across the valley. The Tyler Roses. Laura remembered the city was called the "The Rose Capital of the World". Close to 20% of all the commercial rose bushes grown in the U.S. came from Tyler County. Though it was a beautiful thing to see, she was creeped out even more.

It was another good three miles till she reached Farm Road 1219. From there it was supposed to be a half-mile up. She found her exit and slowly continued up the pitted dirt road searching for some sign of the Naples Processing plant. She was lost. At this point thunder was rumbling all around her driven by huge gusts of wind. Black storm clouds hovered low overhead turning slightly green in the dark afternoon sky as rain fell intermittently. Perfect weather for a tornado. And the GPS said she had already reached her destination. Looking around, there was nothing in sight. Nothing but red mud and rain. Everywhere.

She pulled up to a large oak tree at a crude intersection. A small rusted sign was nailed to the trunk. She rolled the window down and squinted as wet wind rushed into the cabin. The battered sign said Naples Meat Processing and had a faint arrow pointing left.

"Oh, thank God."

She turned onto the narrow mud road and about two hundred feet later she pulled into the pot-holed driveway of a small estate. At the top of a sloping hill was a weather-beaten house surrounded by some smaller structures. Gated pens filled with swine surrounded the main house. She drove slowly up the crude driveway between the pens and pulled up close to the main building. It started raining in earnest again.

Laura opened the car door and wretched. The smell outside was unbearable. She covered her face, slammed the door behind her, and ambled her way through the wet red clay driveway up to the front entrance trying not to throw up. The dozens of hogs in the surrounding pens sloshed and grunted in excitement, smelling her. Gingerly, she made her way up the muddy steps to a splintering wooden door and knocked. No answer. She knocked again. Someone had to be here. She didn't want to have to come back to this place. Ever.

"Whut can I do ye for, *missy*?"

She turned around quickly and almost screamed out loud. Instead, she bit her tongue and clicked her mind into record mode.

A giant figure was hunched over at the foot of the stairs, holding a squirming piglet under one arm and a crusted hatchet in the opposite hand. The man was older, probably in his mid to late 70's. The little hair he had hung in white clumps around the perimeter of his head, the skin of his neck sagging over the stained shirt collar. His hands were huge, sprouting rough, calloused claws that could barely be called fingers. Even with his stoop, his shoulders were broad and hulking, making him a menacing presence standing before her. It didn't help that his overalls were stained black with dried blood.

The man's accent was a thick Texas drawl that almost dripped out of his greasy partially-toothed mouth. Laura quickly forced herself into a business voice, though utterly terrified. "Hi. My name is Laura Milton. I'm looking for Ketter Naples."

"Whut wud a pretty lil thang like yew want wit Ketta?"

"I'm doing research for a story and would like to ask Mr. Naples a few questions, if I could..." She could feel his yellow eyes creeping over her lecherously.

"Not frum 'round these parts, are ye, Ms. Milt'n?"

"I-I was born in Dallas." She mustered what some would consider a proud smile. "My family moved to New York when I was young."

"They calls ye peeple *transplanted.* I calls ye *outsiders.*"

He coughed and spat out a great glob of phlegm on the wet ground.

"I'm Naples. 'Little busy now..." He cocked his head towards the piglet undulating under his arm. The giant smiled a toothless grin and lumbered off into the rain.

Laura carefully scurried down the slick steps after him, almost sliding into the mud before righting herself. Naples trenched through the wet mud road to the far side of the house with Laura close behind trying not to fall. They came to a grassy spot next to a kennel full of barking, vicious-looking dogs. The Land Rover was sitting only yards away from them. At least if something went wrong, she had a destination. The rain started falling a little harder around them.

"Are you *the* Ketter Naples who worked for the Lester Davis family out at White Rock Lake?"

"That no bidness o' yours, missy."

"I'm trying to find some information about Davis' adopted daughter, Rose. You're him aren't you?"

"She's *dead*. Jus' like the rest of em. I gots nutin to do wit dem *animals*..." He turned away from her.

"I'm not with the police, Mr. Naples. I'm just trying to find some informa–"

"That ol' man sealed his fate long 'go. An' th' old *wo*-man wus crazy as th' daze long. Sheet, that po' girl ain't nevah stood no chance..."

"What do you mean?"

Naples approached a large stained tree stump. He turned slowly around and looked Laura dead in the eye.

"Money makes peeple cra-zay, Ms. Milt'n. Wetter yew gots it or not. 'S only a matta 'time 'for it takes yew or sumone takes it *frum* yew..."

"Who was Noel Fowler? Mr. Naples?"

Naples swung the piglet over on its side on the stump and stepped on its neck. It squealed and writhed under his foul boot.

"He ain't *no*-body. Same as you 'n me."

A clap of thunder erupted illuminating the entire hill for a nanosecond. The cold rain was seeping into Laura's clothes and she had to brush her dripping hair from her face just to keep talking.

"Who was Rose's father?" She shouted above the din of the bellowing swine and the falling rain.

"That *wo*-man wuz straight from *Hell*, lil gurl... *Cursed!*"

"She had Rose a year and a half before marrying Davis! Who was the child's father?"

"That *whore* shoulda stayed 'n Houston. Crazy fuckin rich peeple..."

"Who was the father, Mr. Naples?"

"I shoulda fucked that *bitch* when I had da chance like ever'one else..." he muttered under his breath.

Naples raised the hatchet above his head. The piglet squealed.

"Mr. Naples, wasn't Rose's last name really *Hunt*?"

The hatchet came down in a loud chop and the piglet suddenly stopped wailing. Laura looked down and was horrified by the sight of the headless piglet running around spewing blood all over the wet ground. Naples looked up at her with an enraged, blood-splattered face.

"Looka, here, lil girl, thisa here's private prop'ty! Don't you nevah come 'round here talkin' that *God-forsaken* sheet in fronna me 'gain, you unnerstand? Naw git your cute lil ass out o' my site 'for I sic the *dogs* on ye!"

She looked in his eyes and saw nothing but malice, not un-like the mad dogs that were howling to be unleashed on her on the other side of the chain-link fence. She turned and left immediately as the rain began to fall in sheets.

Twenty Six

The drive back to Dallas was unnerving. All Laura could think about was Naples and the horrid scene she had witnessed. It was more frightening than anything else she'd endured since arriving in Texas. As she approached the downtown skyline, she felt fortunate for making it back in one piece.

She was still in a mild state of shock when she pulled into the entrance of the Highland. There were three fire trucks parked along side the building, their blue and white LED strobes firing silently in the rainy afternoon. A large group of probably 60 people stood outside milling about holding umbrellas. It looked like they had to evacuate the hotel.

She pulled up to the valet and handed the kid her keys.

"It'll be a while," he said shrugging towards the fire trucks, "but I'll take care of it."

Laura nodded, took a deep breath and stumbled toward the front doors, walking past the firemen. As she entered the lobby, she noticed two policemen talking to the manager. What the heck had happened? Laura recognized the concierge standing next to him as a group of firefighters were walking towards the exit. The concierge looked up just in time to see her. He leaned over and said something to the manager who in turn looked in her direction.

"Ms. Milton?"

Christ, she didn't want to talk to anyone. She just wanted to take a bath and get in bed.

"Yes?"

His eyes shifted awkwardly between her and the officers. "My name is Mark Gosswell. I'm the manager for the Highland."

"Yes, I've seen you." Just get to the point. "Is there a problem?"

"We've been trying to reach you..."

Her heart began to pound. "What is it?" The manager looked embarrassed. She looked at the officer and he simply stared at her in uncomfortable silence.

She panicked and ran to the open elevator.

"Ms. Milton!" She heard someone call after her but she had already pressed for her floor and the door was closing.

'No, no, no, no, no, no, no, no!' Her heart was threatening to leap out of her chest. She felt dizzy.

Once the doors opened, her nostrils were assaulted by the intense smell of smoke. She ran out of the elevator and down the hall as fast as she could. Turning the corner she saw a small group of people standing in the open door of her adjoining interviewing suite.

Oh. My. God.

She walked up and stared at the scene, speechless. Yellow police tape had been stretched across the recessed entrance. A photographer was taking pictures of what used to be the door. The slab of metal-skinned pine had been split in two by a tremendous force. Two policemen were inside interviewing a Hispanic maid.

The cabinet in the wall behind them was a charred black pit filled with tiny mounds of melted plastic. All of the interview materials, the external drives of media, all her SD cards and secondary media, had been incinerated. The remains of her equipment were a scorched pile of metal and melted plastic fused into the floor at the foot of the bed. Cameras, lights, everything was gone. By the black streaks running up the wall and blooming on the ceiling, it looked like the firemen were lucky to contain the blaze in the room. But why didn't the sprinkler system go off? That would have kept the blaze from getting out of hand...

At least she had had the foresight to send back-ups to Colin, finally, after putting it off for days. Her room next door had been spared though. Thank God at least for that.

As she turned to go back downstairs to wait at the prompting of an officer, she thought this incident meant two things: first, she was definitely on the right trail, but of what still remained to be seen. And, secondly, these people knew where to find her, but who they were and what they wanted was still unknown. She would sleep with the Maglite under her pillow tonight, that was for sure. God, if only Colin were here. She wouldn't feel so frightened.

And so completely alone...

Dallas/Ft. Worth International Airport, Dallas Texas

Amazingly enough, the flight into Dallas/Ft. Worth was only 30 minutes late in landing. It took forever to exit the plane. It seemed everyone and their mother had decided to take the last flight to Dallas tonight. By the time Colin made it into the concourse it was already 12:45 AM.

The place was crawling with travelers. As he headed out of the gate area, there was a heavy-set man in a black suit standing next to the wall holding a card that said 'Colin Jonah'. The man glanced at him, but Colin looked away just in time and pretended to watch a young blonde girl bend over.

Because of the storm, he never had a chance to text Laura what airline he was on. Someone was trying to fish him out. Christ, what the hell was going on? He slowed his pace and stared at his phone as he slid past the stranger.

As soon as he was out of sight, he hurried to the car rental area. Soon, Colin was in a black Acura heading east on 114 toward downtown Dallas.

Traffic seemed heavy for that time of night. A lot of people must have been returning home on military leave from the week. Either that or the weekly business traffic. Then again, there were probably one or two travelers on their way to save their hardheaded girlfriends from getting buried by their own bullshit. Damnit, this crazy sojourn was important to her, but for Christ's sake, you have to know when to say when.

Colin saw a wide right turn in the road ahead, the exit to 114 toward Dallas. He stayed in the right lane and slowed down.

A car suddenly broke out of traffic and boxed him into taking a feeder exit.

"Thanks, buddy!" Colin was now on a service road that didn't seem to reconnect with the main highway, at least not that he could tell in the dark. "Goddamnit."

The roadway veered off to the south-east. This was totally not where he wanted to be. The GPS started squawking at him. Colin reached to adjust the volume just as the interior of the car filled with a blue-white light. Out of the glare, a violent force came barreling out of nowhere, impacting the Acura squarely in the driver's side front quarter panel.

The Acura spun clockwise and slid off the embankment into a small ravine at the foot of a hill. In the rearview mirror Colin watched as the car slammed on its brakes and turned back towards him at street level. It was an old Lincoln Continental, heavy and powerful. Again, its headlights filled the cabin of his car with a bright glow. He reached for the door handle but knew he'd never make it out in time. Colin sunk as far down as he could go into his seat and gripped the steering wheel with both hands, bracing himself for impact.

The Continental flew off the road and sailed into the passenger door, crushing it inward all the way to Colin's right shoulder and shoving the tiny car up the hill. The Continental's front end was literally sitting in the cab next to Colin inches away from his face, the engine revving, trying to get at him like a mad dog. He tried not to panic and see who was behind the driver's wheel but the glare from the headlights was blinding.

The sedan slammed into reverse and pulled out of the Acura's side leaving the car crippled. It sped away and slammed on its brakes, making a 180 degree turn and setting itself up for another run.

Colin tried the ignition but the engine wouldn't turn over. He opened his door to run but his legs fell out from under him, forcing him to grab hold of the door handle. He looked down and saw that the Acura had been rammed to the edge of an elevated embankment with a 50-foot drop over a mammoth drainage system. The earth had been gouged out and cement pipes the size of buildings were half-buried in the Texas dirt yawning up at him like gargantuan mouths.

He pulled himself back up into the car. Through the shattered passenger's window, he saw the Continental about 500 feet away speeding towards him to come back and finish the job. The bluish-white light again filled the cabin of the car. The passenger's door was smashed shut and the front and back windshields were still intact: he had no way out.

In a final effort, Colin pulled himself out and crawled up on the roof. The Continental downshifted and sped up just as Colin made it to his feet.

He jumped at the same moment the Continental struck the Acura, sending both cars spiraling over the embankment. The last thing Colin would remember would be flying through the air and wondering what death would feel like...

January 9, 1970 Colony Club, Dallas Texas

Rose Davis is sitting at the bar of the strip club drinking by herself. She is wearing the beautiful powder-blue strapless dress Kendall had given her from Neiman-Marcus when they first moved in together. The garment fits well but she can still feel her skin through the fabric, the squishy center of her that was so large and warm only a few short weeks ago. Gone is the steady rhythm of the heartbeat, the gentle pressure of the tiny body moving inside of her. Now she is empty, barren, and alone.

Rose blinks her tears away and looks at the clock on the wall. It is 11:30 PM. Louie, the bartender is cleaning up the service well while a dancer finishes her routine on stage for a smattering of patrons.

She shouts over the music. "She hasn't called, has she?"

"No, Rose. Haven't heard." Louie realizes Rose looks dejected. He leans in close to her and says, "Hey, don't wait around here. Take off and enjoy yourself. I'll tell Kendall you're looking for her if she calls."

At that moment, a young man comes up and sits next to Rose. His eyes linger over her until he finally leans towards her and whispers in her ear.

"Do you like cock?"

She can barely hear him over the music. He reaches for her leg and she pushes his hand away. She stands up and walks to the opposite edge of the bar. The boy follows her over. He gets close to her at the bar and while reaching for a drink, he grabs her breast. Rose screams. She pulls back and slaps the guy as hard as she can across the face. He just stares at her and laughs. Louie looks up from the other end of the bar realizing something has happened.

A bulky shadow steps out of a dark alcove and puts a meaty hand firmly on the drunken kid's shoulder. The face of the stranger is hidden underneath the wide brim of a black hat. The kid tries to pull away but can't break free from the iron grip.

"Apologize to the lady," the tall shadow says in a deep baritone, the square jaw under the hat spreading into a vicious grin revealing large white teeth.

The youngster tries to pull away again. "Fuck that bitch. And fuck you, too!"

The mountain smiles maliciously under his hat.

"Oh, you don't want to fuck me," The shadow chuckles under his breath. He squeezes a pressure point on the shoulder and the kid shrieks in pain.

The tall stranger lets him go. Glaring at Rose, the kid puts his hand on his injured shoulder and storms out of the bar before the bartender has a chance to get a bouncer.

The stranger turns towards Rose. He seems handsome under his hat in brutish Centurion sort of way. So masculine and chivalrous. She smiles.

"What's a gorgeous girl like you doing in a dump like this?" His voice is like dark, warm syrup.

"Thanks, I really needed that tonight. Whether you meant it or not." She laughs. She can only see his mouth and chin underneath the shadow of his hat, but he smiles warmly.

"Of course I meant it, doll..." A large, coarse hand comes up and brushes the side of her face gently. "You look like an angel. Has anyone ever told you that?"

"Thank you." She feels herself blush. It feels so nice having him look at her. It's been so long since a man thought she was pretty. "It's my birthday."

"Really? Well, happy birthday, angel. What's your name?"

"Rose. Rose Davis."

The stranger smiled, a row of perfect white teeth appearing between the bear trap jaws. "Rose..." His voice lingered on her name, as if savoring the sound of it. "Rose... Are you even old enough to be in this place, Rose?"

She giggles and brushes against his arm. It was like steel covered in cloth.

"Yes, silly! I'm twenty-seven. Today."

"Well, you should be somewhere classy celebrating instead of this hole." He inched a little closer to her.

"I-I was waiting on my friend... She dances here. I haven't seen her in months."

"It looks like your friend is late." A wide grin spreads across his square jaw. "Why don't you let me take you somewhere nice for a birthday drink? It's the least I can do for a beautiful woman who's been stood up."

Rose takes a moment to think about it. The bar is almost empty and she is restless. At that moment, a song begins playing, an old doo-wop melody that she remembers from years ago. Her eyes go wide with pleasure.

"Oh, I love this song!"

'You don't remember me, but I remember you...'

The song is joyful and full of sadness at the same time. It makes her feel like it was written just for her.

'Tears on my pillow, pain in my heart caused by you...'

She looks up at the stranger and smiles.

"Ok. I'm all yours," she giggles.

The square jaw spreads in a shark-like grin. "I'm the luckiest guy in the joint."

Rose turns to Louie, the bartender. He is looking the stranger over with a critical eye.

"Tab me out, Lou."

"Happy Birthday, Rose. Tab's on the house." His eyes never leave the toothy grin under the stranger's hat.

"Thanks, Lou! If you see Kendall, tell her to call me."

"I will."

"Bye!"

Rose grabs her coat and purse and leaves the Colony Club arm and arm with the hulking stranger...

Present Day. Grapevine, TX

Colin woke up in a wet sandpit, his head pounding. He lay there for a moment trying to get his bearings. The last thing he could remember was being run off the road and a car coming out of nowhere ramming him over and over... He lifted his head and in the pale light saw a huge piece of machinery less than 10 feet away from him. Had he landed a few feet to the right, he would have been impaled on the multiple arms and levers of the burrowing devices without a doubt. He silently thanked the karma angels for watching over him.

Slowly, he carefully crawled to his feet, testing his body to see if anything was broken. Except for some scratches and bruises, he seemed to be all in one piece. It felt like his shoulder was bruised and he had the mother of all headaches, but he was alive.

The sun was glowing silvery white behind the morning cloud cover. Dew was on the muddy patches of grass and the air was chilly. It had to still be very early. Remembering he had it, Colin pulled his phone out of his pocket. The face was smashed but miraculously he could still read the display. It was 7:09 AM Sunday morning. He tried calling Laura, but the phone wouldn't dial. He tried texting and saw that he had no service. Great.

He was surrounded by huge hills of dirt and ravines gouged in the land by super-massive bulldozers. Where was the rental car? Across the construction site he saw the elevation of the highway in the distance, probably a mile or so away. He couldn't remember how he got so far off from the main highway.

Colin turned and slowly walked up the steep mound of earth behind him. When he reached the top, he saw that the ground gave away sharply to a straight drop. Below, four mammoth cement pipes shot out of the black dirt like small skyscrapers. There, 50 feet down or more, the remains of two cars were smoldering at the mouth of the tunnels in the cool morning air. Whoever was trying to get to him last night met his or her own fate in the attempt. Poor bastard...

It was a long walk to the highway. And an even longer one to a landline. At least he might be able to send and receive texts once he found a signal, unless the phone was toast. And speaking of toast, some food would be good as well. He hadn't eaten since he was at Colorado International. And it was probably time to contact the police. That would be fun, explaining all of this... And then there was Laura. If these people could do this to him, what was she up against? He really had no time to waste.

He realized he smelled particularly ripe after a night of playing Death Race 2000 with his new friends. All his clothes were gone, trapped in the wreckage of the Acura lying at the bottom of the pit. But at least he wasn't with them. He brushed the dust off his trousers, zipped up his soiled hoodie, and headed off across the construction fields towards the highway.

Welcome to fucking Texas...

* * *

Laura woke up to a raging anxiety attack. Colin was supposed to have already arrived this morning but there were no messages from him, which only added to her stress. Nothing was going right. She couldn't stop her heart from racing. *'Christ on a yacht, Laura, this is how people have heart attacks. Get a grip.'*

She called Colin and the phone went immediately to voice mail. So either he was still in the air or his phone was off... She didn't want to think of what that could possibly mean...

In a nervous fit she got dressed and left her hotel just before 11 AM. Traffic was moderate on the expressway. While waiting on the entrance ramp, she picked up her phone and dialed Mallory. She heard a click and instead of going to voicemail an electronic female voice came on the line, saying, *'The number you have dialed is no longer in service. If you feel you have reached this message an error, hang up and dial your number again...'* What the fuck? She hung up and dialed him again. The same click and recording came over the line. She hung up, totally frustrated.

Laura called Samuel next. His phone went immediately to voicemail. She hung up and called the main Ghosthunters number. It rang once, twice. On the third ring an irritated female voice answered.

"*What?*"

"Rachel? It's Laura Milton..." Absolute silence. "Is Samuel there?"

Rachel seemed to cover the phone with her hand. There was an inaudible expletive shouted and then Laura heard her muffled voice say, "It's her," in the background.

Rachel uncovered the mouthpiece. "We thought he was with you. No one has seen him in days."

"No. He left the club the same time I did the other night." A creeping feeling came over her. "If you see him, have him call me as soon as he can."

"Sure, Laura. You too." Rachel hung up the phone abruptly. Damnit... Now even Sam's crew had turned against her. Where the hell was he?

Victory Plaza and the W Hotel were just a block away. She knew there was a security door for both the building entrance and the resident's elevator. How was she supposed to get through that?

The Land Rover pulled up to the valet in front of the W Hotel. Jumping out, she threw her keys at the valet and ran toward the frosted glass entrance of the Residences. As she ran up, a young couple walked out of the building and she caught the security door just in time. Across the reception room, the elevator door was closing and she ran to catch it.

"Hold please!"

A male jogger held the door for her and smiled awkwardly as she stepped in. She was suddenly self-conscious of how ragged she probably looked. When was the last time she took her medication? She had no idea.

"Thank you."

When they reached the 16th floor, the door opened and she ran out into the hall. She had to see Mallory. Maybe he would know what was going on. She needed someone to prove to her that she wasn't losing her mind.

His door was the second one on the right side of the hall, #1620. She came to the familiar blue stained door.

It was ajar.

Taking a deep breath, she gently pushed the door open.

The apartment was empty. Even the rugs were gone. The only thing familiar were the polished bamboo floors that stretched throughout the unit. The piano, the couches, everything else had vanished.

She continued down the hall and looked into what she remembered to be Mallory's bedroom. It too was empty. The walls were the same ashen grey but everything removable was missing. Not even drapes hung on the windows. It was like no one had ever lived there.

She heard something down the hall. A shuffling sound. Then the click of heels against the floor. Her head was reeling at this point. Nothing was making sense. Was she losing her mind? Where in God's name was Mallory? Perhaps the people following her had reached him already...

Laura looked around in a panic for anything she could use to protect herself. She picked up a window squeegee that was lying on the floor. It was plastic but was the only thing she could possibly use as a weapon.

She crept into the long shotgun hallway that stretched the length the unit. The shuffling got louder the further she went. And footsteps, definitely... She was not imagining the sounds. Someone was here.

She gripped the plastic handle and turned the corner.

In the sparsely furnished room, a woman was placing books into plastic crates. There were two small folding chairs and a card table. Otherwise, the room was empty. When the woman looked up and saw Laura she was startled.

"Oh! Are you my twelve o'clock?"

"Excuse me?" Laura was disoriented. She put her arm down and pretended to not have been about to strike the woman with the plastic handle.

"Do you not have an appointment to see this unit?"

"I was just–"

"Oh, I'm sorry, we're not taking walk-ins today. You'll have to call and make an appointment through Heritage."

Laura shook her head. "No, I–I'm looking for someone. Do you know Mallory?"

The woman paused. "I don't believe I know what you're talking about." The woman looked at Laura suspiciously and noticed the handle she was gripping in her hand. "I'm afraid I'm going to have to ask you to leave."

"But this was his apartment. I was here just a few days ago."

"I'm sorry but this unit has been vacant for the past seven months. I'm going to have to ask you to leave. Miss?"

Laura's head exploded with waves of chills.

"Miss? Are you alright?" The real estate agent reached out to her.

Laura shook her head. She reached out a hand to steady herself and missed the wall. She fell to her knees with a thud.

"Oh, my goodness! Can I help you?" The woman's voice sounded far away.

Laura forced herself to her feet. She had to get out of there. Her vision blurred and she felt nauseous. This was too much to process at once. Her vision seemed to be getting brighter.

She left the apartment and ran down the hall into the open elevator. The voice of the woman was echoing after her, saying something. Laura pushed the button for the lobby and the doors closed.

There was a sour taste in her mouth, bile trying to come up in her throat. She swallowed hard trying not to throw up. There was a women's restroom in the lobby. If she could only make it, she'd be fine. She prayed that this wouldn't trigger a seizure.

It seemed like an eternity before the elevator doors opened. Stumbling out, she held on to the wall for balance. The bathroom door was just a few feet away. Pushing it open, she fell flat on the white tiled floor, dazed. She crawled to the sink and pulled herself up. The face in the mirror she didn't even recognize. With a thud she fell back against the wall and sank to her knees trying desperately to calm herself down and get on the floor. Her nose was bleeding.

The room went white and Laura slipped into unconsciousness...

* * *

Colin Jonah thanked the driver as he leaped out of the cab of the mammoth Mack truck. It was 12:45 PM when the 18-wheeler pulled away and left him at the corner of Mockingbird Lane and 75 Central just north of downtown. He had been able to catch a ride at the Race Track service station he walked to from the site of his accident. Colin was thankful at least *some* people in this state still believed in southern hospitality and didn't threaten you with vehicular manslaughter at first sight.

The cluster of buildings that was the Highland Hotel and adjacent properties stood before him like some sinister castle out of a medieval fairytale. Even in the light of day, looking up at the penthouse of the hotel gave him that same feeling he got staring at the Bobst Library back at NYU. Something was here, all right. And it wasn't just conventioneers. He could feel a presence, like eyes watching him intently. Whatever it was had honed-in on his frequency as well as his girlfriend's. Colin was suddenly very sorry for disbelieving her. Things *did* exist that were somehow separate from our world. It wasn't just some hallucination or mass hysteria. He had seen it, felt it, and almost died because of it. And Laura had known all this time. He wouldn't make that mistake again. But for now, all he wanted was to take her in his arms and get them both the hell out of Dodge.

He entered the hotel. At the front desk, a young woman glanced up from her computer screen as he walked up.

"Welcome to the Highland Hotel. How may I help you?"

"I'm trying to find Laura Milton. I have no idea what room she's in."

"Your name, sir?"

"Jonah. Colin Jonah."

A subtle smile came across her face. "We've been expecting you. May I see your identification?"

He handed her his ID wondering what in the hell she meant. The girl returned his license along with an electronic passkey.

"Thank you. Ah, is there a car rental service on the premises?"

"Yes. Feel free to stop by the concierge desk around the corner. They'll set everything up for you."

"Thank you." He turned towards the elevators.

"Enjoy your stay with us..." the young woman called after him.

And for some reason he couldn't quite explain, at the sound of those words his blood ran cold.

In the elevator, the exhaustion was overcoming him. He knew there was so much still to do, but all he wanted was to sleep. He was finally here in Dallas and he would be in Laura's arms soon. He just had to hold it together for just a few minutes longer...

When the elevator opened, the scent of burnt wood and metal was unmistakable. What the fuck had happened? Finding Laura's room, he knocked lightly. No answer. He slipped the key in the mechanism and stepped into the lush suite. The aroma of Laura's perfume reminded him of home. God, how he had missed her...

Looking around, he saw the room was in disarray. That was not like her. Laura was meticulous. Something was wrong. Where could she be?

He took his phone out. Miraculously, there was a missed call from her. At least his phone was working. He called her back but the phone went immediately to voicemail.

"Laura, I'm at the hotel. Where are you? Call me as soon as you get this. I love you, baby." He hung up feeling helpless and exhausted.

He would wash up, get a rental car downstairs, and grab a quick bite to eat somewhere while he waited to hear from her. That was the best plan he could come up with.

Something in the pit of his stomach told him that even though he was finally in Dallas, he and Laura were by no means out of the woods...

Twenty Seven

...A small hand submerged in liquid, gently rising and falling with the current, spidery veins of light dancing over pale flesh in the depths... Minnows dart through the water drawn by the flashes of light glinting off a thin platinum bracelet set with dozens of tiny crimson stones... Through the water, a faint melody echoes as if sung by a chorus of blue, rotting lips...

'You don't remember me, but I remember you...'

Laura Milton tried to open her eyes but met a white glare. She clamped them shut, her head pounding with the effort. She covered her face with her hand and slowly the intensity faded. Squinting through her fingers, she realized she was lying on a couch in a room she didn't recognize. There was a figure sitting close to her. She instinctively recoiled but relaxed when the figure didn't move. Slowly her eyes adjusted and she could see the details of a young face staring back at her. It was a chiseled, intense face with deep sad brown eyes framed by a mop of curly dark hair. She recognized him immediately.

"You're the courier." Her mind was reeling a million miles a second. "From the antique dealers. You're the one who sent me to the warehouse on Parnell..."

The young boy with the shaggy hair smiled sadly. He looked to be no older than 18.

"I knew what you were looking for."

Laura sat up, her head still swimming. She looked around the sparsely furnished room. Nothing was familiar.

"Who are you? What happened?"

"Do you remember going to the W Hotel?"

She thought. "Yeah, the Residences. I went to find a friend..."

"You passed out. I found you in the women's restroom on the first floor."

Laura saw the room they were in was empty except for a futon, the couch she was laying on, and a standing lamp. Her head was throbbing and there was an icepack lying next to her.

"I put my bike in the back of your car and brought you here. You've been out for a few hours. I'm just glad I found you before they did."

"They who? Who are you?"

"My name is Ren Morrow. Daniel Morrow was my grandfather."

Morrow. Laura's mind raced. She knew the name. And then it came to her. He was Lester Davis' lawyer in the 60's.

The boy's voice was steady. "Ever since you came to Dallas you've had people watching you."

"How do you know?"

"Because I've been watching you, too." Ren stood up and picked up an old manila envelope off the floor.

"Watching me? Why?"

"My grandfather was killed because of this woman."

"What woman? What are you talking about?"

"The one you're looking for. Rose Davis."

Laura sat back. Her head was pounding. She indeed had a seizure and must have struck her head when she passed out. She had to be very careful not to get too worked up.

"Before he died," Ren continued, "my grandfather left this letter to my father, who hadn't even been born yet. He and his wife separated right after she found out she was pregnant. When my father died three years ago, I found it in a safe deposit box with my name on it. It explained everything."

"Everything?"

"Why both he and my grandfather were killed."

Laura looked closely at Ren. He was thoroughly convinced the things he was telling her were true, whether they were or not. Her head was pounding. She was still having a hard time deciphering what was real and what wasn't.

Ren continued talking. "Rose Davis was raped by one of her employers, probably one of her clients at Neiman-Marcus. In desperation, she made an appointment to get an abortion..."

Laura's memory was coming back slowly. She whispered, "Doctor Noel Fowler..."

"Fowler was a pervert and a cannibal." Ren's voice dripped with contempt. He obviously knew all about the good doctor. "She was lucky she escaped before he made a meal of her or her child. I can't believe he was allowed to violate women for so many years..." His hatred of this Dr. Fowler was intense.

"Then she didn't go through with it?"

"No."

'So, Rose actually had the child...' Laura thought. Even in her foggy state, she knew this was important.

"How does your grandfather fit in this? I thought he was just Davis' lawyer?"

"He was in love with Rose's roommate Kendall, even though the girl was little more than a prostitute. When she began disappearing for weeks at a time, he went into a deep depression. He and Rose knew little about one another until the night she escaped Fowler's clinic..."

June 1969, The Wilson Building, Dallas, Texas

The sun is just starting to sink behind the downtown buildings as Rose Davis pulls into the parking garage of the Wilson Building. She had pulled her dress on over her head but the green paper medical gown still hangs out underneath it in strips. Blood is dripping down her leg leaving a trail behind her of crimson droplets on the cement floor as she gets out of the car and shuffles toward the elevators.

Rose closes her eyes for a moment and then finds herself in the elevator, the doors opening on the penthouse floor. She pulls herself into the hallway, slowly hobbling across the white tiled floor to her front door.

Severe cramps slice through her causing her to scream out in intense pain. She covers her mouth with her hand and starts crying in earnest in the dark hallway. Her sobs echo throughout the deserted top floor of the building.

She takes a deep breath and forces herself to fish her keys out of her purse. She finds them, puts the right one in the keyhole, and turns the lock.

The apartment is completely dark except for slashes of dying sunlight shooting through the bay window. Closing the door behind her, she puts the security chain in place and breathes a sigh of relief.

Shuffling to the couch, she drops her bag and the rest of her clothing on the floor, collapsing with a moan. The room is full of shadows and silent except for the muffled traffic noise from the street far below. White-hot cramps shoot through her abdomen again and she remembers the horror of the clinic. She can still see the blood-smeared face of that man, Fowler, licking his lips, violating her in the most sickening way possible. Rose closes her eyes and tries to stop thinking all together.

She's on the verge of sleep when a loud knock resounds from the door. Her eyes pop open and she hears the sound of keys fumbling in the lock. Rose pushes herself up onto her feet and hobbles to the door just as it opens. The security chain keeps it open only a sliver. She can see a tall dark figure peering into the apartment.

Rose speaks first. "Kendall?"

"No. I'm sorry! I, ah, it's Daniel. Morrow. The landlord." Rose recognizes his voice immediately.

"Oh! Just a moment please..." She pushes the door closed and is instantly flustered. The apartment is barely presentable. Turning the light on in the entryway, she looks at herself in the mirror on the wall. Her eyes are red and swollen from crying. She wipes the mascara off from under her eyes and runs her hands through her hair. Taking a deep breath, she removes the chain and opens the door.

Even in the shadows she knows the man standing before her. He is tall and lanky, his charcoal suit hanging off his body at a strange angle as if he were nothing but bones underneath. He has a matching hat on his head with a wide blue band. It makes him look like a spy or a gangster from television. But his face is young and handsome, though he seems upset.

"I'm sorry to bother you, Rose."

"It's no trouble at all, Mr. Morrow. After all, it's your place. Please, come in."

"Call me Daniel." He cautiously steps into the apartment, closing the door behind him. Fidgeting, he seems more than a little out of his element.

Rose can't imagine why he would show up so late in the day. "Is there a problem with the rent this month?"

“Oh, no, not at all. I was really just checking to see if maybe Kendall was home.”

“I haven’t seen her in a few days.” She doesn’t have the heart to tell him about Kendall’s engagement ring, much less the fact that she hadn’t slept in her own bed for the last three weeks. His face grows dark, as if he is about to cry.

“I don’t mean to bother you with this,” he stammers, “I know it’s not your problem. But she won’t return my calls. You wouldn’t happen to know where she is?”

“She’s very private. She never tells me anything anymore.” That much at least was true.

“I know the feeling...”

They stand there for a moment staring at each other in awkward silence, partners in pain and confusion. He realizes she looks disheveled. Looking down he notices small drops of blood trailing behind her.

“Oh, my God, are you alright? Here, sit down.” His voice is calm and soothing. He walks her over to the couch and helps her put her feet up and sees blood trailing down her leg.

“Where are your towels?”

Rose answers back in a feeble voice. “In the hall closet.”

Morrow leaves her, fetches a towel, goes to the kitchen and runs hot water, soaking it. He returns and wipes the side of her pale face and arms.

“I... can’t...”

“Don’t talk. Rest.” He helps her to lie back.

The last thing she sees is Morrow’s concerned face staring down at her before she slips into warm darkness...

* * *

When Rose wakes she has no idea how long she has been out. The sky outside the vaulted windows is black and shadows dance on the walls of the apartment cast by the streetlights and cars 12 stories below. The lamps in the apartment have been turned on as well as the television, though the volume is all the way down.

A thick white robe has replaced her clothing. Her hair is damp but has been brushed through. She feels clean. Her thoughts are cloudy and fragmented. The last thing she remembers is a man...

Daniel Morrow walks into the room from the hallway, a cigarette dangling from the corner of his mouth. He sees she's awake and takes the butt out of his mouth.

"You ok?"

Rose feels a little self-conscious but nods her head. She remembers his soothing voice. He is a friend.

"You were bleeding. I was afraid I'd have to take you to the hospital."

Rose pulls back the robe. She has clean panties on. Next to her groin there is a thick white bandage taped to her inner thigh.

"It was a bite mark. I finally got the bleeding to stop."

She looks away, thoroughly humiliated.

"It's ok," he says, sensing her embarrassment. "I was pre-med before getting into law school." Her frightened eyes meet his gaze. "I would never..."

"Thank you, Daniel."

She reaches up and scratches at the thick square bandage on her shoulder and winces from the pain.

"It was another bite. I cleaned and dressed it. You should probably get a tetanus shot as soon as possible."

Daniel sits on the couch next to her. Silence passes between them for a long moment.

"You don't have to tell me what happened if you don't want to..."

"I'm pregnant."

He waits just a heartbeat. "I figured." He doesn't have to say anything else. He just sits there listening attentively.

Rose is unsure of what to say. Seeing his face, completely non-judgmental, she feels better about telling him. She has to tell *someone*... "I-I decided to get rid of it. I went to a man by the University. He..." She chokes back angry tears, not wanting to seem like a basket case to him. "He raped me."

"Who is he?"

"His name is Fowler."

Daniel's eyes flicker for a moment and then he's back. He reaches for her hand.

"I-I feel alright. But he tried to..."

"But you're ok?"

"Yes." She looks away. So many thoughts in her brain, so much pain she can't process. "I don't want to lose my baby."

Daniel puts his arm around her. "I can't tell for sure, but you seem fine. You don't seem to have any internal bleeding or trauma, as far as I can tell. Are you in pain?"

"I'm sore, but I think I'm ok." Tears fill her eyes once again. "It was a mistake. I was afraid..."

Daniel is silent for a moment. He knows he has a child growing inside his own wife's belly at this very moment. He also knows since his wife found out about Kendall, he will never be part of either of their lives ever again. His pain is unbearable. He has destroyed his own life and will never be able to pay for what he's done to his own family, but perhaps it was time for him to start thinking of someone else for a change.

"There's an alternative," he says softly. "You can have the baby. And decide later if you want to put it up for adoption." Her head drops into her hands and he hears the wet, shuffling sounds of her crying. His heart swells in the radiance of her pain. “I’ll help in any way I can. You can stay here as long as you want.”

“No. I don’t want to be here anymore. This place scares me at night.”

“I can get you a room at a hotel if you like.”

She feels his sincerity and smiles.

“I appreciate what you’re doing, Daniel. But I don’t want to be a burden.”

“It’s the least I can do.” He smiles gently. “Where else would you want to go?”

Rose doesn’t have to think.

“Home. I just want to go home.”

“There are people watching your father, Rose. Bad people.”

“He’s in Europe for the rest of the year. Can’t I just go back home?”

He thinks for a moment. Anyone watching Davis would be following him around the world, not watching the house of a demented widower. It might be the safest place for now.

“You’re right. I think we should go tonight.”

“I, ah–”

“Grab what you need and I’ll have the rest couriered to you in a few days. Come on.” He gently pulls her to her feet.

“Why are you doing all this for me, Daniel? I’m no one to you.”

He stares down into Rose’s blue eyes. “We have something in common. Kendall meant a lot to both of us...” He smiles in the dark. “I’ve done some things I’m not at all proud of. This is a chance for me to do something right for once.”

“I don’t know how to thank you....” Tears begin to fall down her silken cheek. She’s totally at a loss for words.

Daniel reaches out and pulls her close to him. She wraps her slender arms around him and holds him tightly.

"You don't have anything to worry about..."

Present Day. Ren Morrow's flat, Richardson, Texas

"...Over the next few months my grandfather would go and visit Rose at the house on White Rock every week. He bought her new clothes, paid for all her medical bills, and hired a private nurse to see her throughout her pregnancy... In time, he fell in love with her..."

Laura was speechless. One thing stood out from all the details: Rose kept the baby.

Ren saw her deep in thought. He grabbed his jacket and put it on. She noticed he had a backpack and a duffle in a pile at the door. "I'm leaving town, tonight. I think you should do the same."

"Why? Why would anyone care that I'm here?"

"I don't know, Laura. But you've had people tailing you from day one. You stepped on a hornet's nest. I would suggest you run." He turned his back to her and put the manila envelope containing Daniel Morrow's letter in a secured compartment in his backpack.

Laura watched him, her senses just starting to come back to her. "Where are you going?"

"I have an aunt in the Midwest. She said I could stay there with her and her husband for a while. It's as good a place as any to start over."

"Why did you stay after your father died?"

Ren looked her straight in the eye. "I wanted revenge. There are names and places in that letter that will lead me to the ones responsible for their deaths. I knew if I laid low something would happen sooner or later."

"So you just hung out?"

"My dad left me some money when he died. My mother split when I was a kid."

"Oh..." So many questions she still didn't have the answers to...

"For the last couple of years I scanned the net for anything remotely related to Davis and some of the other things mentioned in the letter. Finally, I saw your Facebook ads for interviews about the White Rock Lady and I knew something was up."

She was confused. "What does White Rock have to do with this? I didn't know anything about these people before I came here–"

"But they knew about you," he said, definitively. Laura sat back in her chair trying to make sense of all this.

"So, why are you leaving?"

"After watching them deal with you, I know I'm not ready. Nothing I can do will hurt them. Not yet."

Laura opened her mouth to say something but forgot what it was. Her head was still cloudy. Ren smirked. "Come on. It's late. You have a lot to do and I have a plane to catch."

"Can I drive you to the airport?"

"Thanks, but the rail is only a few blocks away. I'm safer on my own. And so are you."

He held his hand out and helped her to her feet.

"There's nothing else you can tell me?"

"Only that these people own everything. The police, judges... My grandfather and my father were both lawyers and they never stood a chance. And neither do I unless I get the fuck outta here."

Her belongings were in a neat pile on the floor next to her, including her car keys.

"Your car is downstairs in the garage, first floor. The code to get out is 20101."

"Thanks, Ren." She gathered her things and went to the door. She turned around as Ren looked up to watch her leave.

"I know what you're looking for, Laura, and I sure hope you don't find it." He turned back to his belongings as she walked out of his life...

December 6, 1969, Baylor Hospital, Dallas, Texas

In the early morning, dense fog has rolled in from the low-lying areas. Daniel Morrow is wide-awake staring out of the hospital room window smoking a cigarette, waiting for the sun to rise. Light rain has been falling on and off all night. There is a prevailing chill, even inside the building.

Behind him, Rose Marie Davis sleeps soundly in her hospital bed, tucked into a dark corner of the private room. It has been two days since the birth of her daughter and physically Rose has bounced back almost immediately. But mentally, Daniel knows it has all been too much for her.

After the delivery, the nurses had come to her. The baby needed more physical connection than they were staffed to handle. Of course, after hearing their persuasive argument, Rose offers herself to be the temporary caregiver. Since then, she has spent the last two days holding and feeding the child as if it were still her own. Yes, it is in the baby's best interest, but Daniel knows, in her situation, it is also the hardest thing Rose could possibly have done.

Standing at the side of her bed, he watches her sleep. She is a porcelain angel lying there in front of him, her breathing deep and steady. He gently brushes a lock of blonde hair away from her face. She stirs slowly, feeling his warmth next to her. A wide grin spreads across her face before she even opens her eyes to look up at him.

Her eyelids flutter and a pair of enormous blue eyes open up to him like flowers to the sun. He takes her hand in his.

"What are you doing up so early?" he whispers to her.

"Mmmm, I felt you..." She purrs, pressing the side of her cheek to his hand. "You didn't sleep again."

He smiles. "I'm fine."

"We're leaving today," she says. It is more of a statement than a question.

"Yes. We are." The weight of his words is far heavier than the words themselves. Leaving here means so many different things to both of them. All Daniel can do is hold her close and let her lean on him. The hard part is just beginning.

He reaches into his pocket and pulls out an object. "I was going to save this for later. But at least right now I know we're alone."

He hands her a small blue velvet box.

"Daniel..."

"Open it." He flashes a foxish grin.

Rose slowly sits up in bed and considers the box thoughtfully. She smiles and carefully pulls the top back. Sitting on a small velvet platform is a beautiful bracelet made of delicate platinum chain inset with dozens of tiny red roses meticulously carved out of Rose's birthstone, garnet.

"Birthdays are really for the parents anyway. Happy birthday, Rose."

Tears well up her eyes. She throws her arms around his neck and hugs him tightly. Never could she love another person as much as she loves him right now.

"Put it on."

Rose reluctantly lets him go. Wiping the tears from her eyes, she takes the piece from the box and holds it up to the light. The stones glow like tiny embers in her hand casting glittering reflections around the dark room. Taking the chain in both hands, Daniel clasps the ends of the sparkling bracelet together on her wrist.

"Now," he says, "you will always have something to remember me by."

Rose lays back, content for the moment just having him near.

She catnaps for another hour until the morning shift nurse comes in with her breakfast.

"Good morning!" The woman is always so chipper in the morning. She is totally on Daniel's nerves.

After Rose has breakfast, Daniel goes to find the head nurse to see about checking out. While he is gone, a young candy striper comes in to collect her dishes. Rose recognizes her as one of the young women who assisted during her care-giving sessions a few times.

"Thank you for all your help."

The girl smiles. "It's my pleasure. I hope everything goes well for the both of you..."

"I know this may be awkward, but... is there any way I could tell her goodbye? The baby?"

The young volunteer looks at her slightly confused but replies, "I-I think it would be alright. The convent is on its way to collect her, but she's ready to go. Give me just a sec."

The young girl leaves the room but returns in moments with the pushcart holding Rose's daughter. She gingerly picks the child up and hands the bundled infant to Rose one last time. The baby is quiet, her tiny blue eyes staring out at the new world in wonder. Over the last two days in Rose's care, the child has never cried. Not once.

She is perfect. Staring at her lying there in her pink blankets, Rose wonders what her daughter's life will be like. Will she grow up creative and happy? Will her new parents teach her to be kind and respectful? Will she have a daughter of her own? If only Rose could watch over her, protect her if she ever needed it...

Daniel walks in the room and watches the two of them for a moment without interrupting. He slowly creeps up to the bed and places his hand on Rose's shoulder.

"I will always be with you, little one," Rose whispers to the child, who in turn smiles from the depths of the blankets. "Always..."

At that moment, the door opens and two nuns in black habits enter the room followed by the managing nurse. The young candy striper cowers against the wall as the nun standing closest to the bed clears her throat, gently picks the child out of Rose's arms, and walks out of the hospital room door without another word, her companion and the nurses in tow.

Daniel puts his arm around Rose. She has cried so many tears they will no longer come. He sits on the bed next to her and she melts against his warm body.

After a few moments he says, "The doctor said we can go at any time."

They take ten minutes to pack her things and leave. As they descend in the cold steel elevator, Rose puts her arms around him.

"I love you, Daniel," she whispers, her voice soft and lovely like the tinkling of bells in his ears. At this second, nothing in the world could have made him happier than to be here by her side.

They drive back to White Rock Lake in silence through the intermittent rain. Rose closes her eyes and leans against his shoulder listening to the low voice of the radio.

When they arrive at the Davis house Rose is fast asleep. Daniel gets out of the car and opens the front door. He goes back and picks up Rose, still sleeping deeply, and gently carries to her room. On the way out, he turns the AM radio sitting on the bedside table on very low for her, knowing she loves music to sleep by.

After securing the car, he goes to the kitchen. Opening the refrigerator, he pulls out a can of Pearl beer and pops the top. The gentle rhythm of the rain falling on the roof patters through the house. Staring out the back window of the kitchen, the lake spreads out before him across the lawn, quiet but somehow lifelike with the impact of the droplets animating the surface. He can feel something there in the water, watching, waiting... He laughs to himself. Maybe Rose's mother hadn't been as crazy as everyone thinks...

He takes a deep drink. So much has happened in the last few months, it's almost unbelievable. Never in his life has he felt so much pain and pleasure simultaneously. The taunting he had to endure from Kendall Reece the previous year had been nothing compared to his wife's counter-attack once she discovered he was sleeping with her.

And somewhere in this city his soon-to-be ex-wife, a self-important daughter of a well-known Dallas spinal surgeon, is carrying his unborn child; a child who will grow up to never know him. His wife's deep scorn for his indiscretions with 'that woman', though substantiated, is bitter and absolute. He is cut off from the possibility of ever being part of their lives. Period. That part of his life is seemingly over before it ever had a chance to begin.

On the other side of the coin, getting involved with Rose Davis, even in this, the most harrowing and vulnerable moment in her life, and sharing her joy and grief for the last six months, has been the most painfully exhilarating experience he's ever had. Daniel knows in his heart that he has fallen in love with her, this gorgeous, sincere, broken girl.

Not that she's taken the place of his wife and child necessarily, but she has shown him the meaning of true selflessness. It is because of her plight that he has been reborn. Into what, he still cannot say. But he is different. And for the first time in years he is undeniably happy.

But what can he possibly tell his unborn baby about the choices he's made? A generous trust fund has already been set aside for him or her, so regardless what may happen, the child will be taken care of. But money can never take the place of having a real father. And the thought of another man, a stranger, coming into his wife's life and raising his child as his own makes Daniel's blood boil.

Truthfully, he has no right to feel violated. It was he who chose to get involved with a stripper and destroy the sacred trust of his marriage vows. Throwing himself on his wife's mercy was never an option; she had cut him off completely. With nothing else to lose, he made the decision to devote himself to helping Rose. Rose Davis, the daughter of a known felon and convicted killer, Lester Davis. His client. God, what a world they lived in...

The last six months has been like a lucid dream. Rose and Daniel had been living in their own world as if no one else existed. She would cherish his weekly visits and wait anxiously for him. He would bring her presents; flowers, sometimes tiny gifts that meant everything to her. He had become her confidant, her friend, and literally had become her entire world.

But was this the best place for her, the house she grew up in, plagued by despair and sadness created by her mother so many years ago? Many times he would find Rose sitting on the porch, staring out at the dark water of the lake for hours just like she had...

The only sound other than the rain is the old grandfather clock in the living room, its mechanical wooden click resounding through the quiet rooms. So much history in these walls. The horror that Rose grew up with, the insanity of a parent and the darkness that grows out of such a situation... So much sadness here...

And Rose's victory has been bittersweet. She escaped one horrible situation only to go straight into another. What kind of torture it must be to birth a child and bond with it, only to give it up for adoption days later. He can't imagine how she must feel.

But what he *does* understand is the great joy being with Rose gives him. It makes all the rest of this shit, the risk of certain people discovering his involvement with Davis' daughter, the confusion and danger, *everything*, worthwhile. And as long as he has air to breathe, Rose will be protected.

Daniel reaches down and pulls his briefcase from the floor. Extracting a legal pad and a fountain pen, he starts writing. Somehow he wants to try to explain to his unborn baby that he isn't crazy. He is just a regular man who is starving for affection and affirmation, concepts his child's unformed brain is at least a decade away from being able to fully comprehend. But Daniel has to try.

'I am not a madman,' he writes. *'I am a tool of madmen. The only sin I've committed is to dare to love, with all my heart and soul, one being who needs me more than any other. Even you, my dear child. Here in this sea of corruption I have found my happiness...'*

As he reveals his deepest feelings, hot, angry tears form in the pits of his eyes. He opens his soul, and writes everything. Names, dates... and most of all, why all this is happening in the first place.

'There are groups of people against us. Powerful people. They want Davis wiped out. And we, she and I, are a part of him. I feel like every minute of my life might be my last. But one thing is certain; if something should happen to me because of my

involvement with Rose Davis, I would die with a smile on my face knowing that, for a short time, I have loved with my entire soul...

'My one regret is never having had the chance to know and love you. I would give anything for a chance to hold you. Your mother will tell you truths that will paint me as a monster. But it's not that I haven't tried. She refuses to speak to me whatsoever, much less agree to let me be a part of your life. I love with all my heart. Never forget that. And when you are an adult, remember that no man is without fault. It's how you make amends that matters. And remember, that we all must pay the price for our transgressions...'

He stuffs the pages into an envelope, writes his attorney's address on it, and places it in his brief case. Along with the money he's already set aside, his lawyer will see that his heir receives this letter as well when the time comes. And by that time, maybe this will all make some sense. To somebody.

Daniel then quietly creeps upstairs to check on Rose. Lying there surrounded by pillows she looks so young and innocent. His heart swells. He leans over and kisses her on the cheek while she sleeps. It is horrible what the world puts us through...

Going back downstairs, he locks up the house and checks the heat. On his way out he takes one more look out at the turbulent waters of the God-forsaken lake. If he never saw it again, it would make him all too happy.

The drive into town is in total silence. There is little traffic on a rainy Sunday afternoon. There is only one other car on the road behind him. Daniel doesn't share Rose's love for music; it doesn't make him happy or distracted, it simply annoys him. Instead, he lets the rhythm of the wheels serenade him.

Once he gets to Park Cities, he takes the letter and drops it in the mailbox at the corner of Fitzhugh and Cole Avenue. He pulls away and is driving past a public park adjacent to

North Dallas High School when out of an alley a black Chevrolet sedan leaps out and strikes the passenger side of his car.

"Jesus Christ!" Shocked, Daniel jerks the steering wheel and steps on the gas, fish-tailing his car around the Chevy and speeds away.

He runs the red light at the next intersection and takes an immediate right onto Blackburn, a side street that runs at a steep angle down toward Turtle Creek. The Katy Trail train line runs across an elevated stone bridge that crosses over Blackburn. A thick cement support wall separates the two narrow passing lanes.

He sees the Chevy squealing around the corner in his rearview mirror and steps on the gas, speeding toward the bridge partition. Out of the corner of his eye, Daniel sees a car speeding through the small tunnel in the on-coming lane. As it approaches, the car swerves straight for Daniel. He punches the clutch but instead of speeding past the approaching car and through the tunnel opening, his wheels hit a wet spot, jerk to the left, and the car strikes the stone partition head-on with a brutal, resounding impact.

It seems a long moment passes before the car bursts into flames amid a rain of glass and metal fragments. The few witnesses will later swear the explosion happens instantly, but the reality is Daniel Morrow's body burst from its seat and lodged itself in the windshield on impact, the seatbelt already having decapitated his head cleanly off his shoulders. When the machine finally erupts in flames moments later, Daniel Morrow is already dead.

The forensics doctor will later comment that Morrow's loved ones will be comforted to know, though his body was indeed incinerated, at least he didn't have to suffer the agony of actually burning to death...

Present Day. North Dallas.

Laura's nerves were totally shot as she carefully drove back to Dallas from Ren's apartment in Richardson. The tale of Daniel Morrow and his horrible demise left her feeling defeated and overwhelmed. Her exhaustion was almost debilitating as she tried her best to calm down and focus. After a grand mal seizure she had no business whatsoever being behind the wheel of a car, but there was no other option.

Looking at the dash, she saw it was 6:45 PM. Colin had sent her a text from the hotel hours ago. By now he had certainly discovered that every bit of evidence she had accumulated was now gone. She had been so close to finding the secret of the ghost of White Rock Lake, however, in this ghost story, no one died, no one lived, and apparently no one cared. She dreaded the thought of having to face Colin and admit she failed. And other than her father, no other person's opinion mattered more than his. Laura gripped the steering wheel and began to cry bitter, frustrated tears.

It came to Laura in a painful moment of clarity. She was nothing but a foolish little girl. All of her life she had rationalized everything, doing her best to prove to the world and herself that she wasn't broken. But that was exactly what she was. She was bitter because of the loss of her parents, bitter because of her medical condition, bitter from having to live in a world that constantly reminded her that she was cursed with an emotional deficit. All this time, she fought to prove that she was a strong, independent woman, but she was nothing but a spoiled child hiding from her sadness and fear behind a façade of aptitude and privilege. Even this trip to Dallas was nothing but a self-serving effort to verify that she wasn't falling apart, that she was privy to something no one else could understand. How egotistical.

Even her intelligence, which she painstakingly cultivated all her life, she wore like a piece of armor, a cold, hard barrier that kept her separate from the rest of the world. She wanted to appear viable and responsible, but the reality was she was damaged, worse than the gold-digging girls she knew from college who were happy just being married to average men and having babies. At least they were able to just let themselves exist and be content. But in her mind, Laura thought she was better than them. How delusional could she be?

And her aloofness where Colin was concerned was unforgivable. Here was a man who any woman would be proud to spend the rest of their lives with and she was toying with him like a spoiled debutante. His love was not perfect, but for God's sake it was *real*. And instead of cultivating the partnership, she kept looking for flaws and holding him to some insane code of conduct no man could ever follow.

Her entire life was a lie.

'Oh, Daddy, I have failed you. And I have failed myself. I am nothing...' Even the thought of crying made her feel ashamed of herself. Her kind of self-absorption didn't deserve the luxury of remorse. She deserved to just be banished from life and love like the psychic vampire she was...

At that moment, the sounds of Johann Sebastian Bach's most well-known Bourrée ignited from her purse. Laura jumped in surprise. She wiped the tears from her face with one hand and looked at her phone. The caller ID said "SAM". She answered immediately, driving with one hand.

"Samuel? Where are you?"

Static on the line. A muffled shout, then, "Laura, it's me..." There was panic in his voice.

"Sam?"

"I'm at the lake, the boathouse. Laura, whatever you do, don't come here! Don't–" The phone suddenly went dead. Laura slammed on her breaks and made a U-turn from the center lane sending the cars around her in all directions.

Scared out of her mind or not, she had to help Sam if at all possible. Forget her selfish need for validation, forget her vile self-loathing, forget everything. She had to get to White Rock Lake immediately.

Twenty Eight

The Land Rover skidded to a stop in the graveled parking lot of White Rock Park. The boathouse lay off to the south, on the other side of the hill. Laura looked for Sam's car but saw no other vehicles anywhere on this side of the lake.

Pausing, she sent Colin a text message. "At the lake near the boathouse. Please call. I love you." She tagged her text with her location and hit send.

Getting out of the vehicle, her mind was a jumbled mess but fear was no longer part of the equation. She ran to the very edge of the rickety pier and scanned the expanse of black water.

"Samuel!" She shouted, her voice echoing in the night. There was not a single sound anywhere on the lake. The water was so black in the waning light that it looked like oil. Or blood.

A smooth tenor voice broke the silence.

"The deepest point in the lake is only 10 yards off-shore from here. Who would have thought?"

Laura turned.

Mallory was casually walking across the pier towards her. In her distress, she had not heard his footsteps.

"It's you," she whispered, confusion sweeping over her like a wave. The one person other than Colin she had let into her heart and her bed was standing before her sizing her up like a hungry panther. Her heart disintegrated in her chest.

"I'm sorry, you were expecting maybe the grunge kid?"

"You were gone..." She shook her head. "Where is Samuel?" She was trying to keep herself from panicking, but was failing miserably. Mallory pulled a small digital recorder out of his pocket and pushed a button.

"Laura, it's me. I'm at the lake, the boathouse. Laura, whatever you do, don't come here! Don't–!" Samuel's voice abruptly cut off.

Mallory turned the unit off and smiled in mock thoughtfulness. "Ah, technology... It's truly amazing." The spark Laura had once seen in his eyes was gone. They were now black pits that reflected no light whatsoever; lifeless, like a shark's eyes. Gone was the charming, easy demeanor that she found so attractive. The man standing before her was inhuman; insectile. Reptilian.

"The kid was right, you know," he offered. "Something in the lake is definitely drawing Death towards it..." He chuckled to himself and threw the recorder out into the water. Laura gasped; the only evidence of Samuel's demise was gone forever. And then the cold realization sank in: Mallory had killed her friend. She was dumbstruck.

She blinked hard and visions leapt into her head.

The silhouette of an old woman cursing the black water, pitiful moans of despair leaping out of her throat as her grandchildren lay lifeless at her feet.

Overhead, in a continuous loop, the sun chased the moon in a red sky, black shadows of trees expanding and contracting with the variance of time... Something dark and heavy fell into the cold liquid, gagging on its way down to the murky bottom of the lake...

"How–?"

Mallory laughed casually. "I've been keeping an eye on you, Laura. A man has to protect his interests. You see, little goes on in this city that I don't know about these days. I'm really sorry about your friend, by the way. It was unavoidable."

"Sam," She whimpered, holding back her tears as best as she could.

"He really had a thing for you. He had no idea about us, did he?"

Laura winced at Mallory's cruelty, revolted by the thought of ever giving herself to the monster standing before her.

"I didn't think so." Mallory turned to look out at the dark water. "You know, there've been countless people discarded into this lake over the last century." He scoffed. "Prohibition itself was a massacre. With all the Families against the Fed..." He laughed to himself. "And we think we have it tough now..." He turned toward her, staring into her brown eyes. "So many lives have ended here..."

Laura did not see him, but rather stared inward, into the cavern of her sub-conscience where at least her mind had some shelter from his venom...

Dark silhouettes from decades past throwing a police officer into the lake in the middle of the night, his body hitting the water and sinking fast with the weight of the chains wrapped tightly around him. Fish darting toward him on all sides as the last of his air escapes from his lungs in a panicked gasp...

Men, women, and children tossed into the water, food for the nameless thing that lay waiting in the depths to be fed human flesh. It wasn't something corporal, but rather an ancient spirit from a time when men prayed to a myriad of gods and were humbled by their fragility in a world eclipsed by the unknown. It had taken root here in the valley centuries ago, fed by the blood of Native Americans, long before the state of Texas was even a concept. She saw the lives of hundreds, thousands, burning like tiny fires in the dark; the innocents, jealous lovers and madmen, criminals and saints alike throughout the countless decades, all extinguished here in the cold, black water. Madame Belle, Eva from the Highland Hotel, gutted and robbed by one of her own prostitutes, tossed in the deepest part of White Rock Lake in the middle of the night for the fish to feast upon...

"It all makes sense," Laura said, staring into nothing. So simple, really, she thought in horror. "The reason why all the stories of the Lady of White Rock are different is because... *they're all true...*"

Hideous images were firing like synapses in her brain, snippets of scenes from a past she had never consciously known but that had always been a part of her.

Looking up into the black pits that were Mallory's eyes she spoke the horrible truth: "There is more than just one ghost."

In her mind's eye, the cruel flood of images continued...

Rose Davis, bound with ropes, tossed into the cold water. Her little body makes a splash as she thrashes and slowly sinks into the cold depths. Beneath the undulating waves of White Rock, there lies a graveyard of bodies, some only skeletons, others, masses of rotted flesh still being eaten slowly by the fish. Rose lands on a carcass. She struggles against the ropes binding her, desperately trying to hold her breath. Suddenly Kendall's body bobs up next to her, the flesh of half her face blasted away. Rose screams into her gag releasing the last of her air...

Mallory taunted, "Like I told you, I don't believe in ghosts."

Laura didn't hear him. She was enrapt in visions of the past. She spoke in a soft dreamy voice, her body present but her thoughts decades away. "Rose was just another unfortunate girl in the wrong place at the wrong time..."

"Now, that I *do* believe." Mallory's voice was void of compassion whatsoever.

A Native American staring out at an empty valley. He is painted in colorful stripes and sporting bright feathers in his hair, his skin as smooth and brown as the soil. The chieftain moans, holding his dead infant son in his arms, the tears running down the deep crevices of his face so very long ago...

"It amazes me how many people end up in the wrong place at the wrong time..."

Laura's eyes rolled in the back of her head as the visions took her even deeper.

Black avengers storm into a hotel suite where groups of people are having sex. The demons pull out shotguns from their trench coats and slowly walk from room to room systematically murdering every man and woman in sight... Chel Sheldon sits in his car at a stoplight smoking a cigar after leaving their interview. A motorcyclist wearing a black helmet rides up next to him, pulls out a revolver, and blows his brains out before riding off into the cross-traffic.

Laura looked up at Mallory, and the words she spoke seemed to come from somewhere else. "Please take me home. I just want to go home..."

"Laura, for all your smarts, you really haven't done your homework very well. Why do you think it's been so easy for you to get your information? Haven't you felt like some things have just fallen into place? It's not a ghost calling out to you." He snickered. "Don't you see?"

'*What are you talking about?*' she thought.

He was laughing again. "Davis, that old bastard, really pissed a lot of people off, let me tell ya. When the money disappeared, they decided to take his precious daughter, Rose, as collateral..."

Flashes of a faceless stranger chatting Rose up at a bar... They walk out into the night together. A drive in his car out by the lake...

"It seems the guy got a little *over-zealous* in his assignment..." Mallory's smile, the smile that she so once loved, was plastered on his face like a death mask.

"Why...?"

"After looking for Davis' stash for decades, the old timers thought I could get you to answer some questions. But you knew nothing. Unfortunately, you found out more than you should have about us. And now it's your turn..."

Laura felt waves of chills running through her. She pointed out to the water. "You don't even know it's out there, do you? You just feed it. You are a slave to it!"

"The Lake?" He laughed. "Laura, life attracts death. You should know that by now. They're natural enemies. Dark versus light, good against evil... Take comfort in the fact that it's nothing mysterious or supernatural..." He pulled a knife out of his back pocket. Opening the shining blade, he walked slowly towards her. "It's just business, Laura..."

Her heart sank in her chest. The life she had wasted, the pomposity she had worn like a badge of honor all the while being nothing but a smarmy, whiney little bitch, full of self-importance, pretending to be a hero when she barely had the strength to stand on her own two feet. She deserved this, for it all to end here, at the hands of an ex-lover she had been too stupid to recognize as the enemy. *'God, just let me die quickly...'*

From somewhere deep inside she heard familiar words of encouragement. *'Whatever you do, never give up, Pumpkin! Use whatever you can, but never give up!'*

With the sound of her father's voice in her head, she fought back the terror. He would never have let her quit as a child, not honors English nor Statistics. And, even from beyond the grave, he wasn't about to let her give up on life itself. *'You are not a victim, Laura. You are strong; you are a fighter. Never forget that...'*

In that instant, Laura Milton realized that life was the most precious thing imaginable. And she would have to fight to keep it.

"You're wrong," she growled to Mallory under her breath. Laura stood up straight, her entire body tensing.

Mallory extended the hand holding the knife slightly towards her. She focused on him, aware of the effects of the adrenalin coursing through her. She was conscious of the uneven wood underneath her feet, the mournful cry of a bird somewhere across the lake, the small scar under Mallory's right eye that she had somehow missed before... She could even somehow hear the rhythm of his breathing.

Something bubbled up out in the lake. Mallory looked up for an instant.

That was all Laura needed. Grabbing his wrist, she yanked him towards her breaking his nose with the palm of her other hand with a single fluid motion.

Mallory screamed and staggered backwards, grabbing his nose and dropping the knife. Thick, red blood spurted out, seeping between his fingers, leaving wet trails down the front of his white dress shirt.

"You little bitch, you broke my fucking nose!" He looked up and grimaced, the blood streaming down his face and into his mouth. He looked like a demon made flesh. He shook it off and rushed her.

She moved to her left and he almost went over the edge of the pier. He came back swinging, punching her in the face. She took the hit, crouched, and came up in an arc, her elbow slamming into his right temple. Mallory fell backwards.

He lay on the pier for a moment, dazed. Laura kicked the knife away from him and into the cold water. Everything in her body told her to run but before she had a chance to move, he was on his feet coming at her.

He led with a punch at her face but she ducked. She turned backwards with a back-fist but he easily blocked the blow. He grabbed her hand and pulled her to him, punching her in the stomach with all his might, knocking the wind out of her. She dropped to her knees gasping for air.

Mallory lifted her face in his hand, his breath labored. Blood still poured from his nose, over his teeth, dripping down his chin. He looked into her swollen eyes in a moment of recognition, a moment of remembrance of their intimacy, their connection. She felt the heat in him, felt their mutual desire and admiration that had fostered an amazing night of passion a billion years ago. It would have been a beautiful moment if it weren't for the gore oozing down his face. But in a flash, the sentiment was gone. And only the reptile remained.

He slapped her hard, sending her tumbling to the wooden pier. Pulling back, he kicked her as hard as he could in the side. She screamed out loud, drowning out the audible crack that came out of her body. The air rushed out of her lungs and she rolled onto her back, gasping. Her ribs were broken.

"*Please...*"

Mallory dropped to his knee onto her chest. His left hand wrapped around her throat and squeezed.

"Please, what? Please *stop*? I can't hear you, Laura. You're mumbling!" He started laughing at her, his once-angelic eyes brimming with demonic intent.

She would not let him take her, not like this. She clawed at him trying to get him to let go, her nails digging deep trenches into the flesh of his forearm. He screamed in a long howl, but tightened his grip on her throat. She was thrashing under the weight of him desperately trying not to pass out. She reached blindly behind and felt a sharp piece of wood splintering off the pier. She snapped it free and wildly stabbed it into his side trying to get at his kidneys again and again until he finally rolled off of her, screaming in pain. Laura forced herself to her feet and saw that Mallory was bleeding from multiple wounds in his side.

"You bitch! How dare you?"

She stood up on her own, feeling the strength coming back into her legs. Her side screamed in pain but she slowed her breathing and embraced it. She stared Mallory in the eye, her anger overcoming her sense of fear. The man she once desired was out to kill her and one thing was for certain: she wasn't going without a fight.

"Fuck you, Mallory."

She rushed him and then seemed to stumble. He watched her fall to one knee and descended on her. Just at that moment, she reared up with all her weight, both her fists clenched together, and caught him underneath the chin. The force of her blow took him off his feet and he landed backwards on the pier, unconscious.

She collapsed in agony holding her wounded side. She waited for a moment then crawled towards Mallory's prone body. He was out. With a groan she forced herself up to her feet, reared back and kicked him as hard as she could in the face.

"Just for grins," she said between clenched teeth.

Laura hobbled over to the edge of the pier. She bent down on her knees and gently hung over the edge of the wooden platform, protecting her side. She cupped her hands and got some water to wash the blood from her hands and face. The cold liquid felt good on her skin.

She lurched across the pier violently, her side shrieking in agony. Mallory had risen and kicked her full force in her broken ribcage. She grabbed onto his leg and sank her teeth deep into his shin. He fell over her throwing them both over the far edge of the pier and into the cold water.

Mallory's weight sent him deep into the lake. Above him, he saw Laura's legs kicking upward. Before she reached the surface he grabbed her ankle and quickly pulled her downward, wrapping his arm around her neck, strangling her. Laura clawed at his arm, kicking back at him, desperately trying to free herself but he was simply too strong. She was exhausted and knew she couldn't fight much longer. Her lungs were aching to take a breath, but she knew that meant certain death. As her strength dissipated, the graphic visions once again took over...

A young blonde woman staring out at the lake under a dark sky, her long tresses undulating slowly in a phantom wind. Laura had seen her a million times since she was a girl; the sad ghost figure that had reached out of the darkness and summoned her here to Dallas, to the edge of extinction, the mysterious girl that had occupied the most secret recesses of her soul all of her life...

And in a soft heartbeat of movement, the girl's shoulders began to shift, light glaring around the lithe figure as the apparition seemed to be inverting. All sensation stopped as the beautiful silhouette gently rotated towards her. First, Laura saw the profile of her nose and pearl white cheek, the long shadow of an eyelash... Then the edge of a generous mouth... Slowly the specter turned in a fluid motion and, for the first time, stared directly at Laura, the cobalt-blue eyes searing into her own...

It's Rose Davis. She is absolutely beautiful. And she is crying. She is crying because she sees you hurt, Laura. She sees you are hurt and she knows you. She knows who you are, Laura Milton...

You are ***family****.*

Laura's body spasmed in Mallory's arms as realization came flooding into her. The answer had been in front of her the whole time. If what Mallory said were true, then Lester Davis, was not only Rose's father, but he was also Laura's great-grandfather...

The dominos kept falling...

And if that were the case, then Chesapeake, the half-insane matriarch, was undoubtedly Laura's great-grandmother, making the gentle Rose Marie her biological grandmother... The secret of their otherworldly connection was the blood flowing in Laura's veins. That was why the visions had never subsided.

Laura instantaneously knew it all was true.

'Oh, God...' And with that, she lost consciousness.

Mallory felt Laura finally go limp in his hands. He pushed her away and swam up to get air.

Just as he reached the surface, he felt something catch on his pants leg. It gripped him hard and with a jerk he felt himself being dragged back downward. Looking into the water, there was nothing in the gloom at first, and then Mallory thought he saw tiny red pinwheels of light glistening in the depths beneath him... Then something cold wrapped around him.

The fish-eaten corpse of Rose Davis pulled itself up through the muddy water to stare Mallory in the face. The pure white of the skull's forehead had been penetrated, leaving a coarse, gaping hole. The empty pits where her blue eyes had once been bore down on him as the hideous maw seemed to open on its own volition. Through the water, he heard a diminutive female voice cry out silently.

"Please take me home..."

Mallory screamed, expelling the last bit of oxygen from of his lungs. He grabbed his chest as his heart simply stopped beating. The carcass of Rose Davis gently embraced the paralyzed body of her new lover. Tatters of ice blue fabric danced with the current around her, the red stones of her bracelet glittering like tiny beacons in the night. The cadaver kissed Mallory on the mouth and slowly descended, pulling his rigid form into the deepest part of the lake, a sunken graveyard, decades old, filled with corpses who were just dying to meet him...

...

Colin Jonah's rental car skidded to the mouth of the pier. Sirens of police cars filled the air, obviously close behind. It was still twilight. He leapt out of the car and scanned the area, calling out her name, "Laura!" The sound echoed through the valley, the only other noise audible on the lake other than the sirens.

Out of the corner of his eye, he saw something floating in the water next to the pier. Without hesitation, he jumped into the lake, swimming out towards the body.

Reaching Laura, he turned her over on her back, wrapped his arm gently around her waist, and pulled her to shore. Crawling to his knees in the sand, he laid her head in his lap. Looking down at her, tears spilled out of his eyes dripping onto her face. She was gone. Her cheeks had already turned powder blue, almost angelic. She looked so extraordinarily beautiful. He started to sob as the police cars skidded into the lot behind them...

Twenty Nine

Modern day. White Rock Lake 1:56 AM

It's a gorgeous spring night. A sleek, new Audi sedan is blaring rock music as it races down the lakeside road. The male driver is doing a bump of cocaine and chases it with swig of Red Bull. The car speeds around a curve and suddenly in his headlights the driver sees the figure of a woman standing in the middle of the deserted road. He slams on his breaks and narrowly misses her, skidding sideways on the gravel road past her. He backs up and pulls up next to her.

"Oh my God, are you ok?" He slicks his hair back, nervously. "I'm so sorry–"

The girl is soaked to the bone. She's absolutely beautiful. He's entranced by her thin, muscular arms, the long brunette hair hanging in her face. "Did you have an accident? Can I take you somewhere?"

Her petite blue lips barely move but he hears her voice as if she were in the car next to him.

"Please, just take me home..."

"Sure, baby. Get in."

A tiny wet blue hand reaches for the handle and she lets herself into the back seat of the car. The driver looks in the rear-view mirror and sees a pair of large brown eyes staring back at him.

Had the driver known the circumstances, he would have realized that the presence in his car was the residue of the latest in a long line of unfortunate victims who shared a watery grave at White Rock Lake. Had he known the girl, he would have recognized the dark brown eyes, the high, angular cheekbones, the dark hair. He would have recognized the cadence in her voice. He would have known that the frightened, chalk-white face staring back at him through his rear-view mirror was that of a beautiful young woman once named Laura Milton...

...

The vision faded.

Laura had slipped into something between death and lucid dreaming, the night dissolving into morning in what seemed like an instant. Behind her closed eyelids, everything seemed glaringly bright. She could hear someone calling her name from far, far away. She was so tired, she just wanted to rest. It was warm and comfortable here. Yes, keep your eyes closed and sleep...

'No. Not yet...'

That voice again, coming from somewhere... Calling out to her...

'Laura...'

She carefully opened her eyes. Her vision was blurred, as if staring through a thin veil of a dream, obscuring her vision, keeping her just on this side of her own perception. Slowly, the haze lifted. Laura sensed soft sunlight filtering through an open window, a slight breeze of recognition carrying the scent of honeysuckle and lilacs. It took her a moment to get her bearings. She was lying on an elevated old style twin bed in the corner of a small room decorated in pale colors and modest wooden furniture. Pictures of old movie stars covered the light blue walls, obviously torn from magazines. A poster of a young Elvis Presley hung on the closet door. On the dresser, there were tiny bottles of perfume, a hairbrush, some bobby pins... A stack of Nancy Drew novels and fan magazines were on the bedside table. This must be Rose's bedroom from so very long ago...

Reality hit her, hard. Laura knew she must be dead. But there was a deep warmth radiating through her body, calm and soothing, like nothing she'd ever felt before...

This can't be happening...

'Laura...'

The whispered voice was familiar, tender, coming from all around her. Then she remembered Mallory, like a bad dream. She had been drowning, fighting for her life against someone who was once her lover.

"Laura..."

The sound made her jump. In the doorway, a vision seemed to grow out of the sunlight itself. A shimmering figure, almost a reflection, stepped out of the warm glare. A beautiful, young Rose Davis, sheathed in a gorgeous powder-blue dress, walked through the door. Sitting next to Laura on the tiny bed, Rose took her hand. The milk-white skin felt warm, radiating. Laura saw her face was flush with a hint of sun freckles. This was no ghost.

They sat silently for a long moment studying one another. Finally, Laura broke the silence.

"Are you real?"

"We are... Yes..." Laura recognized the soft voice from countless dreams and forgotten exchanges. It had high overtones and reminded her of the tinkling of bells. A confused look came over Rose's face. Laura could feel her frustration.

"You can't fully communicate with me, can you?"

“Not yet.” Rose seemed to struggle with her words. “But I want you to remember this...”

The soft flesh of the face manifesting before her looked healthy and vibrant. A faint smell of perfume permeated the air...

“It is not your... *time*. You must go back...”

“Go back? To *what?*” Laura was genuinely confused. Rose smiled, as if to a child. She spoke slowly but the sound seemed to come from somewhere else.

“To your life. There is still so much to do...”

Laura’s heart sank. She was being sent away, torn again from the one person who she could identify with. Just like she was torn from her mother and her father...

“But I just found you...” Laura felt her sanity stretching its boundaries. Warm tears were flowing from her eyes as she pleaded with the apparition. “There is nothing for me there. I am alone.” She began sobbing. “Please, don’t send me away... *Please...*”

In the wave of her misery, Laura felt a warm hand rest on her shoulder. And all of her fear evaporated.

‘You will never be alone again,’ the specter told her wordlessly, ‘but you must return. Not just for you, but for all of us...’

‘Who is ‘all of us’?’ Laura wanted to scream in protest, but she felt nothing but love and compassion coming from the young woman...

There were so many questions. Where was she? Had Rose seen Laura’s parents? There was so much she wanted to know. But with a slight nod from Rose, the light slowly began to fade and the radiating warmth was replaced by a wet, cold rush of air.

And then darkness...

* * *

For ten minutes Colin had held her, refusing to let the police take Laura's lifeless body from him. The coroner would be here soon and he would have to give his beloved to them, but until then he held on. The most important person in his life was gone. How could he have ever torn them apart? Without Laura, life meant nothing. He sobbed deeply.

The cold body in his arms convulsed and he almost screamed out loud. He watched her face as the tiny eyelids fluttered like butterfly wings. And with a sigh, Laura Milton slowly opened her eyes wide once more to the world of the living.

The first thing she saw was Colin staring down at her, his face completely overcome. He was a mess. Had she the strength, she would have laughed out loud, but instead gripped him tightly, so incredibly thankful that he was with her, thankful that she was alive.

Once again, she was breathing. And for the first time in her existence, Laura was where she belonged. Her maternal grandmother, Rose Davis, had come from beyond the thin veil of the grave and saved her life. And now, for some reason she couldn't understand, she was back in her body.

There were still so many questions left unanswered. But regardless of all the confusion and pain she had endured, as she felt Colin's arms tighten around her, Laura Milton was content, for now, knowing she was safe.

And she was loved...

To be continued

Born and raised in Dallas, Texas, I have had the good fortune of making a living as an artist in one capacity or another all my life. I've been many different people in my short half-century on this earth: a guitarist and songwriter for an alternative band in the 90's, a freelance camera op for a number of reality television productions, a photographer, a furniture designer/fabricator, a fine artist, a production designer, a bartender, and most recently, a freelance editor and corporate video producer.

However, during all these forays into other artistic professions I have always been a writer at heart, penning songs lyrics, poetry, short stories, a handful of scripts, and a number of unfinished works since the tender age of 14.

White Rock is the initial entry in a compilation I call 'The Thin Veil Series', a collection of novels that follows the life of **Laura Milton**, the brilliant yet flawed protagonist and her uncanny gift of communication with the dead.

Look for the next installment *Black Kiss* in the late fall of 2018. Updates and purchase information at ReneGuerrero.com. Until then, thank you so much for your patronage.

J. René Guerrero

Made in the USA
Lexington, KY
04 November 2017